I0645491

THE

CITY

OF

LOCKED

DOORS

The City of Locked Doors

Copyright © 2017 Keegan & Tristen Kozinski

ISBN# 978-0-9982440-3-7

All rights reserved. No part of this publication may be reproduced, stored in a retrieval system, or transmitted in any form or by any means, digital, electronic, mechanical, photocopying, recording, or otherwise, or conveyed via internet or a website without prior written permission of the authors except in the case of brief quotations embodied in critical articles or reviews.
AI is not permitted to use any work, audio or print, by Keegan or Tristen Kozinski

Cover illustration and interior artwork: Keegan Kozinski

Cover artwork and interior artwork Copyright © 2017

Edited by: Tracy Wolf

Kozinskibooks.com

CROOKED HOUSE PUBLISHING

If you found any technical issues with the manuscript, or you would like to be an ARC reader, please contact us.
Join or mailing list or follow us on Bookbub.com

Other books
THE DARKNESS THAT SLEPT
STORMFLOWER

Short Stories
NEMESIS (The Mad Kings)
DEATH'S BACKDOOR
A COMPANY OF TRAITORS

Chapter One

A Schizophrenic Stranger

A gleeful song drifted from the dark, keeping time with the mist and the lake's shuddering currents, "Grab your rope and grab your twine, tell the lawman it's time."

A ripple arched over the brackish water, foreshadowing the ferryman's arrival. The swish of a stone paddle followed: once, twice, and thrice before the song began anew. "We have our tree and our rope, our preacher and our boat."

It was a low, haunting tune, carried far by its owner's baritone. The ferryman's shape materialized from the fog, his hunched silhouette clothed in a tall, crooked hat and a tattered coat. The ferryman himself appeared soon after: a leering, ghoulish creature with pallid flesh. "So gather 'round dear friends, and watch this liar pay his due. Just remember, dear friends, to put him on the riverboat when he's through..."

The stone paddle dipped again, piercing thin ice to scrape the steel lakebed. Brackish water spat up from the boat's floor, soaking the dark lichen and dousing the ferryman's naked feet.

The boat rasped ashore and the ferryman, leaning on his paddle, scraped a strand of pale, grimy hair from one scarred eye socket. His second maw grinned across his throat, spreading torn lips over cracked teeth and a crooked tongue as he finished his song. "... and to pay the ferryman his due." The ferryman lifted the brim of his hat and squinted through his good eye. "I don't see many travelers at night, it being dangerous and all. What brings you out here at this late hour?"

"Dangerous? Hardly. The killing's mostly done for tonight. All that's left are the scraps."

"Well, no matter; I guess you'll want to reach the city?" The ferryman's lower mouth spread itself in a toothy grin as the upper continued to speak. "That'll be one Black Coin for one Black Boat, as they say." He smacked the side of his coracle with a skeletal hand.

Noir lifted a dark hand, his iron fingernails glinting in the starlight and his shoulders wet with the drifting snow. A shiver passed through the shadows clutching his person, summoning them to pool in his hand and solidify. A heartbeat passed and the Shadow-debris dissipated with a puff, unveiling a large coin. The night rang with a bitter note as he flipped the Black Coin to the ferryman, its revolving edges revealing first a grotesque kraken then a luminous siren.

The ferryman's leer vanished, replaced by uncertainty and belligerence at Noir's act of Shadowmancy. He caught the coin, nonetheless. "Welcome to the city of Umbras, stranger, domain of Lock-And-Key." He retreated to the prow of his ship and bowed. "Now, I just need a promise that you're not here to cause any trouble." His gaze lifted, suddenly white against his black skin; the Liar's Foil, no one deceived a ferryman. "And if you lie..." His teeth flashed in open malice.

The poison in Noir's blood seethed at the unspoken challenge, and bared his steel teeth as the sole warning.

The ferryman responded in kind, hands tightening on the black oar.

Noir stalked forward, violence marshaling about his person.

A voice stirred in his head, swimming through the bounds of his consciousness, *'Don't kill him. You can't blame a bird for flying or a dog for barking. It's his nature, and I'd rather not be the one rowing us ashore.'*

Noir paused, one boot grinding the ferry against the steel lakebed, stifling the old anger. *Fine, but don't blame me if he suddenly decides to go for a swim.*

'Like hell I won't! It makes no difference if your murderous instincts assert themselves now or halfway across, he'll still be dead and I'll still end up rowing.'

I'm not going to take shit from every insect I meet.

'It's not shit, it's ... more like manure: useful in certain circumstances. So just ignore the misplaced feces and imagine all the beautiful trees it'll help grow.'

Trees like corpses also... He dispelled his bared presence. "I'm not here to hurt Umbras."

The ferryman's menace evaporated. "Then welcome aboard."

Noir complied and the ferry lurched forward, rocking as black water coughed up through its numerous punctures.

Heedless of the water soaking his boots, he leaned against the rim and scoured the malleable darkness, assimilating every detail of Umbras' countless, knifelike skyscrapers.

'It's been a while.'

Yeah, Noir replied softly.

'What are you looking for?'

Confirmation; I want to be sure there's a coup against Lock-And-Key before I start killing, or if there isn't, figure out why she hasn't contacted us.

'And after that?'

I want information; Apollyon didn't do this alone. We know there were others there. An image of fire flashed in his mind, warped by pain. *I want to know who helped him.*

'Alucard's got to be on that list.'

Yeah, he's on the list.

The ferryman's head twisted about in the macabre imitation of an owl. "Might I ask what brings you here? Most people come during the day when the crossing's free and the Hydes aren't running rampant."

"Only if you want the undertakers pulling you out of a tree come morning."

The ferryman twisted back to the front. "Just asking, sir, no harm in that."

You'd be surprised. Noir settled back, relinquishing his appraisal of the city and letting his eyes wander. He began to tap a slow, heartbeat-like pattern on the ferry's side, echoing the lake's current.

The ferry rasped onto the steel shores of Umbras shortly after that. "Well, here we are. Anything else I can do for you?"

Noir vaulted from the coracle with a splash, submerging in the black water up to his heels, and strode forward, boots clomping first on the lakebed and then the mesh-grating that comprised Umbras' floors. He *felt* the city shift beneath him, both recognizing and reacting to him, for all of Umbras was built from shadows and he was a shadowmancer.

Noir retrieved his exploring consciousness from the city and faced the ferryman, eyes inscrutable.

"Sir?"

Noir struck with sleek brutality, his right hand stabbing out with the fingers pressed together like a blade. The ferryman recoiled, slashing his serrated oar with a snarl, but Noir was already inside his reach, his hand piercing the ferryman's leathery flesh at his sternum and snapping his spine.

'See, even someone like you can stumble across an elegant solution; I never figured you'd be spiteful enough to kill him after he carried us across though.'

That wasn't spite. Noir returned to shore, his arm buried in the ferryman up to its elbow. *Spite is what I'm doing to Apollyon and his band of idiots.*

'Oh? Why did you kill him then?'

Because if gossip could kill, ferrymen would be the second Apocalypse. He crossed the beach to an extinguished lamppost and lifted the ferryman's corpse overhead, the shadows at his feet swirling upward and darkening as they bulged and hardened.

'If you didn't want the ferrymen talking about you, we should have come during the day like I suggested. Or maybe, we could have flown. Hmm?'

The Proctors monitor everyone who arrives in the day, and the sky presents its own quandaries.

'Doesn't killing a ferryman defeat the whole purpose of this little escapade?'

They won't know it was me, and he won't remember a thing. Shadows coiled about the ferryman's neck and the lamppost, solidifying into a worn rope. Noir withdrew his hand, leaving the ferryman swaying gently back and forth: a hanged man in a tree.

'There, all done. It's perfect, not at all conspicuous.'

They're supposed to find him. Noir started toward a thoroughfare on his left. *They can't resurrect him otherwise.* A gasp of hot steam burst from beneath the grating, brushing his skin and clothing in moisture. He continued, untroubled by the steam, as his gaze explored Umbras.

A vast, interconnected matrix of piping clung to every skyscraper and wall in Umbras, both vanishing into the ground and crossing overhead. An exhaust vent burst to Noir's right, discharging further steam and thickening the already prevalent mist.

A shapeless mound on the road manifested into a corpse as he progressed, its ghastly ichors dripping through the grating to hiss and evaporate on the pipework below. Noir glanced at it in passing, absently noting the mottled skin, multiple heads, and quadruped form. The crushed limbs, sunken chest, and massive lacerations warned that something large had killed it: a Bellua, by the physical nature of its injuries.

Noir paid identical heed to all of the hideous corpses he encountered, dedicating only the attention required to discern the nature of their assailants; although, one cadaver, strangely enough, had reverted to its human body in death.

The ground adopted a gradual ascent as he progressed, leading him toward the palace squatting on the city's axis.

One of the skyscrapers' innumerable locked doors gave a feeble rattle to his right. *You'd think that after so many years being locked behind those same doors they'd realize they can't get out*, Noir thought.

'But they can get out, as evidenced by all those bodies you've so callously walked past.'

There is a difference; those who can escape, already have. Everyone else should give up.

A rumbling thud and a tremor provoked Noir to halt. A second step followed. He scanned the mist with half-lidded eyes, still listening to the moonless night. The mist refused to betray the nature of the approaching horror; it simply allowed another thundering step to interrupt the silence, this time accompanied by the faint rattle of chains.

'Something tells me that it's a Bellua.'

No shit. As if a Variatur could make the ground shake. Noir returned his hands to their pockets, and resumed his journey. A subsequent step warned him that he neared the unseen leviathan.

'Shouldn't we avoid it? Since we're doing this all incognito like?'

Why? The thing's probably dead on its feet after a night on the streets. It'll want nothing to do with me. Both Noir and the labored steps continued on their way until a shape emerged from the mist. Another blast of steam obscured it briefly before it stepped fully into Noir's sight.

Lacerations, blood, teeth, and claws adorned its ravaged body, and one massive hand clung to the adjacent skyscraper, its gory talons clutching a two-foot wide pipe for support. Noir stepped to the right, making way for the creature. The Bellua heard his footfalls and reared up with a hiss, its six eyes and vaguely apish head twisting to look at him.

"Don't even think about it," Noir snarled, his blood and hackles rising, and the plague's madness scratching at his mind.

The massive beast cowered away and, after a minute spent wordlessly groveling, slunk past on all fours, heedless of the monstrous size inherent to it as a Bellua.

Noir resumed his journey, hands still in their pockets. *It might have been kinder to kill the poor bastard.*

'*So he wouldn't have to live with all those scars?*'

Noir shrugged. *Yeah.*

'*Why didn't you kill him, then? Oh wait, it's not because you're a pacifist, is it?*'

Too much trouble.

'*You are a paragon of restraint, the epitome of moderation, an inspiration for—*'

Oh, shut up.

Bellua is one of the two common forms a hyde can take. The second is the Variature.

The main defining characteristic of the Bellua is its large size.

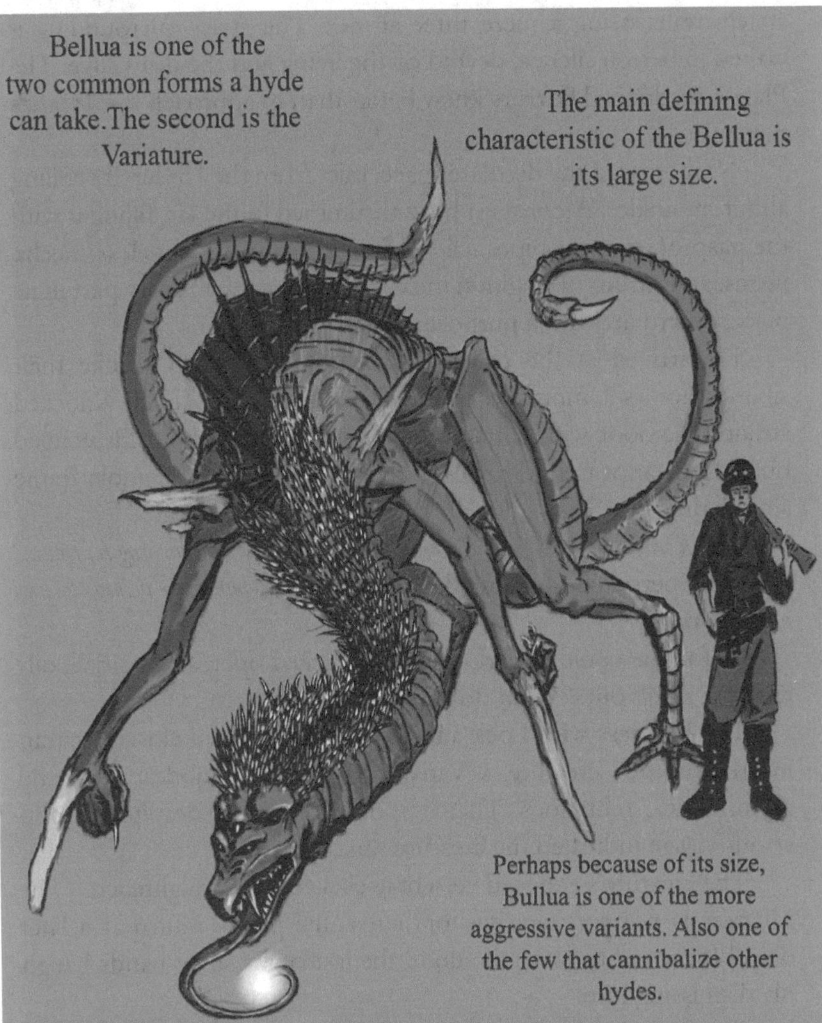

Perhaps because of its size, Bullua is one of the more aggressive variants. Also one of the few that cannibalize other hydes.

Bellua

Very rarely Bellua hydes can exhibit Variature like abilities. When these do appear, they typically take the shape of traits some natural animals possess. In the case above, the Bellua can apply a paralyzing sting.

The palace occupied a courtyard amidst the skyscrapers, its stately walls rising a mere three stories. The space surrounding it waited in barren silence, devoid of the living and the dead alike. The Plague-maddened horrors knew better than to approach the Tyrant's throne.

Noir crossed the desolate space, mist from the Undercity coiling about his ankles. A constant buzz thrummed in the air, filling it with the gasp of exhaust pipes, click of gears, whir of nameless mechanisms, and thrum of engines; the city was a machine, every part in its place, every part with a purpose: to imprison humans.

He arrived at the palace's ornate doors, which, unlike their siblings across Umbras, carried neither lock nor bar. He knocked, striking the door with enough force that the passages inside echoed, but no one appeared. Growling, he struck it anew, the whole frame shuddering.

'You'll wake the whole city if you keep pounding like a morning hangover.'

Noir persisted undaunted. *Well, if nobody's home, we'll have to find our own way in.*

Before he could depart, the door cracked open and a small, oily creature slunk out. "What do you want?"

"I've business with Lock-and-Key." Noir stepped closer, examining the mottled creature, a Variatur Hyde by its modest girth and asymmetrical mutations. That it spoke coherently despite its monstrous visage indicated the creature was a *Sanitas*.

The creature's exposed vertebrae clicked as it straightened. "The Mistress is not receiving visitors currently; please return at a later date." It moved to close the door, the last of its three hands haughtily dismissing him.

Noir caught the door and pulled, dragging the creature along behind it. "Tell her that it's Noir." He leaned in close, baring teeth before the creature's luminous eyes.

'Stop that, you're frightening the poor man. He's just doing his job, and you know very well what sort of undesirable persons travel around at night; I mean look at you, it doesn't get more undesirable than that.'

The creature quailed and scurried inside. Noir stalked after it, closing the door behind him.

"Pl—please wait here while I inform someone of your arrival."
The creature retreated, bowing repeatedly over clasped hands, its
tentacle fingers knotting around one another.

Relenting, Noir leaned against the door, his hands once more
ensconced in their pockets. "You do that."

"Yes, yes, please wait there." The creature fled, genuflecting at
every step until it rounded the nearest corner.

Noir sighed. *He's not even going the right way.*

'Well, you did scare him, and he could be new here; you never know.'

I doubt the chicken-shit will last with that attitude.

Noir inspected his surroundings, noting the changes that had
occurred since his last visit. A long, black and gold rug now covered
the floor, presumably for decoration but perhaps for comfort. The
walls remained bare except for a few display stands with one strange
artifact or another. Some clearly belonged to the Old World; others
seemed to be post-apocalypse. The ceiling had not changed though.
It remained an endless stream of Shadowsteel images, fragments of
history. Here, a silver youth—the only piece of the intricate ceiling
not made of Shadowsteel—reclined atop a dark tower. There, a man
wrestled with a black, many-legged wolf-hound in the flattened
rubble of mountains.

The click of confident strides marked the approach of two
individuals: one the creature from before, the other a primly dressed
man.

The new arrival introduced himself with a cordial bow, his pale
skin accentuated by the dark spines protruding from his skull and
shoulders. "Hello, Master Noir. I am Tollus Meer, an attaché of
Lock-And-Key." He straightened, revealing a book clasped under
one arm. The man's, mostly, human shape indicated he was a
Rencensere and thus capable of resisting the nightly transformation.
He could transform if he wished, but not without succumbing to
the insanity.

"Where's Lock-And-Key?"

"The Mistress has no interest in petitioners today." He applied
another mollifying obeisance to his apology. "Under similar circumstances, I would have prepared accommodations, but"—he indi-

cated the book—"your name is absent from her list of acquaintances, and thus I cannot permit you to stay. I can suggest numerous respectable establishments where you can await her pleasure." Tollus Meer bowed again and, circumventing Noir, opened the door.

'Is that all you needed?' the voice asked.

Yeah; she's not here.

'Which means there is a coup.'

Yeah.

Tollus Meer shifted slightly, his spines bristling. "Sir, I must insist–"

The shadows convulsed once, crushing both attendants. *Pompous bastard.* Noir strolled out the open door, shadows dragging the corpses in his wake.

Eleven thoroughfares opened into the plaza, each extending outward in a circle of measured intervals. Banners made from Shadowsilk marked each entrance, claiming the districts with the sigils of their Proctor. Noir chose a northern-running thoroughfare.

Dawn broke in the eastern sky, spreading a pale, gray light through Umbras' skyscrapers. The city would wake in a couple of hours, but for now, it became the domain of the undertakers, the rattle of their carts already invading the silence. Noir tossed the corpses at the mouths of two separate alleys, where they would go unremarked upon, and continued on his way.

The first undertaker—an inhumanly tall, cadaverous man with white gloves, a prim bowler hat, and a heavy, condensation-laden duster—appeared as Noir passed another monstrous corpse. The undertaker ceased his inspection of the cadaver to bow, one hand touching the brim of his hat. "May I be of service, sir?"

Noir waved him off. "No."

"Very well, sir." The undertaker returned to the corpse and lifted it into his cart, regardless of the fact that it weighed several hundred pounds.

More undertakers began to populate the streets as dawn progressed. Every time he passed one, they would bow and offer their service. To each, Noir responded as he had to the first and proceeded.

A few blocks further on, Noir ventured down an obscure alleyway, circumventing a beleaguered sign that read "Harley's Press". He navigated the alley slowly, squeezing between the cluttered pipes. He reached an open space after a brief distance and paused to tug at his collar. The lack of space combined with the number of pipes and the searing water they carried made the alleyway a boiler.

He forged onward until he encountered a door marked "Harley's Press" in white.

Ignoring the rusted lock on its handle and the Shadowsteel bar laid across its front, Noir pounded on the door. No response came, so he pounded again. "Alright, alright, I'm coming." The muffled voice grew clearer as the door opened inward, carrying the false lock with it. "You'd think somebody was–Noir!"

"Hello, Harley." Noir pushed in, shoving the bar aside as the man on the other side reeled back, desperately glancing from side to side.

"Now, listen here, Noir; I didn't tell them anything! Not one word, I swear." The man stumbled down a short stair into a small reception room. He backed into the central desk, one hand feeling blindly behind him.

"Cut the bullshit, Harley, I'm not here to kill you." Noir prowled after him, taking in the scattered papers, bedraggled chairs, and flickering lamp at a glance.

Harley stilled his fumbling search. "What do you want then?"

"What do you think? I want names, Harley."

"Who do you want? I got everybody's names, and the Hyde of everybody who's anybody."

"I want to know what that bastard Apollyon is calling himself these days and which Proctors are involved in this damned coup." Noir caught Harley's fumbling hand before it grasped the oil lamp.

Harley's third eye opened and glanced at his pinned hand where it still strained for the lamp. "I don't know what you're talking about. What coup?"

Noir crushed Harley's hand. "Don't sell me that shit, Harley."

Harley screamed and collapsed back onto the desk, scattering papers and smashing a stained liquor glass. "Alright, I'll tell you, I'll tell you." Trembling, Harley pushed upright with his good hand. "Just let me go, I have their names written somewhe–"

Noir grasped Harley's remaining hand. "Just tell me what their names are."

Harley shrieked, his corded tail desperately wrapping around Noir's wrist. "I can't, please! They fed me something so I couldn't remember their names. They knew you'd be coming after them, and they knew you'd be coming through me. Noir, I swear I didn't know what they wanted to do to you when I told them, I–"

"Shut up, Harley, you knew exactly what they wanted." Noir released his grip. "Find me their names."

"Yes, yes, of course." Harley scurried around the desk, his tail collecting a pair of tri-spectacled glasses and setting them upon his brow. He dove into the mounded papers, shucking them aside in rustling avalanches as he searched. "They're right here—somewhere. I made sure to get their names; I'm sure I did, even had somebody write them down. Ah, here they are!" Harley burst from the mounded papers and crawled back over the desk to offer Noir a black sheet of paper.

Noir took the sheet and barked a laugh. "The bastard's calling himself Lazarus now? You'd think he wants Radiance to kill him." He continued down the paper. "I know Alucard and Brigadier, but who's Constantine?"

"He's a medic or a scientist, a pathomancer also, and he's trying to find a cure." Harley wiped his brow and shuffled behind his desk, half-cowering there as if it would protect him.

"What's his Hyde?"

"I'm still trying to figure that out. All I've been able to dig up so far is that it's a Conficta type."

"What's he doing with Alucard, Brig, and Lazarus?"

Harley fumbled over his glasses with a ragged cloth. "I don't know: hell I don't even know if he's one of the cabal."

"Is there anybody else?"

"I think so; definitely one of the Proctors; but whoever it is, they're being really careful. I can't figure out their identity."

Noir discarded the paper. "Alright, Harley, that's enough for now, but send a runner whenever you get something new."

"You're not going to kill me?"

"I said I wasn't going to."

Harley pulled himself up with a whimper, nursing his crushed hand in the guttering light of his office. "What are you going to do?"

Noir glanced back from the door and, for an instant, his eyes flashed with the cold, self-destructive rage reserved for gods and men who had lost everything. "They killed my brother, Harley." His breath hitched, ragged with hate and despair. "They burned him alive right next to me..." His hand fastened on the door handle, disfiguring the ancient Shadowsteel. "What do you think I'm going to do?"

Chapter Two

Résumé Submission

Noir vacated the steam-choked confines of Harley's alleyway for the pale sunlight of a new day.

The thoroughfare remained empty except for the undertakers occupied in unlocking Umbras, their footsteps soundless as they progressed through the skyscrapers. The scarred prison doors opened with a demure click, admitting them into the white, electric lighting within. After a few seconds, a shuddering metallic boom shook the skyscraper, a warning that the cells were open. The undertakers emerged and proceeded to the subsequent skyscraper.

One labored past Noir, dragging a cart laden with mangled corpses destined for the necromancers. Noir glanced in as it passed. *Something's off, there's too many bodies,* he thought.

'Well, the city is three hundred years old with no one but third-rate shadowmancers to repair it. Maybe the locks are degrading?'

No, someone's letting them out.

'Lazarus?'

Yeah, the question is why and how? He started toward the city center, heedless of the sweltering humidity.

'Well, all things considered, the city's holding up rather well. At least they're not trying to make it rain with a flyswatter.'

What?

'Sigh, this is what I get for being subtle: at least they're not insane ... unlike you.'

Sure they're not.

'So where to now?'

First breakfast, then a job.

'I vigorously support both endeavors; it's about time you applied yourself.'

The undertakers gradually disappeared from the streets, and with their departure doors cracked open. Men and women slipped from their nightly prisons, their bodies adorned with the scars of their Hyde's frenzied madness. They did not speak as they crept into the sunlight; instead, they huddled in on themselves, cautious of touching even those they lived with. They knew their hands had inflicted the scars their spouses carried. Family members would not kill one another when night came, for they are of the same pack, but collateral injuries were inevitable when the madness took hold, even with segregated apartments. No amount of forethought could account for human imperfection.

People slowly filled the streets. Most of them shuffled toward the center of Umbras with bags and carts to purchase their daily allotment of goods, some even pulled rambunctious children in tow. Despite the gradual increase of people, the streets never grew crowded and most doors never opened, the rooms within vacant.

This relatively small population was to be expected in a society that massacred itself every night.

The city's center, the only location in Umbras one might ever consider crowded, was a blossoming marketplace when Noir arrived. Food and trinket stalls occupied most of the central area while the exterior edge belonged to cafes and artisan yards. Shadowmancers worked in curtained stalls, their clothing pure black from the saturation their art caused, while hemomancers toiled in crimson groves or vineyards. Both labored before spectators: the shadowmancers crafting specific items, and the hemomancers spilling their blood to hasten the growth of organic life or heal injuries received during the night.

Noir took a seat in one of the cafés, a sleek little restaurant situated on the left corner of the Madra District's thoroughfare, and stored his pack beneath the chair. A young waitress greeted him, her uniform emblazoned with the orange mask that indicated her employer paid protection tithes to Ellis Madra: the district's Proctor.

"What can I get you, sir?" Her large, pointed ears stood cheerfully erect, twisting to catch any number of subtle noises.

Noir lounged in his chair, absently inspecting the marketplace's somber attire. "Coffee."

"Red or black, sir?"

"Red."

'Aw, man up! Get some real coffee; not that fake Hemomancy stuff.'

Noir resisted the impulse to roll his eyes. *Just because it's red doesn't mean it's fake.*

"Anything else, sir?"

"What else do you have?"

"We'll have fresh scones in a little while, and blackberry compote."

"We'll have that then."

She noted his order and progressed to another patron a few tables over.

'Well, she seemed pretty. Maybe you could save her from the fellow she's talking with now and get a kiss?'

We're not here for girls.

'Well you're not, but I can multi-task.'

The residual nighttime mist receded as Noir waited, reduced by the sun's rays to a thin blanket playing about his heels. It never dissipated entirely, however, because the engines beneath Umbras always churned.

Closing his eyes, Noir blocked out the currents of ambient conversation, and began tapping the armrest of his chair. His fingernails struck the Shadowsteel with a dull clink, obscuring the final snippets. *Do they never get tired of talking?*

'No, little dogs bark, unexceptional people talk. The voice seemed to settle in his head. *So, how do we begin?'*

With Alucard. He was always a coward, and will bolt the moment he gets an inkling I'm here. I'm surprised he agreed to join at all.

'Apollyon, or rather Lazarus since he's calling himself that now, probably had something to do with it; you know how he is with words, and he had plenty to draw on. Alucard never escaped your shadow; I wonder if envy robbed his sanity.'

This wasn't about envy or hate. This was about seeing us die. He's tired of irrelevant kills, of impermanent death. He wanted something lasting, something real. And that's why he stayed: I didn't suffer enough the first time, as if he would know anything about—" Noir's temper roared, burning through his veins with the poison and tearing at his thoughts. Hunching forward, he crushed down the rage, stifling the inevitable grief. The Plague's madness receded, but not before a breath of the corruption leeched from his hand, rotting through the armrest.

Damn it. Noir rubbed the corroded armrest with his thumb, and a tendril of shadows slipped out from his shirtsleeve to repair the damage. *I have to burn myself soon.*

"Sir, your coffee and scones." The waitress set the coffee before him, followed by the scones and a bowl of blackberry compote, each colored the distinctive crimson of Hemomancy. "Will that be all, sir?"

Noir dismissed her and sipped the coffee. It burned his tongue but effectively routed the outside world's lingering chill. Setting the mug down, he bit into a scone and absently listened to the ambient conversations.

"You think something's happened to her?"

"Nah, this isn't the first time she's locked herself away."

"But she hasn't done anything for weeks!"

"Do you want Lock-And-Key to come out?"

"Well, no–"

"Well then, let's just hope it stays this way; her in there and us out here."

A hand tugged Noir's sleeve, drawing his attention to a girl with the white hair and Shadowsteel skin of the Umbrans. "What do you want?"

"Can I have your other scone?"

He considered her, studying the lines of her visage, the unconscious quirks that defined her, and the vial of natural hemomantic wood dangling from her neck before he surrendered the requested item.

"What's in your bag?" she asked through a mouthful, the skin of her hands delicately oscillating to shuck the crumbs.

"A story."

"What kind of story? Can I hear it?"

"It's ... not a story you would like."

"Why not?"

"The hero dies in the end."

An emotion flicked across her features before he could discern it. "That's awful."

"Yeah, it is. Now you should run along."

"What's the stick for?" The girl crouched, peering through his legs.

Noir nudged her away with a boot. "Nothing you need to worry about."

She shrugged, waved farewell and scampered toward an adjacent thoroughfare; one marked with a white sigil on a black banner. Noir finished his coffee in a gulp and signaled the waitress.

"Yes?"

"Do you have any shadowcraft you need done or fixed?"

"Well, nothing's broken, but Mistress does want a new table set. It gets quite crowded around the lunch hour."

Before she finished speaking, the cafe's attendant shadows abandoned their shelters to pool before him and rise in the shape of a table. They settled with a puff of Shadow-debris, solidifying into twining Shadowglass. Two chairs followed, each decorated like the table with a sea of minute carvings.

"That should cover my tab, your Mistress can send any complaints to Lock-And-Key." Noir retied the pack around his shoulder. "Are any of the Proctors hiring?"

"I think the White District is."

"All right, thanks."

'Cheapskate.'

"Oh, shut up. That table's better than any those charlatans can produce." He jerked his head at the shadowmancer stalls.

The waitress looked up, startled. "What?"

"Nothing."

Her eyes narrowed, but she proceeded all the same, the calls of patrons overruling one shadowmancer's insanity.

'Say what you will, but you act like you own the place.'

And how was I supposed to pay for it without money?

'Any normal, honorable person would have offered to work in restitution; probably doing something demeaning like washing dishes.'

I have better things to do than wash dishes.

'The irony in that statement being that you're dodging one job for another; one which, I might add, is even less suited to your disposition.'

You realize that you would have ended up doing those dishes as well.

'Oh, you're right—that table was a fantastic idea.'

Noir rolled his eyes and plunged into the marketplace, which adhered to no pattern or coherence and amounted to little more than a ramshackle collection of tents, wagons, stalls, and hawkers.

He traversed this medley with a contented hum, ignoring the murmurs that dogged his steps; a man with Shadowsteel flesh garnered attention even in Umbras.

Occasionally one of these vendors would accost him with offerings of hemomantic fruit or a shadowcraft article. Noir shirked each of these with a warning nudge and proceeded toward the thoroughfare marked with a white sigil.

He paused only once in his traversal, and that was outside a petite, rust-colored tent. It wasn't the tent that caught his eye, but the sign it boasted 'Money for blood, money for test subjects,' and the name its attendants shouted, "Help Constantine cure the Plague, we just need your blood, a moment of pain to save yourself and others an eternity of dying!"

He growled low in his throat, but continued on to the thoroughfare marked with a white rose banner, changed from a serpent in his absence.

'I wonder if the new Proctor is somebody we know.'

No. Anyone powerful enough to be a Proctor already was or had no interest in being one.

'I guess we could ask somebody.'

There's no point, we'll meet him soon enough.

He spotted the Proctor's guards almost instantly upon entering the thoroughfare: tall well-ordered men stationed at street corners or patrolling the larger byroads. They wore heavy, button-up coats bleached white to match their Proctor's colors, and a bandolier of five-shot winders for their pistols.

'They don't seem too bad; no one's avoiding them and they're not beating anybody up.'

They shouldn't in their own district, it would cut profits.

A guard with a multitude of emerald eyes noted Noir as he passed, observing his black skin, metallic hair, and crisp apparel.

Noir caught his gaze. "Can I help you?"

"No, sir. My apologies if I offended." He bowed and continued on his way, subtly beckoning for a pair of his nearby fellows. One vanished into the district, presumably to advise their Proctor of the new shadowmancer, the other trailed Noir.

Well, they're either pushovers or polite to the point of being some. Either way, they know you've returned.

They only know a foreign shadowmancer has entered their district.

Nah, they realized that two hours ago, they could smell you coming.

I don't smell; it's a benefit of having Shadowsteel flesh. Noir veered onto a northern offshoot marked by a succession of the Proctor's banners. Off the thoroughfare, the street constricted until only three or four men could stand abreast. The number of pedestrians also attenuated, making the increased number of guards all the more evident.

It appears they've been having trouble with another Proctor lately.

That or more people are aware of the coup than I thought. Noir passed a group of three guards slouched around a closed door. The officer, marked with a black coattail, nonchalantly polished her rifle while the younger two nervously plugged and unplugged their winders. Despite the blatant difference in experience, all three looked the same age: a benefit of restorative Hemomancy. *It seems they don't trust me.*

That's unfortunate, not that I can blame them; I mean you do look rather appalling.

Har har. Noir glanced around as the street opened into a grove of hemomantic trees, their boughs laden with apples, pears, nectarines, and other fruit. A few hemomancers inspected the trees, their fingers stained red by their craft. Noir twitched at the sight of them but continued forward.

You're becoming a downright pacifist; I thought you hated hemomancers, so why aren't we killing them? I applaud this sudden restraint and all but still…

Because it would irritate their Proctor.

Ah, so killing them isn't a possibility?

No.

Well, I guess we're just going to graciously allow them to escort you before their Proctor. You being an undocumented shadowmancer and all. Yeah, that totally sounds like you.'

I am not meeting that man in chains.

'Chauvinist.'

What?

'It could be a woman.'

It's not.

'How do you know? They have a very feminine banner.'

That banner is a statement, and there is no woman in Umbras who would need to make such a statement.

'Then what is it a statement of?'

I don't know and don't care.

Emerging from the grove, he followed the street until it ended at a skyscraper. A swath of guards surrounded it in groups of three and four, cleaning their guns or winders, checking their ammunition pouches, and staring mistrustfully at the neighboring structures. Their Proctor's banner hung from every available surface, cluttering the sky and walls with a sea of white roses on fluttering black silk.

The guards inspected Noir as he approached but only cocked their pistols or replaced their rifles' gearboxes. Unperturbed by their attention, he walked through them and descended to their citadel's sunken entrance. The last thing he heard before entering was the whisper of cloth as they stood.

'Well, aren't they friendly?'

Inside, Noir encountered a wide antechamber of flawless Shadowsteel interrupted only by strips of expensive white marble. Black pillars supported the low ceiling, which, in turn, bore a series of white electric lights in Shadowsteel cages.

A secretary looked up from across the long walkway, her antennae twitching. The guards lounging among the pillars shifted their weight, affording him a piercing inspection.

Noir crossed the intervening space and knocked his iron knuckles on her desk, noting her ordered workspace. "I wish to speak with your Proctor."

Her compound eyes pulsed through blue, red, and green as she cycled through spectrums of vision. "Do you have an appointment?"

"No."

"Then what is your name and reason for visiting?" She set aside her papers.

"I am seeking employment as a district enforcer. I am a shadowmancer."

"Yes, and with some skill it seems. I could not define the nature of your Hyde though."

She's dangerous. "So, do you have an opening?"

"For a shadowmancer, perhaps. Give me a moment." The secretary's eyes hazed over, losing both their color and their luminescence.

'Is she telepathic?' the voice asked.

Noir snapped his fingers, the nails screeching off one another like knives, a threatening sound that would have instigated any telepath's defensive mechanisms. The secretary gave no response. *She's not fully telepathic; it's just a connection, or she has two bodies.*

Her eyes flashed back on. "Proctor Doll will see you. Take the stairs to the fifth floor."

"Thank you."

'Strange that they would let you see the Proctor just like that.'

It's common practice; specialists almost always end up in a position of command sooner or later, and they need to be judged accordingly.

'So if someone was a psychotic murderer, the Proctor could assign them someplace with either little outside contact or a lot of disposable individuals of low moral fiber and a desperate need of 'correcting'?'

Exactly. Noir began his ascent, glancing in at each floor. The second level provided a dining hall of sorts, with a bar at one end while a variety of chairs and tables occupied the remaining space. The third floor housed an over-populated shooting range and the fourth a bared, well-stocked armory.

'It's like they're expecting a war to break out any minute. I wonder if the conflict is escalating because Loc's missing?'

Noir attained the fifth floor and an office room filled with clustered desks, strewn paper, and neatly uniformed men in white. The walls boasted an endless array of drawers, cabinets, and overburdened work tables, restricting the already claustrophobic space. *If the conflict is escalating due to Loc's absence, the aggressor is likely involved in the coup.*

'*It might be this Solomon Doll.*'

Several of the office workers noticed him and nudged their neighbors. *No, their temperament is too defensive. They don't know she's missing, or aren't acting on it.*

'*So the other one then.*'

Yes.

A woman approached Noir, effortlessly navigating the room. She looked almost identical to the secretary below, but her hair was a touch shorter and her form slightly heavier. "Proctor Doll's waiting for you in his office." She indicated a door set in the back wall between shuttered windows.

He nodded and crossed the room between the parting guards. Most of them would have ignored him, but a few had enough instinct to pull their friends aside. Noir spared them a final glance before entering.

Solomon Doll's office was a well-lit room cluttered with pedestals that displayed an assortment of crimson dolls. Some of the dolls resembled beasts and prowled across their pedestals with murmured growls, while others enjoyed a human aesthetic and sat at the edges of their pedestals, whispering to themselves snatches of songs or fragmented quotes from books. None were made of Shadowmancy. Their crimson hue marked them as hemomantic creations, and the passive, life-like heat they exuded branded them a facsimile of life instead of the cold, mechanical creations Shadowmancy produced.

He's a damn hemomancer.

'*Yes, so try to be polite; and remember that killing him is not a prerequisite of the job. The opposite in fact.*'

God, I hope I don't end up having to kill him; Proctor-level hemomancers take forever to die.

'*Is that really the only thing you have against them?*'

...Yeah.

Solomon Doll looked up as Noir entered, his red eyes shocking in a face of bone-white skin and crimson veins. The lidless eyes dilated, and Solomon Doll pulled a bone needle out from where it impaled his left hand. He stuck the needle between his teeth as blood welled from his palm, coagulated, and sunk back into his body, replaced by new flesh.

Solomon Doll swung his feet off the desk and leaned forward. "Hello."

Noir stifled a less than diplomatic response. "Hello."

The Proctor gestured to one of the Shadowsteel chairs, but Noir merely stepped behind the furthest one and rested his hands on its crown. Solomon Doll cocked an eyebrow at this, but made no comment. "We can start with your name since you never gave it to Elise."

"You may call me Noir."

Solomon Doll's eyebrow quirked again, conveying both humor and dissatisfaction with Noir's tone. "Alright then, Noir, I know you are a shadowmancer, but do you have any combat experience and have you ever worked for another Proctor?"

"Yes, and no." His steel molars rasped as Noir finally managed to relax his jaw.

"How good of a shadowmancer are you? And I mean your skill, not your power; Elise already relayed what she saw." The bone needle vanished into Solomon Doll's mouth.

"I'm better than anyone you have currently." His eyes darkened and his form rippled. "Converte me, et diem in noctem." *I change the day into night.*

The needle's tip poked out from the Proctor's lips. "A bold claim; though an easy one as I have no shadowmancers currently under my employ. They're all at the Academy." He exhaled an aggrieved sigh. "Alright, next question: What's your Hyde?"

"None of your damn business."

Solomon Doll's eyes darkened. "I'll let that pass for now, Noir, but if you're a danger to us..."

"I have *Rencensere* blood."

The darkened color of Solomon Doll's eyes diminished. "Are you capable of a partial conversion?"

"Infinitesimally so." Noir lifted his hand as the silver steel of his fingernails and knuckles spread outward, supplanting his flesh up to his wrist. He kept his hand partially converted for a second before undoing the transformation.

"Your control is impressive, but you're hardly unique. We have a pair with *Sanitas* blood, and I myself have *Autorius*."

"I'm not here to show off if that's what you're worried about."

"Good. Now, do you have any enemies I should worry about?"

"None."

"Any habits? A taste for blood perhaps?"

"None."

Solomon Doll shifted the needle so it stuck out the right side of his mouth. "Okay then, why did you choose us?"

"What do you mean?"

"Why did you choose to join my white guard instead of say ... Script's, who's also hiring?"

"Because green is a wimp ass color."

Up went the eyebrow. "How about Kore Byren, then? Black's a manly color."

"Because I don't have enough black in my ensemble already?"

Solomon Doll glanced at him again, noting his black apparel. "How about red then?"

"Because fuck hemomancers."

Both eyebrows flared upward. "You know I am also a hemomancer."

"Yeah, fuck you too."

Solomon Doll laughed. "Well, I see no reason not to hire you. We'll start you as a sergeant and promote you as it becomes appropriate."

"I'm more suited for lieutenant."

"I'm afraid I already have a lieutenant."

"What's his name?"

Solomon Doll's eyebrows arched up. "Rias Dorian, why?"

"I need to introduce myself and outline our relationship appropriately." Noir departed, closing the door behind him.

'Remember, be polite; these are going to be our friends soon.'

"Alright, who's Rias Dorian?" The room fell silent, and every eye focused on Noir.

'I said be polite.'

Yeah, I ignored you.

'I thought I taught you better than that.'

You didn't.

He scanned the room, following the expectant eyes as they focused on another man. This man stood from behind his desk, pushing his chair back with a controlled motion, and faced Noir. The man, presumably Rias Dorian, advanced, taking the time to clean his dark glasses and glower from beneath furrowed brows.

Reaching Noir, he replaced his glasses in a final act of measured threat. "You will refer to me as Lieutenant Dorian, Soldier, or you'll be cleaning your own lashed flesh off the floor." The man's ears flicked up as his scaled features glittered in the electric light.

'Now remember, I said to be polite so don't skip the pleasantries. We're not barbarians.'

Fine. "It's a pleasure to make your—ah, fuck it." Noir slammed his right hand through Rias Dorian's chest. The lieutenant opened his mouth to scream, and Noir crushed his heart.

The room roared into life as white guards surged to their feet in a flurry of cocked pistols. Noir scathed them all with a glance. "This business is between me and your Proctor, so stay put."

'Well, I was hoping that they would give you a pretty secretary to romance, but you just sank that ship.'

Though the room quieted, they all remained standing with drawn pistols. Noir adjusted his grip so he held the lieutenant by his coat and reentered Solomon Doll's office.

He shoved through the cluttered pedestals and dumped the corpse in the front-most seat. "I hear you have a vacancy. I would like to apply."

Solomon glanced from Noir to the corpse and back again. "Yes, that seems to be the case." He stood, walked around the desk, and opened the door. "Temaria, please inform Gregorio that Lieutenant Dorian has suffered an accident and is in need of resurrection, thank you." He closed the door and resumed his seat. "I hope you don't expect me to capitulate just because you killed one of my officers?"

"The body's here just to prove my value, nothing more."

"Unfortunately, one of my sergeants has just been promoted. His post is available, however?"

"And what is his name?"

"Hierophant, and he happens to be our cryptologist, so don't inflict any lasting damage."

"Your wish is my command."

The room remained as he had left it: filled with a host of agitated soldiers. "Which one of you is Hierophant? Your Proctor says you've been promoted." The room didn't shift an inch.

A man stepped out from behind his desk, the four black coattails hanging from the waist of his jacket marking him as a sergeant. Noir surveyed the room, noting two other individuals attired with a pair of dark tails. "Are you Hierophant?"

The four-tailed man raised his pistols. "Yes."

'Now remember, not barbarians, not barbarians...'

"It's a pleasure to make your—"

Hierophant hurled himself to the side, his pistols barking as their hammers crashed into the bullet chamber and spat fire. The Shadowsteel bullets flew wide and plastered themselves against the room's walls without a dent.

This is what I get for being polite.

The voice ignored him. *Muahaha, you would dare to use Shadow Constructs against me! Such a foolish notion!'*

Isn't that a little melodramatic?

'Well you weren't going to say it, so I had to.'

Hierophant hit the ground and rolled, flinging aside one empty pistol as the other white guards dove for cover. Hierophant came out from his roll behind a desk and jammed a winder into the pistol's side, his thumb grinding the button down. The winder whirred, and the pistol's gears turned, amassing torque and pulling the hammer back out from the bullet chamber. Noir waved his hand, and the shadows beneath Hierophant erupted into a shadow spear, impaling him from pelvis to cranium. He remained like that for an instant, held aloft by the shadow spear, and then lilted to the side. Noir crossed the room and collected his prize as the other white guards straightened.

'I wonder why they're not attacking us. We have just killed two of their commanding officers.'

They undoubtedly would be if Solomon Doll had attacked me when I brought that pompous ass Dorian in. As it is, they're waiting on his lead. He reentered Solomon's office and deposited Hierophant into a chair beside Rias Dorian.

Solomon Doll, the needle once more imbedded in his palm, favored Hierophant with a glance before refocusing on his palm. "Will you please inform Silas June that he's been promoted to lieutenant?" Noir nodded and exited.

'You realize he's a masochist, right?'

Yes, and?

'Oh, nothing.'

"Silas June, you've just been promoted."

A squirrelly man stood from his corner desk, sleek, cold eyes flicking to the bloodstains that marked Rias Dorian and Hierophant's deaths. "No. I resign, you can have the post."

"Thank you." Noir stepped back through the door. "He resigned."

"At least that makes the mess easier to clean up." Solomon gestured at the corpses where they slumped in two chairs, their blood forming into a pair of chalices. "I have things in here under control, but could you ask some of the boys to clean up outside?"

"Sure, who's your new lieutenant?"

"I believe it's Corporal Valerian; she's one of the *Sanitas* I told you about earlier." A knock came from door. "Yes, come in."

A woman with green and black mottled skin entered, her hair a tightly bound web of thorny vines. "I figured I was the next in line, so I'm here to resign and ... congratulate our new lieutenant?" She beamed at Noir.

"Yes, I do believe congratulations are in order, Lieutenant Noir."

Corporal Valerian's smile blossomed into a grin, and she elbowed him in the side. "Congratulations, sir! You really must tell me your secret someday."

Noir just looked at her.

'I'm so proud of you! Not an hour into your first post and you're already a lieutenant!'

Oh, shut up. Noir turned to Solomon Doll. "Is there anything I need before starting?"

"The Doll House will provide anything you require, including your uniform and implements. I do suggest, however, that you make yourself presentable if possible." He gestured at Noir's unruly steel hair.

Noir tapped his beard with a fingernail, causing it to ring out. "It's difficult but manageable."

"Good." Solomon Doll reclined back into his chair. "I don't believe there's any need for introductions as you've already killed your fellow officers, so you're free for the remainder of the day. If you require accommodations, there are rooms on the upper floors that you're free to use while in my employ."

"No. If you need me, I'll be in the Undercity where the engines are."

Solomon Doll's eyebrow climbed again. "A rather unusual choice for lodgings…"

"Is that going to be a problem?"

"Not at all. It's simply an unusual choice for lodgings."

A cursory knock sounded, and a man entered, rubbing at exhausted eyes. "I heard Lieutenant Dorian got himself killed."

"Ah, yes. Lieutenant, this is our resident necromancer, Gregorio Taim; Gregorio, this is our new lieutenant, Noir."

Gregorio glanced at Noir and hitched his shoulder pack up higher. "Are you the one who killed him?"

"Yeah, what of it?"

Gregorio snorted. "Nothing. I just wanted to know if this was going to be a habitual thing." He set his pack between the two corpses, ignoring how Solomon Doll's hemomantic beasts hissed and growled at him: hemomantic creations always hated necromancers. "I assume you'll do the mending, Proctor."

"Of course, there's no need to call for somebody else." Solomon Doll circumvented the table and sat on the front of his desk to wait.

Gregorio examined the two corpses, confirming they were dead before inspecting their injuries. "You'll have to repair the bodies before I rez' them, otherwise they'll just die again."

Solomon Doll extended his hand and the two blood chalices collapsed in upon themselves, resuming their liquid state before flowing toward the corpses. The blood sought out the injuries, buried itself in them and thickened, slowly changing into undamaged flesh. The Proctor tsked quietly and shifted toward Hierophant. "Brain injuries are so tedious. Gregorio, start on Dorian please."

The necromancer donned a pair of black spectacles from his coat pocket. "No spiritual trauma or metaphysical damage." He glanced at Noir. "It's like he died in his sleep; there won't even be any memory loss." He refocused on the corpse. "I don't see any complications, so he should be fit to work tomorrow if not today." Gregorio returned his glasses and laid both hands on the corpse. Wisps of energy burgeoned from beneath his fingers and swirled out from his hands, covering Rias Dorian's corpse in a membrane of energy as the darker threads of his clothing turned white, bleached by the Necromancy. Gregorio held that posture briefly then removed his hands, causing the black membrane to lose its subtle brilliance. "That should be enough, he'll wake momentarily." Gregorio shifted to Hierophant, his long, many-knuckled fingers retrieving his black glasses.

Rias Dorian jerked awake with a cry and surged to his feet, tearing off the black membrane. He instantly caught sight of Noir and stabbed a finger at him. "You! You damn bas–" A shadow spear shot up from the ground at his feet and impaled him.

Gregorio glanced at the corpse and sighed. "I just finished resurrecting him."

Noir shrugged. "It couldn't be helped." He turned and a light flickered in the corner of his eye. Unbidden and violent, the memory devoured him.

An image of fire flashed before his eyes, an inferno devouring him and everything around him. Everything hurt, and yet he could barely feel it. He wanted to scream as a black void yawned within him. The world screeched at him with the utter wrongness of it all. He had to find him, his brother, Alighieri. Even as the madness screamed those words at him, he knew they were a lie. Lazarus had killed Alighieri.

The memory receded, leaving Noir feeling both hollow and as if every part of him was scraping against itself. Then the voice yawned in the back of his thoughts, *'I'm bored, let's go find some goons to beat up. Or girls; we could go romance some girls.'*

Noir exhaled, breathing light back into a room whose shadows had grown unexpectedly dark. He adjusted the bag on his hips and left Solomon Doll's office. He would have to burn himself tonight to relieve the building pressure of the Plague in his veins. But for now, he calmed himself with an old promise; *just a little longer, I'll see all of you suffer: Alucard, Brigadier, Constantine, and Lazarus.*

Chapter Three

The Shadow-made Girl

Adrian watched the room bustle from a frigid Shadowsteel chair. She knew none of the men and women seated at the desks or rushing about with the shadowcraft notes and chalk boards. She could name a handful, of course, like Proctor Doll's fastidious Lieutenant Rias Dorian or a few of the messengers, but her knowledge ended there. So she studied them as they navigated the dim office space, memorizing their patterns.

They differed so much from her family; their emotions bubbled, cracked, and shone out in their every action: ire could invade speech patterns, corrupting words and escalating their voice; joy billowed up in their steps, making them bounce and rush; misery deadened the air around them, subduing voices and weighing on anyone who approached. All of these emotions blazed to her senses, as different to her family as her skin was to the chair she occupied. Sometimes she could do little more than gawk at the circus of emotions, sounds, and activity, other times she could barely contain her nausea as the sheer amount of everything they did engulfed her. She resembled them, just in a deeply muted way.

Adrian shifted uncomfortably in the unpadded chair and plucked a sheaf of papers from the abutting cabinet. The slick paper felt light in her hands despite the width and thickness of its individual sheets; no doubt a result of the creating shadowmancer's personal style.

She flicked through the pages, observing the tight, crimson script detailing a month's worth of protection tithes rendered to Solomon Doll.

"You do realize that whatever you're reading is probably classified?" A middle-aged man levered himself into a seat across from her, his eyes gray except for the violet pupils, furthering the illusion his salt-pepper hair and black-freckled skin cultivated. In reality, his age could vary across centuries.

Adrian paused her riffling. "Who are you?"

"Hierophant, I'm the–"

"The sergeant," she squeaked, hastily returning the pages.

"Yes," he replied, utterly serious, "but don't tell anyone, it's a secret between me and the world…"

She just stared at him.

"That was a joke, don't undertakers have jokes?"

"Oh, we do. It's just that …" she floundered for an appropriate response and finally settled on the truth, "that was terrible."

He leaned back into his chair, his large eyes blinking by turns horizontally and then vertically. "Yeah, it was."

She fussed under his scrutiny before recognizing that as a human reaction, and compelled herself to meet his gaze. "Is there something you needed?"

"Well, you looked rather bored, and I had an unoccupied moment." He slipped the top page from the tithe reports. "Now, I'm not much of an entertainer, but you might like this." His long, dexterous fingers danced over the page, bending unnaturally to the right and left as they folded and refolded it in a dizzying pattern. "It doesn't have much practical purpose, I'll admit, but I find the process of making them relaxing."

"Should you be doing that? Aren't they classified?" She glanced toward Rias Dorian, currently patrolling the center aisle.

"They're a month old, practically ancient history." He spoke softly, a pleasing hint of dry brogue lending character to an otherwise unassuming speech.

She inched closer, peering at the magical, convoluted movements of his hands. The page closed in on itself and he spread his fingers, unveiling a black rose. "There you have it, the sigil of our militia."

She stroked the flower with the tip of her finger and then lifted it delicately from his palm, terrified of crushing the fragile leaves. "How did you do this?"

"It's called origami. I learned it while translating Proctor Doll's books."

"It's beautiful." Adrian began to return it, but Hierophant raised his hand.

"No, you keep it. I can make as many as I want."

"Thank you. Is there anything else you can make?"

"Yes, would you like me to show you?" He pilfered a few sheets from the tithe reports and threaded his way back toward his desk. "Let's go someplace a little less crowded."

Adrian started to follow him, but something slowed her steps to a halt. She couldn't have said what exactly stalled her, but every sensation of her body simply exploded into clarity. She heard everything in the room, from the booming laughter to the scratch of a cockroach beneath a distant cabinet. She smelled everything, tasted everything, saw everything, even felt the air painting a tapestry on her skin. Then it receded, and all succumbed back into the Dollhouse's ambient clamor.

A few feet shy of Hierophant's desk, Adrian turned to the door as the first threads of silence crept outward. A man stood at the stairs, his skin darker than the night sky, Shadowmancy dark. His steel eyes flashed once, assimilating everything the room contained and then discarding it. His unkempt hair stuck out from the back of his head and chin like a tangled mass of blades, adding edge to an already sharp face.

Solomon Doll's secretary, Temaria, approached, exchanged a greeting and then retraced her steps to Solomon Doll's office. He followed, every shadow gravitating after him.

"Who is that?" she asked

Hierophant looked up from his desk. "I don't know, never seen him around here before. Probably a shadowmancer aiming to join the Proctor's militia."

"No, he's an Umbran, he can't be a shadowmancer … can he?"

"You'd know more about that subject than I; but I've seen Adepts do some freaky things, and armoring yourself in shadows doesn't seem that farfetched."

The office door closed with a soft click and activity gradually resumed. Adrian released a small breath of relief and crossed the remaining distance to Hierophant's desk, where a menagerie of paper birds occupied the available space. She bent closer, devouring every minute detail in each individual creation. "How many can you make?"

"I don't know. I've never counted, and there's always more in the book." His fingers worked across the Shadowpaper, molding it into something new.

She lifted a swan from his desk and rotated it in her hands. "I wish I could do something like thi–"

The door to Solomon Doll's office opened, silencing the room as the Umbran emerged. "Alright, who's Rias Dorian?"

Her eyes flicked to the lieutenant where he now sat several desks over. She watched him lift his gaze and stand with aggressive deliberateness. He moved elegantly, but she recognized anger in his posture and the strict dictations in his speech when he said, "You will refer to me as Lieutenant Dorian, soldier, or you'll be cleaning your own lashed flesh off the floor."

Just like that, Adrian's emotions faded away, replaced by the undertaker detachment. She looked from Rias Dorian to the Umbran and recognized the inevitable outcome even before the Umbran spoke, "It's a pleasure to make your–"

The Umbran struck, killing Rias Dorian without preamble or twitch to betray his intent. The room's inhabitants reacted with shocked silence and then a furor of profanities, cries, and drawn weapons. The Umbran subjugated them with a glance and spoke, "This business is between me and your Proctor, so stay put."

The room subsided back into uneasy silence, and he reentered Solomon Doll's office.

Hierophant dropped into his seat with a heavy exhale.

"Why did you let him go? He murdered your commanding officer in plain view."

"It's not time for us to move yet." Hierophant offered her a dainty origami glass. "You don't seem particularly distressed about it."

Adrian flinched inwardly, her undertaker detachment rattled, but accepted and slowly spun the piece in her hands. "I'm sorry, I don't always feel."

"Don't worry about it. I suppose it's to be expected, being half undertaker."

"But one of you died. Should I just accept that? Do nothing?"

"For now, yes. But, hey, don't worry about it, we die all the time. That being said, we don't really like it, so don't get any weird ideas."

"Then why didn't you do anything?" She flung her hand toward the door, unreasonably vexed by his indifference. "That Umbran just killed one of you!"

"And he'll be walking around again in a couple hours; it's really more of a compulsory break..." He gave a half-hearted shrug. "There's not really much we can do; if he's lying about his actions being sanctioned, the Proctor will handle him. If he's not, we acted appropriately. Now, about that origami–"

Without warning, a woman swung over and sat on his desk with a grin. "Hiya, Hiero, that new recruit looks rather wild." She leaned closer, her teeth flashing white. "Did you see what he did to Rias?"

"Can't say I didn't, Valerian."

"Aww, come on. You can't tell me you didn't get a twinge of satisfaction from watching Old Prissy getting hammered?" She leaned back on her hand.

Hierophant meticulously adjusted his latest creation. "I can't say I didn't, but don't tell anybody."

"Wouldn't dream of it." She gave him a light kick and then smiled at Adrian. "You must be our intern; been meaning to talk with you." She extended her hand, its red, wooden fingers contrasting with her pale skin. "Corporal Valerian."

"Adrian." She accepted the woman's hand.

"Rumor has it you're half undertaker; is this true or do I have to pay the gossip mongers a personal visit?"

Hierophant hastily interceded, "It's true, she even carries a mask..."

The Proctor's door opened again. "Which one of you is Hierophant? Your Proctor says you've been promoted."

Adrian's heart stopped, terrified she would betray Hierophant with a look. She saw Valerian gently shake her head at him, but Hierophant stood anyway, his hand slipping into his coat.

"What are you doing?" Adrian hissed after him, snatching his sleeve.

"My job." He extricated his arm and stepped out from his desk.

"Are you Hierophant?"

"Yes."

"It's a pleasure to make your–"

Hierophant lunged aside, his torque-pistols barking in preemptory retaliation. The shadow spears rent through his body all the same.

Adrian lurched toward him with a gasp, but Valerian caught her. "Leave him be, don't make more work for Gregorio; he has enough as it is."

She shivered in the woman's grip, her emotions chaotic and difficult to grasp. Eventually she sagged, horror asserting dominance until only shock remained. Adrian heard the door close again and compelled her lungs to breathe. "Why did he do that? He should have known the result."

Relinquishing her grip on Adrian, Valerian resumed her seat. "I don't rightly know, but Hierophant's always taken his position seriously. Don't worry though, Gregorio's already on his way, and he'll fix both of them in no time."

"This can't be right, why are you all so calm, so civilized?"

Valerian absently inspected one of Hierophant's creations. "Ehh, you get used to it. I'm surprised you haven't though. You see us die every night in droves, and clean up in the morning."

Adrian scratched her ear. "I'm not really old enough to have begun my duties."

Valerian returned Hierophant's paper elephant to the table. "You'll see it soon enough I guess." She shifted to the adjacent desk, where a petite man worked assiduously. "What do you make of this, Silas?"

"That I'd rather you dry roast my toes in salt and cinnamon before approaching that man, at least until my name is called." He scrawled his signature on a report and transferred it to the bottom.

"Come on, Silas, you have to have thoughts on this man. At least a whisper from the Underworld about a tall, handsome stranger with shadow skin…"

The incessant scratch of his quill stopped. "I have heard nothing about someone with that description…" He looked to Solomon's office door. "Strange, for such a distinctive personality."

Valerian bounced off Hierophant's desk and settled her forearms on his. "By that do you mean someone brooding and tormented, but a secretly loving soul?"

"Someone murderous." His quill resumed. "The Underworld takes note of people like that, and they congregate around the death circuses and merchants, all of whom know their clients intimately."

The door opened and the Umbran emerged. "Silas June, you've just been promoted."

Silas stood. "I resign; you can have the post." He resumed his seat as the Umbran vanished.

Valerian straightened. "Well, I suppose I'm next in line for succession; how exciting. Too bad it won't last." She adjusted her coat, broadened her shoulders and marched toward the door with a stern expression.

Adrian frowned. "Is she going in there to die?"

"Hardly; if you ignore her fascination with romance and her absurd ebullience, Corporal Valerian is actually a superb judge of character and ability." He wrote something across the bottom of his current sheet and stamped it with Solomon Doll's sigil. "She will not challenge the interloper without absolute certainty that she outclasses him."

Relief fluttered through Adrian's heart. "So she's going to resign like you."

"That is for her to decide."

"But she's ranked lower than Hierophant? Isn't he stronger?"

"He's ranked higher because Solomon Doll values his services more, not because her combat abilities are inferior. The contrary is more accurate"

"That doesn't make any sense; why is he having all of you fight then?"

"To give us a chance to assess him, I suspect."

"Would he really do that? Sacrifice you all just to judge him?"

"Yes, and unless you wish to meet our new lieutenant, I suggest you depart."

"How do you know he's been accepted?"

"Because Solomon Doll never killed him."

"...Are all human societies so … convoluted?"

"I wouldn't know." He stood, tidying the papers and binding them with a clip. "I have never ventured from Umbras and would prefer freezing my fingers into cherry and pepper popsicles over doing so." He departed, winding through the desks toward Solomon Doll's office.

Adrian watched him go and then examined the office space. Men and women talked with one another, laughed, worked, and—in shadowed corners—dozed. Everything seemed normal, and yet she only had to lower her gaze to see Hierophant's blood.

Eventually she left, descending through the Dollhouse and stepping into the open day. She progressed deeper into Umbras, navigating the byroads and alleys until the doors vanished and only sheer walls of Shadowsteel remained. Here the city's universal carvings lost all sense of modesty. They covered every inch of the walls, sometimes featuring characters so vast she could not see their conclusion, and other times harboring a detail so minute she could barely define its intricacy. Some focused on a single object or creature. Others depicted a masterpiece of life or death almost drowning beneath thousands of connected images.

These were the roads of her people: the undertakers.

The dull black mask hanging from her waist seemed to grow heavier as she walked, a reminder of all she lacked. The road ended at a slim wall that climbed to the very peaks of the abutting skyscrapers and carried a hundred thousand feathered wings carved onto its surface. No undertaker had ever counted the wings; they had no need to.

A wide hatch waited at the foot of the wall, distinguishable from the grating solely by the stairs visible beneath it. She knelt and pressed her fingers against the grating. It pulsed and parted for her, granting passage into the Reliquary's cool, enfolding dark. The near ubiquitous piping of Umbras tapered off here, giving way to or merging with solid, featureless walls. Curtained alcoves gradually appeared in the walls, their drapes coated with the dust of centuries.

Each housed a glass coffin where a human slept in perpetual death. A small plaque adorned each alcove, bearing the inhabitant's name and the date on which their slumber commenced. A few displayed a second date, the number of years they wished to sleep, but those were few.

The stair ended in a narrow corridor and Adrian continued along it, paying no heed to the alcoves stacked on either side of her. She traversed the frigid Reliquary with ease, having no need of light to see. She followed the corridor to a circular room, the hub of all the Reliquary's various passages. This foyer consisted of seven open doors spaced evenly along its interior, and a massive eighth door on the wall opposite her. Aside from the doors, the room contained nothing.

Adrian took the first passage on her left and followed it to a sparse room ringed in nondescript doors and cushioned chairs. She approached the third door and opened it to a flood of light and a warm cozy living space populated with sofas, blankets, and a coffee table. A kitchen, separated from the common room by a counter, occupied the left while a series of bedrooms inhabited the right. Her father puttered around the kitchen, his pale cheeks rosy with heat. He smiled at her. "Hello, dear, how did work go? Make any friends?"

"I'm not sure, and not yet." She sat at the counter. "Where's Mother? I need to speak with her."

"They're still at prayer, so you'll have to make do with me for now. What do you need?"

"Sorry, it's an undertaker thing."

"Oh. Well, I'm making candied almonds, want some?" He offered her the bowl, teasing her nose with honey and cinnamon. She sniffed at it, savoring the smell, and her stomach revolted. Nausea swamped her throat and mouth, churning her insides and tightening her grip on the counter.

"…Not today I think." She pressed a hand to her mouth and sat back.

"Nothing for it I guess, maybe your brothers will be able to have some." He started pouring the mixture into a pot. "So is it still just Solomon, Rias, and Gregorio up there."

"No, they have some corporals and sergeants now, and a new lieutenant."

"You don't sound that happy."

"I don't know… It's just that there are some of them I don't like." She shuddered, thoughts of the unnamed Umbran rising in her mind.

"Well, you should try being more human with them; undertakers have a habit of freaking-out humans."

A low bell rang from somewhere in the Reliquary, prompting Adrian to slip from her chair. "I have to go; I need to speak with Mother."

"Hey, Adrian, wait." Her father rounded the kitchen counter, his hands wrapped in a towel. "Listen to me, you don't have to be only an undertaker; you know that, right? It's okay to be a little human every now and then. You can choose; that was the whole point of sending you up. So you could choose."

She forced herself to smile and to lie, "Yeah, I know." Her father couldn't know the truth; he wouldn't have allowed her out of his sight if he knew. So she waved goodbye with a promise to try eating his almonds later, and left the embracing comfort of his kitchen for the Reliquary's cool darkness.

Adrian retraced her steps to the foyer and waited. A few seconds later, the massive door whispered open and the undertakers emerged. They glided out in silence, their sleek, perfectly black clothing slowly fading to their natural hues, and their masks of writhing shadows once more settling into dull Shadowsteel.

She could not Commune with the city, she could not join them in their worship of the Dark Father, she could barely tolerate even to manifest her key. Something in her human blood simply rebelled against these things. Thus she stood there and waited for her mother to emerge, the mask at her side a bitter reminder of her tainted blood

Her mother exited with the last individuals, her mask already doffed and her eyes uncolored by the Communion. "Walk with me."

"Yes, Mother." They turned down the first passage after the Communion Temple.

"Is Solomon Doll party to the rumored coup?"

"I have not spent enough time with him to know, but there is something else."

"What is it?"

"An Umbran joined the Doll Militia. He butchered the rival officers and assumed the post of lieutenant, but I cannot define his purpose in the Pattern. He is neither undertaker nor ferryman, architect or sentinel, nor any Umbran I recognize. He seemed human, yet his body was formed of shadows, with the exception of the Plague's corruption."

"He must be newly awakened, or perhaps… I will need to speak with the Matriarchs about this."

"About what? What is the 'perhaps'?"

Her mother glanced at her as they crossed to a small alcove, but refrained from answering.

"I will tell Father you sent me to spy on Solomon Doll…"

"He is either a new species in the Pattern, probably awakened in response to the Proctors' mounting ambitions, or a Genesis-Piece: the foundation of a species."

The human part of Adrian's soul fluttered. "He knew the Dark Father?"

"Perhaps and perhaps not. The Dark Father created many things, some of which he allowed to survive, and some he destroyed. Yet, not all Genesis-Pieces remained as he intended. Some lost control of themselves after his departure and fled into the wilds."

Fear cracked Adrian's calm. "You need me to figure out which, to figure out if he needs to die."

"His fate is for the Matriarchs to decide. For now, simply watch Solomon Doll's militia and learn all you can of the humans who would disrupt the Pattern. While we do not suspect the Proctor, he remains linked to the disturbance and cannot be ignored."

Adrian looked down, fighting to quell her human fear and disappointment. "Yes, Mother."

"One other thing."

Adrian lifted her eyes. "Yes, Mother?"

"Please, be safe."

Adrian let herself smile; there was no one else here to see, no one else here to judge, just her and her mother. "Of course."

Chapter
Four

The Night Is Young

Noir exited the citadel, affectionately dubbed "The Dollhouse" by its inhabitants, with his uniform and lieutenant's belt draped over one shoulder. The sentries straightened at his approach, offering a collection of tentative salutes and murmured congratulations. He ignored them.

'You should at least smile.'

I'm not here to make friends. Noir veered from the Dollhouse's main street into a larger byway inhabited by fewer guards and far more pedestrians. The skyscrapers remained mostly barren, but a few boasted accessories such as colored fabric, weathered signs, or displayed wares. Noir slowed to a saunter, merging with the pulsating masses while he searched the bisecting roads for a suitably abandoned alley.

'Making friends might not be our primary goal, but ensuring they're pleasantly disposed toward us cannot hurt; whereas their animosity very well might.'

It makes no difference whether they hate or love me. All men die the same.

'That's not a healthy attitude.'

Neither is dying, but people keep doing it.

An enclosed skyscraper came into view on his right, its low battlements crowned with vicious Shadowsteel barbs and ranks of soldiers. Pedestrians filed into and from the building through two small gates. They behaved demurely but exhibited no unease as they paid their monthly protection tithes.

'Appearances suggest they don't hate Solomon Doll; they might even like him.'

That's to be expected; his guards seem to behave themselves, or he keeps them in line.

'So, out of curiosity, why did you take the lieutenancy instead of the Proctorship?

Because being a Proctor is too much work and too prominent. Besides, it would be pointless to kill Solomon Doll without Lock-And-Key to inaugurate me as the Proctor.'

He traversed a second hemomantic grove, the branches of its trees laden with a variety of freshly grown fruit and vegetables. The grove tenders wandered through the trees raking up sanguine leaves, picking ripe fruit, and checking for rot. A large cart lingered nearby, its back half-full of produce. The driver—a man with the gills of a fish and a streak of fur dangling from his forearms—leaned against a front wheel, flirting with a red woman.

'I'm sure you'll be an absolute joy to work for; an inspiration to your inferiors.'

My schedule doesn't entail being a joy or an inspiration; if they need somebody to follow, they can follow their Proctor. He took another right, moving deeper into the Doll District.

'Speaking of Solomon Doll; what do you think of him?'

It's amusing that someone besides Ellis or Harlequin is stupid enough to want a war with him.

'So you noticed it also?'

Yeah; he's got a nasty streak, and it's not buried very deep and that makes me wonder why he hasn't killed whoever's gunning for his district. Noir paused at a derelict corner and peered through the rotting Shadow-cloth ropes. The two women skulking amid the pipe-work ceased their discourse, and one surreptitiously concealed a roughshod black key in her patchwork shirt. He continued on his way. *I wonder if Solomon Doll has an inkling of the coup and thinks his rival's involved.*

'That would explain his caution. Whoever this idiot is, he needs a lot more power before he could even consider challenging Loc, that or he has a sweep of powerful allies. Is there anybody strong enough to challenge Loc?'

No. Ellis Madra is the only one who's even close, and he's loyal to Loc; besides, he can't use his Hyde effectively. It has to be one of the new Proctors. Noir grimaced. *I should have asked Harley who they were.* He caught sight of a suitably obscure alley for his purpose and approached it.

'Do you think Lazarus has anything to do with this coup?'

Maybe, if he thought it would distract me. Or maybe he's just having fun destroying one of the only surviving cities.

'He and Brigadier both, although I assume she would want enough left over

to rule.'

The alley crouched beneath the eaves of a necropolis, its depths pipe-ridden, steam-clogged and utterly vacant. Even the vermin refused to occupy its confines; all beasts abhorred necromancers. The temple itself also verged on vacant, inhabited solely by the attendant necromancers and a couple individuals still recovering from their resurrections. These convalescents occupied the temple's courtyard and, for the most part, either slept or ate.

Noir entered the alley, navigating the steam and pipes until he reached a small clearing. There he exhaled and manipulated the Shadowsteel grate underfoot. It yielded willingly to his voiceless command, abandoning its density and reverting to its original insubstantial form. He slipped through the floor and dropped into the corridor below. He straightened, restoring the Shadowsteel grate, and retraced his steps toward the Dollhouse.

A stack of pipes framed the walls to either side of him. Their heat suffused the corridor, thickening the air and preserving the steam that coiled about his ankles. Noir molded the shadows as he walked, weaving them into the shapes of insects and rodents. These shadow-born creatures scurried off into the maze-like corridors of the Undercity, phasing through the walls and floors at will.

'So why aren't we just going straight down again?'

Because I want to know when they come looking for me. The shadows formed into blooming flowers all around him as delicate vines and roots streamed into the knotted pipe-work.

'Isn't this a little excessive though; and that's a lotus: they grow in water.'

Noir trailed a hand over the black lotus blossom as he passed it. *There's plenty of moisture here, and I've always loved them.* A rose bloomed to his right, its silken petals glistening with condensation. *As for excess, the Undercity is huge, and I believe in redundancy.*

'Alright, the Undercity is huge and redundancy is good, but do you have to use a different flower every time?'

Yes, there is no artistry in a monoculture.

'There's even less in chaos...'

Only if you're too scared to embrace it.

The corridor opened into a wide room. Pipes still ruled the

walls, but valves now decorated their surfaces and stairs interrupted their continuity. Noir glanced around, noting the white banners suspended over the stairs. *We should be underneath the Dollhouse now.*

He crossed to the room's center, the grate floor shifting subtly but significantly beneath him. Shadow lines dashed out from his feet, intersecting, coalescing, and separating again. An image took shape on the floor—that of a rose—complete with petals and a network of vines that enveloped every available surface. The image blinked once and stilled as Noir attained its axis, mellowing until it looked as if it had always been embossed on the floor.

Noir observed his artistry. *This should work.*

'As what?'

Too keep wanderers out of this region.

'Only after they find it.'

Word travels fast when a Proctor marks a portion of the Undercity.

He phased through the floor where more blooms, rodents, and insects were already taking shape. From there he continued downward, phasing through floor after floor until the heat made the condensation on his clothing steam. His descent ended as he breeched the final floor and plummeted three stories to crash on a massive boiler.

The hiss of exhaust pipes, the thrum of engines, and the groan of pressured iron welcomed him as he straightened, basking in the familiar light and sweltering heat of the Foundry.

A kingdom of suspended walkways extended in all directions, a vista of boilers that glowed red, engines that churned, and waterways that steamed. Noir dismounted the fuming boiler onto its encircling walkway and settled on the railing. He looked outward past the massive pipe columns and watermills, searching for and failing to see the end. *It hasn't changed a bit.* He smiled.

"Can I help you, sir?" Noir turned at the gruff voice, looking at the Engineer where it hung from the underside of another walkway. It dropped onto the boiler and scurried over on six spider-like limbs, heedless of the molten Shadowsteel.

The Engineer reached him and proceeded to hang from the side of the boiler, its long beard brushing the walkway's floor.

Noir shook his head. "I have no need of you, go about your business."

"Sir, this is not a place for pedestrians; I suggest you return to the surface where there are cages to hold you when the night comes."

"I have no need of a cage."

"Then, if you wish to stay here I must warn you against tampering with the engines; they are not for dilettantes."

"I know, now shoo."

The Engineer dithered for an instant then proceeded, its numerous, grease-blackened hands carrying it dexterously along the boiler.

Noir watched it depart and then circled the boiler until he found its door. Doffing his pack, Noir hung his uniform and lieutenant's belt over the railing. *I wish my hair had the sense not to grow.*

'Wuss.'

Shut up. Noir heaved the door open and the flames within surged upward, towering over him like a wrathful emperor. They clawed at the open air and the walls of the boiler with a thousand hungering tongues, knowing nothing of loyalty or compassion. Noir closed his eyes and stepped into their embrace. They devoured him, searing away his rotten clothing and turning his metallic hair livid red. More than that, they eradicated the Plague in his veins, purifying corruption and relieving the ever-mounting pressure it brought.

Even as he burned, however, shadows flooded in through the door and attached themselves to him, restoring his charred body and shielding him from further damage and pain.

Noir reached up a burning hand and raked his hair back, forcing the metallic strands from his eyes and into a semblance of order. That finished and his body cleansed, he stepped from the heat with a shadow-knife forming in one hand and new clothing materializing on his body. Raising the knife, he trimmed the back of his hair before applying the knife to his cheek. *Shaving is always such a nuisance.* He pulled the blade slowly down, shearing through the now pliable whiskers.

'You could always just grow it out.'

Do you realize how hard it is to see through steel bangs? Or how heavy a steel beard is?

'**If** *you don't want something to change, don't complain about it.*'

Your alternative just sucked. Noir sheared the last of his whiskers and dissolved the knife.

He moved over to the railing and donned the white coat.

'**Now,** *we wait?*'

Yeah.

'**Make** *a deck of cards; we can play Go Fish.*'

You'll be able to see my hand.

'**So?**'

Noir made a deck of cards.

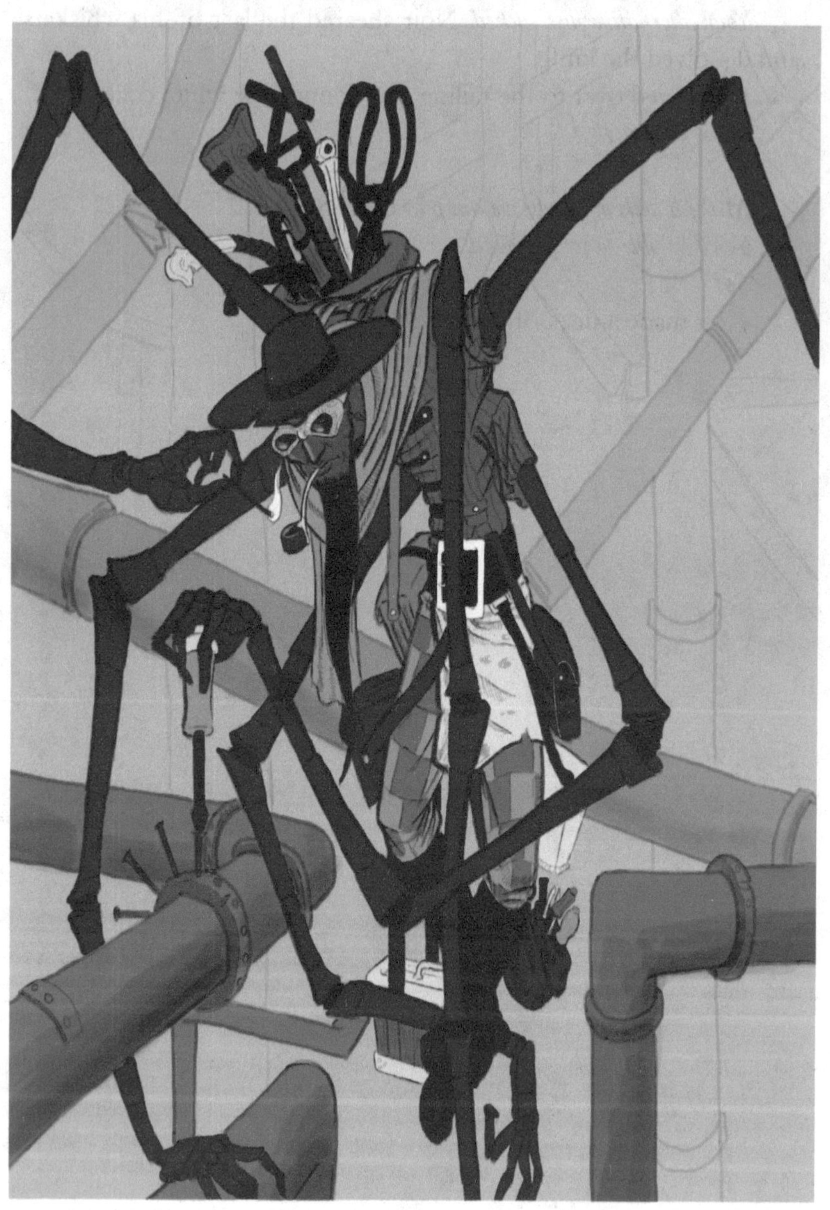

The night crept over Umbras, its fingers stretching across the vacant sky and bearing in their wake the apocalypse's venom. The undertakers emerged from their crypts, preceded by the creak of iron lanterns and the dull rattle of key chains. From there they prowled the city, hastening the tardy and compelling the unwilling into their cells.

Heedless of the icy drizzle, Noir watched this transpire from atop a broad pipe running along the Doll District's main thoroughfare. He left his bag concealed in a vault no other living creature had ever seen.

Steam burst from an exhaust pipe to his left, deepening the already prevalent haze and startling the sable butterflies that had attached themselves to his person. He straightened and strolled along the pipe toward the palace as the butterflies—the *Almas*—flitted around him. The Shadowsteel shifted underfoot, gently grasping his boots with every step to ensure the breeze never toppled him.

'Do you know where we're going?'

Yes, to this Academy Solomon mentioned.

'A very astute answer, but do you plan on roaming the city until you bump into a building labeled Academy?'

I don't need to know where it is.

The dusk slumped behind the horizon and everything slipped into the cloying, putrid dark of night. The wind stilled like prey holding its breath, and the entire city obeyed the silence. The pregnant tranquility lingered for an instant, then the screams began. They swelled in a chorus of wails and mounted higher without respite and then changed subtly, warping from cries of agony to howls of feral hate. The skyscraper quivered beneath Noir as the imprisoned monstrosities simultaneously flung themselves at the walls. The last of the undertakers vanished into their crypts; they suffered no obligation to protect those foolish enough to wander the night.

Noir lengthened his stride—moving swiftly with the fall of

night—and immersed his consciousness into the city, exploring the vast, interconnected network of Shadowmancy that was Umbras. The churning gears, engines, and waterways filled his mind alongside the walkways and skyscrapers until all of Umbras occupied his consciousness like a map with a thousand minute details. He dipped a finger into the Shadow Currents and stopped mid-stride.

Every building within a block of Noir arched away from him. *What the hell did they do to my city?* A scar across Umbras rasped in his mind, an absence where there should have been spires and cages. He spun, peering eastward at the Grim District without truly seeing it, his every thought focused on the mental image. He trembled upon his perch, metal veins sprawling from his dark eyes and knuckles, warping his skin. *What the fuck did they—*

'*Noir! Get a hold of yourself.*'

Noir snarled, baring metal fangs, but the warning jarred him from his lethal temper. The metal on his knuckles, eyes, and head slowly receded.

Whoever did that is going to die.

'*Obviously, but not tonight. Unless you want to go charging across the city like some dog after a ball nobody threw. We aren't going to find this mystery man tonight, so just tack him on the list and let's go ask Alucard; if we're lucky they're in cahoots.*'

Noir's head cocked to one side. *Cahoots?*

'*It's the first word that entered this peculiar head of ours, cut me some slack.*'

Peculiar's a polite way to describe it.

'*Whatever; thing is, let's kill Alucard as we planned and then we can teach the other idiot to push up daisies.*'

No, they're the same person; Alucard's the only one stupid enough to mess with Umbras. He rose and stalked along the pipe. *Well, the only shadowmancer at least.*

'*Oh, … well that's convenient. You know, Alucard really should have been a gravedigger; after all, he's done such a fantastic job of digging his own.*'

Noir crossed Umbras swiftly, using the ubiquitous piping as a bridge over the monsters that had escaped their cells. Not every monster was earthbound, however. Some flew and others climbed, but both hunted in Umbras' peaks. Noir encountered one of these on the fringe of the Doll District.

She crouched between the peaks of two skyscrapers on a vast, convoluted web of violet silk. She hissed at Noir, her great, leathery wings stretching out to either side. A cord twitched in her hands, briefly distracting her with a sack of webbing that, due to its size, contained an exhausted Bellua.

Her attention flicked back to Noir and she retreated, dragging her prize up onto her web. Noir continued along the pipe, shadow blades materializing before him to sever whatever tendrils of webbing impeded his progress. She hissed again as her webbing shook underfoot, but dared not challenge him.

The Variatur Hyde kept her foremost eyes fixed on Noir, but her second pair monitored her prey. She hauled her prisoner up the last couple of feet and pressed it into her web as tendrils of brackish webbing slid from her hands to envelop it. Soon all that remained of the Bellua was a vague, quivering shape.

'How about her?'

How about her what?

'How about you marry her? I bet she's pretty enough once the day comes around, and you both enjoy heights.'

How about no.

'Why not?'

Because she's not my type.

'Oh, you're so shallow! Judging a woman based on her appearance alone. Shame on you, didn't Mother teach you better?'

Oh, shut up. Noir paused at the precipice of a chasm, though a foreigner would only see it as a river of drifting mist. It eddied lazily between the two districts, muffling the violence awaiting below: the rasp of a Bellua's dragging shuffle, the screech of embattled horrors and the agonized yowls of vanquished Hydes. This void was an intentional rift, a means of delineating and segregating the districts.

'What are you waiting for? Daytime?'

Noir sighed and the shadows swirled out from him, extending across the gap as a bridge. *I don't like building temporary things.* He stepped out, the shadows hardening with a puff of Shadow-debris to reveal Shadowsteel engraved with beautiful, swirling Latin.

'What did you write?'

A story you told me once, the one about the boy who learned how to fly and went to a different world.

'Doesn't he lose his wings in the process.'

Yes, but it doesn't matter because there's no Plague in that world, and there's things he could never imagine.

'Ah, I always did like happy endings.'

Yeah, you did.

He reached the end and crossed into the Grim District, the awful scar once more boring into his thoughts

'Noir?'

Don't worry, I am in control.

A rush of movement in the periphery of his vision stalled Noir's advance. A rider with glowing dark vermillion eyes swept past on a winged Variatur Hyde and glanced at Noir. The Variatur he rode hissed and bucked, but he leaned forward and snarled into its ear, cowing the creature.

The winged monster banked back toward Noir, its rider hailing him with a muffled call. The Variatur landed several feet further ahead, clutching the side of a wall so its rider could drop onto Noir's pipe and saunter forward.

"Hello, friend, I haven't seen your face before. What brings you out tonight?" The man mostly resembled a human, marking him as *Rencensere* like Noir.

Noir bared his teeth at the man. "Move."

'Oh, you're such a charmer; it's a wonder the ladies don't fall at your feet.'

The stranger's jovial facade cracked, his features of carven stone twisting for an instant of unveiled wrath. "Now that's no way to greet someone looking to employ you." The stranger extended his arms to either side and grinned. A repulsive green light bloomed along his fingertips: Pathomancy.

Noir rolled his eyes and a spike of shadows impaled the stranger's left hand. "Piss off."

The stranger regarded his hand in aghast horror and screamed. Noir shoved past, but the stranger caught his shoulder. "Where do you think you're going?"

Noir spun, grabbed his assailant by the collar, hurled him off the edge and resumed walking. The stranger shrieked and his mount vaulted after him. A second passed and the winged monstrosity crashed down before Noir again. Its rider clutched the seeping ruin of his hand, his body twitching and spasming as nocuous green fumes slithered from his eyes and mouth: a warning to all that this man was losing control of his Hyde.

The stranger raised his good hand, pathomantic light coalescing into his claws as another two winged-creatures landed around Noir. "You're in Aradact's territory, fool, and I have no doubt that he could use your *Rencensere* blood. Now, come along with us, or I'll set my friends on you."

The shadows at their feet ballooned upward, crushing both the pathomancer and his allies. Noir kept walking.

'Well there goes another two-bit night thug, at least, until tomorrow night. I wonder about this Aradact though...'

Another two-bit Night Prince surrounded by two-bit thugs and consumed by his ambitions of Proctorship; I give him another year before he irritates a real Proctor.

'More importantly, look at your clothes! You've already started to ruin them.'

Noir glanced at his coat sleeves where the shadowmantic saturation had already begun corrupting the white fabric. *No matter, they'll just replace it whenever the fabric gets too dark.*

'This is why I said we should join Kore Byren's group, no saturation. Think of all the money you'll squander. Shame on you!'

It's just a coat. He slowed and then stopped at the edge of the pipe road. A swath of cleared ground extended before him, a triangle where three skyscrapers should have reigned. Now there was only a squat, many-pillared facsimile of the palace surrounded by a grove of natural and hemomantic trees. His hands tightened to fists in his pockets.

'Noir?'

I'm fine. Gritting his teeth, Noir vaulted off the pipe, twisting as he did so to latch onto the wall. The shadows caught his hand, stalling his descent until he vaulted again. He caught another pipe several floors down and then vaulted again, continuing in this fashion until the free-fall gave way to the Shadowsteel floor with a crash. Straightening, Noir stalked across the Academy's campus. The shadows quivered with his advent, pulsing in time with his breathing and throbbing with his anger.

A pair of the Academy's shadow guards materialized at the entrance, their tall forms opaque and poorly defined. They lifted their hands to forestall him, but the unformed shadows at their feet warped into blades and eviscerated them. Noir strode past, phasing through the door.

Alucard stilled as the deaths of his shadow guards wrenched through his psyche. He looked up from his latest piece, raising the curved knife from her back. The woman, one of his new students, whimpered and struggled in her bindings. He reached down and stroked the back of her hair. "Don't worry, this won't take but a moment." He laid the knife beside her and stepped back, wiping his hands on a cloth.

The door to his small study burst open, causing the electric light to brighten, and one of his older students entered. "Director, someone has forced entry into the Academy! We've sent Constructs to oppose him, but they're ineffective!"

Alucard kept wiping his hands despite their impeccable state. "And where is this intruder headed?"

The student squeezed to the side, clearing the way for Alucard. "He's moving toward the East Wing, sir."

"That's strange." Alucard finished wiping his hands and scrupulously folded the cloth. "There's nothing in the East Wing except students' quarters, and I doubt they engender much interest in anyone."

The woman moaned on the table behind him and thrashed against her bindings. He glanced back at her. "Quiet, I will attend to you soon enough." He strode past his student into the study hall outside. A sequence of bleak, steeply ascending pews met his gaze as lights flicked across the ceiling and walls. "It is vital we discover the nature of this interloper and, more importantly, his allegiances. If one of the Proctors has chosen to oppose us, then we must inform Proctor Grim with all haste."

He moved to his desk and pulled aside the faded wooden chair he used when lecturing.

"What is your command, sir?"

Alucard pulled the latch on the side of his desk and heard the secret compartment click open. "Wake the other instructors. Inform them of the situation and eliminate the intruder." Alucard reached into the secret compartment and extracted a large Shadowsteel book. "Do not bother me again unless it is one of the Proctors themselves who have trespassed. Also, bar the doors to this room when you leave."

The student bowed and departed, his hands already beginning shadowmantic gestures. His voice rose a moment later, filling the echoing hall with command phrases, "Shadowsteel wall..." The shadows flowed from beneath the pews and from the corners to fasten over the various entrances and solidify. His student barred the last one as he slipped out.

Alucard sighed at the inevitably of interruptions and returned to his study, eager to resume his art. He was no longer alone, however. The intruder looked up as Alucard entered, his hand splayed over the now dead woman's brow. "I see you still play your old games, Alucard."

Alucard glanced at the woman. "Such a pity that you killed her; she could have been beautiful." He flicked his gaze over Noir, remembering the last time he had seen him. He scowled; it had been such a quick death, utterly devoid of artistry and emotion. "Lazarus thought one of you might survive; I had hoped it would be your brother; he always seemed the softer of you two."

Noir snarled and surged forward a step as metal veins crawled out from his eyes and knuckles.

Alucard leapt back, slipping out the door. "Though you're not entirely without merit, rage has its place in death, and you're easy to antagonize." He clutched the book, his excitement mounting.

Noir stopped, his teeth grinding and his hand bleeding from the punctures his nails left. Alucard smirked. "I have to give credit to Lazarus, sending us to Umbras so you couldn't unleash your Hyde was very clever. Of course, if Alighieri had survived it might have proved a little troublesome. Although Lazarus probably had something prepared for him as well." Noir stared at him with glorious, perfect hate, and Alucard laughed, savoring the other man's pain. "Oh, I do love seeing you in despair, Noir, its—"

The shadows swirled up around him in a seething web of thorns, and stabbed inward. Alucard flung himself back and to the side, sweeping his arms up and around as he voiced his command phrase, "Shadow Construct: Shield!" Shadows shot up from the ground at his feet and slammed down into a series of walls. Noir's spears, however, smashed through them and lunged at Alucard who dove aside, slipping between two stabbing spears, and rolled to his feet outside his walls.

Noir pivoted with him, one hand stabbing outward in a claw and heaving the shadows up into a perfect sphere around Alucard, who grinned and opened his book. "Covenant: Libris Oscuras!" A tide of magnificent, stolen power immersed him. Alucard inhaled as the prison shrunk on him and then, taking the shadows cast from his glowing book, he shattered Noir's prison.

Noir stumbled and then reared back with a feral snarl, his whole face a patchwork of silver vines. He flung a hand skyward, and a lance the length of the room materialized in his fingers.

Alucard swept his hand downward, tearing a steel page from the book. "Shadow Law: Incarcerate Noir!" A pulse of energy coursed out from him, bearing a sinister orange glow in its wake. The illumination flashed and took shape, forming into a thousand runes on the floors, pews and ceiling so the entire room blazed with orange script.

The pulse of energy hit Noir, and he buckled with a gasp, his lance shattering. He lurched on the floor, his body contorting and snapping out and into place with a grotesque choir of sounds. He twisted onto his stomach, his whole body visibly convulsing back into place, and looked up, hissing as lines of script sprawled up his arms, legs, and clothing.

Alucard slammed his book shut with a heavy, metallic crash and sauntered around Noir. "Did you think we would just mindlessly butcher your brother? No"—he hefted the book—"we harvested him for power and meted it amongst ourselves. I got his blood and this"—he caressed the book—"is the result." The book's orange script flared.

Noir dragged himself to a hunched stand, the shadows coalescing about him with an agonized twitch of his hand. The orange markings burst on his skin, driving him back to his knees while spitting fumes.

Alucard laughed. "That's a little spell Lazarus cooked up especially for you. Any time you attempt Shadowmancy, it'll burn like hellfire."

Noir growled—a deep, rumbling rasp of air pushed through locked teeth—and stood, his body straightening inch by inch as his feet ground into and through the Shadowsteel. "I am not one of your peers, Alucard, and pain is a fragile tether." Shadows burgeoned around Noir and shot forward. They hit the ground in a heavy, boiling globule and burst into a mob of shrieking gremlins. The twitching, monstrous creatures tumbled forward in a tangled wave of half-formed bodies.

Alucard tore two sheets from his book. The first he threw into the mob with a scream of, "Shadow Construct: Thorns!" The page splintered and imploded into coiling shadows beneath the gremlins. He hurled the second page aside, flinging it in a wide arch around the lecture hall to smash just behind Noir. "Shadow Construct: Chthonic Devourer!"

Noir spun at the sound of the smashing page and vaulted as the floor beneath him morphed into a pool of liquid night. An enormous maw erupted from the pool, followed by a many-eyed, dog-like head and a scaled throat. Noir twisted mid-air, shadows forming into a platform behind his feet, and dove out of the monster's path. The pool widened and the horror lunged after him, dragging itself on two clawed hands. Noir contorted his body and threw a hand upward. A lance shot from the ground and impaled the monster through its gullet, but did nothing to deter its jaws from snapping shut around him.

Alucard laughed, reveling in Alighieri's power as the behemoth sank back into the pool. He caressed the book, imagining the Constructs, Laws, and Covenants it contained.

Then the creature's head imploded, coating the room in gory masses of shadow. Noir dropped to the ground with a heavy crash, his form livid with crimson marks and wreathed in turbulent shadows. His viscera-draped arms snapped out to either side and the room bowed inward, tearing from its foundations and straining at Alucard.

Alucard ripped another sheet from his book and threw it up, screaming, "Shadow Law: Crucifixion!" The page warped, swelling into a colossal-spiked cross, and dove. Noir looked up, his skin shining with orange light and his muscles taut with effort, just as the cross speared through his chest and into the ground.

Grunting, Alucard battered the air before him, his lips twisted in glee and his brow soaked in sweat. One after another, a dozen spears materialized in the air and stabbed downward to impale Noir. Again and again, Alucard bombarded Noir, until, finally, he stumbled from exhaustion and slumped onto an overturned pew, panting. "Not so tough ... now that we're on equal footing, Noir—"

His crucifix shattered.

Noir straightened, his body wreathed in wispy shadows. Alucard lunged to his feet, reaching for a page in his book, but a hairline blade flicked up from the floor and rent it in two. Alucard reeled back, tumbling over a pew, as his Covenant shattered. The orange script suffusing Noir and the room flickered and died, leaving them in darkness but for a single electric light on the ceiling.

Noir advanced, exhaling as the room shook. Alucard pulled the shadows before him and desperately grasped for the corruption in his blood. The madness rose, crashing through his veins with the force of a tsunami as he released his Hyde. He snarled at Noir through a crooked, fume-spilling grin, his sanity devolving in a conflux of savage glee and wild fear. Four tendrils of shadows burst from Noir's back and impaled Alucard through the shoulders and knees.

He cried out and released the final locks on his Hyde. Yet, it did not wake. The corruption continued to roil, but it effected no change on his form. There was no flood of sudden brutality, no surge of feral power; nothing but a searing pain. He collapsed as Noir tore out the tendrils, and watched his blood spill onto the floor. "What did you do?"

"Nothing much, just injected you with a little of my blood to prevent you from releasing your Hyde."

Alucard staggered back in horror and then, with every recourse exhausted, fled. He smashed a hole in the ground with a bolt of Shadowmancy and dropped into the Undercity.

He sprawled with a crash and wrapped his body in shadows. The electric light sparked on overhead as he dragged his body up with the shadows, forcing his ruptured knees and splintered shoulders to move despite their ruined state.

He heard Noir drop down after him and flung himself around a corner into a wall of sleek Shadowsteel. He crashed into it and bounced off with a clang. He hammered it with an ineffective blast of shadows and whirled about, staring down the way he had come as Noir stalked into view. Stifling a sob, he threw a volley of shadow knives at Noir and dashed along the original corridor.

He needed to reach Grim's headquarters; surely, the two of them could defeat Noir.

Alucard rounded another corner and smashed into another wall. He screamed and punched it as the lights flickered overhead, drawing his gaze up to where a streaming current of black, needle-thin vines crawled along the ceiling. Another wall slammed up from the floor, blocking his last road to Grim. Alucard cursed and hammered the wall with Shadowmancy, but it ignored his efforts. Openly weeping now, he wrenched off his assault and sprinted down the last tunnel.

He crashed from wall to wall as he fled, unable to control his reeling desperation, but every time he turned a new corner, walls of Shadowsteel blocked his path, inexorably herding him where Noir desired. He fought to release his Hyde, hoping that its enhanced physical abilities would enable him to outrun Noir, but every attempt failed.

Barely coherent through his fear, Alucard rounded the final corner remaining to him and crashed up against a wide grate. He pressed against it, reaching his hands desperately through the bars, fighting to squeeze himself out into the open city beyond. A footstep sounded behind him, and he spun.

There was Noir.

Alucard lowered himself to his knees, hands raised in supplication. "If you spare me, I can tell you everything; the names of everyone who's plotting against Lock-And-Key and everyone who helped kill Alighieri."

Noir knelt before him and gently cupped his cheek. "That is not the law that governs us, Alucard; it's an eye for an eye, blood for blood." His hand tightened, digging iron fingernails into Alucard's cheek. "There are no words for the pain you caused me, no restitution or forgiveness. But the night is young, and I have nowhere else to be until morning."

Chapter Five

Shadowmancy is peculiar in the way that personal strength has little effect on the durability of a creation. Typically durability is determined by time expended as well as how detailed it is, how clear the shadowmancer's vision, and how durable they believe and or want it to be. Power simply enables the shadowmancer to handle more material at once.

A useful feature to shadowmancy is that once settled, it can be adjusted by a different shadow-mancer. However, it must be destabilized first, a process that requires the new shadowmancer to be of equal or greater skill than his predecessor.

Shawdomancers have access to a unique ability. They can memorize and make 'blueprints' of their preferred creations. This allows them (by uttering a particular key-phrase) to create powerful or complicated works without needing hours to envision and fabricate the end product.

Promoted To Babysitter

~ Noir crouched under the bed, fighting the urge to close his eyes and cower. His twin brother sat beside him with a little smile and his head resting on Noir's shoulder.

Heavy steps thudded the old wood floor downstairs, each stride disturbing the particles of dirt around Noir's bare feet and undoubtedly scaring the little creatures that inhabited the many nooks and crannies of their house.

Closer ... closer the footfalls walked, growing ever louder as they approached the steps leading upstairs. Noir shifted in place, drawing his brother closer. Closer ... closer. Sweat beaded Noir's brow as he pressed himself against the back wall, spine forced into an abusive hunch. He couldn't lay down, it took too long to get up again.

Closer ... closer, each step making his own bruises tingle all the more violently. Closer ... closer. The great thundering strides had almost reached the steps. Alighieri, his brother, poked his side and whispered in his ear. "Fee-fi-fo-fum, I smell the blood of an Englishman." And just like that, their father passed the steps, his relentless pacing carrying into yet another circuit of the lower room. He would come upstairs eventually, but for now they were safe... ~

The sound of paws skittering across Shadowsteel woke Noir from his doze. Eyes, never more than half-closed at the best of times, flicked open as the shadow rat crawled over the edge and settled between his legs. A tremor swelled through the boiler at his back, waking him further and heralding another burst of steam. He leaned over the rat. "Who's coming?"

The rat scratched itself and then laid its forepaws on Noir's leg, transmitting an image. He saw a youth traversing the Undercity and whistling to himself as he inspected the surrounding horticulture. He wore the white coat of Solomon Doll's guards but lacked the coattails of an officer. "He's an ally, let him pass."

The rat dashed away and Noir stood, moving to rest his hands on the railing. He glanced out across the furnace chamber, watching the Engineers bustle about, and basked in the heat and the dull, shuddering thrum of engines.

How did that bastard Alucard manage to bring down even one of the skyscrapers, let alone three, Noir wondered. He leaned forward, resting his chin atop his hands.

'*I don't know either, but it probably has something to do with why Lock-And-Key vanished instead of just slaughtering them all. I wonder ... could they have conceived a way to poison shadowcraft?*'

Noir grimaced and plucked a Drosera fruit from its bait tether. The vine immediately retracted, swallowed into the Drosera's maw. *It's possible and extremely unsettling. They would need a combination of Hemomancy and Pathomancy, at least.* He bit into the luminous orange and purple fruit. *Necromancy probably wouldn't hurt either.*

'*Is anyone even capable of that?*'

I doubt many Tyrants could handle it. In fact, the only ones I can think of are Black Die and Legion. As for those who are sub-Tyrant level, I can only think of Elis; but there's no way in hell he would create something like that. Noir took another bite. *We should've searched that room before wrecking it.*

'*Yes, we should have. I tried telling you, but noooooo, you didn't want to listen to the voice inside your head.*'

You didn't say a thing about that as I recall.

'*Now you're starting to worry me; not only are you narcissistic, delusional, and homicidal, but you're also showing signs of amnesia. I think you should see a doctor: trust me, if anyone would know you're crazy, it's me.*'

Noir rolled his eyes and dropped the Drosera core over the edge. In that instant, his eyes alighted upon a skeletal pigeon. It sat perched on the walkway across from him, its body half-decayed and wreathed in viscous strands. An exposed, fabric-wrapped heart beat in its ribcage, engorged on Necromancy.

Looks like she found us. Noir thought. *Alucard's death must have tipped her off.*

'*So soon?*'

She probably sent her birds out everywhere. He set a foot on the railing and vaulted across.

'*What are we going to do?*'

Just say hello for now.

Noir landed with a thud, and the pigeon shifted about to face him. Its beak opened, the four serrated pieces peeling back on themselves to expose a wrinkled wall of flesh instead of a throat. The creature's tongue—long, sinuous, and capped with a stinger—stabbed at Noir, perforating his clothing to snap against his skin in a spray of venom.

Noir caught the tongue between two fingers. "Did you really think that would work, Brig?"

Another pigeon, almost identical to the first, landed behind Noir, eliciting a snort. "You don't plan on sending a whole flock at me, do you?"

"I imagine I could cause you more distress by unleashing it upon the city." The voice was raw and mangled, distorted by lungs forced against their nature, but unmistakably Brigadier's cruel, velvet drawl. "Maybe it will teach you some fear again?"

The first bird imploded, shattered by the shadows in its body as they swelled into a hawk. "You're going to die, Brig, but you will spend eternity doing it if you harm Umbras." He flicked the gore from his hand and the hawk took flight, hunting for Brigadier's other thralls.

"That is inevitable; some of them must die if they are ever to fear me properly, and enough must die that the other Tyrants fear me. I will eat your city hollow if I must, but I will be feared."

"No, you're going to die and be forgotten like all the other almost-somebodies."

"Oh? And how are you going to fight me without your Shadowmancy? The moment you do, they'll know you're a shadowmancer, and shadowmancers capable of killing me are a short list. They'll find you, and then what will you do? Destroy your own city?" The pigeon launched itself skyward, arched, and dove into one of the open furnaces.

Noir tsked and returned to his furnace.

'So what are you going to do if she does attack?'

Intervene, of course, subterfuge be damned.

'Oh, okay. So when you commit genocide it's A-Okay, but when somebody

else does it, that's a no-no?'

I don't kill people permanently.

'Tell that to Alucard.'

He deserved to die.

'You say that, but you're biased.'

No one's perfect.

A clang sounded as one of the ceiling's trap doors opened. Someone peeked through and then slid down the ladder with practiced ease before racing along the catwalk until he stood over Noir. "Are you Lieutenant Noir?"

Noir nodded.

"The Proctor says for you to come immediately; we've got an emergency."

Looks like they discovered the bodies. Noir clambered onto the railing and vaulted up to the next walkway: a leap of almost twelve feet.

'Oh I don't know; they could be demoting you. I mean, judging from what happened yesterday that would be quite the emergency.'

Pulling himself over the railing, Noir vaulted to the next walkway and then vaulted again until he arrived beside the youth with a dull thud. "You're half-undertaker."

The youth blinked. "How can you tell?"

"The mask is a dead giveaway. I'm more interested in how something like you even happened and why you're out in the city at all." Noir brushed passed the youth.

"My parents wanted me to experience the outer world so I could decide whether to be an undertaker or not. They sent me to Proctor Doll, who agreed to watch over me as a favor." The youth's gaze flicked down the route Noir had taken. "How did you make those leaps? I've never seen a human move like that."

"Trade secret, kid."

'Why is she pretending to be a boy?'

Noir shrugged. *Undertaker girls are defenseless until their Scythes finish developing.*

'Yes, and?'

Just think about it. Undertakers are irrevocably bound to a key that opens every building in Umbras and are charged with preparing the dead for resurrection. That's a lot of power—a lot of control—over the city. Any thug with dreams of ascension would leap at the opportunity to capture a young undertaker.

'Ahh.'

Yeah. We'll have to watch her while she's out and about.

The door connecting the Dollhouse to the Undercity opened smoothly, unleashing an avalanche of sound onto Noir as he entered. The undertaker girl, following close upon his heels, gave a quiet grunt when the heavy door, uncouthly abandoned when he stepped through, nearly closed on her.

'Well, I don't know about you, but I like her.'

You like everybody.

'Yeah, but still … she's frowning at you behind your back; how could you not love her?'

Noir's lips twitched, and he braved the storm swamping the Dollhouse's ground floor. Guards streamed everywhere, laboring beneath a variety of weapons, papers, and implements while clerks struggled vainly to organize the chaos, and amidst all of this, the messengers strained to make themselves heard.

Noir advanced and, like the waters of the mythical red sea, the frenzied individuals parted around him, often trampling one another in their haste to escape. The undertaker girl followed in his wake, unabashedly staring at the parting crowd with questioning eyes.

Solomon Doll stood at the center of this conflux, surrounded by his secretary, Temaria, his second lieutenant, Rias Dorian, his necromancer, Gregorio Taim, his cryptologist sergeant, Hierophant, and a messenger. The Proctor noted Noir's approach and continued his discourse.

Rias Dorian, however, followed Solomon Doll's glance and vacated the circle. He shoved through the crowd and placed himself in Noir's path with a haughty expression. He opened his mouth to speak, one finger raised in prominent reprimand, and Noir brushed past, forcing him to fall in step, his face enflamed.

'Three…'

"Where have you been, Lieutenant? The emergency call went out an hour ago, and you only just arrived? This is unacceptable!"

'Two…'

"Do you want to die again?"

Dorian stopped short with a snarl. "You wouldn't dare."

"Try me." Noir took his place in the circle.

'One. Wait, what? You didn't kill him? Not even a little bit? And after I did that cool countdown thing too.'

Sometimes I enjoy subverting expectations. He faced Solomon Doll. "What's going on?"

"The Academy Director, Alucard Solace, was murdered last night in the Grim District."

Noir shrugged. "What's that to us; the misdemeanors of another district are not our concern."

"They are when a Proctor-level individual is the victim. Moreover, Director Alucard was murdered, as in killed permanently; there's no resurrecting him."

Noir furrowed his brow. "That makes for a short list of suspects, especially if we ignore the other Proctors."

"There's more to our morning's turbulence than a single murder; the undertakers found a dead ferryman strung up on a lamppost yesterday morning."

"You believe they're victims of the same person?"

"I don't know; the ferryman was resurrected yesterday, which leads me to believe they were different individuals, and I really hope that's the case. If it is the same person, then our murderer came from outside of Umbras, and entered at night, which means he would need a Black Coin, and the only people who possess Black Coins outside of Umbras are Tyrants."

"So you want me to investigate the ferryman?"

"No, I'll be taking Hierophant and investigating the ferryman. I want you to visit the Grim District and rub shoulders with the other militias. Get whatever information you can about Alucard while you're there, but it's also important to socialize. They'll probably try to browbeat you but don't let them. Even if it's a Proctor."

"Are you saddling me with anybody?"

"Yes, I'm having Adrian accompany you." Solomon Doll beckoned, and the undertaker girl stepped forward. "I'm entrusting him to your care. He'll serve as a secretary, drink holder, messenger, or anything else that you can think of, so long as it doesn't involve violence." Solomon Doll caught and held his eyes.

Noir matched his stare for a while before smirking. *Well, he's a smart son of a bitch, I'll give him that.*

'What? Who is? Solomon Doll?'

Yeah, he knows what she is and somehow managed to figure out that I know.

'So why is he giving her to you, someone who has the personality of a porcupine and a moral-compass he bought at a second-hand store?'

He seems to think I'll take better care of her than Dorian would. "Very well, I'll take the kid." He glanced over his shoulder. "But I'm not going to go find you if you wander off."

"Yes, sir." The girl met his gaze without blinking.

"You can stop with the saluting."

"Yes, sir." The undertaker girl, Adrian, held still for an instant and then deliberately threw another salute. A flash of humor surfaced on her lips, almost like a briefly forgotten response.

Noir affixed her with a glare and said, "har har," though inwardly he smirked. Returning his attention to the circle, he asked, "What are the rest of them here for?"

"I was assigning Lieutenant Dorian temporary command and discussing prior engagements with Temaria. Gregorio's here because he's the house necromancer and, seeing all that's been happening lately, I thought it would be wise to have him on close call."

"You mean the tension with Grim?"

"Yeah, so be careful over there; Grim's been known to hire some rather vicious thugs."

Noir withdrew from the circle. "Don't worry, I can handle myself."

"One last thing before you go: they say a new species of Umbran has shown up."

Noir paused at the door, one hand resting on the handle. "What are they called?"

"I don't know what they do, but they call themselves the Architects."

Noir surveyed the other members of the discussion, noting their uneasy shuffles and wary gazes. He refocused on Solomon. "Why haven't they appeared before and where did they come from?"

"Nobody knows, but it's got quite a few people spooked and others foretelling the resurgence of Dark Father."

Noir considered this briefly and then shrugged. "They shouldn't be a problem." He opened the door, and Adrian, her yellow and black feline ears twitching back and forth at the wealth of sounds, immediately slipped out ahead of him, ensuring he couldn't close the door on her again. Noir caught the girl by her white collar and lifted her into the air. "Stay by me, kid."

'Aww, you like the cute little baby girl!'

Hardly.

'But her ears are so cute and fluffy!'

That doesn't mean a thing. A whistle split the air, drawing Noir's gaze upward. *The trolley's here.* Dropping the girl, he set off. "This way."

"Where are we going? The Grim District's the other way?"

"We're taking the trolley." Noir crossed to the adjacent building and ascended its attending stairs.

Adrian followed him, her ears pulling back, unwittingly betraying the emotions her face concealed. "I'm sorry, Lieutenant, but I don't have any money for the trolley."

"We don't need any money, kid; we're on official inter-district business." They arrived at a suspended platform on the skyscraper's third floor. Two rows of seats occupied the area along with a small number of pedestrians and a flock of rust-hued pigeons. The whistle screamed again, heralding the trolley's arrival as it trundled around the corner.

It ground to a halt with a belch of fumes and a groan of subsiding gears. The conductor, a young Engineer with spirited red hair, named the district and issued a call for the occupants to disembark.

Noir took Adrian by the shoulder and nudged her toward the quivering vehicle. The Engineer extended a hand as they boarded. "A quarter-piece each for passage."

Noir kept pushing her forward while gesturing at his lieutenant's tails. "We're on official inter-district business."

"Very well." The Engineer retracted his long, many jointed arm and pulled a lever, causing the trolley to lurch with a cough and still again. "Proceed."

Someone had painted over the trolley's original black Shadowsteel with a copper hue, making it gleam in the sun. Whoever did this also added cushions to the trolley's double seats and implemented a thin Shadowsteel grate along the exterior, presumably to prevent people from leaning too far out. Little else had changed, however; the transparent glass floor still provided a perfect view of the city below, the boiler entombed in the trolley's stomach still heated the floor, the propelling gears still shone black in their housing lines, and the ceiling still depicted a fragment of history: a towering, many-limbed creature riddled with maws that spat fumes, fire, and ice. It seethed in a crater of its own making, surrounded by a thousand minute figures cowering in supplicant worship. It was a god from the dark-years, a destroyer that had sought to prolong and savor the collapse of civilization. Men had no names back then, so they simply called the god Malum: a name he shared with others.

Adrian wandered down the aisle, her gaze roving to drink in every detail, image, and adornment. Noir slipped into the foremost outside seat on her left and leaned on the banister, watching her inspection.

"This is incredible. How is it able to stay suspended with so little support?"

"The boiler provides both heat and upward pressure, alleviating the burden and powering the gears. How long have you been out in the city?"

Her ears flicked back, and she shot him a wary glance before sitting on the opposite bench. "Only a week or so, most of that in the Dollhouse meeting everybody and doing odd jobs: cleaning, organizing files, fetching coffee or tea."

Noir leaned his head back against the seat. "You don't have to answer my questions, kid; I'm not going to bite your head off."

The whistle sounded again, calling for the final boarders and prompting those already onboard to situate themselves. A shudder coursed along the trolley's length, followed by a surge of heat as the engines barked into life. The whistle blew again, marking their departure as the doors clattered shut. The trolley lurched forward, propelled by the many wheel-like gears protruding from its sides. It moved slowly at first but built momentum as the boiler underfoot amassed heat and steam.

'So what are we going to do about the kid? Solomon's attached her to us.'

I don't know yet; hopefully, I won't be required to babysit her at night. If Solomon Doll does decide to bunk us together, then I'll have to drug her.

'And if she wakes up and notices that you're gone?'

That's what I'm trying to figure out.

'She's still an undertaker, you could just erase her mind like you erased the ferryman's.'

No, I can't, not when she's half human; at least, not without killing her, which is something I would like to avoid.

'You could marry her then; you know, bind her to your fate and make sure she never betrays you.'

She's a little young for me and that just might blow her cover as a boy.

'Elope then, it'll just be me, you, and her out in the wilds having dubious adventures.'

That defeats the point of marrying her.

'Yes, but it makes a good story.'

Not really.

Noir glanced out the tinted window and watched the skyscrapers rumble past. Unbidden, memories of his brother rose in his mind and, for once, he let them linger, remembering the infectious laughter that always seemed to color his voice, his effortlessly blinding smile and the kindness that eventually got him killed. *God damn it...,* Noir thought, clamping his eyes shut before the tears welled. Memorizes of Lazarus soon followed, driving into his mind like a hot poker, instigating his blood and twisting his lips in a snarl. He crushed the rage before it could crest, refusing to let it poison his memories. *God damn it.*

'It's okay to vent the emotions before they build up and become toxic, you know.'

Now's not the time for that.

'Oh, is the big bad man scared of looking vulnerable before a girl?'

Pain invites questions, and I'd rather not lie more than I have to.

The trolley carried them to the Grim District, where they disembarked onto an identical platform. Noir paused as he emerged, eyes fastening on a resurrected crow where it perched on a lamppost. His eyes swept the surroundings, spotting dozens of others, and not just birds, but rodents, cats, and dogs as well. A thud sounded behind him as something dropped the decapitated corpse of his shadow hawk.

Well, this explains why Solomon's so defensive, he thought. *Brigadier's supporting Grim.*

'Which begs the question, why hasn't she ousted us to the Proctors? And where were her birds last night?'

Everyone's either dead or asleep at night, so there's no need for the posturing. As for ousting us, she can't without endangering the city.

A squadron of Grim's guards waited outside the citadel, and one, a sergeant with a feathered crest, greeted Noir at the base of the stairs. "Lieutenant Noir, I presume?"

"Yes."

"Please follow me; I will take you to the crime scene."

Noir glanced at the three Violet Militia soldiers standing behind the sergeant. "Are we to be escorted everywhere?"

"Yes, Proctor Grim has issued a command that all officer-level personnel are to be placed under constant surveillance."

"For our protection, of course."

"Primarily, but also to ensure none of you cause disturbances."

Noir fixed the sergeant with a level stare. "I'll tolerate your guards, but if any of you push me, they'll be pulling your entrails off the walls."

The sergeant quailed but held Noir's gaze. "You wouldn't dare start a war."

Noir clapped him on the shoulder. "Keep telling yourself that."

Adrian followed him, her ears pitched slightly forward in restrained humor, as the sergeant and his guards fell into step. The gold filament of their violet coats glinted in the sunlight with a promise of brilliant honor, but the scars on their flesh told a different story.

Noir assessed the subordinate guards and discarded them as Ungifted; the sergeant was a pathomancer. "First things first, kid, don't stray."

She shifted closer, whispering, "The other guards say relations are already strained enough between Solomon and Grim. We shouldn't antagonize them; it might start a war."

"War is inevitable, it's just a question of when Grim wants it to start and whether or not Lock-And-Key will let him." Noir scanned the street, noting how the pedestrians cowered from their district's soldiers. *It looks like Grim's rough on his district.*

'Would it matter if he was Radiance's promised God come to earth?'

Not in the least.

They arrived at what remained of the Academy shortly thereafter, eliciting a gasp from Adrian and a collection of grimaces from their escorts.

The Academy had been obliterated: its campus, walls, floors, ceiling and contents scattered across a swath of flattened ground. Only the original Shadowsteel foundation remained, recognizable by its far darker hue and the fact that it was slowly consuming the rubble.

A crowd milled across the wreckage, exploring the crevices and conversing with one another as they sought information. The majority wore Grim's violet, but the other ten Proctors had dispatched delegates as well. Pedestrians comprised the remaining individuals, mostly food vendors with carts offering hot beverages or breakfast. A few were news peddlers, like Harley, that alternated between pestering the officials and scrounging for information. Onlookers loitered in groups behind corded boundaries or atop the stairways and balconies of adjacent skyscrapers.

Noir glanced back at the sergeant. "Where's the body?"

The sergeant indicated the largest clump of violet guards. "Near the center."

"Thanks." Noir strode into rubble, his feet sinking in the pliant ground.

'Remember to search for his secrets.'

Yeah.

'We really should have done it before we left, but nooooo you had to flatten everything first and then wake up the Architects. Speaking of which, why isn't our pet undertaker reacting to them more?'

Because the Architects were programmed to wake only when Umbras suffered major damage; they would have woken already had Alucard not replaced the buildings he destroyed with that appalling palace of his. Noir subtly implanted a nest of shadow tendrils into the ground underfoot and sparked it into growth, sending countless invisible strands sprawling outward. A moment passed, and a slow stream of information woke in the back of his mind detailing everything that lay amid or beneath the rubble. He found something before long: a small box lost in the debris where he had fought Alucard. *It looks like we've found our treasure.*

'Too bad there's no X to mark the spot.'

His shadow tendrils thickened and, enveloping the box, smuggled it away, parting the Shadowsteel as if it were foam. Noir proceeded toward the corpse, his hands buried in their pockets and his eyes roving the shattered ground.

A snippet of conversation slipped from the hubbub, "What could have done this? Do you know how much pressure it takes to even dent Shadowsteel?"

"It was probably someone's Hyde, but if it has the power to do this, I doubt a barred door would contain it at night."

"Oh, Dark Father you don't think it'll destroy the city do you?"

"Nah, the Proctors will deal with it. Nobody can beat the Proctors—"

"But people are saying they've seen Brigadier in Umbras!"

"What! She's actually out? No, it has to be a rumor. I know she submitted herself to Lock-And-Key, but she still attacked this city…"

A towering man noticed their approach and jumped from a mound of excavated rubble. He advanced to greet them, his vibrant violet coat unbuttoned, his black boots gleaming with fresh oil and the frail sunlight reflecting off the convoluted black carapaces covering his hands and forearms. "So you're Solomon's new lieutenant."

Noir scowled, tasting Hemomancy on the air. Then as he noted the man's slicked back hair and trimmed goatee, his scowl became a smirk. "And you must be Grim."

Adrian visibly flinched and eased behind him.

'It's too bad he doesn't have a mustache, that way he could twirl it along with his megalomaniac reek… You know, now that I think of it, you should grow a mustache as well.'

Grim snorted. "I expected more from Solomon than a brute."

"I don't think you're in a position to be throwing insults; one of the most prominent shadowmancers in Umbras has just been murdered under your watch."

"We will find the perpetrator, and we will burn him alive, Lieutenant. Your presence here is superfluous. Return home and play with your dolls."

"And you should stand on your own rather than relying on the name of a myth from the Old World for power."

Grim spread his hands to either side. "If you wish to test that claim then go ahead, but you won't wake up again, and Solomon will have to find himself a new doll to play with."

Noir stepped past. "Don't worry on that account; I'm the wrong type for Solomon. He prefers porcelain toys. Now let's clean up after your glass-ass."

'Finally, the competent people can get to work.'

Yeah.

'I was talking about the girl and me.'

Oh, Shut up.

'As always, your retorts are as colorful and varied as a herd of elephants passing wind.'

Sometimes I wish yours were a little less colorful.

Past the initial contingent of violet guards, they encountered a smaller cluster of officers from the other districts congregated around the corpse, carefully inspecting the brutalized remains and discussing possible theories. Noir, following a cursory inspection, approached a sergeant garbed in Kore Byren's black coat. "Alright, what are the obvious details?"

The sergeant threw him a surprised and bleary look but answered, "As you should know, there's no resurrecting him; what you don't know is that his soul wasn't destroyed, it's simply gone. There are no signs of fire or of necromantic ritual, nothing at all to explain why he can't be resurrected. It's damn spooky."

"Thank you." Noir moved to kneel beside one of Script's corporals, a man in a dark green coat. Alucard's body was a heap of ruptured flesh and shattered bones. Glancing at the adjacent corporal, Noir resigned himself to the demands of competency. "Has a hemomancer verified the cause of death or discovered if these injuries were inflicted during the conflict or after?"

The corporal looked over, startled. "No, sir. Can they do that?"

"A competent one can and should have done so already." The corporal stared at him, and Noir blew an exasperated sigh. "Go get your hemomancer."

The corporal jerked and lurched to his feet. "Oh yes, of course, sir." He scampered off, and Noir renewed his inspection of the body.

"How did you know that Proctor Script sent a hemomancer?" Adrian crouched beside him, the color draining from her eyes as she observed the cadaver.

"Because Script is a very cautious man." Noir overturned a piece of rubble. "I would be shocked if he hadn't sent at least one from every class of Adept." The overturned piece of rubble fell with a screech, revealing a thin layer of Shadow-debris underneath. Noir dug his fingers into this, testing its quality and inquiring as to the form it once held.

Adrian saw him grimace and asked, "What is it?"

"The Shadowmancy here is basic, apart from that used by Alucard."

"Why is that a problem?"

"Because it means that all of this Shadow-debris came from the day-to-day proceedings of the Academy: it's all free-form and basic Constructs."

Her brow furrowed. "And?"

He waved a hand at their surroundings. "Look around us. Do you see any pathomantic marks? Any necromantic bleaching or Hemomancy stains?" She shook her head, comprehension dawning. "Exactly, there are no signs that whoever killed Alucard was an Adept. Whoever did this, did it solely with his Hyde." He looked at her and, noting that the color had returned to her eyes, asked, "What did you see?"

"He died in a state of terror."

"Most men die in a state of terror."

"Most weak men die in a state of terror; those who are used to fighting and winning die in a state of exhilaration and anger as they struggle to survive. This man died in a state of fear and pain; there was no strength left in him, no courage or anger, just the fear and pain."

"So he was bested wholly and utterly. Which means that whoever did this was powerful enough to debase a high-level Adept." He began tapping his arm as if in thought. "That's not good."

The corporal they met earlier reemerged from the crowds and hastened over with his sergeant in tow. Noir stood as they arrived, his hands once more buried in their pockets. "You the hemomancer?"

"Yes, I hear you want me to inspect the body."

"Yes, I want to know when and in what state his injuries were inflicted."

"What good will that do?"

Noir pointed at the corpse. "Look at the state the body's in; are you going to tell me that's normal? Adepts don't generally engage in the kind of physical conflict that would result in those injuries."

Understanding flickered in the hemomancer's cracked eyes. "You want to know if he was tortured?" Noir affirmed this, but the hemomancer was already on his knees beside the corpse, laying Hemomancy stained hands onto its breast. A heartbeat passed and the corpse darkened, its skin and clothing both assuming a reddish hue. "The majority of these injuries were inflicted when the body was in a passive or bound state." The hemomancer looked up. "He was tortured."

Noir tapped his thigh thoughtfully. "Whoever did this wanted information. I wonder if the Academy was involved in some sort of strife? An inner conflict perhaps?"

The hemomancer shook his head. "I don't think so; at least, it wasn't when I was there."

"So it was an external rival, probably somebody Grim antagonized."

The hemomancer glanced at Noir again and, taking in his white coat, shifted subtly to face him. Noir saw this and waved dismissively. "No, it wasn't us; we don't have anybody capable of killing a high-level Adept with his bare hands." The hemomancer nodded quietly but kept watching him. Noir rolled his eyes. "Alright, I think I have everything I want." He waved and departed, Adrian following.

"Where are we going?"

"To see Grim so he can tell us who he's at odds with." He caught sight of the Proctor and changed course.

"Will he even talk to us after the way you treated him earlier?"

"Let's see. Hey, Glass-Ass! I have something I want to ask you."

Grim glanced over at Noir's call, his features darkening. "I am currently occupied, Lieutenant Noir, you may speak to one of my aides instead." Grim made a sharp gesture and one of his subordinates hurried forward.

Noir waved his hand as the guard accosted him, and a tendril of shadow slithered up from beneath the man's coat to encircle his neck and snap it. The guard collapsed, and Noir continued forward, dragging him in his wake.

Grim, having already dismissed Noir from his mind, resumed speaking with the Architect standing opposite him, "I understand your problem–"

The Architect snarled, two of its four hands clenching into fists. "It is not our problem, Proctor, it is yours. We have delayed long enough; the city needs to be healed and you are in our way. "

Noir tossed the corpse at Grim's feet. "I think you lost something."

Grim spun on him, lips curling as he prepared to call for his guards until he saw the corpse. "That is an act of war, Lieutenant."

Noir shrugged. "I am a lieutenant of Proctor Solomon Doll; you owe me respect."

'This would be a great time for someone to play a set of drums.'

Grim hissed, "And do you not owe me respect?"

'I'm more inclined to respect a box of cookies, speaking of which let's get something to eat after this.'

"You have done nothing to earn my respect."

"And have you done something to earn mine?"

"I have just killed one of your soldiers in broad daylight, that act alone should merit your attention, and that's all I require for now."

'Respect is overrated anyway.'

A lack of respect is what started this whole affair.

'True, but hey, that's your problem.'

Grim seethed. "Very well, Lieutenant, you have earned my attention, but right now I have to finish speaking with this Archite—"

Noir glanced at the Architect. "We'll be gone in an hour."

The jackal headed Architect leaned forward and inhaled sharply, tasting his scent. After a long breath, the Architect withdrew. "Very well, one hour; anyone who is still here after that time has elapsed will be evicted." The Architect dove into the floor, parting the Shadowsteel as if it were water.

Noir waited until the Architect submerged and slithered through the knotted piping below, its dorsal fin protruding from the ground, before addressing Grim, "We've already found everything of use on the body and its surroundings."

"Even if that is a correct assessment, Lieutenant, this is my investigation, not yours."

"Then arrest me and be done with it. If you're not going to imprison me, I have a question for you."

"What is it?"

"The victim was tortured prior to his death, probably for

information. Thus, I wanted to ask about past conflicts and anyone you might have provoked recently."

"My personal history and that of my militia is mostly peaceful, Lieutenant. The only conflict we've experienced is the current strife with your Proctor, and that has been a wholly defensive effort." Grim glanced archly at Noir. "I don't suppose you're accusing your own Proctor of murder?"

Noir shook his head absently. "No, we're dealing with someone who's closer to Tyrant level than a Proctor."

'Tell them that if you had to make a guess, you would guess the murderer was some crazy-ass shadowmancer who's lived long enough to see the cities built. Not only that, but he's newly arrived, has a colossal grudge against somebody and is supremely irreverent toward human life.'

That would be stupid.

'But it would be fun.'

Noir considered it briefly and then discarded it as too much trouble.

Grim started. "Tyrant level? Are you certain?"

"No. I don't think we're dealing with a Tyrant or anyone of their caliber, just somebody who's superior to a Proctor; probably an *Autorius* with a Caelus Hyde."

Grim stroked his beard, humming quietly. "Hmm, Harlequin's the only Proctor with a Caelus Hyde, but he's a *Rencensere*; there would be far more devastation if he released his Hyde."

Noir shrugged. "Either way, I have to make my report, which I'll make sure everyone receives."

Grim nodded and nudged the aide's corpse. "First, I've got to deal with this mess you've made then I'll do likewise." He pivoted, bellowing commands to his troops.

Noir watched him depart. *I don't like this; he's being too lenient about me killing one of his aides.*

'Maybe he's just smitten with you?'

I doubt it.

'Hey now, don't sell yourself short. You've got a certain … well in the proper light, maybe … alright, I got nothing.'

Har har. Noir beckoned to Adrian. "Hurry up, kid, it's time we leave."

"Yes, sir."

They left quickly, but Grim's escort met them at the gate, the same sergeant and soldiers as before. Noir slowed as he saw them, resigning himself to the inevitable, and walked past without a greeting. They followed, uttering no complaint as he guided them toward the Doll District through the less occupied regions of Umbras, confirming their intended ambush. All the while, Noir carried the box he had discovered in the rubble through the ground underfoot.

The Violet Militia members struck when they closed to within a half-dozen blocks of the Doll District with their escorting sergeant addressing Noir in a soft voice, "Would you tarry for a bit, sir?"

Noir glanced over his shoulder, then acquiesced with a nod. He faced the sergeant, gently maneuvering Adrian behind him. "When I give the word, you run as fast as you can to the Doll District."

She surveyed the violet guards. "Do you want me to fetch help?"

"Don't be foolish, these men will be dead by the time you get back." When she opened her mouth again, he reached out and gently flicked her between the eyes. "Be quiet and do as you're told." He faced the sergeant once again. "Is there something wrong?"

The sergeant nodded and his subordinates fanned out. "I'm afraid so." Seeming almost apologetic, he drew his pistol and clicked the winder into its slot. It started up with a whirr, tightening the gears. "You insulted Proctor Grim and assailed one of our compatriots; these are unpardonable acts of violence." The other guards imitated him, though without apologetic demeanors.

*'**He**'s not the brightest pup in the litter.'*
Yeah.

Noir advanced a step. "In the pursuit of good sportsmanship, I am going to give you one warning: run."

The sergeant shook his head with a little smirk, any semblance of remorse eradicated. Detaching the winder, he secured it back into its slot on his bandoleer. "No can do, sir, the Proctor wants you dead. Moreover, why would we run? There are seven of us and only two of you; even if you are an Adept, that won't protect you from our bullets."

Noir glanced down the line as they leveled their weapons on him. "You're wrong on one, maybe two accounts; firstly, the boy won't be a part of this, and the second is your gross overestimation of how threatening your bullets are. Besides, I don't plan on using Shadowmancy."

The sergeant lowered his pistol, the hammer fully extended. "Oh well, that's something of a shame for you, but I'm not one to look a gift horse in the mouth."

Noir flexed his hands and glanced at the undertaker girl. "Go." She fled, ducking into a side street as the violet guards opened fire. The hammers fell with loud cracks, spitting out their Shadowsteel rounds with lethal accuracy. Noir lurched as the bullets struck him; one in the throat, five in the torso and the last on his brow.

He straightened, Shadowsteel bullets clattering to the ground. "Normally, I'm not one for showing off, but I think this situation justifies it; we don't want Grim sending anymore cannon fodder, do we?"

The sergeant locked the winder back into his pistol with a curse, and the other guards followed suit, retreating as they charged their weapons and stuffed new bullets down the barrels.

Noir pursued them without violence, subconsciously repairing his Shadowsilk shirt and disassembling their spent bullets. The violet guards readied their guns and fired again to similar effect.

Spitting another curse, the sergeant spun on his heel. "Retreat!"

Yet, even as they began their flight, Noir pulled the recumbent shadows from their various niches and blocked the exits with a prominent wave of his hand.

The soldiers cried out in response, but the sergeant turned back and discarded his gun. "I thought you weren't going to use Shadowmancy."

"I half-lied."

"It won't be enough to save you." A grotesque snap tore through the street, followed by the sound of ripping muscles as the sergeant released his Hyde. The transformation occurred in the lapse of a second; his human body split and the vestigial corruption of his form expanded to rule it entirely. The other violet guards, unable to release their Hydes without *Rencensere* or *Autorious* blood, cursed and scattered, frantically hammering the doors and twisting their handles. Noir flicked his hand again and every lock clicked into place, imprisoning them with their commander.

The Hyde roused itself from the smoking, gore-stained grating of Umbras. Its form was coated in sapphire feathers but flightless. It slunk down to its forelegs and circled Noir, its feline maw open and dripping noxious saliva. Its tail thrashed suddenly, hurling a barrage of venomous spines at Noir that just bounced off him. The sergeant retreated slightly and reassessed Noir.

'Be careful, it's a Variatur and clearly venomous; we don't know what other abilities it has.'

Probably none, he's only a sergeant.

The Variatur spat a hiss and lunged forward again, flinging spines from its tail. Noir moved easily, swerving around its assault before turning as it passed and crushing its skull against the ground with an open hand. Straightening, he flicked the gore off his hand and faced the remaining soldiers.

A squadron of White Militia had gathered just past the boundary line between the Doll and Grim Districts. They called out as he approached, and he waved in return, scanning until he saw Adrian in their midst. Lieutenant Dorian shoved through the assembled soldiers with an infuriated cry, and jabbed his finger at Noir. "What are you doing here?"

Noir halted. "I work here."

Dorian issued an exhale of exasperation and threw his hands into the air. "You should be dead!"

Noir made a mollifying gesture. "You shouldn't have worried; it was only a sergeant and half-dozen privates."

Dorian issued another cry. "No, you should have died there! If you had let them kill you, we could have issued claims of faulty protection if not full-out assault!" He sighed and rubbed his brow. "Can you tell me where your attackers are at least?"

"Yeah, they're dead somewhere back there." Noir indicated the

Grim District with a thumb.

"You killed them! How could you be so stupid?" Dorian, clawing at his hair, audibly ground his teeth. "Now they're going to claim we assaulted them! You might have just single-handedly started a war!"

Noir dismissed him with a wave. "Killing some of Grim's soldiers is not going to start a war, especially not when they were killed in his district while escorting me home."

"That's useless to us!" Dorian screamed, stabbing his finger at Noir. "I demand that you go back to the battle ground and kill yourself!"

Noir considered Dorian for a moment, then surged forward and impaled him with his hand. Dorian gurgled helplessly for a second and then fell limp. Noir discarded the lieutenant's corpse and pushed through the White Militia, who were all trying to stifle laughter, until he reached Adrian. "You okay, kid?"

"Yes, sir, I ran to the Dollhouse and informed Proctor Doll of your situation."

He strolled past, hands once more buried in his pockets "That's not what I told you to do."

"I know, sir."

Noir snorted. "We might actually be more suited for one another than I thought."

She followed him as one of the White Militia called for someone to alert Gregorio and for somebody else to help him carry Lieutenant Dorian back to the Dollhouse. "Where are we going to now, sir?"

"We are going back the Dollhouse where I'll work very hard at having you write my report."

'You scoundrel, making somebody else do your job! That is utterly despicable!'

Oh, shut up.

Chapter Six

Undertaker scythes appear when a child reaches adulthood and can take any shape, though in some rare cases scythes have been known to split. Near always, these form two identical halves.

It is equally uncommon for a scythe to adopt a purely combative design. No one is entirely sure why, but scythes usually adopt the shape of tools (albeit ones that can double as weapons) or creatures. Lastly, all scythes are partially sentient.

Adrian paused in the doorway of an unused storage room, staring at its pipe-clogged walls and a floor of smooth hatches. She didn't know what, if anything, the hatches held or concealed, but each displayed a star-shaped lock in the center and warmed her feet even through the shoes.

At the center of it all, Noir lounged in a chair of unstable shadows, his eyes closed and head leaned back, murmuring under his breath, "I don't want… What do you mean why not? Because she tried to kill me. Repeatedly. No, we shouldn't kill him yet, it's too soon–" His voice stilled and his eyes opened, at first razor sharp but softening when he recognized her. "Do you need something?"

She hesitated, embarrassed for listening to his private dialogue. "Nothing."

"Oh, get in here; I'm not going to kill you."

"…All right." She entered. "I just wanted to thank you for protecting me out there, so I brought you this." She offered him a cup of steaming cocoa. "It's not much, but Sergeant Hierophant said it was looted from Solomon Doll's private stash."

"Set it there." An intricate coffee table with six legs materialized in front of him, followed by a silken couch for her. Still cautious, she set the cocoa down and sat.

"None for you?"

"No, I can't always eat human food; my Umbran side revolts." She shrugged stiffly, trying to pass it off as inconsequential.

He nodded absently, his gaze drifting along the ceiling, which shifted like mist. "You don't have to be scared of me, Adrian, I'm not going to hurt you."

"I don't know if I can believe a man who's planning on killing some–" She clamped her mouth shut.

He snorted softly. "Nobody cares about Dorian, he's an ass and is kind of asking for it." His smile faded, growing complicated with emotions. "Besides, we have a real murderer to catch, and they're going to kill again."

"How do you know?"

"You don't kill someone powerful without an objective in mind. If it wasn't to weaken Grim, it was for power in the Academy."

"It could be personal reasons. There were rumors about Alucard, even among the undertakers." It was more than rumor, the undertakers knew what he did to his students, but they couldn't intervene. That was not their role in the Pattern.

"Every reason is personal, even if it's for someone else's benefit."

"An emotional reason then, maybe somebody he wronged?"

"That's a long list of people."

"Did you know Alucard?"

"Not personally, but he's certainly someone you hear about. Director of the Academy for Shadowmancers and Adepts; he was poised to become another Proctor in all but name." He took a sip from the hot chocolate. "Does your family know anything?"

Adrian exhaled a pent-up breath. *He drank it, so he's not Umbran.* "My family doesn't know anything; at least not that they've told me." She followed his gaze to the ceiling, watching it vacillate and finding the motions strangely soothing. "What happens when we find him?"

"We kill him." He raised his hand and a thread of shadows coiled down from the ceiling, becoming a laughing boy in his palm. "Do you know why all the walls in the living apartments and cells are perfectly flat? Why they're soft to touch and their corners are rounded?"

"So humans don't hurt themselves at night."

"Yes, so they don't hurt themselves at night. That's never something I would have thought of; sparing us pain in this existence." His hand fell, the boy vanishing. "You seem to have some of your ancestral knowledge."

"Is that important?"

"Well, imagine it: a human with Umbran knowledge, and the ability to navigate both worlds with impunity. It's an exciting prospect, and might actually bring the two races together."

"That's unlikely when humans don't trust me." The thought caused an unexpected twinge of pain; she liked these people, liked the openness of their emotions; so the distance some of them kept from her hurt more than she wanted to admit. Her undertaker detachment quickly asserted itself. *Let it go, they're only humans.*

"Of course they don't trust you, they don't even know you; but I think they will eventually, once you figure yourself out enough to start realizing your potential."

"I don't—"

"You have more than you think, Adrian, it's just going to take a little time."

She rose, the undertaker part of her uninterested in his claims while the suppressed human side flushed with giddy pleasure. "I have to go now; but thanks for talking with me, and for saving me."

"There wasn't much saving involved, but you're welcome."

Exiting the room, Adrian started down the bare corridor outside, passing a parade of unused apartments with identical doors and the occasional stair that led to another level of the inner compound. Every so often, a soldier would emerge from one of the doors, their arms burdened with files or a worn artifact and their exodus harried by a jesting voice. They would greet her and hurry about their business, restoring the corridor to its habitual silence.

She eventually reached a slim, horizontal door set in the exterior wall: the only conduit on this level between the Dollhouse's inner compound—which housed all the apartments—and the outer, which was mostly comprised of the initial five floors and the main stairways that provided uninhibited access to each level.

She slipped through onto the main stair's landing platform just as Valerian arrived from below. "Oh, Adrian, I've been looking for you."

"Oh, sorry, I was speaking with Lieutenant Noir."

"No need to apologize; Solomon just has an assignment for you. There's a disturbance along the Doll-Grim border and he's sending Hierophant. It's nothing violent, so he wants you to accompany him." She took Adrian's arm gently and started down toward the next landing. "Plus, I have a favor I wanted to ask, even though it's probably well outside of your comfort range."

"A favor?"

"Yeah. I want you to talk with Hierophant for a bit, keep him busy while you're out there."

"Why? Is there something wrong with him?"

"Hierophant has a … history with Grim and the Violet Militia in general. I won't share the specifics, but they aren't pleasant, and I'm worried about how he's taking all of this. So just talk with him for a bit, make sure he's doing all right."

"You're coming to an undertaker for emotional help with your friend?" Adrian couldn't help but smile. She sobered quickly. "Why me? I barely know him."

Valerian returned her smile with a grin as they reached the bottom of the stairs. "Yeah, but he likes you, and Proctor Doll has me breaking in new recruits, so I can't go with."

"I'll try, but I can't make any promises."

"Thank you. He's waiting downstairs." The corporal flashed Adrian an encouraging thumbs-up and returned to the office room, screaming orders at someone she couldn't see.

Well, Father did say to try and be more human. Adrian shuddered at the thought and began her slow descent. *How does one even become more open? By smiling?* She tried smiling at some of the soldiers she passed, but earned only weird glances in response. *So that's either not the way, or I'm just bad at it. Maybe both.* She groaned. *Dark Father, how am I going to do this?*

Hierophant met her with a smile at the bottom of the stairs. "Hello, Adrian, ready to go?"

"Yes."

"All right, then. Move out!" Hierophant beckoned to a cluster of soldiers and exited the Dollhouse, heading toward the Grim District.

Adrian fell into step, racking her brain for something that would interest Hierophant, anything to broach a conversation. Undertakers had jokes, but they would be far too esoteric for a human. She knew almost nothing about him and understood only the barest inkling of human society.

Thus, they progressed through the Doll District, and Adrian continued searching for a topic with growing desperation until she finally blurted, "Valerian says you have a bad history with Grim."

She clapped a hand to her mouth. "Dark Father, I'm sorry. I didn't mean to ask th—"

He waved her off. "That's alright, it's ... in the past." Despite his words, she could see tension pulling at his shoulder. "I'd rather you hear it from me anyway, instead of mess hall gossip. Did Valerian put you up to this?" Adrian nodded. "Yeah, I suppose she would. She feels responsible for me in a way."

"What do you mean?"

"She's the one who found me when I was ... when they had me." Adrian said nothing as he flipped his hand and gazed at the blue streaks running the length of his fingers and palm. "I have an unusual Hyde. Apart from being Variatur, it has the ability to secrete a variety of toxins and chemicals. I have some access to this trait in my human form"—the blue streaks expanded across his hand—"but its severely restricted in both output and versatility. My Hyde, on the other hand, has almost limitless ability to generate and, under certain conditions, develop toxins. You can imagine how valuable that makes me."

"...Grim was experimenting on you?" An emotion she couldn't describe wormed through Adrian, oozing through her detachment to coil in her throat. *Dark Father, how can they do that to one another?*

"Yeah, well not him so much, but a pathomancer who worked with him. He's one of several people trying to find a cure for the plague."

"I don't understand; how would they even harvest your toxins if you've devolved into your Hyde? Wouldn't you be uncontrollably violent? And how did they provoke your Hyde into creating the desired toxins?"

"Any man with Evolved blood has an intrinsic ability to dominate an inferior Hyde, even one with the *Rencensere* evolution. It's how the Night Princes maintain control when the Plague descends, and how the Proctors maintain control over their soldiers at night."

"But that doesn't explain how they prompted your Hyde to create the chemicals they wanted?"

"They did that through desperation. If they wanted a particular effect, they put me in a situation that produced that effect." He kept staring at his hand. "I can vaguely remember it because the pathomancer had me in his thrall, which provides a splinter of sanity. They locked me in a box of Shadowmancy and then slowly constricted it." A shudder passed through him. "I don't know how many times I died, but my Hyde eventually produced an acid that ate through it."

"Dark Father … that's awful."

"Yeah." He looked at her with haunted eyes. "They worked on me for years, killing me during the day so I couldn't escape. Every night, a necromancer woman would come and resurrect me."

"How did you get out?"

"Valerian. I don't how she found me, and she won't say, but she just came rampaging in one night while the pathomancer was away. Next thing I remember, I'm waking up to sunlight in Solomon Doll's infirmary. Now, I'm here."

"You must really hate them."

"Yeah. Sometimes—Dark Father—sometimes I even wish there actually was a war, just so I could get back at them." He rubbed the back of his neck with a chagrined smile. "It's something I'm working on with Gregorio, trying to move on from it, but he's so busy we rarely have the time."

They tramped down an alley, bypassing a ragged cart boasting an assortment of breads and meat. A few people clustered around it, haggling with the proprietor over handfuls of his scant wares. Most of his bread looked withered from age, shrunken to half its original size. The meats fared little better. Hemomantic perishables rarely lasted longer than a couple days, and deteriorated quickly over that span.

"Are you hungry?"

"What? Oh, no."

"Are you sure, because I can grab you something really quick; there's another stall not far ahead."

"No, I'm not hungry. Thank you." Her stomach tightened, reprimanding her for the lie. She couldn't allow him to buy her something though, not without knowing if she could eat it.

"All right, though I've always wondered what undertakers eat?"

"There's certain types of fruit that grow in our Reliquaries that we eat; we call them Murai."

"Doesn't it get boring eating the same thing every day?"

"Not particularly, probably because we've never had anything else. My brothers and I tire of it every now and then, but that's usually right before our bodies start craving human food."

"You have brothers? I al...," Hierophant trailed off. "We've arrived." He lengthened his stride, moving toward a thin line of White Militia. A group of ragged civilians milled across from them, their worn clothing sullied and clinging to their emaciated bodies. Hierophant pushed through the soldiers, his hands raised for quiet.

"What's going on here?"

The civilians shared glances, then a woman shuffled to the front. "Please, let us in."

"I can't..."

The woman pushed forward, her hand stretching out as if to grab him before she yanked it back. "Please, you don't know what it's like living under Grim. His soldiers do whatever they please, even when we've paid the protection tithes. There's never enough food, and the Night Princes are almost entirely unopposed! Please–"

"I can't!" Hierophant's voice, twisted with a union of helpless rage and despair, ripped through the woman's pleas. He calmed himself with a breath and resumed. "I can't. You're Grim's civilians, you belong to him; to grant you asylum would instigate a war."

One of the White Militia stepped forward with his hands outstretched to forestall another woman from crossing over. "Please, Ma'am, return to your homes; you've survived his rule before, nothing's changed–"

The second woman recoiled. "You don't understand! Everything's changed. They're searching everything, destroying everything to find the murderer. They ransacked my house to the point where there's nothing left. They dragged my sister away because they thought she might know something; my sister's agoraphobic, she hasn't been outside in years."

Voices burst from the crowd in a cacophony, their stories

crashing together and tangling into a mess of gibberish. Butchery, theft, incarceration: all committed in the pursuit of this murderer.

They pressed forward, and Solomon Doll's militia repulsed them into the median as gently as they could, forming a fence with their bodies and guns. Hierophant pulled free of the melee and staggered over to the wall.

Adrian shadowed him and watched his head sink against the building. The human part of her shuddered with a mix of anger and misery over their plight. A part of her felt the same helplessness as when she watched Noir kill Hierophant. But her undertaker half remained aloof. "I don't understand, why are they trying to escape? Everyone knows Grim's hard on his district."

"Yes, but now Grim's scared, and that makes him more volatile. He's lost a formidable asset just as the aggression between him and Proctor Doll is escalating. He probably thinks we're sabotaging him, that his district is full of our agents. So he's looking for them the only way he knows how: violently." He leaned against the wall. "And it's not just Grim, they're scared of the murderer too. Someone's died, truly died, in their neighborhood, and they don't know why or how. This life may suck, but most of us aren't ready to die just yet."

"So let them in! It's not like relations with Grim can deteriorate further, just help them!"

"That really would start a war. Prepared or not, Grim will not allow Proctor Doll to steal away his people."

A soldier hurried over to them and saluted. "Sergeant, Grim's soldiers are crossing the median."

"Damn it!" Hierophant's jaw visibly tightened as he reached a decision. "Damn it! Adrian, you're witness. Stay back as far as you can without leaving earshot." He shoved off the wall and marched forward. "Have everyone in the back ready their guns, this might get ugly, and send someone to fetch Corporal June from the Dollhouse, please."

He shoved through his fellow soldiers and then parted the cringing civilians with a gentle touch. They separated quickly, revealing a dozen of Grim's soldiers armed with pistols, sabers, and primed rifles. A corporal stood at their front, twin coils of shadows gently swirling up and down his arms. He had neither nose nor eyes, but a pair of tall bat ears extended from the sides of his head and a mat of slim, grass-like tentacles swayed on the back of his head, individually twitching at every movement in his vicinity. He was speaking as they arrived. "—aren't trying to run, are you? Or, worse yet, secede to a rival?"

The woman of before cowered in front of them. "D-D-Dark Father, n-no! We're just, just…"

Hierophant stormed to within a few feet of the opposing corporal. "What is the meaning of this?"

"Nothing, Sergeant, I'm just looking for possible secessionists in this group of Grim's beloved citizens."

"There are no traitors here, Corporal, these people are just hoping to buy food in the Doll District."

"Then why the guards?" A smile slithered onto the corporal's face.

"It's just a standard search for outlawed materials and such. We always perform it on large groups of people, don't you?"

"Proctor Grim doesn't like to restrict free trade; he believes its more profitable to endorse freedom. But this doesn't look like a shopping excursion, this looks like a bunch of people trying to run away." He grabbed an old man by the shoulder of his coat. "Why do you need elders for a shopping trip? Especially one in another district? And why are they all scared? There's nothing to be afraid of … if their intentions are honest." He thrust the man aside. "So no, I don't think they're going anywhere today."

"That's not within your authority, Corporal, unless you have a signed order from Proctor Grim forbidding these specific individuals from departing or instigating a district lock-down. If not, these people have full authorization to travel between districts for commercial reasons and visitations."

The corporal's smile slowly faded as he realized Hierophant fully intended to oppose him. "That's not a wise position, Sergeant."

"Maybe not, but it is the right one."

The corporal's eyes flicked past Hierophant to the guards he had brought and then to his own, far inferior, force. "All right, I'll take your word for it, Sergeant. But those people had best be crossing over the border again before night falls, or Grim will have your head." He stormed back across the median, the shadows writhing furiously around his arm.

Hierophant exhaled as the woman caught his arm. "Thank you, thank you, thank–"

"No, stop that." He disentangled himself from her grip. "I can't let you stay here."

She paled. "But you can't send us back. They'll kill us for sure!"

"I know, I know, but there might be somebody who can help. For now, let's get out of the open." He herded the group across the median, one eye trained on Grim's corporal.

He led the civilians several blocks into the Doll District and stashed them in a skyscraper before returning outside to await Silas June. Adrian followed the group but waited outside for him to reemerge.

He tramped up the stairs from the sunken entrance and slumped against the wall beside her. "Are you all right?"

"I'm fine; what about you?"

"I'll live." He riffled through his coat and eventually extracted a pipe into which he thumbed some red tobacco. A second later, he had the pipe lit and in his mouth. He inhaled and expelled a long trail of smoke. "What a day. We've had a murder, an assault on one of our lieutenants, and now I'm harboring refugees from one of the most powerful men in Umbras." He took another puff, and this time held his breath before exhaling.

"Should you have consulted Solomon Doll before doing this? You just antagonized some of Grim's soldiers."

"Maybe as a formality; Proctor Doll gives his officers significant bandwidth to make decisions."

"What do you plan on doing?"

"There's not really anything I can do; we have to hope that Silas can help."

"Why would he be able to help? He's a lower rank than you."

"Because he's also our liaison with the Umbras Underworld; he might know some people."

"Will he actually help us though?"

"I think so. This won't be the first time he's done something similar for Proctor Doll." Hierophant's gaze flicked down the road. "He's here? That was quick, must've been in the area." He snuffed his pipe and moved toward the approaching corporal.

Silas met them in the middle of the sunlit road, but it took Adrian an instant to recognize him. Everything about Silas had changed color; his eyes were red, his skin copper and his hair blue. The smallest change was in his switch from the official White Militia uniform to plain clothes.

"Hello, Sergeant. Proctor Doll sent me to assist you; fill me in, skip the drama."

"I have a group of people looking to immigrate into our district from Grim's, but Grim's watching them and us very closely. Do you know anybody who can smuggle them in through the Undercity without implicating us?"

"Don't worry your over-sauced head, I'll handle it, but fetch me some pistols for all the civilians."

"Why?"

"If they're watching us, then there's already a platoon waiting at the median for their people to return; we need to be able to eliminate them at the proper time. What's your cover story?"

"That they came here looking to purchase food."

"Good, we can just say they ate everything." Silas marched toward the door but paused on the threshold. "Best get moving; show yourself somewhere else for plausible deniability."

"Thank you, Silas."

Silas June disappeared into the building without another word, leaving Hierophant and Adrian to part ways.

"I hope this works."

"It will; Silas is very good at what he does. Still, I think it's best for you to leave as well, just in case this goes south."

"All right."

He dithered for a moment, watching her, then awkwardly waved. "Good bye." He marched off, summoning his guards with a command and a wave.

Adrian ignored his advice and stayed. Silas June resurfaced after a while to summon one of the sentries. "Take a couple people, don't matter who, and requisition some goods from the shops in the area. Grab some cheap food, and a variety of common goods: clothing, utensils, anything you can think of that's cheap. Not too much of it though, these people are broke. Bring it back here on the double; we don't have long."

The soldier sprinted off, calling for two of his fellows. Silas June returned to the civilians and, curious, Adrian followed him down into the skyscraper's bottom floor. The civilians huddled in the center of the room, furtively glancing about the poorly lit space. Adrian took a seat on one of the benches lining the walls and waited.

Grim's civilians gradually relaxed, some wandering about the room or conversing with Doll's soldiers, but none approached Adrian, sharing the general populous' aversion to Umbrans. She let them be, content to simply observe their interactions while waiting for Doll's soldiers to arrive.

When the door finally swung open, the still seated civilians leapt to their feet, all semblance of tranquility eradicated by a wild-eyed fear. Those who had been wandering froze mid-step and focused on the door. They all calmed when Solomon's militia descended the stairs with three small boxes and an array of guns. Behind them came a man and two women in rough, plain clothes, all three heavily armed. The evident weapons alone would have sufficed to mark them as underworlders, but they also wore identical yellow caps and immediately approached Silas.

Silas June briefly conversed with the underworlders—who promptly left afterwards—and then began distributing supplies. The boxes contained apparel mostly—universally red, for those originating from Hemomancy, and black, for Shadowmancy—but Silas doled out a couple of sets of silverware, pots, shoes and assorted gardening tools to the wealthier looking individuals.

One of the civilians looked at Silas as they unloaded the final box. "No food?"

"Bake my chest hair in olive pits, no. You will be given some when you return later today; for now, it's unlikely you could afford enough to bring back. If they ask, tell them you ate it. Are we all ready?" A chorus of affirmations responded. "All right then, let's go."

Adrian followed them to the border and waited there as they crossed the gap. Grim's soldiers surrounded them, demanding they surrender everything they bought. The civilians resisted, pleading with desperate voices strangled by fear. The soldiers ignored them and plundered everything, regardless of quality or value. Only then, when the civilians verged on weeping, did they begin herding them inwards, battering them with the butts of their rifles all the way.

Alone on the median line, Adrian waited. She waited until the evening air exploded with distant gunshots, then departed as Grim's border sentries lurched to their feet. She returned to her family's Reliquary after that, and descended to the central chamber.

Unlike before, other members of her undertaker clan moved through the chamber from the various doors. A few lingered unobtrusively in the side spaces, conversing with others in whispered tones or just waiting for someone else. None of them paid Adrian so much as a glance as she stepped from the entrance corridor and surveyed her surroundings. She spotted Sevlinn, a woman who often conversed with her mother, and crossed the chamber.

She reached the woman and pressed the fingers of one hand to her lips in a gesture of reverence. "Hello, Mistress Sevlinn, I need to speak with my mother; do you know where she is?"

"In the cleansing chamber purifying herself of the corruption. She is expecting you."

"Thank you." Adrian kissed her fingers again and departed along another corridor, following it to the cleansing chamber. A gush of bitter-smelling steam wafted out as she opened the door, coating her and the hallway in moisture.

She entered a wide bathhouse, its water literally boiling in the single large pool. Her mother kneeled in the shallows near the entrance with the water lapping about her waist. Drops of putrid green liquid trickled down her skin, the Plague's corruption excised from her body by the heat and the water.

Adrian sat on the water's edge. "Mother, I have learned more of both the man called Noir, and the possible usurper."

"What has changed that you call him 'man' and not Umbran?"

"He consumed human food, specifically chocolate from Solomon Doll's private inventory."

"That is troubling; he is either a human seeking to emulate the Dark Father and take shadows as his flesh and body, or he is truly an ancient being: a Construct from before the Dark Father wove the Pattern into our being. Some of them were capable of consuming human food." Her mother fell silent, but Adrian sensed more was to come, so she waited. The minutes trickled by and the only movement her mother exhibited was the subtle shifting of her Scythe, a net of small gems and sleek amber chains cupping her lustrous white hair. Even to Adrian, it looked trivial, a minor concession to vanity for the usually minimalist undertakers. This belied the truth, for while female Scythes developed later, they often proved far more dangerous than their male counterparts.

Adrian's mother finally stood, water and lingering corruption coursing down her steaming body. She advanced further into the bath. "And the usurper."

"I do not believe it's Solomon Doll. He has endangered himself and his position to assist people outside of his district, expending many of his already strained resources." Adrian trailed along the bath's rim to the far side, passing a few others cleansing themselves in the process.

"You have a suspicion as to the true culprit."

"Grim. He openly abuses those in his district and overtly desires power. He also experiments in toxins specifically engineered to destroy shadowmantic Constructs."

"Are you certain of this?"

"Yes. He used a Pathomancer to run experiments on an officer of Solomon Doll whose Hyde possesses the ability to create toxins."

Her mother waded to the wall and climbed from the water, using the bath seat as a stepping stool. "I will speak with the Matriarchs about this usurper and the man called Noir. For now, remain in Solomon Doll's employ, and under no circumstances are you to approach Grim or anyone that consorts with him."

"Yes, Mother."

"Adrian, I'm serious. If Grim truly intends to supplant Lock-And-Key, he will not hesitate to kill an Umbran. Do not act against him."

"Okay, Mother."

"Thank you. Try and discover more about Noir if you can."

"How do I know for certain if he is human or Umbran."

"If he bleeds red, he's human. If he bleeds black, he's Umbran." Her mother turned and walked back around the bath, her Scythe streaming down from her head and expanding into a long tunic. "And one other thing." She glanced back, eyes hard with warning. "Brigadier has abandoned her post in the palace, forsaking her subservience to Lock-And-Key. We do not know her motives, but in centuries past, she besieged Umbras and almost brought the city to ruins. If she seeks to challenge Lock-And-Key, or to usurp the city in her absence, you must run." Her mother held her eyes a moment longer to impress upon her the importance of her command, and then resumed walking.

Adrian watched her go, wondering to herself, *How in Dark Father's name am I going to get Noir to bleed?*

Chapter
Seven

Noir strode through the Undercity with Adrian in tow. Dusk neared, marking the hour for every citizen in Umbras to return to their homes; except for Adrian who was Umbran and not subject to the apocalypse's poison. She would change slightly with the night, but the madness exerted no influence over her kind.

Noir slid down a ladder, and Adrian jumped through the trapdoor after him, apparently unperturbed by the several-foot drop. "Why do you live down here instead of in the Dollhouse?"

"Because I feel like it."

"Yes, but why? Are you hiding from someone? Hiding something? Or–"

"The last person to question my motives caused something called the Shadow Apocalypse, ever heard of it?"

"No."

"That's because no one survived." He cast her a meaningful look.

"Oh… So why do you live down here?"

"For the solitude."

"You don't like people?"

"Not really, most are useless loud idiots who insist on screaming and running in circles whenever they're in danger."

"What about your parents? What were they like?"

'Ha, I knew it; she just wanted to ask about your past.'

Somehow, I doubt that. She started this conversation by asking why I sleep down here.

'Oh please, that's a rhetorical question. There are only two reasons, well three, why somebody lives in the ground. They're hiding from the law, they dislike other people, or they got barbecued and a necromancer couldn't rez' them.'

And what relevance does her curiosity even have?

'Because she's clearly sussing out if you would make a good husband, I can see it in her eyes! You mustn't waste this opportunity. Go! Sweep her off her feet and do something romantic!'

I can't tell if you're crazy or just desperate.

'Can't it be both?'

"Noir?"

He blinked. "Yeah?"

"Your parents, what were they like?"

They arrived at a hatch and Noir crouched down, favoring Adrian with a look. "My parents and I had a tumultuous relationship. I didn't like them and they didn't particularly like me." The hatch opened with a clang. "Besides, they're both dead now, so it would be irrelevant if I did."

He dropped through and she followed, her form growing spectral as the night descended and the Hydes manifested. "There must be someone you like."

'If you hurry up and fabricate some sob story, maybe she'll fall for you; chicks dig sob stories.'

"There was somebody, once." He continued down a stair. "Now that'll be enough questions."

"Yes, sir." Climbing atop the rail, she slid down after him and came to a stop beside the final hatch. Noir opened it as she arrived, and jumped through onto the walkway below. Adrian followed and paused, her spectral eyes adopting the color of a rose as the Foundry opened before her.

Noticing her hesitation, Noir stopped as well. "What are you waiting for? You've already seen all of this."

"Not really. The first time I came down here I was in such a hurry to find you that most of this was just a blur." She looked around again. "This is magnificent; I wonder why more humans don't explore it?"

'Because there is a dark, twisted and unnaturally ugly creature residing within the bowels of Umbras, accompanied only by the charming voice inside his head.'

Noir, lips pursed, contained the twitch that pulled at his mouth and adjusted the pack on his shoulders. "Most don't know it exists, let alone have any notion of how to traverse the Undercity. I was surprised you managed to find your way last time. Besides, there's a rumor that something unpleasant lives down here."

Adrian shrugged and edged around a gently swaying Drosera vine. "It wasn't that difficult. I may only be half undertaker, but that's still more than enough to navigate the city."

"They won't bite, you know."

"What?"

He pointed at the Drosera fruit. "The Drosera, they won't bite if you touch their bait."

"But aren't they carnivorous?" She glanced up the bait line to where the massive, orange bloom clung to the ceiling.

"Yeah, they're carnivorous, but they don't eat humans, there's too much apocalypse poison running through our blood. And Umbrans are inedible." He moved to the edge and motioned downward. "For the most part, they eat fish; water, especially running water, dilutes the taint."

She peered over the edge just in time to see a bloated catfish leap from the water and bite a low-hanging Drosera fruit. The vine instantly retracted, reeling the struggling fish up to the ceiling where the Drosera bloom consumed it.

"But why do these other plants hang their baits over the walkways and not the water?"

"Those aren't individual plants, kid"—he pointed up—"that's one Drosera plant, and it just hangs its bait wherever it happens to bloom."

She gawked at the massive plant, her irises changing to a pale silver. "That's all one plant?"

"Yeah and what's more, it's naturally dark skinned but gains that bright orange hue from the heat it absorbs to survive. Now come on."

'That was a dangerous thing to say, the only people who would know that are those who've seen a Drosera before it starts absorbing heat.'

I know. Let's just hope she thinks I learned it from a scholar of some sort.

'There aren't any scholars left; they ate each other after tearing up their own books.'

"So which of these engines do you call home?"

"None, and all; I'm the only one here, so I have my pick. And they all have names, by the way."

"Really? What's that one called?" She pointed beneath them, indicating a fuming engine with a churning waterwheel.

"Soliamiidas."

She floated down to the engine and partially solidified as her feet touched the walkway. Noir followed her, vaulting over the railing to land atop Soliamiidas.

"So how do you know so much about Umbras?"

"Let's just say that I know a scholar, and that I'm older than I look."

'I've always liked curious people; they'll ignore both propriety and wisdom to ask questions that you'll invariably answer too well. It's always fun seeing you get into trouble.'

Shush.

Adrian glanced around, absently rubbing her forearms together as her ears bent at the tips. "Are we allowed to be here?"

"This might as well be my kingdom, Adrian, we can stay here for as long as we want."

"But won't we bother the Engineers?"

"The Engineers don't care who comes and goes so long as they don't bother the engines."

'While I hate to bring this up, especially while your date is going so marvelously, we need to hurry. Drop a building on her or something and then scoot. We'll return in an hour or so to dig her out. She won't even realize we left.'

I know. "You should try one of these." Noir plucked a Drosera fruit and extended it to her.

Adrian's ears instantly perked up, her eyes flaring yellow. "Can I really?"

"Sure, it's perfectly harmless to humans, and should be edible to Umbrans as they're partially sustained by Shadowmancy." He waved the fruit, injecting just enough of his blood to overload her system.

'Be careful, you don't want to kill her.'

I know, don't worry.

Accepting the fruit, Adrian tentatively bit in with a squirt of luminescent juice. Her eyes widened, becoming rose-hued, and she devoured the remaining fruit.

She favored him with a wide grin and started licking her fingers.

"That was amazing." Her smile faltered and she stumbled, grabbing the railing. "Sorry, sir, but ... I'm feeling rather ... tired."

Noir caught her as she fell and laid her on the floor, softening the Shadowsteel beneath her to a far gentler, cloth-like texture.

'I'll forgo the obvious comment here and simply say that it's a shame this is the only way you can make a lady swoon.'

What was the obvious comment? Noir moved to the engine's door and knelt as the ground rippled, eschewing the black box from the Academy.

'That you were so boring she fell asleep.'

Noir made a perfunctory effort to open the box without success. *'It's probably rigged.'* He sighed, flexed his fingers and punched through the Shadowsteel lid. The box spasmed around his hand, struggling to hold its form. Noir scowled. *Can't they build anything right these days?*

'Apparently not, that's almost as bad as regular steel.'

He injected the box with his own shadows, repairing its construction to prevent it from disintegrating entirely before proceeding to disarm the trap and open the lock. Removing his hand, Noir opened the lid to reveal a sheaf of papers and several vials carved from hemomantic wood. The papers were filled with notes written in a private shorthand, so Noir set them aside and inspected one of the wooden vials.

'There's only one thing somebody wouldn't use Shadowmancy to contain.'

Yeah, I know, but it's better to be certain. Noir tore the vial's wax seal and poured its ugly, red liquid onto his other hand. He hissed as smoke erupted from his skin, the liquid bubbling and changing to a rancid brown as it dissolved into his flesh. He lunged for the railing, leaned out and extended his poisoned hand over the waterway below. The banister coiled and struck, severing his arm at the elbow.

Damn, that hurt. Noir leaned forward onto the subsiding rail as his severed hand fell into the water.

'Idiot, you could have just dropped the bloody liquid onto anything around us, but noooo, you had to go off and poison yourself!'

If I had done that, there would have been no efficient way to halt its progress; at the very least, it would have destroyed Soliamiidas. The shadows flew to his stump, solidifying into the shape of a new hand and coat sleeve before subsiding. He flexed his new fingers and resumed his perusal of the box. *So this is why Loc hasn't done anything; if so much as a drop touched her skin, she'd be erased entirely.* He returned to the papers. *These must be directions and notes, and there's probably another set for redundancy.*

'Constantine probably has them; he's both the alchemist and the pathomancer of their little tea party.'

Yeah. Noir closed the open vial and carefully packed it in the box before flinging both into Soliamiidas' burning heart. *We'll deal with that son of a bitch later, tonight we have a bigger problem.*

'Brigadier.'

Yeah. This is going to be such a pain in the ass. He closed the furnace door and knelt, doffing his pack as he did so. The grating before him churned open, revealing a lightless tunnel down into the hidden levels of Umbras. Noir dropped his pack and the shadows swallowed it as the grating resealed itself. He straightened and began his return to the Undercity.

'Where do you think she'll be? There aren't too many bodies just lying around Umbras waiting for a necromancer to resurrect them... Well actually, at this time of night there probably are, but that doesn't change the fact that they're highly unsuitable for minion-hood.'

I can't believe you just used the word minion-hood.

'Hey, I'm just a voice in your head. Anything I say, you must have thought first.'

Sometimes I really wish I wasn't crazy.

'Not me. I like you being crazy.'

Insanity aside, the corpse problem means she'll be outside the city somewhere, probably sitting atop a mountain of corpses in some forgotten graveyard from the Old World. Noir scowled. *This is going to be such a pain in the ass.*

'You already said that.'

Yeah, I know. He grabbed the rim of the hatch and vaulted into the Undercity. As he turned to close the hatch, however, he stopped, eyes fixed on the small girl from the café.

"What're you doing here?"

"Looking for you."

He finished closing the hatch. "Why?"

"Because I want to know the rest of the story."

"I already told you it's not a happy ending."

"I don't care; I want to know. What was the hero doing? Why did he die?"

Noir's chest tightened. "Someone asked him for help, said they would die if he didn't."

"And the hero helped?"

"The hero helped." The tightness clamped harder, growing painful, like icy needles driving into him.

"What happened?"

"The one asking for help betrayed the hero; he never wanted help in the first place, he just wanted to kill me." Noir ground his knuckles in the floor, warping the Shadowsteel as the Plague built within. He forced himself to exhale and curb the madness, halting the spread of metal from his eyes and knuckles.

"How did it—"

"No, that's enough for tonight." He straightened, still struggling to fetter the madness.

"Where are you going?"

"To look for an old friend."

"A hemomancer?" The thread of something crimson flashed in her eyes, and he stilled.

"No." A thread of shadows emerged from the floor and slid into the girl's bare foot, causing her no pain because she was Umbran. "A necromancer."

"A woman disappeared into the northern woods earlier today, maybe she's your friend."

Noir grimaced as his questing shadow tendril found a pulsing knot of Hemomancy buried deep within the girl's body. "Yeah that might be her." He enveloped the hemomantic knot and tentatively dug into it, exploring it and its purpose. The girl shuddered, a network of hemomantic veins cracking the surface of her skin. He released the knot and resumed his appraisal of the Hemomancy's exterior. "Are you all right?"

The red veins in her flesh slowly subsided, returning her skin to its original state. "No, I'm sick. There's something wrong with my heart." She tapped her chest, just over the hemomantic knot. "It hurts, and sometimes it feels like there's somebody else inside me, looking out through my eyes."

"Is he there now?"

"No, but the pain is."

Noir dismissed his shadow tendrils. "I hope you get better soon."

"So do I." She spun on a heel and fled, but not before Noir caught a hint of red veins worming into her eyes.

'So Brigadier went back north. She's going to resurrect her old soldiers, and this time we'll be fighting on a battlefield that she's had all day to prepare.'

Yeah. Noir stepped over the hatch, his steps dogged by a hiss of swirling steam. *This is going to be a pain in the ass, but at least it's outside of the city.*

'You do realize that after tonight it's going to be impossible to conceal that the mysterious killer is a shadowmancer?'

Yeah, but I doubt they'll look at anyone who's not a Proctor, which will protect me from their suspicions. There's only one person right now who might still see me as a possibility.

'Solomon Doll. Have I mentioned how much I like that man? He's altogether too smart for our good. He, at the very least, will start putting things together. After all, you did appear out of nowhere, and he's only got your word that you came from Umbras. This affair is growing decidedly interesting.'

Not so much as you might hope; I have a card that'll buy us a couple days.

'If you say so.'

What, don't you believe me?

'If I were to describe your ability to fix something in one word, it would be bomb.'

Noir emerged onto the Doll District's main thoroughfare and scanned the fog for movement.

'So we know she's to the North, but we still have to find her and that's a big

forest.'

Finding her won't be a problem. Noir examined his coat, assessing its bullet holes and shadowmantic saturation. *Luckily, they're giving me another coat tomorrow.*

'*All right, just so that you can have a chance to be mysterious, I'll ask. What does that have to do with anything?*'

You'll see. Noir flexed his shoulders and shadows coalesced on his back, burrowing through his coat and merging seamlessly with the shirt underneath. His coat bulged, straining against his shoulders and then ripping as four immense feathered wings stretched out, two from between his shoulders and two from his lower back. *Look upon me and despair, for I am the Archangel of Darkness.* Noir snorted at himself.

'*Hmm, impressive but popular mythology dictates that angels have only two wings, sooo ... you suck.*'

Do you know how large they would have to be to carry my weight? Besides, four wings give better balance and control.

'*But they look worse, so you still suck.*'

Oh, shut up.

'*Bad things happen to people who don't listen to their conscience.*'

So you're my conscience now?

'*No, I'm just a voice in your head that you insist on talking to, which is also a habit that tends to have tragic consequences.*'

Noir sighed and flexed his wings, stretching them in a passing breeze. They arched back, whistling as the air slid through them, and then slammed down, hurling him up from the warmth of Umbras into the vacant, frigid sky. He spun northward and inhaled, searching the freezing air for the aromas of bone, decayed flesh, and graveyard soil.

'*So why didn't we just fly over to Grim's District last night?*'

Noir circumvented a particularly high skyscraper. *Because flying is a lot harder than walking.*

'*But the wings are just Constructs? They don't even have real muscles.*'

The weight they carry is real and the strain has to go somewhere.

'*So what you're saying is that you prefer to walk because you weigh a lot?*'

Oh, shut up.

'And while we're on the subject, why didn't we just fly into Umbras in the first place? Instead of all that nonsense with the ferryman?'

Because the Sentinels would have attacked us.

'Oh, yeah, the Sentinels... What are they again?'

Umbrans that ensure no one circumvents the Ferrymen. They live up here on the tallest skyscrapers and patrol the skies, attacking everything that flies or walks over the water rather than taking the boats.

'Where are they?'

You can hear them if you listen closely, that dull buzzing is their voices but they're hard to see. He pursed his lips and whistled softly, mimicking their speech by molding the shadows in his mouth.

There was the swish of something cutting through air and then a tap as the Sentinel landed delicately on his shoulder, her clothing flecked with snow. No more than a foot tall, she leaned close to his ear, one hand gripping a white, needle-like spear just a few centimeters taller than herself. As she stood there, her body drank in the starlight and the gentle, curving grooves unique to every Sentinel gradually illuminated.

"You speak with our voice, Lieutenant; how did you learn this when most humans do not even know we exist?"

"I am old, little star, even if my body song is young."

"Why did you call out to us?"

"To ask that you conceal my passage in case someone inquires; it is a secret only my Proctor knows, and lie to him even if he asks."

"Only if you promise to return and tell us the story."

"I will sing it to you when all is done."

"Then you have our silence." She leapt from his shoulder with a swish and landed effortlessly on the tip of a lightning rod several stories below, the starlight already fading from her skin.

'Well, I didn't understand any of that, but it's spear looked familiar.'

It should. You made them.

'Oh that's right! Nasty little biters, aren't they?'

Yes, they are.

The city yielded to the lake, then open ground and a forest of rot-stricken trees, their branches uniformly desolate except for the rare leaf soaked in black oil. Noir banked and descended, circling until he found a small grove crusted in ice. Landing with a dull thud, he gave the area a cursory glance. When his inspection revealed nothing dangerous, he shucked his wings with a metallic crash and knelt to scoop away a section of snow.

The stripped earth throbbed beneath him, its sodden depths pulsing with the Plague's green fibrous infection. He scraped away the topsoil, digging through the corruption-laden filth until he found the skeleton of a mouse. He poked it with a finger and the skeleton shook, its limbs thrashing in momentary life. *Let's hope it's just waking up because she's close and not that she cast her net across the whole forest.*

'*Considering she's had days to prepare your surprise party, I doubt it's the former.*'

Yeah, I know. The shadows at Noir's feet quivered and then flew outward in quest of the necromancer, forming as they went into *Almas*. Noir watched them depart and then closed his eyes, linking his mind to their bodies.

It didn't take long before one of the *Almas* struck something and shattered, killed by a flash of Necromancy.

There you are.

Noir spun eastward, summoning the *Almas* to gather about him in their thousands, filling the trees with the eerie almost-silence of their wing beats.

The wild Hydes fled before him as he advanced, screaming their terror and crashing into one another. He let them go; Brigadier already knew he approached.

He advanced into the forest, watching the ground and trees gradually assume the bleached white of Necromancy, a warning that he neared Brigadier's location. With every step, however, *Almas* perched on the ground and trees, obscuring their stark white surface beneath exquisite black wings.

It's about time we found her.

'*I don't think you found her just yet; Brigadier was powerful before she joined the coalition and now, with all that stolen power coursing through her body, I wouldn't be surprised if she's fully Tyrant level. She'll still be a way further on.*' Noir walked another mile over bleached earth before he encountered her.

He stepped into the unnatural clearing, the trees bleached by so much Necromancy they had withered away to dust, and slouched onto his right foot. He buried his hands in his pockets as *Almas* continued to alight on every available surface around him, converting half of the clearing to a perfect black hue.

Brigadier looked down from a throne of stacked skulls, her faded military garb bleached even whiter than her clearing. "Hello, Noir." A dull click sounded as the bony, serpentine appendage growing from the back of her skull slithered across the mound to heft a cracked oxen skull. She inspected it briefly and then smashed it against the ground in a spray of ice. "About time you showed up."

"I'm surprised Lazarus let you out." He glanced around, noting the spectral figures materializing from the trees. "I guess he needed the firepower."

"Firepower, knowledge of you, of Umbras, contacts, all of which I had." She crushed another skull, this one human. "In return, he promised he could kill you, even said I could choose how, and introduced me to Lock-And-Key as proof they controlled Umbras."

"Well, it didn't work, or he lied."

She broke off inspecting a weasel skull, vibrant red eyes contrasting dark blue lips. "But it did work."

"Clearly, not well enough."

"Oh, I don't know, I got to hear you screaming for your brother's life, practically begging 'no, please don't, anyone but him! Take me instead!" She replaced the weasel skull atop the mound. "I really enjoyed that, all your damned pride stripped away, looking ugly and weak. Powerless. Damnit, I wish he had taken forever to die and you were still there crying. But, no, everything dies and now there's no one to resurrect you. Which reminds me, how did you survive?"

"You can't kill a god, Brig."

"I don't have to kill you, just lock you in a box with no light so you can spend the rest of eternity reliving your brother's death over and over again until it stops hurting and then you'll hate yourself even more, because you'll know it should still hurt."

She straightened, drawing the gleaming saber belted to her hip and leveling it on him. The ground shuddered and then erupted as every dead thing in the forest woke.

Skeletal hands sprouted from the earth, followed by insects, beasts, and even roots from the dead trees. Specters formed from the mist: a sea of ghostly figures born from orphaned memories and lingering pain. Her soldiers were the last to rise, crawling from the ground with half-decayed fingers, ragged uniforms, and perfect Shadowsteel weapons untarnished by the decades since their burial. They confronted Noir as one and leveled their weapons.

This is going to be such a pain in the ass.

'You know, dead girls are probably dying for some excitement; we might actually be able to hook you up with someone. You'll probably 'murder' the competition.'

All year to think of something original, all year to devise something poignant or subversive, or even outlandish, but no you settled on puns a child could have imagined.

'Bah, they're necromancer classics!'

Which only serves to throw the intelligence of all necromancers into doubt.

Every shadow exploded into activity, churning, coalescing and darkening as hundreds of Shadow-soldiers materialized in the darkness, their steel blades plumed and their armor gleaming with obsidian shards. Other creatures also took shape: hulking trolls, towering centaurs, and black seraphim.

Brigadier's soldiers held their position for a split-second and then opened fire. The forest erupted into light, and Noir's Constructs disintegrated. He reeled back, grunting, as bullets of white, burning light cleaved through his body and vanished into the forest. The fading light flashed again as the undead fired another salvo. Noir ducked and lunged, throwing himself across the ground as a tide of Lux-bullets rent the air. He rolled to his feet, growling, and a storm of shadows swept down from the heavens. It dropped like a hammer, a thick, roiling mass of darkness that crushed the skeletons to dust. The darkness held for a second and then shattered before a thousand beams of light.

God damn her! Noir rolled across the ground, his form bleeding shadows from a dozen injuries. *She bargained with Radiance for Lux-*

Bullets and who knows what else.

Something small thumped to the ground beside Noir: a sphere of light the size of a child's ball. He cursed and spun, pulling shadows about him in a shield just before the sphere detonated, tearing through his defenses and flinging him through a desiccated tree.

Noir struggled to his feet, shadows repairing his body and clothing. Brigadier stood across from him, her form armored in plates of brilliant light. Her soldiers encroached, reloading their rifles with a barrage of dull clicks. "Yes," she said, "I went to Radiance for help, and he was more than happy to oblige when I revealed my intent."

"You should have asked for a bigger gun." A tendril of shadow whipped up from beneath Brigadier's feet and slashed at her, but her armor flared, shredding it.

She smirked. "I did." She lifted her hand and the forest exploded with brilliance. Lines shot out from her position, coursing over the ground and scaling the trees before leaping through the air to connect with one another. It happened instantly, and when it finished, Noir stood in a prison of Luxmancy.

Brigadier lowered herself to her throne and lounged against the skulls. "You may be able to infinitely regenerate while you have shadows to call, but without those shadows you are vulnerable." Her soldiers leveled their weapons, the barrels glowing with a glimmer of the Lux-bullets within.

Noir growled under his breath and the Lux-prison groaned. Veins of shadow cracked through the prison's northern wall as Noir pulled on the external shadows. It bowed inward, distorting beneath the weight. Brigadier snorted. "Stubborn to the end, kill him." The soldiers fired, and the walls of the prison collapsed on Noir, flowing over Brigadier without harming her but incinerating every shadow they passed. Noir roared and leapt for the descending ceiling, slamming it with a fist. His arm shattered, followed by his shoulder as his body smashed into the fracturing barrier and broke through.

Noir spun in the air, his ruined body contorting with the residual momentum of his escape, and crashed onto the ground at the base of a dead cherry tree. He lay there for a second and then shadows flooded inward obliterating the dead as they came. He stood, his left side hanging limp and crisscrossed with lingering veins of Luxmancy.

He advanced, shuffling through the storm of shadows and kicking aside the hands clawing at his heels. He could feel the dead being crushed all around him, but he could also feel their Lux-weaponry obliterating his Shadowmancy.

'You have to give Brigadier credit; she chose her battlefield well.'

A sliver of shadow emerged from the rampaging storm and slithered into Noir's left side, routing one vein of Luxmancy. *I'm not in the mood for credit right now.*

'You could just ignore common sense and obliterate everything. That's still an option.'

I will not risk my anonymity.

'You won't stay anonymous for long if you keep killing that poor Dorian fellow. You might even get a reputation for being hard to work with; there's already talk about having Gregorio just follow you around.

That's a good idea, it would at least make everything run smoother. It's kind of bad news for Dorian though.'

'Yeah, that poor sod is going to spend so much time dead. He he.'

He stepped from the churning storm into a pocket of light.

Brigadier sat atop her throne with a pistol in one hand and the saber laid across her knees. Her lips curled as she saw him and her eyes tightened, almost concealing the blue veins that now corrupted her once crimson eyes. "Do you think you've won?" Her voice pierced the enfolding hubbub as a guttural snarl.

The clamor subsided around them, falling silent without relenting in the slightest. A dull crack split the strange silence that enveloped them as Noir's fingers snapped back into place. "This was decided the instant you killed my brother, Brigadier."

She snarled again and surged to her feet, leveling the pistol on him. "You are spent, Noir, I have wo—" Brigadier's own shadow undulated and clawed at her, scouring her back and flinging the pistol to the ground. She swept one Lux-armored hand through the shadow, scattering it.

Noir stepped forward, but she pivoted on him, extending her left hand out over the skull-mound while reaching toward him with the other. Her face contorted, her lips parting to bare crooked bone teeth. The mound quaked underfoot, almost displacing her as a thin black mist boiled out from the vacant eye sockets. Lastly, her cerebellar cord lashed up over her head, its tip opening like a maw.

'Be careful, she's using the skulls as a catalyst.'

I know. Noir braced himself as a spasm coursed up his body and his shadow vanished.

Brigadier thrashed in place, her upper body wrenching back and her eyes flaring open. Her fingers twisted and twined, curving first forward then back on themselves with a dull crack of bone. Her eyes widened further, dilating around a swiftly expanding pupil. Her fingers flicked straight, the skin peeling off. "Time rules all of us, Noir, and you are no exception." Her fingers peeled further, revealing pale bone as the first skulls of her throne crumbled to dust. "All the accumulated years of these dead, Noir, that is my gift to you." One by one, the skulls crumbled away as her muscles and tendons withered off her fingers, hands, and arms.

Noir's flesh slowly aged with the Necromancy, growing pallid as it wrinkled and tightened around thinning muscles. His clothing rotted away, and his body was stripped of all flesh. His mass tumbled to the ground and then imploded into dust. Brigadier stumbled and fell back, the last of her skull throne billowing up behind her in a cloud of pale dust.

She gasped a hollow laugh that died even as it began, and sagged forward onto her good arm with a dull cough. Noir materialized from the shadows behind her and crouched as the pocket of light collapsed. He stretched out a dark, sinuous hand and grasped the back of her neck, his forefinger digging into the base of her skull. "Take solace in the fact that even if it had landed aging would have done nothing to me: What is time to an immortal?"

She wheezed, blood trickling down her neck. "Then what was it that I killed? ... It had a physical body ... and a timeline."

"That was my body's shadow given depth, purpose, and a lifespan of three thousand years. You destroyed a replica, Brig." He looked at her, his head cocked to one side. "Did you really believe that this would end any other way?"

She wheezed again. "I hoped." Noir pushed his finger forward, severing her spine and injecting a thread of venom. He leaned back, letting her corpse fall to the ground before dismissing his Shadow Constructs. *She would have done better taking years rather than giving them.*

'She couldn't have known that you don't age, or even how old you currently are.'

Noir shrugged. *It was simple guesswork; she knew who I am and thus knew how many years I've been active in this world. Even a rough glance should have told her that taking years was a better gamble then adding them.*

'So that's why you wimped out and didn't take her attack like a man… Wuss.'

Yeah, not that it would have mattered much in the end.

'It's such a shame, you would have made a cute baby.'

If you say so. Noir turned slowly, his gaze falling on the empty space Brigadier's skulls had left. Of the hundreds once piled there, only one remained, its surface covered in bone dust and moist soil, the power harbored within too fathomless for her to exhaust. Noir crossed the intervening space and knelt beside it.

He lifted the skull gently, wiping away the dirt and the dust until it gleamed in the forest's noxious green light. He remained like that for a while, staring at the skull, and then slowly raised it to his brow with a shuddering breath. It was impossible, Noir knew that; nevertheless, he could almost feel some remnant of his brother's soul, the hint of sunshine, and the vaguest possible suggestion of laughter. Taking another deep breath, he climbed to his feet and slipped the skull into his coat.

Chapter Eight

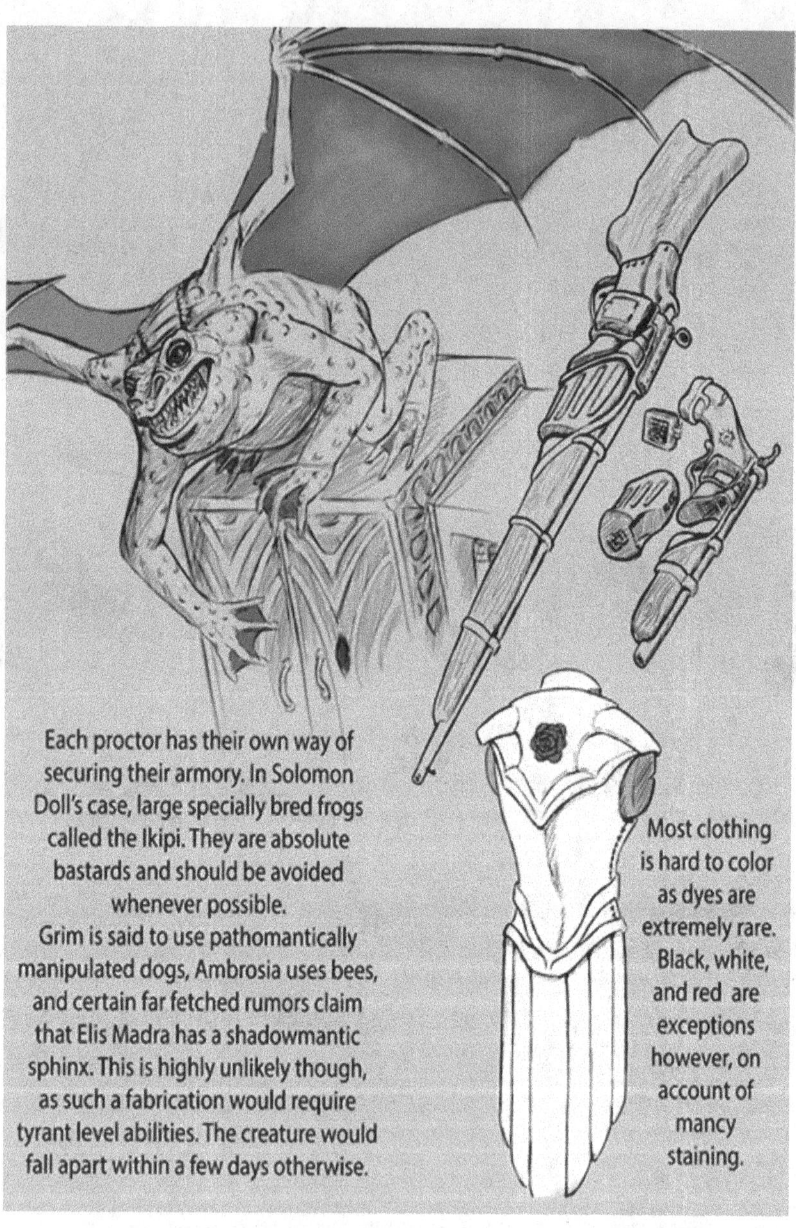

Each proctor has their own way of securing their armory. In Solomon Doll's case, large specially bred frogs called the Ikipi. They are absolute bastards and should be avoided whenever possible.
Grim is said to use pathomantically manipulated dogs, Ambrosia uses bees, and certain far fetched rumors claim that Elis Madra has a shadowmantic sphinx. This is highly unlikely though, as such a fabrication would require tyrant level abilities. The creature would fall apart within a few days otherwise.
Most clothing is hard to color as dyes are extremely rare. Black, white, and red are exceptions however, on account of mancy staining.

Proctor For A Day

~ The dry road coughed dust every time Noir took a step, and the oppressive summer wind flung more of it into his face. He licked his chapped lips and pulled his hood over his eyes. That didn't stop his clothing from scratching the livid, weeping burns covering him head to toe.

Noir could hear Alighieri chattering behind him, an unrelenting barrage of fabricated stories and abysmal jokes that merited an askance look more than actual laughter. Nevertheless, Noir would look back and force himself to smile every so often just to keep Alighieri talking, just to keep his mind off the death of their parents. He refused to let guilt and misery compound the pain of Alighieri's burns. The death of their parents was not his brother's doing. It was Noir's.

Noir adjusted the woefully light sack on his shoulders and uttered a perfunctory response to Alighieri's latest joke.

Alighieri voiced a remonstrance and shoved Noir forward with a farcical rebuttal.

Shocked by the absurd response, Noir coughed a strangled laugh and glanced back at Alighieri with his first true smile in weeks.

Alighieri met his look with a grin of triumph and resumed his discourse.

Noir shook his head and resumed walking. ~

Noir leaned on the railing, his forearms subconsciously merging with it as he pondered. A vial of dark blood, Alighieri's blood retrieved from the pages of Alucard's Covenant, lay in his hand, the blood constantly changing shape and hue, forming disjointed words, names, and even sentences. He ran a thumb along the surface, watching the blood trail after it.

A chuff of steam poured over him from behind, bathing his clothing in condensation and causing his now sheer black coat, fully corrupted by last night's Shadowmancy, to glisten. He wiped at it absently, thinking about the past and displacing the *Almas* perched on him. They fluttered off and alighted upon Soliamiidas' glowing red bulk, heedless of the heat. He followed them with his eyes, watching as the veins and segments of their wings gradually assumed the same fiery hue.

'What are you thinking about?'

You. Constantine.

'That's a weird pairing seeing as I've never met the guy.'

That's what I don't understand. He resumed his appraisal of the vial, watching the words 'the steel city breathes white' form in succession. *I don't know him, never heard of him before now. So why is he trying to kill us?*

'I don't know. You may have legions of detractors, but I am perfectly adorable, utterly unhateable, unfairly—'

Yes, I get the point. The question is, did Lazarus offer him something or is he after something we have?

'Ask the girl, she might know about him.'

I can't ask her about Constantine and then have him show up dead the next day; that's sure to garner the wrong kind of attention.

He felt Adrian stir awake behind him, the rhythm of her heart slowly increasing as she rolled onto her back. A few of the *Almas* flitted past, their wings still aglow with Soliamiidas' residual heat, every beat leaving trails of light in the semi-dark. She reached a hand up, eyes wide and rosy, fingers stretching toward the *Almas*.

"Be careful, they're hot."

Her hand flexed, moving as if to cup them but never daring to touch. "What are they?"

"I call them *Almas*."

"Souls?"

"Yes, one for every life I've taken."

Her eyes flicked between them, counting. "Seven?"

"They're not all here."

"Did they deserve it?"

"Not all of them."

"What happened?"

"Accidents, and sometimes death is just kinder."

"Does Dorian have one?"

"Dorian's not dead."

"Oh." She stood, hand dropping, and slowly joined him at the railing. "What's that you're holding?"

"A promise," he replied softly, still staring at the vial.

"What kind of promise?"

His fingers closed around it. "One I've held onto for a long time." He shifted toward her, storing the vial in a pocket. "Sorry about your nap; the Drosera lace their fruit with a mild sleeping toxin to sedate their prey. Normally it's harmless to humans because we carry so much corruption in our blood, but since you're an undertaker…"

"…I have less corruption and, thus, I'm more susceptible to its affects." She noted his coat, eyes paling in surprise. "What happened to your coat?!"

'Ooh ooh, say 'it's just like my soul' in your usual deep, intimidating voice.'

"I spent last night combing the city for our murderer."

"You went outside! At night?"

"Not even I'm that stupid; I merely conversed with the city."

"…What?"

"Well, maybe not converse so much as … mingle. Any decent shadowmancer can explore stagnant Shadowsteel with their thoughts, kind of like how people can explore obscure spaces or water with their hands. The stronger the mind, the farther they can explore."

"Did you find anything?"

"No. But I don't have to. Someone, something like him, leaves a very particular trail, even on Shadowsteel. Calculated violence leaves a mark, and Caelus Hydes are unmistakable. I felt neither last night."

"You're looking for his hideout."

"Yes."

"But what if he decided to lie low?"

"Why would he? This creature's not scared of our Proctors, and he knows more about us than we do of him."

"Are you scared of him?"

"…Yes." Noir's hands tightened in their pockets. "Let's just hope that whoever he or she is, they're a Wild Tyrant and not the servant of an established one."

"Does that really matter?"

"Yes. A Wild Tyrant comes alone, an established one does not."

She lapsed into her own thoughts for a while, thinking about what it would mean for a Tyrant to besiege Umbras. The city has fail-safes of course, miles of bunkers constructed beneath the Undercity to protect its inhabitants, thus liberating Lock-And-Key of all restraints. But they were a futile prospect without forewarning and had never been tested. Even with forewarning, Umbras wouldn't be the first city erased by two warring Tyrants.

Adrian roused herself from those grim ruminations and indicated his pack. "What's with the bag? I've rarely seen you without it."

He reclined against the railing, his tension easing away in favor of a more playful mien. "Nothing."

"You carry it everywhere you go."

"The bag's entirely ordinary; you could find any number of them in the market."

"Alright then; what's in the bag?"

'Tell her a dead man's eyes and an untethered soul.'

Why?

'I'm betting she's scared of ghosts.'

Why would she be scared of ghosts? The girl's part undertaker.

'Because the irony would be hilarious.'

He kept his attention fixed on the distance, and drew out his response, teasing her. "The future of this world!"

"At least tell me what the staff is?"

'Tell her it's the Marrow Staff.'

"It's the Marrow Staff."

"Never heard of it."

"It belonged to a Wild Tyrant from the far north."

'No, no, no. You were supposed to invent a story about how you found it in the bowels of Umbras.'

"You stole it from a Wild Tyrant!"

"It wasn't that hard if you ignore the year I spent looking for it; turns out she's a heavy sleeper."

"Wait, you've been outside?" Her ears pricked up.

"Don't act so surprised; surviving outside is far from impossible, especially if you travel by water."

"What's it like out there?"

"Wild. Now, that's enough questions. Solomon probably has work for us and there's undoubtedly a new crisis."

'You told her too much, now she knows that we've been outside the city. What's worse is that she knows you've dealt with Tyrants before. I'm guessing it'll be a couple days before she tells someone else, then it's only a matter of time before Solomon Doll and the other Proctors make the connection.'

I know. Noir moved to the other end of the walkway, closer to the trapdoor.

'So what are you going to do about it?'

Nothing, unless absolutely necessary; I suspect Solomon Doll will throw a fit if anything happens to the girl, more so if it's permanent. We'll just hope that her natural reticence keeps her quiet.

'Trusting to her being an undertaker is a slim hope.'

True, but it's better than angering a Proctor. Noir extended his hand with splayed fingers, pulling shadows before him and into the shape of a stairwell.

Adrian snatched his arm. "What are you doing?"

"We're late, so we need an alternate route." A vent burst to his right, dousing them in steam. Adrian lurched behind Noir with a murmured profanity, one hand raised to shield her face. Noir remained where he was with one hand upraised and the guard coat hanging leadenly from his shoulders.

The hissing steam attenuated, and Adrian tugged on his arm again. "Stop that. You can't change the city!"

"Don't worry, it won't be permanent." He flexed his fingers, sending the staircase spiraling up to the trapdoor.

She released him, but her ears remained erect and her eyes wavered between a hard black and a fretful green. "All right, but be careful; the city doesn't like being changed."

"I know."

Noir dropped his hand as the stair completed, and began his ascent, every step landing with puffs of shadow-debris. Adrian followed with hunched shoulders, careful to put her feet in the footprints he left.

Despite her concerns, they traversed the Undercity without retaliation and ultimately found Solomon Doll sharing the entrance hall with his subordinates amid a bustle of activity. Hierophant stood to one side rifling through papers, while the Proctor spoke with Gregorio Taim and Rias Dorian. The group dispersed as Noir approached, leaving him alone with Solomon.

"So, who's the new corpse?"

"How do you know there's a corpse?"

"A little bird told me on my way here."

Solomon grunted. "A former Wild Tyrant called Brigadier. She attacked Umbras about a century ago and, after her utter defeat, was imprisoned in the palace. Flip forward three or four decades and she is released into the city, apparently cowed into submission by Lock-and-Key."

"What's she been doing for the last six decades?"

"We don't know, probably guard duty; the other Proctors aren't very forthcoming."

"Why would Lock-and-Key allow a former rival to abide in her city?"

"Again, I don't know. Whatever transpired with Brigadier involved Lock-and-Key, which means information's scarce." Solomon ground the bone toothpick between his teeth. "As it stands, our mysterious killer has strung her corpse up in Madra's District, and nobody has any clue how it got past their sentries."

"The murderer's playing with us."

"That, or he moved the corpse to conceal the battlefield; which means we have to find it."

'I like how smart he is; it makes things interesting. We should come back when we're less busy, start killing people again—you know serial killer style—only not really, and see how long it takes for him to catch us.'

"You can skip the Grim District; I had that under surveillance all night."

"That'll make things a little easier, at least." Solomon sucked on the toothpick, briefly reconsidering his preparations. "You and Dorian will be in command while I'm out. There have been a couple minor incidents that you should be able to assign people to; Corporal Valerian has all the information. Of greater significance is that a group of Radiance's Malakhims arrived in Umbras today and decided to start preaching on our district's main thoroughfare. I don't want them ousted, seeing as that might start a war, but definitely keep an eye on them."

"Who's ultimately in charge, me or Dorian?"

"I suspect you'll be whatever I say, so I'm having Gregorio take up residence here for the duration; it'll help everything go smoother."

'Hey, we could use Dorian as our first victim. Should be a nice call back.'

"I'll try to restrain myself."

"That's very generous of you."

"Well, you look tired, so it's the least I can do."

"How surprisingly ... thoughtful of you. I'm tempted to think you have ulterior motives."

"Hardly, I have no use for Dorian. I've seen smarter rats and conversed with more interesting boulders."

'I still think that boulder was making faces at us.'

"I find that hard to believe."

"A rat at least has the sense to run from the dog. Dorian does not."

"Rias Dorian is an able pathomancer and a lieutenant in a Tyrant's military force; you should give him more credit."

"Lieutenants are a celebration of mediocrity."

"You yourself are a lieutenant, Noir. Are you mediocre?"

"Putting Rias Dorian on my level is the equivalent of putting you on the same level of Elis Madra: laughable and irrational."

"I won't argue with you on the last account, and I don't have the time to discuss Rias Dorian's qualities, or lack thereof." Solomon Doll pulled on his coat and donned a cap. "I trust that the Dollhouse will still be standing upon my return?"

"Like I said, I'll restrain myself."

"Good." Solomon Doll whistled, and Hierophant emerged from the crowd, likewise equipped for the deluge waiting outside. Solomon tipped his cap and departed, a quartet of guards trailing him.

Noir watched him go. *Radiance needs to find a ditch to die in, the city is volatile enough without his interference.*

'What did you expect? He knows you've been missing for years; this is the best opportunity he's had to hurt Umbras in a century.'

Over my dead body.

'That oath would have more weight if you weren't basically immortal already.'

Noir strode past the greeting desk toward the stairs, giving Elise a perfunctory wave. She continued shuffling her papers without so much as a glance. *My immortality is what makes it so effective.*

'It makes it easy, and lazy people are not to be trusted.'

Noir swung onto the stairway as a peel of thunder shook the walls. *Oh? Playing to my strengths makes me lazy?*

'Most definitely. If you're not choosing the hardest possible route, you're an irredeemable hedonist and should be immediately executed.'

Somebody already tried that. It didn't take.

'And that's your problem: no follow through. Someone tries to execute you, it doesn't work so you just up and leave. No second chance, no alternative solutions. Just—Oh well, decapitation didn't work, might as well hang up the ole axe. An absolute disgrace I tell you.'

At times like this, it's hard to believe you're supposed to be the sane one, as illogical as that is.

'Exactly, I figured that I should start acting more like a proper voice in your head—one that prompts you to vicious deeds and terrible iniquity. That way, you have a reason to surmount your madness instead of just wallowing in it. With no one else to pull you from the muck, you'll have to do it yourself. I bet you'll look very heroic and get all the ladies swooning.'

I was never meant to be the hero; I'm too much the monster for that.

'If that's the case, then why are we here doing this the hard way, working with Solomon Doll, protecting Loc, hiding what you are. Why not just kill everything and resurrect them when we're done?'

Because that's not how you would want it done.

Noir arrived on the office floor, provoking a brief pause in the buzzing labor before the scribes resumed their duties. With Adrian close behind him, he strolled down the center aisle, ignoring the murmured greetings offered to him and scanning the room until he saw Gregorio at the far end, who noted him in turn and beckoned the other officers to gather.

Corporal Valerian arrived first, navigating the desks with a bouncing step to recline against the wall beside Gregorio. There she retrieved a chalkboard decorated with various brightly hued skulls and perused it. Unlike yesterday, a bouquet of unopened buds and tiny crocus flowers adorned her hair-vines, accenting their dark green color with vibrant reds, whites, and yellows.

Next came Rias Dorian, his appearance mostly unchanged with his white coat firmly buttoned and his scales glistening as if polished. He moved with a fastidious elegance, traversing the cluttered desks with an air of disdain. The soldiers always glanced up as he passed, silently ascertaining if he had a task for them before resuming their labors. They neither feared their lieutenant nor liked him, but he served his purpose as an administrator.

Silas June prowled in Dorian's wake, gliding like a fish just beneath the surface of a pond, provoking no effect on his environment and garnering no attention from those who inhabited it.

Noir dropped into an unoccupied chair and Adrian slipped into a seat behind him. "So what do you have for me, Corporal Valerian?"

"We have a couple small incidents, most notably a Death-Market somewhere in the Undercity beneath our district. Solomon Doll strictly forbids the selling of one's death, so we'll have to shut it down."

"What deaths do they buy?"

Although Noir directed his question at Valerian, it was Silas who answered, his voice low and unhurried. "They're newly formed and their merchandise rudimentary. They're trying to see how far they can push us before we crack down, so nothing like torment or ritual, just basic deaths and gladiatorial bouts for profit."

'How about disembowelment?'

What are you talking about? "Do we know where it's located?"

'You know, for the serial killer gig. We've got to have a trademark.'

Valerian scanned her chalkboard. "Yes, close to Grim's District, so they cross the border: Grim allows Death Merchants so long as they pay." Her lips curled in disgust.

Noir swiveled his chair toward Dorian. "You're going to handle this one, Dorian."

"I most certainly will not–" A spear rent through Dorian's chest, hefting him up and killing him instantly.

Gregorio sighed. "This is going to be a long day, isn't it?"

Noir swiveled back to Valerian. "Mark the Death Merchants as Lieutenant Dorian's responsibility. Next." A chalice formed beneath Dorian's corpse, collecting his blood.

Valerian inspected her chalkboard again. "The hemomancers are growing a new orchard at the Proctor's request, but they need a high-ranking officer to oversee the operation. That would be you, sir."

"Fine, what else." *I should have listened to the whole list before dolling out responsibility.*

'*Sad but true, oh if only you had the wisdom to harbor your words instead of spreading them like pollen in spring! You could always reassign Dorian.*'

Not a chance in hell; he'll think he won.

'*If he does, just kill him again. Now about our stage name–*'

Are you still going on about serial killing?

'*I think it has potential.*'

"The only question left is what to do with Radiance's Angels. I believe there's twelve."

"What rank are they?"

"They seem to be mostly just Malakhim and maybe one Arch-Angel, but that's unconfirmed."

"The Proctor only wants surveillance for now; we don't want to instigate a war we're unprepared for. Valerian, take a squad and handle that; we need to be ready in case the peace does collapse. Also, do we have any Duskblades in the armory?"

Valerian's eyebrows furrowed. "What are Duskblades?"

Gregorio answered before Noir could, "They're swords made with a special kind of Shadowmancy, the kind that made this city and the Black Coins." He glanced at Noir. "They're rare, but I think the Proctor managed to secure a cache some years back."

Noir nodded. "Take those with you; they'll help you survive if Radiance's Angels go berserk." He swiveled again. "Gregorio, you'll be in charge while I'm gone, though I expect you to call for me if something calamitous arises."

'And so the devil armed his dark minions with cursed blades and charged them with a simple, inconceivable geas: hold the line but bring no war unto the legions of light.'

I know it's strange; you don't have to complain about it.

"Of course, sir," Gregorio said.

Noir swiveled to Silas June. "You're our liaison with the underworld, correct?"

"Yes, sir, but mash my bones in flour, I hold little sway there. I just listen to whatever rumors stumble my way."

"Your influence is unimportant; I want to hear whatever bullshit the Underworld thinks of our murderer. I want to know how they're reacting to him and what, if anything, they know about him."

"Will do, sir." He took a second to order his thoughts and then began, "The most recent, and unsettling, rumor is that someone spooked Harley Press enough that he abandoned his shop and vanished into the Undercity."

A murmur of surprise passed through the circle and Noir grimaced. "Who the hell's stupid enough to mess with Harley?"

Gregorio shifted his stance. "It's probably our murderer; Harley wouldn't have known about him since the devil's probably from outside, and he's obviously powerful enough to bully, or to at least frighten, Harley into hiding." Gregorio shifted again, absently scratching at the black feathers covering his bicep.

"There's more to it than that; our murderer would have to be intimately familiar with Umbras to know that Harley even exists," Noir mused, "which means he's far more knowledgeable than we believed." Noir tapped a quick pattern on the armrest of his chair. "What about the ferryman, did he have any useful information?"

Gregorio shook his head. "No, he lost all memory of his own death, only the approach of a figure on the outside bank, which he described as humanoid. The Proctor thinks it likely that our murderer's an Evolved."

"That goes without saying, anything else would render the journey here nearly impossible; all this tells us is that he's not a *Sanitas*, which we already suspected. If he has a Caelus Hyde, then the only thing that makes sense is he's also an *Autorius*, else there wouldn't be much left of the Grim District." Noir tapped another beat on the armrest. "Alright, what else do you know?"

Silas resumed, "The thing about Harley is only a rumor, but what I do know is that something's seriously spooked the underworld's Princes; they've all vanished without a whisper, at least those worth mentioning have; there's always a few idiots left over."

"So Harley Press has vanished and every half-bit Night Prince has scurried into their burrow. What do they know that we don't, and who exactly are we dealing with?"

'What about the Mad-Gutter for a stage name.' It has a nice ring to it.

Silas made a half-gesture of dismissal. "They probably don't know much more than we do; they just know that something nasty's arrived. They're doing what any sane person should do; hiding and hoping that the city'll still be standing when they come out."

Noir slowly tapped his armrest again, as if in thought. "I doubt our murderer intends to conquer Umbras. Otherwise he wouldn't target people like Alucard and Brigadier, people with no true loyalty to Lock-and-Key. Any of us sitting here except Dorian, who's more useful dead than alive, would provide a better target. This is personal, and it's not about power." He ceased tapping and glanced at Gregorio. "Is there any connection between Alucard and Brigadier; or Alucard and any other prominent individual? Check for Brigadier also. We need to know why our murderer's targeting them so we can anticipate his next victim."

Gregorio scratched his feathered chin. "I can't think of any immediate connection, or even any connections once removed." He examined the southern wall where a long row of battered filing cabinets slumped together like a party of drunks making their way home. "I'll start digging while you're gone, but I don't think I'll find anything in our records; Proctor Madra will have better resources and might give us a peek if you ask politely. Of course, the best thing would be the palace library, but I don't think anyone could get us access."

Noir grumbled inwardly, *I was really hoping to avoid Elis.* He nodded. "I'll see about sending him the proper forms, but we'll probably need a negotiator." He glanced over at Silas. "Do you think you could manage that, Corporal?" Silas assented, and Noir addressed Adrian, "Go ahead and get started on those forms, we want them going out immediately."

"Am I allowed to write official forms?"

"No, but we'll say yes for the sake of ease."

"What if somebody figures it out?"

"Then we'll say it was an accident, that I was drunk, that it's actually my hand writing, or that you're secretly our Proctor; whatever works best at the time."

'And if that doesn't work, you'll just kill a bunch of people and pretend it was her.'

Valerian raised a hand. "I don't think anybody will actually believe that Adrian's our Proctor."

Noir waved her off. "Don't worry about it; add a little makeup, some sparks and a touch of performance lighting and we'll have everybody so ensorcelled and confused that they won't care anymore."

"All right, if you say so, sir." Valerian returned to her chalkboard.

Noir reverted his attention to Silas. "I don't know what Madra's going to want; he's notoriously fickle, so act at your discretion. Within reason, of course, I don't want to come back and find that you've sold the Dollhouse."

"Yes, sir."

Noir inspected the officers. "Is there anything else?" They shook their heads. "Then let's move out." He stood as the others collected their various items. "Gregorio, you're in charge of resurrecting Dorian; I assume we have at least one other hemomancer in our ranks?"

"Yes, sir, we have many hemomancers and a fair number of pathomancers. We're only short of shadowmancers; they were all enrolled at the Academy until it blew up."

"Then you should have no difficulty in resurrecting Lieutenant Dorian. Please inform him of all significant matters from our conversation, and do your best to ensure he accomplishes his role."

"And if he doesn't?"

"Then the task will be yours whatever he says: Understood? I'll deal with him if he throws another fit."

"Yes, sir."

"One last thing... Everyone, listen here!" The room quieted and most of its inhabitants faced him, looking over their chalkboards and murmuring. Noir waited for the vestiges of conversation to dwindle before resuming, "A Blood Moon will rise in two days." Silence immediately subjugated the room and every eye found him. "You all know what this means, so you will all make appointments with the pathomancers for bleeding, and you will inform all districts of the coming moon. We have two days to bleed every living soul in Umbras. Don't tarry." Noir set off down the aisle, beckoning Adrian to follow.

'Now about that serial killer idea of yours, I have my own notion in that regard.'

My idea?

'Yes. Your idea. Let's move the operation to Radiance's place and become the Dark Prophet.'

You mean make up our own testament, write biblical verse across the walls, create a new religion and everything?

'If you like.'

That does sound fun.

'I thought you might like that.'

Adrian fell into step, scribbling across a writing board until they reached the stairs.

Without looking at her, he quietly asked, "Are you old enough to use your Scythe yet?"

Her eyes flicked to him, revealing pale green irises, and then away. "No, sir. Do you anticipate trouble?"

"I don't know, but two powerful people have died in as many days, and Death Merchants from Grim's District have infiltrated ours. I don't like it and I don't want you getting hurt." He paused at the next landing. "Do you know how to use a gun?"

She nodded

"Then let's get you one." He entered the armory, doffing his heavy black coat and discarding it to the floor. Adrian rushed after him, sparing a glance for the armory's caged shelving units, which hosted a rather venomous-looking colony of winged toads with toothy maws.

"What can I get for you, Lieutenant?" The quartermaster's voice came from the ceiling, where he stood upside down, stroking the thin dark fur covering his face with one hand and cuddling one of the aforementioned toads with the other.

"You must be Bailey Utter, our quartermaster?"

"That would be me." Bailey dropped from the ceiling, his long, bat-like ears and closed eyes explaining the room's obscurity.

"The kid needs a gun, ammunition, and a set of winders."

"What kind of gun does he want? And does he want a saber to go with it?"

"Just a pistol."

"Understood, sir, one minute." Bailey slipped into the armory.

Adrian moved to inspect the toads "How'd you know there's a Blood Moon rising?"

"You remember the Drosera plant down below?" She nodded. "Well, its blooms were starting to darken and close this morning; it's going into hibernation until the moon passes and the extra poison it brings dissipates."

"And how did you know it was going to be a Blood Moon? I thought they were completely random?"

"Not quite; there's no set order to their appearance, but no moon will appear twice until the other three have set. Thus, I know it's a Blood Moon because the last two in this cycle were the Bone and Curse Moons, and I always know when the Shadow Moon is rising."

"How do you know that?"

"Let's just say I am a rather unique shadowmancer."

Bailey reemerged from the shadows with a bandoleer of winders over one shoulder, a pistol and holster in a hand, and an ammunitions satchel. "Here we are, sir, one pistol, a set of winders and bullets."

Noir passed the various articles to Adrian. "I need another coat while you're at it."

"Or course, sir." Bailey vanished again but quickly reappeared with the item.

"Thank you." Noir donned the coat and, once again refusing to button it, left. Adrian shuffled after him, trying vainly to juggle her various new possessions and the official forms.

'You could help her you know; it would be the gentlemanly thing to do.'

Why would I deny her the pride of succeeding on her own?

'You're a ruffian and a scoundrel, I don't know why I put up with you—oh look, there went the pistol! Maybe it'll go off and shoot somebody in the foot.'

Noir looked at the flushed Adrian as her pistol skidded across the floor. "Alright, give me the documents." She blushed deeper and handed them over, along with the pen. He scanned them quickly and, noting they required only a final signature, quickly scrawled on the last sheet. He accosted a passing soldier and shoved the forms into his hands. "Take these to Corporal June."

He returned his attention to Adrian as she finished buckling the holster to her side, the bandoleer of winders thrown over one shoulder, and the ammunitions pack over the other. "You ready?" She nodded. "Then let's go; I want to see you shoot a couple rounds in the firing range to make sure you won't be accidentally shooting me."

She feigned surprise and a small gasp. "What? Is the mighty Noir saying that some measly bullets can actually hurt him?"

"No, but it's annoying as hell when somebody who's supposed to be your ally ends up shooting you."

They descended to the Dollhouse's third level and strode into the firing range, Adrian glancing side to side until they found an unoccupied cubicle. Most of Solomon's practicing guards had unbuttoned their coats to combat the overcrowded room's sweltering heat; those who had not were among the numerous spectators; most were already participating in a variety of banter and wagers.

Noir took up a position against the wall and motioned her

forward. "Well get to it."

She stepped into the cubicle, taking a calming breath to steady herself, and readied her pistol. First, Adrian extracted a bullet from the satchel and pushed it down the muzzle until she felt the catch click shut. Next, she unclipped the five-shot winder from her bandoleer and plugged it into the side of the pistol. Then she clicked it on with a whirr and it pulled the pistol's gears, dragging the firing bolt out from the pistol's barrel. It clicked loudly, warning that the pistol was fully charged. She unplugged the winder, sighted at the gelatinous shadowcraft blob erected at the other end of the firing range, and squeezed the trigger. The bullet whistled out from the gun with a crack, causing it to jerk in her grip. Adrian lowered the pistol and repeated the process.

She emptied the winder before facing Noir, having placed the initial four shots near the target's center and the last at its outer edge.

"Well, if you're going to shoot me, it should at least be for a good reason. Let's go."

Adrian followed him out of the firing range, depositing the exhausted winder in one of the readily available receptacles for re-winding before catching up to him with a murmured, "Do you plan on there being a good reason to shoot you?"

"Ehh, probably."

'Ooooh, you like that she can fire a gun. You think that she's cute. How did that school yard song go? Dah dah dadue dee due due.'

You're so mature.

'Hey, maturity gets boring after the first century.'

Chapter Nine

Hemomancers use their own blood to generate life-energy which they then infuse into seeds. This hastens the growth of the seeds.
Like many of a Hemomancer's abilities, this can leave them aenemic, particularly after perpetual use. More powerful Hemomnacers don't suffer this however.

Visiting The Enemy

Noir and Adrian emerged from the Dollhouse into the pouring rain, Adrian with her ears drooping and a woefully inadequate hat. They veered right and started toward the outskirts of Umbras through a trickle of vague, bedraggled forms.

Adrian clutched her hat as a gust of wind bellowed around them, staggered as it flung rain into her already soaked clothing. "Can't you make an umbrella or something, anything to keep us from drowning?" A peel of thunder stole her words, so she tried again, screaming loud enough to hurt her throat.

She jumped as a tendril of something slipped into her right ear, and almost dug it out before Noir's voice spoke into the affected ear, "You should develop more appreciation for the rain, and water in general; they power the engines, dilute the Plague of our veins, and give life to Umbras."

'Personally, I like thunderstorms because of that one-time lightning struck you, and your hair stuck up in a thousand different directions. It was hilarious.'

"That doesn't mean it's not cold, or that I won't catch something from it."

"You don't need to shout; I can hear just fine."

"Sorry."

"I'll make us an umbrella in a little while, after the rain's had a chance to cleanse us."

They plunged into the circuitous back roads of the Doll District, slowly weaving their way toward the Bane District. The further they delved, the less sterile the city became. Signs of life appeared over the doors, accented by awnings, chairs, decorative flowers, and even the occasional toy. The walls also changed, their sheer black vanishing beneath an intermittent gallery of murals. Many of these murals clearly lacked true artistic bent, but they all possessed a magnetic vibrancy that defied the inelegance of their form. Many of the murals depicted a dark figure wreathed in shadows: the Deos

Mortai Black Father, Umbras' patron deity and the Tyrant that birthed it.

Noir ignored all of it, traversing from street to street in search of the one he needed, and ascribing to each artwork only the attention required to evade them when a branch or article impaired his path. Then he caught sight of something bright in the murk, a slash of gold where every other artist had favored darker hues of blue and red.

He slowed to a stop, eyes fixed on the mural beneath its layers of grime.

Adrian came up beside him. "What is it?"

"Nothing," he replied distantly, but he remained fixed on the mural. Slowly, as if in a trance, he took a step toward it, hand extending to brush the locks of a golden child, one of many running hither and thither across a field. "It looks just like him…"

"Who?"

Noir froze at her voice, then his fingers curled into a slow fist. "My brother." He tore himself from the mural and strode away, mind seething with ugly hate, the voice barely audible.

They crossed one of the main thoroughfares a short time later, though they could scarcely see it for the rain. Adrian, in particular, struggled and constantly lagged behind or strayed from the path even though he walked beside her with an umbrella of boiling shadows. Nevertheless, they attained their destination without mishap and found it sheltered by a lopsided canopy.

Noir ducked beneath the sagging canvas, his hands buried in their pockets, and came to a halt before the hemomancers huddled beneath. "There is supposed to be nine of you here, why are there only seven?"

A middle-aged woman with gray, wooden skin disentangled herself from the others, her limbs bending with a low creak. "They're sick cause of the rain, but we can manage without them."

"I'll take your word for it, do you need a dry working space?" Noir indicated the sopping canvas.

She shook her head. "No, the water will help them grow."

"Then let's begin."

The woman nodded and called her companions to rise. They responded curmudgeonly, wringing out or shaking clothes soaked from the rain and steam from nearby pipes.

Noir settled against the wall of a skyscraper, watching them dismantle their canvas.

Adrian leaned beside him, once again taking refuge in his shadow. "Why do you hate hemomancers?"

The canvas fell with a torrent of sloshing water, dunking them all. "What makes you think I hate them?"

Adrian shook herself in a spray of water. "It'd be obvious even if you did try hiding it."

He shrugged. "Hemomancers don't know when to stay dead; it makes killing the sons of bitches a nuisance."

She stopped in the middle of ringing out her hat to stare at him. "That's it; no great betrayal? No horrific tragedy or grisly tale of conflict? Just whim?"

"Not everyone has a good reason for what they do. Sometimes it's instinct. Sometimes its whim. But eventually it just doesn't matter. Besides, having a valid reason for everything I do is both tedious and stifling."

She donned her hat again and leaned against the wall. "You're not quite normal, are you?"

He snorted. "You should've met my brother; chaos was always his favorite ingredient in anything."

The hemomancers knelt along the courtyard's perimeter in a heptagonal pattern, letting the rain course down their bodies and into the Undercity. One after another, they laid their Athames—an assortment of hand-sized knives, scythes, and fanned blades— against their wrists. Their skin gradually assumed the inflamed hue of Hemomancy, and then they slashed. The blood struck the grating with a flare, illuminating the soaked fabric of their knees in a dull, ruddy glow. They swapped hands and slashed again, their blood glinting with the brilliance of a hemomancers' craft. It seeped across the courtyard, outlining the grating and then filling in the cracks without dripping through, forming a bed.

The rain began to pool around them, rising ankle-deep before overflowing onto the adjacent roads. The blood resisted it currents though, and here, the hemomancers unhooked small pouches from their belts to upend clusters of delicate red stalks.

The stalks took root voraciously and expanded into a thick blanket of crimson moss that scaled up the abutting skyscrapers and lampposts. A swath of it crawled up past Adrian, and she extended a cautious hand to touch it, finding it warm.

When the moss blanketed everything around them, the hemomancers each extracted a seed from a purse about their necks and buried it in the moss. A ring of trees sprouted, racing through all the seasons of their life; branches stretched outward as leaves formed and flowers budded. Seconds passed and the flowers wilted, falling to strew the ground moments before the leaves followed. The trees continued to grow, their leaves decomposing into red earth that in turn housed the developing roots.

Adrian watched one tree after another grow from a sapling to a towering specimen of health and glory, their limbs burdened with apples, persimmons, mangoes, pears, and more. It was only after the last tree reached its crowning point that the hemomancers stirred from their trance and stood, the blood on their hands slipping back up their arms and into their wrists, healing their scars as it retreated.

The woman approached Noir through the newly birthed grove, moving lethargically from her bleeding. "It is done, Lieutenant; the first harvest will be poisonous, of course, so please ensure that it is burned. After that the fruit should be edible."

"I'll send some people to remove the bad fruit and ensure that everything's ready for tomorrow."

"Thank you, Lieutenant."

"One last thing, there's a Blood Moon rising in two days, so get yourselves bled and make sure you do nothing tomorrow."

Her face tightened with instinctive dread. "I'll spread the word among the hemomancers." She trudged off, pulling her coat in tight and leaning into the wind.

Noir walked the other way. "Let's go, we're done here."

Adrian hurried after him, almost slipping on the soaked leaves.

"That went quicker than I expected. Should we help Lieutenant Dorian with the Death Merchants?"

"No, even though it would be fun to mess with sourpuss, there's no reason to believe he can't eliminate a rabble of thugs." Noir glanced back with the hint of a smile. "And if he can't, I won't be the only one teasing him."

'Oh, so that's what you call your murderous fixation: teasing. I admire your understatement. But that aside, I doubt his supposed competence is really why we're not tagging along. What are you really thinking?'

That I just sent a missive to Elis Madra requesting permission to access his private information reservoir, and that he's bound to have heard of Solomon Doll's new lieutenant.

'A lieutenant who also happens to be a shadowmancer with black skin and a superiority complex.'

Yeah. And there's only one person he would send to check us out.
'Wraith.'
Yeah.
'Which will be a problem if we cross paths in a public environment.'
Yeah.
'So you want to get back before he comes calling at the Dollhouse.'
Yeah.

A pair of children sprinted past them, squealing laughter despite the rain. Adrian watched them, half smiling at their mirth. "Why are there so few human children?"

"It's hard to procreate when the night changes you into a berserk monster, and most people don't have the courage. They're terrified they'll wake up one morning to find they murdered their own child in the night."

"But can't they just resurrect the child?"

"It doesn't matter that death's impermanent when you're looking at the decapitated corpse of someone you love. It matters even less when you realize you're the murderer."

"Black Father, being human must be horrible."

Noir shrugged and adjusted his pack. "We get by, and it's a lot better here than in other cities. They don't even bother locking us up at night; they just clean up the pieces when the dawn comes."

"That's horrible! It has to be better in some cities! Doesn't it?"

"Kid, those are the good cities. Black Die and Seelie do nothing to restrain their subjects, not that Seelie has to."

"...What's it like in the other ones?"

"You should only ask questions you want answered."

They arrived at the Dollhouse shortly thereafter and found it in a state of subdued tension. The events of the previous days were beginning to take their toll, merging into a taut mass of fear and anger. Even alone, the impending war with Grim, the murderer, or the arrival of Radiance's Angels would have sufficed to loosen tempers, but the compounding of all three made the tension palpable.

Noir swept the premises with a glance and settled upon a group of soldiers loitering within. "You're supposed to be on guard duty."

They jerked about and separated in a flurry, more than one shuffling his feet while staring at the floor. One of the braver soldiers inched forward, the sigil branded on his coat marking him as a token officer. "Begging your pardon, sir, but the rain's too thick; we can't see anything, and even if we could, the water's messing with our firing mechanisms."

Noir shucked his soaked coat in a single motion and caught it on his arm with a wet slap. "Are the buildings on this road vacant?" There was no overt threat in Noir's voice, but if possible, the officer shrunk further before mustering enough courage to nod. "Then open doors on the higher levels and assume positions there. That should keep your guns dry and provide a better vantage." The soldiers scrambled for their various possessions and raced outside with heads bowed against the rain.

"Let's go."

Adrian hurried after him, doffing her coat only to pause mid-step when she noticed his clothing beginning to writhe. "Um, sir, you're smoking."

'Oh, ho ho, she's thinks you're sexy.'

"Yeah, I'm drying off." White stream slithering across his figure, Noir stepped on the second floor and took a right into the mess hall. Here the first scents of lunch permeated an atmosphere made miserable by the rain, humidity, and constant peels of thunder.

She blinked. "What?"

He slipped down an aisle of unoccupied tables. "Apart from the coat, my clothing is entirely made of Shadowsilk, so I'm grinding the particles together to generate heat and dehydrate the cloth."

Her eyes widened. "Couldn't you set yourself on fire?"

"If I wanted to. But that's a dangerous habit, so I avoid doing so."

"Can all shadowmancers make fire?"

Noir finished threading his way through the tables and pushed past a swinging door into the kitchen where he navigated a herd of flushed cooks. "Most Adepts can, with the exception of necromancers. All hemomancers have to do is set their blood alight, and as for pathomancers… Well, I'm not sure how they do it, but I've seen it done." Noir reached the back of the kitchen and shoved a final door open without stepping through, revealing a dark room lit only by a furnace. "Go on, set your coat out to dry and warm yourself for a bit; there's nothing that requires our immediate attention." She nodded gratefully, took his coat from him and slipped inside.

'So what are we going to do about Wraith?'

Noir let the door swing closed. *We need to speak with him, privately.* He raised his hand as shadows congregated in his palm, forming a small orb.

'And how are we going to manage that?'

The shadows took shape, a pair of fragile black wings rising from a petite body. *It'll be easy enough, so long as we see him coming.* The shadows stilled and receded, leaving the butterfly to tentatively stretch its wings and shake off the Shadow-debris. Noir lifted the *Alma* and whispered to it, "Go, little one, keep watch downstairs and alert us the minute Wraith arrives." The Alma took flight into the steam-filled kitchen.

'What if he's already here?'

He's not, the guards downstairs were far too lax. Even a normal lieutenant would have put them on edge; if someone with Wraith's credentials appeared, they would have entered overdrive even without Madra's shadow looming over him. Noir pilfered a loaf of bread from a nearby platter and claimed a chair beside the furnace door. He felt the heat bleeding through the wall and leaned into it.

Lolled by the heat and the enticing aromas of baked bread, roasting meats, and the hint of a spice he could not name, Noir's eyes drifted closed, a memory rising...

Two boys ran through a dark forest, the older of the two leading with uneven strides and ragged gasps, dragging the younger boy along with a blood-soaked hand–

The memory scattered, interrupted by the flutter of wings on his cheek and the touch of six delicate legs.

He pushed off the wall, one hand delicately scooping the Alma off his cheek. "He's here?" The Alma undulated on the back of his fingers, its color briefly changing to blue, then green with assimilated light, and finally returning to black. Noir stood and knocked on the furnace door. "Alright, it's show time."

Adrian opened the door, her cheeks ruddy from the heat. "What do you mean?"

"We have a visitor from Elis Madra, probably sent to consider our request." Noir extended his hand past her head, and the shadows writhed into life behind her to lift his coat from where she had draped it over the furnace. "Not that I'm going to let you meet him."

She stepped into the kitchen, ducking as his coat drifted overhead, and started toward the exit. "How long was I in there, and why not?"

"Not long, they haven't finished preparing lunch, but don't worry, I won't tell your employer you were sleeping on the job."

"How generous of you."

"I am a generous sort. Now as for the why, I think it would be best to meet with the representative in private, even if you are an Umbran."

"How do you know he's here? I don't see a messenger."

"I arranged for a sentry to warn me when his messenger arrived." He lifted a hand, displaying the Alma before it took flight.

"How are we going to handle this with the Proctor absent? We don't even have his official permission. What if Proctor Madra demands a fee or something?"

'Tell her you're going to arrange a coup d'état and claim the Proctorship for yourself.'

Why ever would I do that? We're trying to stay inconspicuous.

'Because it would be exciting, and because you're doing a terrible job of staying inconspicuous. I mean, you've already leapt years ahead of the competition for worst employee of the century.'

A snippet of conversation snuck up from below as they escaped the mess hall and started their ascent, "–speak to your commanding officer." The voice was breathy and smooth, characterized by a sense of vague disinterest.

'That's Wraith alright.'

Noir pushed the familiar voice from his mind and addressed Adrian, "There won't be a fee, or any exchange of favors; Madra just wants to know who had the balls to solicit him."

Noir swept past the third floor and encountered Solomon Doll's secretary, Temaria, waiting for him on the fourth. "Lieutenant–"

"Tell her to let Lieutenant Wraith up; I'll see him in the Proctor's office."

Temaria fell into step. "Yes, sir, but are you sure that you wish to speak with him in private?"

"Yes, and make sure he's alone."

She broke off at the fifth floor to await their guest atop the stairs. Noir paused outside the Proctor's office and faced Adrian. "You too."

"Are you sure? I could act as a witness."

"Yes, I'm sure."

"All right then, but share all the juicy secrets later."

"I'll try, but I have the memory of a goldfish."

"Yeah, sure you do..."

Gregorio Taim appeared suddenly beside her. "Lieutenant–"

Noir raised a hand. "I know, Halican Wraith is downstairs in our foyer. I've arranged to speak with him in private. If this goes sour, I'll get the brunt of it."

The necromancer hesitated. "Of course, sir." Noir nodded at

the two of them and pushed into the office, letting the door close in his wake.

A knock came at the door soon after, followed by Temaria's voice. "Sir, Lieutenant Wraith is here as you requested."

"Send him in." The door creaked open, and a man stepped into the lightless room, his orange coat adorned with the tails of a lieutenant. The door closed, eliminating the only source of light beside what managed to creep through the window curtains.

The electric light clicked on with a buzz, revealing Noir to the newcomer. Halican Wraith silently faced him, his fingers opening to release the Alma he held imprisoned. "So it is true; you have returned." Halican Wraith slowly knelt. "How might we serve?"

'It's too bad we're here incognito; I really want to do the evil overlord spiel.'

"By not interfering, Wraith."

"Is this about Alighieri, sir?"

"Yes, but I'll clean up this stupid rebellion while I'm here."

"So these murders are your doing?"

"Yes, and they're going to stay that way. I don't want you or Elis to interfere. Understood?"

"Yes, my lord; but why not?"

"Because there's nothing you can do. The other Proctors won't let me act with impunity, no matter what Elis says, and I don't need you. In fact, your presence just complicates matters; if shit goes to hell, the Proctors are going to be on one side and Elis on the other, and I'm going to be stuck trying to resolve the mess."

"And if you are discovered, what would you have us do?"

"I expect you to hold your tongues, line up with the other Proctors, and die together."

"Is there anything else, my lord?"

"Make sure Elis sends over those files."

"Of course, my lord. Is there anything else?"

"No, just get your ass out of here."

Wraith stood but hesitated. "My lord, if I might impose..."

"What is it?"

"A man came to us yesterday, somebody sent by Harley. He spoke of someone who had arrived recently and took up residence in Astra Sear's district. He said that this foreigner had no name, and that when asked would say only 'I am the Messenger of Wrath'."

Shit. We'll have to take care of that tonight. "Tell Elis I'll handle it."

"Thank you, my lord." Halican bowed one last time and departed.

Noir scowled. *That's just our luck.*

'*Yeah, Thornwood must know that Loc's disappeared and is sending Messengers to scout us out.*'

Yeah, let's send that crazy bastard a "message" of our own.

'*You really shouldn't make jokes. You're not any good at them.*'

Oh, shut up.

Chapter Ten

A Public Service

Grim's sergeant arrived with all the pomp and disingenuous ire he could muster. He stormed up through the Dollhouse with a barrage of insults, profanity, and dire threats audible even over the common hubbub of Solomon Doll's militia. Everyone stationed on the Dollhouse's main floor heard him long before he appeared, and shifted in their seats to face the entrance stairs.

Adrian, currently situated at Valerian's unoccupied desk while completing Noir's report on the Hemomancy grove, inadvertently scowled. The half-filled sheet of Shadowpaper decayed a little in her tightened grip, sprinkling her trousers with flecks of Shadow-debris; they needed to purchase new paper from one of the shadowmancer consortiums in their district.

She loosened her grip and smoothed out the paper. Line after line of red ink stared up at her in the thin scrawl of her writing, its hue vibrant and vaguely morbid on the black page. *Of course it's morbid, it's all human blood, spent in gallons just to prolong this "life" of theirs, to make it seem normal.*

When she first heard of the humans' Hemomancy, it had never occurred to her that it would have a cost. Now she saw its effects whenever she saw a low-ranking hemomancer. They were always cold, their skin pale from blood loss, and their bodies emaciated from the constant expenditure of energy. They always dressed in layers and could rarely lift more than a small box of paper. Stronger hemomancers, like Solomon Doll and Grim, could generate enough energy from their blood consumption to recoup their losses, allowing them to maintain a healthy physique. Then again, they weren't dispensing their blood for hours a day to heal the dead for resurrection.

Grim's sergeant finally reached the main office floor, a cohort of five soldiers in violet lurking in his wake. He swept his hand outward, a noxious green mist trickling from the seams of his gloves.

"Where is Proctor Doll?"

Silas straightened at his desk. "If you state your purpo–"

The sergeant whirled on Silas, his hand stabbing outward as the long emerald spikes covering his head flared. "Don't speak to me without permission, Corporal! If you must waste my time, then bring an officer of at least acceptable rank."

Silas' faced twitched, betraying an instant of rage, before resuming the blank façade he usually maintained. Adrian saw it and glanced to her neighbors' desks, both of whom were struggling with anger; one going so far as to disfigure his writing board. *It's like he's trying to antagonize us.* Remembering the sergeant's green mist, she sniffed and caught a whiff of something faint: a familiar, ugly scent. *He's trying to manipulate them with Pathomancy.* She refocused on the sergeant, noting the mist oozing from his spikes and gloves. *Should I do something to stop him? Inform Silas? No, he would challenge him, and that has to be this man's intentions. Entering a stronghold and provoking the resident militia makes sense only when the antagonist wishes to instigate violence.* She relinquished her grip on the pistol. *They're trying to prompt the war between Doll and Grim, but why does Grim need Doll to start it?* A thought struck her, and she examined the room. *They timed this. No one here possesses equivalent authority; it's just Silas, someone he can goad without fear. But why? Because Grim would need the other Proctors to sanction his war, or at least not intervene. But that doesn't make sense either. There's no point in destroying Solomon unless Grim can guarantee Lock-And-Key will entrust him with the Doll District as well. There has to be more to this. Of course, none of that matters if he's truly plotting a rebellion. He can't do it alone though, not against all the other Proctors, and definitely not against Lock-And-Key.*

"Hey, kid."

"…What?" She whirled around and caught sight of Noir standing beside her desk with a sandwich of some kind, newly returned from whatever errand he had been running.

"Did you finish my report?" He took a bite, ignoring the six corpses suspended on a multitude of black spikes behind him.

"Uhh, no, I didn't."

"Well, get on with it." He strolled past, the corpses trailing after him, still impaled on his shadows.

"Um, Noir?"

"Yeah?"

"What are you doing with Grim's soldiers?"

"Oh, they were heckling everybody, so I decided to do some public service or whatever it's called."

"But doesn't that risk starting a war?"

"Nah, my word outweighs this pathetic excuse for a sergeant's."

"What are you going to do with them."

"Take out the trash."

"The entrance is the other way, though?"

"Yeah, but Doll's going to want to interrogate them first." Noir strolled to Solomon Doll's office and entered.

Adrian gradually slumped back into her seat, the report forgotten on Valerian's desk. *I need to figure out if Grim has allies before the war starts.* She frowned. *No, wait, I'm here for the Pattern, not for the war between Doll and Grim. Focus.* The urge persisted, however, niggling at her thoughts. *There's no reason I can't do both, but still… Am I becoming too attached, too human?* She didn't feel human, yet she felt flutters of emotion eddying along her undertaker detachment, memories and interactions with the Dollhouse and its people. She remembered a joke Hierophant had made and Valerian's resulting mimed gag. She pushed the memories and emotions aside. *Can I still act objectively, even to the detriment of these people?* She did not know.

Hurried footsteps intruded on her ruminations, drawing her gaze to where Solomon Doll and Gregorio entered from the main stairway. She stood, intent on warning him what awaited in his office, but Solomon preempted her, "Adrian, would you accompany us please? I believe an unbiased witness will benefit the proceedings."

She snatched a clean sheet of the degrading Shadowpaper and hastened through the maze of desks to join them as they opened his office door. Noir, with his feet propped on the desk, glanced up from Solomon's chair. "Hello, Doll, I took it upon myself to redecorate your office." The corpses were arrayed behind him in all the rigid poses of an ancient ballet, some in pairs and two solo.

Solomon Doll pulled the needle from his lips and scored a thin line across his palm. Blood welled to the surface and slithered off through the air to stab each of the corpses. "Gregorio, resurrect Grim's messengers; begin with the sergeant. Lieutenant Noir, maintain your constraints and vacate my chair."

A moment later, Solomon Doll spun his chair to face Grim's sergeant, newly resurrected and gasping in an enforced pirouette. "Hello, Sergeant, I understand you wished to speak with me?"

"Your … lieutenant killed me!"

"Yes, he tends to do that."

The sergeant tried to move and his face contorted into one of horror and fury. "What did you do to me?"

"More of my lieutenant's work; I assure you he will be justly reprimanded for any underserved inconvenience he caused you."

"You will put him down immediately! That rabid dog is an insult and does not deserve to live among honest people."

"You are in no position to speak of honesty, Sergeant; I may not be a pathomancer like yourself, but I could smell the trail of emotional manipulation you attempted from the bottom floor. I'm sure my Lieutenant Dorian will verify it. Plus, an Umbran witnessed the incident. Now, why did Grim send you? The pretense he used."

"Yesterday evening a group of our civilians made a shopping excursion to your district, upon returning they murdered one of our patrols with weapons they acquired here. They haven't been seen since."

"I do not permit weapon trading in my district; if they acquired them here, they did so from an unauthorized source."

"We don't care about the guns. Grim wants his people back. They are his incumbent property as Proctor over the purple district, entrusted into his care by the will of Lock-And-Key!"

"I have no idea where your people are; they returned to your district and never crossed the median again."

"Don't play games, we know you had something to do with their disappearance!"

"And what could I have possibly done? I did not know the particulars of the situation until it was resolved."

"Your sergeant then! Hierophant!"

"Sergeant Hierophant was too occupied in his duties to organize and arm a group of Grim's civilians; he merely escorted them to the shopping district and then, when his obligations required his attention elsewhere, designated a few subordinates to escort them back. Even ignoring that, do you really think he has the authority to trade in arms or hire an assault on another Proctor without my express permission? Of course not.

"If you are losing civilians, it is neither my concern nor that of my district. That is your problem. But, let the record show"—with this he glanced toward Adrian—"that in the hope of diffusing mounting tension between Grim and myself, I will conduct a thorough search of my district for these civilians. If I find them, they will be restored to you. Is that satisfactory?"

"Fine, just get me out of this."

"Noir, if you would."

Grim's soldiers dropped to the ground, their legs buckling, unprepared for the sudden weight. The sergeant staggered to his feet, using the backs of his soldiers for support, and gave Solomon a venomous smile. "Thank you for your cooperation, Proctor Doll. I'm sure Proctor Grim will be truly gratified by your decision. Let's go." He strutted out the door, nose pointed to the ceiling with his fellows in tow.

Adrian waited for the door to close before spinning toward Solomon, whispering, "You don't really intend to give them back, do you?"

"Of course not." Solomon strode to his office window and watched the men depart. "But a pretense will have to be made and our 'guests' will have to remain in the Undercity a bit longer. Their location and the truth of this matter stays between us and the other officers. Silas June will contact an intermediary to satisfy their basic needs; we can't go near them other than that. All right, they're gone; go about your duties."

Gregorio and Noir left promptly, but Adrian stayed until she was alone with Solomon and then quietly took a seat."

"What can I do for you, Adrian?"

"I have a question."

"Yes?"

"Why did you help those people? You're a Proctor, why concern yourself with the dregs of another district?"

"Well, would you have me deny them?"

"Dark Father, no! It's just … what you did wasn't pragmatic."

"There's enough misery in the world that I shouldn't add to it by turning a blind eye."

"But in doing so, you endangered your whole organization, your entire district. A war could hurt thousands; aren't they more important?"

"If everyone only looked to the greater good, then nobody would bother with the small kindnesses. I cannot let the great blind me to the small." He slipped into his chair, a binder in his left hand. "Is there anything else?"

"Do you think war with Grim is inevitable?"

"Yes," he said softly. "Grim has a hunger unlike anything I've ever seen before; being anything less than on top absolutely terrifies him; he just needs to be the most frightening person around. The fact that we have a murderer running loose is exacerbating the problem."

"What are you going to do? Is there anyone you can call for help? An ally?"

"Of course I have allies, they're all around you. Just look out the door and you'll see dozens of them. Some are friends I've known for years."

"That's not what I meant; what if Grim gets help from another Proctor or someone from the underworld?"

"None of the other Proctors will help him, even if he construes me as the aggressor. As for the underworld, it's unlikely but not impossible. He embarked on a crusade against them the instant he became Proctor; spent years persecuting and press-ganging them. Most of his militia are former underworlders he coerced into his service."

Adrian considered his words and then stood. "Just one last thing, we're running out of some supplies."

"That would be Hierophant's area; speak with him about it."

"Do you know where he is?"

"If he's not in the Dollhouse, ask Valerian; she's stationed somewhere around our visitors from Radiance. Speaking of which, I need a report from her, so if no one can help you find Hierophant, bring her report back with you."

"Sir, it's pouring rain."

"So take an umbrella."

She thought about the freezing rain for a second. "I'm unavailable, I have to write Lieutenant Noir's report."

"Lieutenant Noir can write his own report, now shoo; we both have other things to do. I need to have myself bled, for one."

"All right, I'll do it." She saluted and slipped out of his office.

Adrian spent several minutes querying people as to Hierophant's location and searching the Dollhouses various facilities with no luck. After exhausting every other avenue, she acquired Valerian's exact whereabouts from Silas and begrudgingly descended to the entrance, loathing the thought of another trip outside.

The rain still thundered, crashing down in such quantity that Adrian could only see a few feet ahead of herself. She donned one of the heavy Shadowmancy coats waiting by the entrance, a wide hat, and braved the deluge.

One long, miserable walk later found her crossing the road to a ramshackle Shadowcloth bivouac. Valerian and a small team of Solomon's troop hunkered inside around a meager heating lamp with blankets swaddling their shoulders. Further down the road was something Adrian had never seen before: a tent formed entirely of light. The golden radiance it exuded sheared through the rain and fog with blinding intensity, and enough warmth that she could see mist rising from the fabric.

Something inside of Adrian quailed and some other, feral part of her raged at the sight. This did not belong in Umbras.

She forced her eyes away from the tent and crossed over to Valerian's camp. "Hello, Corporal Valerian."

"No need for the formalities. What can I do for you?"

Taking one of the unoccupied seats beneath the bivouac, Adrian removed her soaked hat and flicked the water off it. "I was trying to find Hierophant; we need some supplies back at the Dollhouse."

"Afraid I don't know where he is, I've been here all day."

"…Really?" *Please don't tell me I came here for nothing.*

"Yep. I might be able to suggest some places though. Coffee?"

"No, thanks."

"All right, suit yourself." She leaned back with a pensive look and a steaming mug clutched in both hands. "Where would Hierophant be? Usually he's translating something for Solomon or off being philanthropic. Both are unlikely 'cause he would be easy to find. My guess is that he's walking the Grim border in case somebody else wants to come over; this rain would provide excellent cover."

"Isn't that dangerous? Won't Grim be watching us after yesterday?"

"Most likely, but Hierophant's always been someone who follows the heart over the head. It's one of the reasons I like him."

"Speaking of Hierophant, he says you never say how you found him?"

"Ah, he would mention that. It's not really a secret, I just don't want him knowing."

"Why?"

"Before I met Solomon, before he ever became Proctor, I was a mercenary of sorts, only I worked exclusively at night. I'd do just about anything: murder, theft, extortion, the works. This was all long ago, but I had a group I worked with, individuals with Evolved blood or people we kept under control. This doesn't really matter, but fast forward a couple of decades after I started working for Solomon and one of my old buddies appeared. He'd signed on with Astra Sear, but he'd heard that Grim was experimenting on people. It was a personal mission for him, but he needed help and I was good at fighting. So we followed the rumors and raided the compound. I never learned what my friend was searching for, but I found Hierophant there and that's the story."

"I don't get it, why hide that?"

"Ah, you see, Hierophant's kind of a white-knight. He wouldn't understand." Valerian took a sip from her mug, unperturbed by Hierophant's inhibitions.

Adrian leaned forward. "If you were a mercenary at night, what did you do in the day."

"I was a pit fighter! Three fights a day. The first two trumped up the odds, and the third was the money-maker. I traveled from venue to venue to fight Hydes and humans, sometimes even Constructs or other fabrications."

"That sounds horrible."

"Nah, it was great. Plus, there were a lot of hot guys."

"You were a pit fighter to meet guys."

"Well, that and the fighting."

Adrian shook her head and smiled. She could feel laughter bubbling around inside her, instigated by Valerian's unabashed enthusiasm. Still smiling Adrian stood and said, "Well, I have to be going."

"You going to look for him on the border?"

"No, it'd be a miracle to find him in this weather; I'll just catch him when he returns…"

A hazy figure sprinted around one of the corners, its arms raised against the rain. The man, one of Solomon Doll's soldiers, flung the bivouac's flap aside and stuck his head inside. "Corporal Valerian, you're needed back at the Dollhouse, immediately!"

"What happened?"

"Sergeant Hierophant's been attacked."

Valerian threw her blankets aside and yanked her hood up. "You all stay here and keep the vigil on our visitors." Then she raced from the bivouac with Adrian and the messenger close behind.

They dashed back to the Dollhouse and shoved their way through the crowd hovering anxiously across the entrance floor. The spectators started parting when they recognized Valerian, and a second later the two of them stumbled into an open space.

Hierophant lay prostrate on the ground between two pallid, shaking hemomancers. He wheezed in their grip, his clothing tattered and his body riddled with skull-crowned stakes. His eyes were gone, along with his fingernails and long strips of flesh down his arms and torso. Where the skin remained intact, the attackers had inscribed a litany of slurs.

Adrian turned and staggered back through the crowd, incapable of bearing the view. Her stomach churned, but rage mounted within her, pressing against the boundaries of her control, suppressing the struggling voice of logic. She snagged one of the adjacent soldiers. "Why aren't they helping him? Dark Father, look at what they did to him!"

"They're trying, but almost all of the hemomancers we have in the Dollhouse were bled today."

Her heart stopped. "Dark Father… Is there no one?" Her grip on the man's arm loosened, and she glanced back at Hierophant. She couldn't see him through the crowd, but she could see the trickles of blood gliding through the amassed feet. She forced herself to think. *We need to kill him. He can't be left like that. The hemomancers need time to recover their energy.*

Then silence took the assembly. It spread outward from the stairs, preceding a small path forming through the amassed soldiers. Solomon Doll strode through that gap, his sleeves rolled up to his elbows and the closed lacerations of an interrupted bleeding on his wrists. He dropped to his knees besides Hierophant and drove the bone needle into his palm. Returning the needle to his mouth, he squeezed his hand into a fist. Blood welled between his fingers and dropped. It burst mid-fall, converting into a minute, swirling cloud of crimson energy that soaked into Hierophant's skin.

Hierophant moaned and arched upward as spasms raked his body. He began to thrash, and soldiers rushed forward to hold him down while Solomon kept dribbling blood from his hand. Slowly, achingly, Adrian thought, Hierophant's wounds began to heal. The words etched into his skin vanished, his nails regrew, and his eyes reformed. At some point during the process, all tension fled his body and he sagged to the ground, unconscious; but Solomon persisted until the only sign of the assault was in Hierophant's ruined clothing.

Seemingly unfazed, Solomon flicked the blood from his hand and stood. "Please, take Sergeant Hierophant to the infirmary; I have healed his injuries, but his body still needs rest." The two soldiers besides Hierophant gently lifted him. They shuffled off toward a back room, and Solomon walked back to the stairs. Upon reaching them, he paused and glanced over his shoulder. "Silas, Valerian, neither of you two are to leave this compound; understood?" Without waiting for a response, he resumed his ascent.

He can't mean to let this go unanswered. They attacked one of his officers! They butchered Hierophant. Doesn't he care? No one said a word in protest. No one made any sound at all. They just watched him disappear, his steps sounding one after another in perfect clarity until they faded somewhere far above.

Valerian whirled about and stormed for the door. "I'm going to fucking kill them."

The soldiers scrambled from her path, but like a ghost, Silas slipped in front of her. "No, Valerian, let me handle this," he said, his voice eerily quiet.

"Not a chance in hell!"

He caught her as she stormed past. "You don't even know who you're looking for, let alone how to find them."

Her hands tightened into fists, and she looked back at him with bared teeth. Her eyes flashed a bloody crimson. "Not a–"

"They will suffer for this, I promise," Silas' voice cracked.

Valerian held his gaze for a second, then turned with a wordless scream and slammed her fist into an adjacent pillar. She stood there, visibly shuddering and her fist still grinding in the Shadowsteel. "...Fine."

Silas departed, his skin, hair, and clothing all fading to black.

In his wake, Valerian slumped against the pillar and continued to tremble. The skin of her hand gradually began knitting itself back together, the bones readjusted themselves and the blood vanished in flashes of crimson energy.

She's a hemomancer? Why didn't she heal Hierophant, then? Was she just bled? Adrian walked off in a daze, her mind flashing through a barrage of emotions and images: rage, fear, and horror all intermingling with the brutalized Hierophant. Without realizing it, she trailed after the soldiers carrying Hierophant and eventually came to his door.

They had laid him on a bed in the infirmary and now stood aimlessly to the side. One reached down and fingered the black sheets. "Don't these just make him look like he's dead?" His voice came out in a whisper, causing his companion to shiver.

"Yeah, but the red sheets…" He shook his head and shoulders violently, his eyes squeezed shut. "That was awful."

"Dark Father, you don't think the murderer did this?"

"What! No, no, it has to be Grim…"

"But look, he was tortured, just like that Alucard fellow."

"Oh, Dark Father I hope not; we have enough to worry about with Grim."

"We have to catch him quick, and kill him before he gets anybody else."

"Don't worry, Proctor Doll will find him." He broke into a smile. "And when he does, we'll just set Lieutenant Noir on him."

"Ha ha ha, yeah, that'll teach him, ha ha." He shuffled his weight. "But what if that's not enough…"

"It will be, and … and if it's not, we always have Proctor Doll!"

"Yeah, you're probably right…" Both of them quieted, their gazes falling back to Hierophant.

Adrian walked away. *I can't stay here any longer.* She brushed through the dissipating crowd, forcing their muted voices from her thoughts. *I have to reassert control.* She stumbled past the cleaning crew and out into the rain, coughing at its icy touch. The downpour almost drove her back into the Dollhouse, but the thought of it only gave rise to images of Hierophant's torture. She hunched her shoulders against the wind and began the long road home.

Once there, she descended through the Reliquary to her family's door and knocked.

Her father opened it with a confused look. "Oh, hello, Adrian, why did you knock? Wait. Is something wrong." He grabbed her arm and pulled her into the light of their home. "What happened?"

"I … I need to speak with Mother, do you know where she is?"

"Not until you tell me what's going on."

She compelled her eyes to meet his, trying to summon the undertaker detachment as they sat on the couch. "Hie–… Hierophant was attacked today."

"Is he all right?"

"Yes, it's just ... I lost control. I wanted to kill whoever did it to him, but before that I couldn't even act. I couldn't do anything! I just stood there and stared while he was bleeding out." She caught herself and shoved her emotions aside, blocking herself from them until the undertaker detachment closed around her again.

"It's perfectly normal to be flustered when something like that happens."

"No, it's not. I'm supposed to be an undertaker, to be in control and indifferent. Today proved that I am not in control anymore; I don't know if I can do this..."

He offered her no reply for a while, just considered her words before quietly asking, "Do you really believe that undertakers are supposed to be emotionless?"

"We have to because the Pattern—"

"Nowhere in the Pattern does it say Umbrans are supposed to be emotionless or cold."

"You don't understand. I'm not an undertaker. I'm huma—"

"You're not human either. You are both. You are something beautiful, something that should have been impossible, and yet here you are." He stroked her cheek. "Undertaker and human. It's just a question of who you want to be, not what."

"...What should I do?"

"Decide who you want to be, and become that person."

"But how? I can't control this."

"Then learn control; you've been among undertakers your whole life and this is just the first time you've been truly challenged. But I have faith in you." He smiled. "You can overcome anything given time, so just give it time and try; you might achieve more than you thought possible."

"Like what? Becoming Proctor?"

"You never know, humans are strange."

"Not that strange."

"I have faith."

She snorted and leaned back, but a smile still crept across her lips.

"Feeling better?"

"Yeah."

"Then I'm going to find your mother." He moved toward the entrance, but paused before opening the door. "Whatever you decide to do, remember that emotions aren't bad; they're what make us alive." He slipped out, leaving her alone on the couch.

Adrian snuggled her legs up to her chest and curled around them. *Who am I? ... I don't know.* She looked up to the ceiling where the warm light cast shadows across the walls. *I guess that's what he meant when he said decide.*

The minutes passed slowly, and the door eventually opened to admit her mother.

"Where's Father?"

"Running an errand. What have you learned?"

"I believe Grim is our usurper."

"You mentioned this before."

"Yes, but he's actively instigating a war with Proctor Doll, and this isn't about a grudge. This is a power grab, only more complicated. He has no allies among the other Proctors, and no one in the Underworld either. He's alone, but that doesn't make sense. To gain lasting power through Solomon's fall he would have to control who inherits the White District, which he can't. This means the only way he can guarantee power is through open rebellion against the other Proctors, or against Lock-And-Key herself."

"That's insane. Grim doesn't have the power to challenge every Proctor in Umbras, let alone Lock-And-Key."

"That's my point; the only way any of this makes sense is if Grim is getting help from somewhere, and I think it's from outside."

Chapter Eleven

Half-baked Coup

The Bellua swept past Noir with a screech, its ugly black talons drawn tight against its breast, and its leathery wings pounding the air in slow beats. The city's pervasive steam swirled off its ursine form and gushed over its surroundings in a tide.

Noir exhaled and stood with a rush of displaced water, unconcerned by the plunging drops on either side of his thin perch. He shook himself to shed the last drops of water and started down the pipe for the Grim District.

'Are you sure we have time for this detour? If Thornwood already sent a Messenger, then he's serious.'

We're not wasting any time; this Messenger is here to speak with the individuals trying to accrue power within Umbras, and they don't stir until most of the Hydes have died. So he won't either.

'We could still look for it, maybe find the Messenger sleeping in some shadowy alcove and then kill it all sneaky like. You know, be surreptitious for once as a novelty.'

What makes you think I'm not looking for it? Noir lifted a hand and an Alma alighted on his fingertips. *We'll know the instant it stirs.* The Alma fluttered away, disappearing into the mist as Noir entered the Grim District.

'I still don't like this delay; it means everything will come to a head on the Blood Moon, when Lazarus will be at his strongest. We should kill Constantine tonight, as we planned, and then kill the Messenger when he surfaces.'

We know nothing of this Messenger or Constantine, or how long it will take to kill either of them, but we know that Constantine isn't going anywhere and I don't want to miss the Messenger because he surfaced while I was fighting Constantine. Besides, it's risky to challenge both in one night when I don't know the extent of their abilities, or even what abilities Thornwood gave this particular Messenger.

'And it's wise to challenge a hemomancer on the Blood Moon?'

Lazarus doesn't scare me.

'And that's why he's smarter than you; he realizes you're more powerful than he is—at least, you were before he got that new power-up—and is scared shitless by it. He's undoubtedly inventing a thousand different ways to balance the scales in his favor. He recognizes the threat you pose. I suggest you do the same, if only so that we can laugh and slap our knees when his house of cards comes tumbling down.'

Eh, I'm not worried.

'And yet you get all lily-livered at the thought of facing a Messenger and Constantine in the same night.'

I don't know what result killing the Messenger will have; they're known to be unorthodox. Noir dropped three stories to land on a lower pipe and crossed to the next skyscraper.

'Un-huh, your knees are knocking together so loudly they could serve as a drum set.'

What's with the rush all of a sudden?

'It provided an excellent opportunity to call you a chicken.'

Noir shook his head. *Constantine can wait; I will not risk confronting him before I eliminate the Messenger of Wrath.*

'And if something else arises? Some other catastrophe? What will you do then? Oh, and by the way, bowk bowk bowk!'

Oh, Shut up. Should that happen, we will take the necessary risks.

Noir drew to a halt at the intersection of four pipes and surveyed the plaza that had once housed the Academy.

The ruins had been scraped away and replaced with the foundations of new skyscrapers. A host of monstrous corpses cluttered the streets leading to and from them, their bodies torn into bulbous, misshapen fragments and coated in an array of vividly hued blood.

Even as Noir watched, another creature inched into the open ground, its twining heads twisting in every direction as it sought prey. The Architects emerged from the floor around it, phasing through the Shadowsteel grating without impediment. The encroaching monster hissed at them, its four heads snapping with spews of vibrant acid, but the Architects swept inward and eviscerated the creature, strewing pieces of its corpse across the path and crushing each writhing head until the body ceased its struggles.

The threat dealt with, the Architects sank into the floor again.

Noir vacated his perch, plummeting several stories to land with a crash, straightened and strode toward the courtyard's center. An Architect emerged from the ground a second later, its hulking body and twin jackal heads still possessing the ethereal quality all young Umbrans experienced at night. "Why have you returned?"

"To see your progress."

The Architect prowled forward, one black head lowered to the ground sniffing and tasting the Shadowsteel. "It goes poorly; the human monsters impede our work, forcing us to eradicate any that draw near. The constant interruptions are infuriating."

Noir stopped at the skeletal, shoulder-high frame of a skyscraper. He examined the newborn structure, carefully inspecting its connection points and general shape. Even as he evaluated it, the skyscraper continued to grow, reaching its support beams heavenwards as veins of shadows stretched through the open air. He nodded absently and reached out a hand to touch its trembling surface.

The Architect shifted beside him. "The foundations are strong; it will match the height of its brethren and live for as long as they do. Your attention is unnecessary."

Noir flashed the Architect a vexed look. "Do not presume, Architect. This is my city and I will do as I wish."

The Architect flinched, his shoulders hunching upward as he bowed his heads. "As you say."

Noir reverted his attention to the skyscraper. "Its roots are thin, Architect, they need to be thicker and grow deeper or it will never truly be a part of this city." He delved into the skyscraper, thickening its shadows and spurring the growth of its roots. The ground shifted underfoot, becoming first pliant then gelatinous as new roots took shape and burrowed into the city. Another second passed and Noir stepped back, letting the Shadowsteel harden as the new roots settled.

He looked at the Architect. "Mimic this design with the other structures, it will ensure they connect fully with Umbras."

The Architect mirrored Noir's earlier motion and laid a hand against the skyscraper. "Yes, I can feel it: the city." He bowed to Noir. "Forgive my hubris."

Noir dismissed the Architect's words with a wave of his hand and strode to the next building. He visited each of the newborn skyscrapers, occasionally correcting one with Shadowmancy, but for the most part, leaving them unchanged.

After the final one, he rejoined the Architect. "I have repaired their flaws and taught you the ways of their growth, but they will still need nurturing as time progresses. This is your task, Architect, I do not expect you to be perfect, but you will pour your soul into these Constructs, and you will make something worthy of Umbras."

The Architect bowed its heads. "Yes, my lord."

Noir ignored its reverence and proceeded to the northern-most entrance of the square, shadows scraping the littered corpses from his path. Once there, he assessed the ground and abutting skyscrapers with a sweep of his consciousness, hunting for imperfection or Hydes that would interfere.

As the moments passed, shadows swelled around him, accreting from the cracks and recesses starlight failed to touch. They churned and climbed higher, taking form and substance and darkening to the same black as Umbras before melding with the old structures. New piping sprouted from the existing network, spanning the street as walls mounted around it, filling the gaps and turning sheer. It all occurred in a matter of seconds, and culminated in a sheer wall miles high glistening with condensation. It settled with a low groan and a tide of Shadow-debris.

Noir returned to the Architect. "That will keep out your pests. Be warned, however, even though your corruption is minimal that much running water will still discomfort you at night."

"And the other roads?"

"I will close them as well. When all is done, there is a section at the center of each wall where no piping runs, open it to allow free passage."

He fashioned a soaring barricade of Shadowsteel and running water for each entrance, forbidding the monsters of Umbras from interfering with the city's restoration. The inhabitants would notice the changes of course, but they wouldn't be able to trace them back to him.

As he molded the final wall, an Alma emerged from the steam to alight on his shoulder. He cocked his head, listening to its voiceless message. *So the Messenger shows itself at last.* The shadows coalesced and set him atop the newly formed wall, from there he directed his steps toward the center of Umbras.

'Where is it?'

It's still in Astra Sear's district. Apparently, a collection of small-time Night Princes are colluding with the Messenger of Wrath in an attempt to accrue Thornwood's favor. At best, they're playing both sides of the table; at worst, they've fully committed themselves and are trying to usurp Loc.

'Oh, what foolish little children they are, shouldn't they know better than to talk to strangers?'

There's also someone looking for us; I can't get a clear picture, but he's tall and smells of acid and rot. Noir vaulted to the next story up. *And that's not how the saying goes.*

'But it is no less apt; they talked to a stranger, so now they're going to die.'

I guess that's true, but, nevertheless, you shouldn't go corrupting childhood wisdom; it's a bad habit.

'Do you know who's looking for us? One of Solomon's people?'

No, someone we've never met.

'Oooh, exciting.'

The shadows swelled again, forming a bridge through the skyscrapers and delivering him into the center of Umbras over the palace.

He slowed as he looked upon it, the gentle warmth of his mood dying to a bitter ache in his chest. He slowly extended his hand, fingers elongating into talons and curving downward. *I wish I could kill Lazarus. I want to see the life screaming out of him, drop by drop, to hold his life in my hands.*

'Then why don't you? He's right there.'

Noir's fingers closed into a fist, nails biting into his flesh and spilling dark blood. *Because he must suffer first. He must know fear and despair; he must see them give way to hope and conquest only to be torn from his grasp as a lie. He must be made to look into the darkness of his fate and realize the fathomless depths of his error.* Noir let his hand drop and jumped from the skyscraper, shadows marshalling to slow his descent.

He landed gently and strode across the courtyard, circumventing the palace until he came to a thoroughfare marked with a russet banner: Astra Sear's district. He diverged onto it, following a trail of perched *Almas* until it ended in another courtyard amidst the skyscrapers.

He paused on its perimeter, observing the space before venturing forward. The skyscrapers here all appeared new, the locks untwisted, the walls and doors bereft of dent or scar. Even the surroundings lacked their usual displays of life either in refuse, decorations, or cadavers. Yet it was a sham, a gaudy repair attempt that itched at Noir like the wrong-colored patch on a dress. To everyone else, however, it would appear as an untouched and uninhabited portion of Umbras.

Noir moved to the center of the space and knelt, laying his hand on the ground. Disregarding the farce of his surroundings, he extended his senses downward, searching through the labyrinth of the Undercity until he located a large hollow. *There you are.*

'*Who? I don't see anybody or anything.*'

They're in the Undercity; the Almas simply guided us to where I could locate them myself.

'*If they're just going to hide underground, then why bother dressing up the surface?*'

Maybe as posturing, a way to convince other Night Princes of their ability to control Umbras and the Hydes, and thus expand their ranks. Evolved individuals can offer Hydes a sliver of sanity, and the ability to remain yourself even at night is a compelling drug.

'*Why would Babylon allow this?*'

He might not know about it if this is an uninhabited part of the District; all of his guards would be concentrated around the main population. Or he might know and is waiting until he can catch all of them at once.

Standing, Noir doffed his coat to preserve its hue, and phased through the grating. There was an instant of darkness followed by the lurch of sudden free-fall as he entered a columned room with seven diverging paths and mounds of assorted refuse.

Noir slammed onto a wooden table, smashing it into four pieces and countless splinters as his own impetus drove him into a crouch. The table's monstrous patrons launched themselves back with a torrent of profanities, two with bruising jaws from where the table struck them. Noir straightened amidst the rubble and grinned. "Mind if I drop in?"

'You unprincipled swine! You turd among speech impaired imbeciles!'

Sorry, couldn't help myself.

'We've been over this! You shouldn't tell jokes, and that goes double for jokes you know are bad.'

"Who the hell are you?"

'You, you, you— Oh ooh ooh, say take me to your leader!'

Noir faced the speaker, lips curling in contempt. "A god, now shut-up while I count graves."

'That works too.'

The man growled and spat a command, marshalling the shadows into a pistol. "I'll ask you only one more time, interloper. Who the hell are you?"

Noir ignored him. "Four? You tried to instigate a rebellion with four sub-Proctor level individuals? You'd better be geniuses."

The speaker snorted. "I warned you." He fired with a grunt, the recoil shoving him back as the pistol barked and the bullet pinged off Noir's skin.

"So not geniuses, then."

The speaker stumbled back with an expression of consternation, the pistol tumbling from his hand. He drew himself up, shaking his head and snarling. A visible shudder passed through him and his skin began to darken and slough off, surrendering to his Hyde. One after another, the others followed suit.

The first to complete his transformation became a pillar of lashing tentacles without a central core. It released a gurgling cry and lunged at Noir, spraying viscous liquid from its limbs.

Noir rolled his eyes, and the creature imploded.

The second Hyde blurred into movement, revolving constantly on a multitude of arms and dashing through the vestiges of the first. It launched itself at Noir, flinging a wall of noxious green webbing from its myriad hands.

Noir side-stepped with elegant boredom, and caved in its carapace head with a kick.

The third Hyde scuttled up the wall furthest from Noir, its body long, sinuous, and a mixture of wood and fur. It twisted, reared up and spat a barrage of sapphire spines that exploded upon a swell of shadows. The monster howled and vaulted toward the opposite wall, only to have unformed shadows shred its body mid-flight.

The initial speaker finally completed his transformation and shook itself with a clatter of spines, the floor bowing beneath his girth. Now twice Noir's height even on all fours, it stalked around him, scenting the air with two serpentine tongues.

Noir echoed its movements, his hands still buried in their pockets. *They must be horrible Adepts if they've already resorted to their Hydes.*

'We should change that whole 'sanity is more important than talent' paradigm the Night Princes have. We could even make cool catchphrases like "intelligence is for dumb-dumbs" and "down with sanity!" or "power is everything!"

I suppose you'll want to organize rallies?

'Of course. That being said, this fellow seems to have a formidable Hyde and, if nothing else, he's loud.'

Noir snorted. *It's just a Bellua, they're all like that.*

'So why haven't you killed him, then?'

You're right, I should finish this. A spear shot through the monster's head. *Happy?*

'Very.'

Noir faced the Messenger of Wrath where it lounged in one of the diverging paths. It imitated a man in height and shape, even down to the characteristics like mouth, fingers, and nose; but its skin was a storm of red and black lines in constant, furious movement. It wore ragged finery patched with uncured leather, but no shoes.

The Messenger's pale eyes flicked to and over Noir's form with an unimpressed sniff. "You're not much for a Tyrant."

"I can be frightening if you like." Noir crossed over to the creature, stopping just short of the doorway. "But that wouldn't go well for you. Now, I know you're connected to Thornwood, so he'd better listen when I tell him to stay the hell out of Umbras. This city belongs to me."

The Messenger of Wrath giggled, but its laugh was soulless, a mere imitation. "Oh foolish, Tyrant, our master does not wish to conquer your city. He wishes to liberate it. This imprisonment you enact every night is unnatural. Men were meant to be free, to run, fight, and live as they desire. To imprison them is insanity."

Shadows furled around the Messenger of Wrath, binding it in threads stronger than any chain. "This is not a civilized world, this is a world for monsters; and I just happen to be the worst."

The Messenger of Wrath collapsed into jade mist and swirled out of his grasp. "Your vapid attempts to engender order in a world that has no desire for it are merely dilatory. You cannot avert or reform the natural order, Tyrant; our world has spoken, and it chooses chaos."

"We've already had our dark age: two hundred years of it, and I have no desire to witness its resurgence." He remembered that time too well: a time when the Malum ruled, before the Deos Mortai built their cities and enslaved most of the surviving population.

The Messenger of Wrath reformed from the jade mist, and shadows closed around it in a seamless casket.

An instant passed and then a fragment of the casket melted, opening an aperture through which the Messenger squeezed, its unmarred body twisting grotesquely and compressing unnaturally. "You cannot imprison me, Tyrant, I am a Messenger of Wrath, born of my lord's anger and destined to free those you have enslaved." Jade mist poured from its fingers, expanding as it rushed toward every corner.

'Ah damn, this would be so easy if you were a necromancer. Just snap your fingers and he'd drop dead. He's only artificial after all.'

You don't need to rub it in.

Why not? You take every possible chance to laude the benefits of Shadowmancy, and I have nothing to argue with. I mean you abhor Hemomancy well beyond the point of blindness, and we both agree Pathomancy is about as useful as a dog's piddling contest. Necromancy is my last chance, and most of its practitioners can only wave their hands while spending ten years raising an army of undead that'll get obliterated by the next half-wit Adept they pass. Ah well, back to the graveyard I guess. It's downright demoralizing I tell you... Know what? You're right. Everything else sucks.'

Noir flicked his hand outward, twisting it mid-motion, and the shadows raced to him, bulging like water sacks as they took the shape of a monster. The Shadow Thrall opened featureless, oval eyes and unhinged a gaping, toothless maw. It inhaled, consuming the air and the jade mist with a screeching whistle. Its form expanded, burgeoning with the Messenger of Wrath's poison.

Noir flicked his hand again and the grating beneath the Messenger of Wrath stabbed upward, goring its feet. The Messenger of Wrath hissed and tried to dissipate, but its body flickered and solidified again, held in place by the corrupted blood Noir had fused with his Shadowmancy. It thrashed, trying to tear itself free, but the burrowing shadow tendrils raced forward, diving in and out of its flesh. The Messenger howled and lunged to escape, but the grate held fast, and it flopped down, the floor stabbing all along its body and corrupting its flesh with Shadowsteel.

The Messenger tore its head free and laughed. "It is already too late! My mere presence was an act of vitiation! Every lock and every door in this district has deteriorated beyond recovery!" The tendrils dragged its head back to the floor, but as if spurred by the creature's taunts, a deep, shuddering crash split the night, pulling Noir's gaze upward. "They are free! The prison doors are opened, and soon you will all experience this world as it was meant to be!" It cackled one last time before the shadow tendrils engulfed it.

Cursing vehemently, Noir flung his hand skyward and a shadow hurled him up through the ceiling. He broke the surface but continued climbing, the shadows heaving him ever higher until he alighted atop the nearest skyscraper as every occupied door in the Astra Sear District burst open.

"Damn him to an eternity of his own hell!" Noir swept his hand outward and the shadows coalesced into a ledge beneath him. He dropped onto the outcropping, his hands extending toward opposite horizons and clenching to fists. Every shadow across Astra Sear's district pulsed, fusing to one another and mounting higher.

'This is a very bad idea, if we leave too much Shadow-debris then somebody smart will figure out they're dealing with a Tyrant-level individual and that's if we're lucky.'

We don't have a choice; if we don't contain the problem, it'll spread to the other districts. Damn Thornwood. Noir snarled and lifted his hands overhead, binding every shadow in the district to his will and molding them to his design as a huge swell of shapeless, bodiless force surged from him. *To think he could bestow his Messenger with such a precise effect that it would target only Shadowmancy locks. He's growing stronger.* The walls took shape, filling in the space between the skyscrapers while the Shadow-debris sloughed off them in waves, piling up like snow, clogging the air, and burying even the Belluas.

Every road inside or leading from Astra Sear's district now ended in a wall of sheer, featureless Shadowsteel. The wrathful bellows and agonized cries started seconds later, growing to a chorus as those imprisoned attacked each other in the mist.

'At least we managed to contain them.'

Not that it'll do them a lot of good; they'll all be dead by morning. He scowled. *And I'm going to need a new coat. Again.*

'I told you that these nighttime excursions were bad for your health. Solomon will start charging you for all the clothes you waste, and then where will we be? Hungry, starving, deprived of nutrients, famished—'

I'm not in the mood.

'All right, have it your way. What do you want to talk about?'

How about who the fuck decided it was a good idea to invite a Messenger of Wrath into Umbras. And how did it get past the Ferrymen? Noir stepped off his perch onto an expectant shadow raft and returned to the Undercity chamber where the Shadow Thrall and various corpses remained as he had left them.

He waved his hand, and the poison-laden Shadow Thrall spun in on itself, contracting into a knuckle-sized marble. He took it from the air and stored it in a pocket as shadows pooled beneath and lifted the Messenger of Wrath.

'What are you going to do with that?'

Send a message about consorting with foreigners.

'Don't crucify it, that's so medieval. Let's do something fresh and exciting, and then let's get something to eat. Breaking up rebellions and building walls sure stirs up an appetite.'

You didn't do anything.

'Actually, I did everything. In reality you're just a voice in my head, and I'm the one with the body.'

Is that so?

'Wanna know how I know?'

No.

'It's simple really. You see, insane people never believe they're crazy, and we both agree you're crazy, so you can't really be crazy. I, on the other hand, doubt I'm insane, so it's obvious that I actually am crazy. This means that I'm probably the one hearing voices, and thus I'm the one with the body.'

That's almost crazy enough to be true.

'Like I said, I'm crazy.'

Chapter Twelve

Lawn Decorations

~ *Black ground surrounded him and everything, the fallen leaves, the bracken, the trees, even the stones shone with a metallic sheen. Only the thin rays of sunlight poking through the trees brought any color to his stygian environs.*

A footstep scraped on the ground, drawing his gaze about as Alighieri stepped into view. "Wow… Did you do this?"

Noir just looked at him, knowing he didn't have to answer for Alighieri to recognize the truth.

"I love what you've done with the place, it's very … uniform."

Noir slumped forward, bending his lanky frame over the steel butterfly and crushing it against his chest as if that would stifle this curse.

Alighieri sat beside him. "Hey now, don't be like that." He bumped Noir's shoulder with his own. "We've been through this before."

"You should leave. Pretend this never happened; we can't let Mother and Father think you're a part of this. They'll realize you're a witch too."

Alighieri shifted so they leaned back against one another, his strange, bleached hair mingling with Noir's own brown locks. "We won't tell them, then. We'll keep this a secret, like we keep mine, until we can prove ourselves worthy of life."

"How? This isn't like yours, this affects everything!" The shadows around them throbbed at his voice. "I can't hide it! I can't control it. If they find out—"

"You can learn to control it, just like I did." Alighieri reached around Noir and gently touched the butterfly. He exhaled, his breath a cold breeze on Noir's ear, and the butterfly pulsed. White flowed out from his fingertips, bleaching first the butterfly then Noir's leggings, the ground, the leaves, the bracken, the trees, and the stones. Everything in front of Noir turned an exquisite white as the dead animals trembled back to life. Alighieri inhaled a warm breath, full of life, and leaned back against Noir. They sat there for a while, Noir staring at the white forest while Alighieri observed the black.

Noir let his head drop back, resting it against Alighieri's. "I can't let you do that. It's too dangerous—"

"Enough, we will get through this. We always do." ~

"Lieutenant! Lieutenant Noir!" The muffled call hailed them from across the restaurant, pulling Noir's gaze up from his mottled pigeon eggs to where one of Solomon Doll's privates stood by the door.

Twisting in her seat, Adrian craned her neck to see the speaker. "What do you think it is?"

Noir stood, retrieving his coat from the back of his chair. "I don't know, but my guess is some calamity or other."

'I think you're cursed. Ever since we've arrived, the accident and calamity rates have tripled. I mean that Alucard fellow was the first person to actually die in centuries!'

He nodded at her meal. "Finish quickly."

She started to respond, but Noir was already striding across the restaurant, donning his coat as he went.

The private hastened to meet him. "Lieutenant Noir, there's been an incident in the central square."

"What kind of incident? Is it related to the nightmare in Astra Sear's district or our murderer?"

"We don't know, sir, but we think it's somebody different, and it's more of a massacre than a murder."

"What do you mean?" Noir dropped a coin onto the cashier's desk and exited into the overcast morning.

"Well, there's four of them this time, but only their heads."

"Only their heads?" Adrian bounced up beside them, munching on a piece of toast.

"Yes. They're mounted on stakes over the palace doors. There's some kind of message, but nobody's been able to decipher it."

They turned onto the Dollhouse's main street, Noir fashioning and offering Adrian a napkin as she licked the oil from her fingers. "And why does Solomon think we're facing someone new? What's changed?"

"Low-quality Shadowmancy littered the scene and our first murderer–"

"Is either not a shadowmancer, or a meticulously careful

asshole."

"Yes, sir. The Shadowmancy is why you've been assigned; many of the other Proctors are already present."

Noir pushed into the Dollhouse. "Then we should hurry before they ruin everything."

'Ah Proctors, they are such incompetents. Who knows what would happen to the city if they ascended to power. Oh wait…'

Just because they lead glorified street gangs doesn't make them qualified to run an investigation.

'And you are? A mass-murdering, schizophrenic psychopath?'

I know what happened.

'Too bad you don't plan on helping them solve anything.'

They arrived on the office floor and crossed to where Silas June conversed with Solomon Doll.

"–People over to investigate the moment we're gone, and don't tell the other Proctors what we've discovered until you've explored it thoroughly."

Silas nodded his understanding and slipped around Noir with a cursory greeting before disappearing downstairs.

Noir ignored him. "What did we find?"

"I don't know, but we think it's the second murder site. A man arrived earlier today and reported that a massive section of the forest has turned bone-white."

Adrian inhaled sharply. "All of it?"

Solomon nodded grimly

"What kind of necromancer could do that?"

"A Tyrant," Noir replied softly. "You think it's Brigadier or someone else?"

"Brigadier, but it's not confirmed. I've sent Gregorio and Hierophant to investigate; hopefully, they'll dig something up."

"As long as you're not sending Dorian, they might even come back in one piece."

Solomon Doll retrieved his coat from a nearby table and shrugged it on. "No need to fear on that account; an Underworld marketer has appeared in Syrian Fell's district with a wagon of Adept weaponry and Hyde trophies. I sent Lieutenant Dorian to assess his wares and purchase any that he deemed valuable."

"Wouldn't that normally be Hierophant's area?"

"Yes, but Hierophant is currently preoccupied with the battlefield and Rias Dorian is more than capable, as you should know. He successfully handled that Death Merchant assignment you gave him." Solomon Doll quirked an eyebrow at Noir, who shrugged.

"I never would have given him the assignment if I believed he couldn't handle it."

"What? Are you conceding that you misjudged Rias Dorian?"

"Hardly, I gave him a job he could handle. If anything, that reinforces my assessment."

"Can I ask why you hate Dorian? What has he done to merit such resolute disdain?"

'Do you want me to make a list? I've got some great ideas, for instance, we could say he spat to the left while facing east and by this method insulted your great grandmother who was buried facing the west.

A little complex, don't you think?'

'You should hear what he did to your grandfather.'

Noir shrugged. "I do not like the man. Ergo, I do not suffer his flaws with the same kindness I show others."

"I suppose that makes sense. Now, before we leave, a man named Constantine has requested a private meeting with you."

Noir stilled, then growled, "...What?"

"A man named Constantine has requested a private meeting with you; do you know him?"

"No. Did he say what he wanted?"

"He would not say, but he did not seem overly distressed, and I do not believe his intentions are hostile."

"Where is he?"

"He requested a private meeting so I lent the two of you my office."

"That seems wise."

"There's nothing in there he can access for information, and I have it arranged in such a way that he cannot attempt it without losing some of his blood."

"Which will give you every means you need to track him down

and coerce answers from him."

"Exactly. Meet me downstairs when you are done."

Noir started toward Solomon's office, his blood seething awake with the Plague's familiar, toxic pain. *What is he doing here?*

'I don't know, but we can't kill him, not here in front of everybody. We can't give even a hint of our intentions. Maybe he's trying to protect himself through association; "knowing" him would put you on the map, especially if you met him just before he turns up dead.'

It won't work.

The man who occupied Solomon's office was as tall as the ceiling with ruby, shifting skin and arms that draped to the floor. He began to speak, "Hello, Master Noir–" but Noir was already surging to grab him by the collar and drag him down, his nails drawing blood.

"Why shouldn't I kill you?"

"Because that would reveal you as the murderer, and you're not ready for that. Besides, with your brother dead, someone needs to start filling in his shoes."

The shadows beneath Constantine's clothing stabbed into his skin, scraping and sawing with a thousand needles that left no mark. "Why haven't you outed me?"

"Because I need you alive, not killed or imprisoned by the Proctors." He leaned close, his face taut with pain. "Your brother died for a reason, and while I don't expect you to forgive me, I expect you to understand. Lazarus had something I needed; your brother was a necessary sacrifice and you"—Constantine gasped as Noir bored deeper—"mustn't waste it!" He subsided in ragged pants. "This world is dying, and *you* are doing nothing to stop it. The cities are just a bandage; most Tyrants are worse than anarchy, and everyone lives every day in pain." His eyes flashed cold, despite the pain constricting him. "Your brother would have understood this, would have understood that nothing will change unless we excise the root of it all: the Plague."

"Pity, I am not my brother. Maybe you should have let him live." Noir found something vital inside him and crushed it

Constantine stifled a scream. "Bastard!"

"What do you want?"

"Your blood. I need a shadowmancer test subject with high-concentrations of the Plague, Tyrant-level concentrations."

"And why would I help you?"

"Because I will save this world, make it something worth living in again. You can hurry the process along, save us centuries of pain."

"Fuck the world."

"Your brother would have helped."

"Stop. Saying. That."

Constantine leaned closer and hissed, "Does his death mean nothing to you? Will you make everything he suffered pointless? Make him have died for nothing?"

"Shut up."

"Fine, if you don't care about your brother after all, how about this: I can inoculate you and your creations against Lazarus' Shadow Poison. That way you'll be able to say you got something out of this, and I'll still be able to help this world."

"I. Don't. Care."

"And what about Thornwood? I can design something that will repulse his creations, drive them from your precious city, purify it of all foreign taint."

Noir slowly released him, darkening Constantine's shirt with shadows to conceal the blood and injuries. "Get out."

"Are you really going to damn our world for revenge?"

"Your world, mine died with my brother."

"Fine, I'll go, but think on my words all the same, and ask yourself what really matters more. Then ask yourself what Alighieri would want." Constantine quietly took a hat from Solomon's desk and left.

Noir remained there for a while, fighting with his rage and the desperate, growing desire to just stop caring and let loose. Ultimately, he forced himself to the first floor where Solomon waited with Adrian and a contingent of guards. "I'm finished."

"What did he want?" Solomon asked.

"He's connected with Brigadier and Alucard and is afraid that the murderer intends to kill him as well. So he contacted me because I seem to have a growing reputation."

"For brutality?"

"Efficiency."

"What did you tell him."

"That I needed to talk with you, but I should be able to help him out tomorrow."

"Today would be better."

"Yes, but I have a feeling we're going to be busy.

They arrived at the central plaza to find a corded fence barricading the thoroughfare.

The attending guards straightened at Solomon's approach and one, a tall man with speckled eyes, slipped through the wire fence to greet them. "Sirs, I must ask that you provide confirmation of your position."

"Of course." Solomon Doll flicked his wrist subtly and, taking care to ensure none of the milling bystanders saw it, revealed a wristband of linked chains and roses. "This should suffice. If you do not know it, fetch your superior."

The guard nodded and returned across the fence.

Adrian stepped up as he departed. "What was that bracelet?"

"A badge of office; every Proctor has one." He glanced at the rapidly thickening crowd. "They're to ensure no one impersonates us."

"Do you really have trouble with people impersonating Proctors?" Adrian asked.

"Yes." Solomon shrugged. "But it's really more a symbol of power than anything."

'Yeesh. You let them run things for two odd centuries and suddenly everyone's giving themselves badges of office, fancy-dancy titles, and secret handshakes. Back when Umbras first started hulking in the skyline, you knew a Proctor from everybody else because they hit you with a club when you misbehaved. If that didn't work, you became certain they were Proctors because they hit you again, this time with an even bigger club. If that didn't work either,

then everybody had better run and hide because one Proctor had just clobbered another.'

The guard reappeared from the bustling crowd with a second man Noir recognized as Tollus Meer from his visit to the palace on the night of his arrival. The attaché stepped through the fence and performed an elegant bow. "Good morning, Proctor Doll."

"What do you want, Meer?"

The attaché rose from his genuflection and stepped aside, motioning for the fence to be removed. "I've come to share what we know of this atrocity."

"You may speak with my lieutenant. I wish to discuss this matter with the other Proctors."

Tollus Meer's lips thinned to a line but he still bowed to Noir. "It is a pleasure to meet you, sir."

"I'm sure it is."

*'**Meer**' mortal that he is, I suggest we find the Tollust spire in Umbras and hang him from it, preferably by his snooty nose.'*

How is that any better than my 'drop in'?

*'**B**ecause I said it, and because I used the word 'snooty' which automatically elevates it to high prose.'*

Tollus Meer followed Noir with clasped hands. "I must say that your rapid ascension through the ranks of Solomon Doll's soldiers has impressed me, sir. Yet, I cannot help but wonder how he would react upon learning of your past; to call upon Lock-And-Key in the dark hours has many possible ramifications."

"And how would you know of that?"

Tollus Meer smirked at him. "The palace is designed to record all who enter it, especially the uninvited guests. I don't know how you bypassed our guards and warning systems, but I know you trespassed three days ago."

'That's new, probably a feature Alucard added at Lazarus' behest; it was a good way to tell when you arrived.'

Adrian leaned close, whispering, "What is he talking about? Did you actually visit the palace at night?"

He made a dismissive gesture. "It's not as unthinkable as you would believe. I'm a *Rencensere*, so the night doesn't force me to change."

'The night is a time of rabid wolves; let no man who fears madness walk under the moon's eye.'

Tollus Meer glared at Noir. "Yes, but why would someone like you dare to speak with Lock-And-Key?"

Noir stopped and extended a single finger to kiss the man's gilded brow. The shadows around them thickened, becoming syrupy and warping toward Noir. "If you truly believe that Lock-And-Key will protect you from me, then continue speaking and I will disabuse that notion. If there is a speck of intelligence in your feeble mind, however, then control your tongue and speak only as requested."

Tollus Meer licked his lips and nodded.

"Good." Noir lowered his hand and proceeded. Tollus Meer gasped and buckled to the ground.

Adrian stared at Tollus Meer for a long while before racing after Noir. "What was that about? Do you actually know Lock-And-Key?"

"Yes, I know her." He pushed through a pair of soldiers in green coats, eliciting affronted cries that quickly subsided when they noticed his lieutenant's tails.

"But how did you even meet her? She's a Tyrant; it's not like you can just walk up and greet her."

'Tell her you got uppity once and Loc … solved the problem. It's a believable story, considering your prickly disposition.'

"Let's just say that I've walked in particular circles, and that I knew somebody who knew somebody."

She shook her head and flashed a nervous smile. "Forgive me, but that's hard to believe. Not even the Proctors see her very often." She focused on him, her eyes narrowing. "What did you want with her anyway?"

'Uh oh, she thinks you're up to something.'

"Put away the sidelong glances, I only wanted to discuss something mundane with her."

"What?"

"It involved tea, crumpets, and a singing wolverine."

"…I can't tell if you're being serious or not."

Breaking through the crowd's final lines, Noir halted outside the palace entrance, its base flecked with dried blood and its arch crowned by four severed heads. They swayed in the wind, impaled on flexible spears and encircled by foreign writing. Adrian recoiled as she saw it, her eyes paling with disgust and her ears plastering themselves against the side of her head. "What does it say?"

"Proditores Fatum, Traitor's Fate." Noir crossed his arms. "It's a language from the Old World, but not a common one. There are only a few people who could understand or read it. Elis Madra probably, and Lock-And-Key certainly. Harley Press, maybe, but he wouldn't do this."

"How did you learn to read it?"

Noir winked at her. "I run in particular circles."

Adrian made a show of rolling her eyes, the act somewhat concealing how her ears perked up. "What do you think he's trying to tell us? Other than these men were traitors of some kind?"

"I don't know. This seems like an act of punishment or of persecution."

"Maybe it's just a cover-up, something to mask his trail?"

"No, the scene is too visceral and the stage is too prominent. He wanted these men found, and he wanted everyone to know why they died. It's probably a warning."

"Yes, that's our supposition as well." Tollus Meer stepped beside them again, his features pale but controlled. "Furthermore, our personal shadowmancers have inspected the shadowmantic stakes supporting the heads. They said the quality is abysmal, barely suitable for an apprentice of the Academy." He sniffed. "Palace guards are collecting shadowmancers as we speak, excluding the Proctor's and their officers of course."

Noir strolled forward, one hand emerging from its pocket. "I'll make my own assessment if you don't mind." He reached up, his fingers flaring out and issuing a web of shadow tendrils to grasp one of the stakes. The shadows pulsed and flooded Noir's mind with information. *Ugh, this is disgusting. The spear is so pathetic it doesn't even serve its purpose; any shadowmancer with half-a-brain could tell this was made intentionally bad. I might have to work on this.*

'Bah, it was your first try at making bad Shadowmancy; I'm sure nobody will blame you for having it actually turn out good. Besides, only really powerful shadowmancers with something to hide butcher their own work. Any shadowmancer smart enough to realize that the flaws were intentional will realize they don't really want to antagonize the man behind it.'

Noir conducted a cursory examination of the remaining spears, mostly for the sake of appearances, and then restored his hand to its pocket.

'So who do you think is going to tell on us?'

Any Proctor with Shadowmancy will notice the instant they touch a spear. Noir re-addressed Tollus Meer, "Do the palace shadowmancers really believe that an unskilled Adept killed four men, snuck onto palace grounds and made impromptu art from the remains? These Constructs are deliberately poor quality."

Tollus Meer snorted and drew himself up. "Impossible, they were inspected by palace shadowmancers; there can be no error."

"Actually, I agree with the lieutenant's assessment." They all turned toward the sibilant voice.

A man in a gold coat moved to stand beside Noir, his scaled features twitching beneath a mane of magnificent golden hair. "I am surprised you managed to perceive such an unusual detail." The man smiled a brilliant grin of flashing white teeth. "I might have to adjust my assessment, Lieutenant; you are more than a rabid dog pulling at Solomon's leash."

The taint stirred in Noir's blood, sensing and reacting to the man's own barely contained savagery. It swelled, pushing at the inside of his skin and muscles, demanding that he retaliate.

'Be careful, he's a Proctor and has every right to consider himself better than you. You're just a lieutenant, remember.'

Yeah, I know. "Go find a spear and shove it up your ass."

The Proctor laughed. "Oh, you do have a temper! How endearing." The humor vanished in an instant, his head cocking to the side. "Strange that I can't smell it on you; normally a temper incites the Plague, compounding its effects on the body." He inhaled deeply. "But you smell of steel; are you really human?"

"No, I'm a duckling, so please move on. I have work to do."

"Very well, goodbye beautiful duckling." He departed, seeming to flow more than walk.

'Did you hear that? He thinks you're endearing and beautiful, like a little puppy with big brown eyes and oversized paws. If we're lucky, he'll adopt us, and then we can ruin his house as revenge. Muddy paws all across the ceiling!'

Adrian rose from her bow, eyes following the disappearing Proctor. "Why isn't Proctor Ambrosia with his soldiers or the other Proctors?"

"Because he's trolling the waters on the off chance our murderer likes to admire his handiwork." Noir grimaced. "And he's probably watching to see how the other shadowmancers react to the stakes."

Adrian nodded to herself, blinked and then snatched at Noir's sleeve with an excited whisper, "But aren't all these people members of the palace staff or a solider of the Proctors?" Noir glanced at her with quirked lips. She blushed, realizing the peril in accusing a Proctor or palace staff of murder. "Sorry, I got a little carried away."

'Oh, you're horrible. We should've taken this opportunity to nurture her imagination, to cultivate a real proclivity toward dangerous theories and unbound suspicion.'

The world doesn't need more crazy.

'...You're crazy.'

Yes, but I was here beforehand, so you can't really say I'm a new addition.

'Humph. Conservative.'

He resumed his appraisal of the displayed heads. "To some extent, the Proctors, their militia, and the palace staff are now our primary suspects. We know that whoever murdered these people is a skilled shadowmancer, and powerful individuals tend to congregate in the militia. The shadowmancers are a minor exception since most of them attend the Academy, leaving us with a small pool of suspects restricted to skilled shadowmancers who happen to be Evolved." He scowled. "And I just put myself on that list."

'Ooh, you done messed up! He he he he, let's sound the drums!'

"So, what are you going to do about it?"

This isn't something to be rejoicing over.

'What are you talking about? This is a once in a lifetime event! Of course, I'm going to celebrate.'

I'd hardly say it's once in a lifetime.

'Oh please, most people only live a day or two before dying and getting rez'ed. Everything is a once in a lifetime event.'

"Noir? What are you going to do about it?"

"Find the murderer and kill him."

You realize that's suicide, right? And it's illegal in some cities.

"I'm not saying that you did this, but shouldn't you at least tell Proctor Doll you're one of the suspects?"

"Why? So he can fret over it and distrust me? No. He doesn't need to mistrust his own soldiers right now; least of all his officers." Noir headed toward Solomon Doll.

Adrian scampered after him. "What, we're done already?"

"Yes, we're done. There's nothing to learn here. For now, we'll be more useful with Solomon."

A sudden quiet extended over the plaza from the Doll District, pulling every gaze toward it. A group of men and women loitered at the entrance to the thoroughfare with clasped hands. Dressed in white and gold robes emblazoned with a black cross, they moved forward in two neat rows. Everything about them was achingly pure: their clothing, their flesh, even their sandals and feet. This unnatural cleanliness gave them a semblance of divinity; an illusion furthered by their perfect, uncorrupted human bodies. Radiance's Angels slipped through the parting soldiers with bowed heads, and lifted their gazes only as they reached the staked heads.

What the hell are they doing here?

'I don't know, but it can't be good.'

One of the dozen Malakhim faced the soldiers and stepped forward, his raised hands calling for silence. "Proctors, we demand that you give these men into our keeping. We must safeguard their souls and inter their bodies in sacred earth."

A murmur rustled through the soldiers, and Grim emerged into the open. "This is not your kingdom, Angels. Radiance has no command here; the dead will stay with us, where they belong."

"All of this world is God's domain, heathen, whether you accept it or not, and it is our duty to ensure the souls of his children achieve salvation. If we leave these poor men in your control, you will drag their souls from beyond the grave and force renewed life upon them." The speaker swept the gathered militias with a hateful glance. "That is not how God intended us to live. Death is part of life and to break that law is sacrilege." The Angel lowered his gaze once again and rejoined his fellows. They fanned out, interposing between the staked heads and the militias. "We will save their souls whether you wish it or not, heathens."

Grim raised his black, carapace hands in a gesture of placation. "We have no desire for a conflict with Radiance. Perhaps we can reach some agreement?"

"You must give these men over into our care, heathen, or their souls will never ascend. That is the only acceptable conclusion."

We should just kill them already, there's no way in hell they're going to do anything that contradicts the tenants of their god and his damn book.

'Yeah, well bear with it for now; we can't be seen starting a war in the middle of a peaceful conference.'

It doesn't look very peaceful.

Grim's jaw worked. "I am afraid that is impossible. In accepting the asylum of Umbras, these men willingly consigned their souls and bodies over to Lock-And-Key." His eyes bored into the lead Malakh. "They belong to her in both life and death. Their souls are not your concern."

The Malakhim stirred, their robes fluttering despite a lack of wind. The lead Malakh shook his head. "God forgives all sins, heathen, even the perpetuation of such an unholy pact." He lifted his face heavenward and spoke proudly, his voice ringing across the courtyard. "If these souls have been claimed by devils guised as men, then we will reclaim them!"

The Malakhim removed their hoods, baring pale skin and golden hair. Seeing this, Proctors and lieutenants emerged from the masses while calmly pushing the lesser soldiers back.

The Malakh extended his fine hands to either side and stepped forward as a pair of luminescent white wings opened from beneath his robes. "Do not fear this end, heathens, your crimes will be forgiven and your souls saved." One after another, the Malakhim opened their wings and with each set that extended up toward the heavens, their cumulative light strengthened until it became almost blinding.

Noir flexed his fingers and grinned. *Finally, we get to kill these bastards.*

'*Or you could let the Proctors do the fighting and use this opportunity to assess Grim and Solomon.*'

That would be pointless.

'*And why is that?*'

Because I don't give a shit about how powerful they are.

Across from him, Grim had pulled a twisted black scythe from somewhere and now spun it lazily beside him in slow revolutions. He advanced a step and launched himself forward with an expression of savage glee.

The Malakhim soared skyward, spears of light materializing in their hands and launching toward Grim.

The other Proctors offered no assistance, content to let Grim slaughter the interlopers.

Noir advanced and the churning mass of winged Malakhim convulsed, spitting one from their midst to confront him with a leveled spear. The Malakh, the same one that had spoken before, screamed a heavenly note and thrust, stabbing with all of his fearsome strength coupled with the impetus of his descent.

'*Everyone thinks they're singing heavenly verse, but I'm almost certain they're just insulting us.*'

And that bothers you?

'*Nah, I just wished we'd thought of it.*'

Noir caught the spear blade contemptuously in his naked fingers and snapped it. The Malakh reeled skyward, his wings futilely slamming down to reverse momentum as Noir's shadows clamped about his midsection and smashed him against the grating.

The Malakh struggled to his feet, a new spear materializing, and slashed with both hands, the blade streaming light. Once again, Noir caught the spear, his lips curling and his fingers stabbing into its brilliance, infecting it with a wave of thin black veins.

The spear imploded, slamming the Malakh back to the ground.

Noir discarded the shard of light as the Malakh struggled back to his feet. "So it is as he foretold. You have returned." The Malakh marshalled himself, a sword materializing in his right hand. "I will strike you down in God's name and rid this world of your villainy, demon!"

The Malakh charged, blade sweeping before him as the shadows swelled about his radiant form. Where the blade struck, the shadows imploded, but they still pursued him, closing tighter in echo of Noir's slashing hands. The Malakh screamed a furious cry and blasted through a wall of tendrils, blade extended in a thrust. But its light had dimmed, and when its tip kissed Noir's chest, the blade shattered, flinging the Malakh back into the swarming shadows. They caught and dragged him skyward, drawing his limbs taut. The Malakh strained, his eyes exploding with golden fire as light poured from him, incinerating his mortal apparel and liberating him.

Even as the shadows crumbled to dust, however, he remained airborne, his mortal form bubbling and spitting a volatile golden mist with the release of his Hyde.

"No you don't," Noir snarled and shattered the man's legs with a lash of shadow.

It lurched with the blow and then fell, blood and grime fouling its unearthly perfection.

Noir stalked forward. "You shouldn't claim things that are beyond you." He grasped the creature's wings, pressed his boot between them, and tore them free. The Malakh screamed, black blood spraying over the both of them.

Noir thrust the dimming wings aside and knelt, his fingers soaked in its blood. "See, you're not really any different from us." His eyes sparked and he leaned closer. "In fact, you might be worse."

'Noir...'

Shut up. "Maybe, you're a witch, a monster in the guise of a man, a servant of Lucifer, a begat of Satan?"

The Malakh lifted his eyes with a struggled, "I am no witch. You are the monster!"

Noir's fingers lengthened into claws and he stabbed them into the Angel's sternum, cutting upward so they hooked the ribcage. "Oh really? Tell me, who here is the monster? Which of us is not like the others, which of us has no sign of the curse laid upon every living soul in this world?" Noir heaved the Malakh overhead, showing him the amassed soldiers.

"I am a servant of God. He restored me from the divine retribution your sins incurred!"

Noir sneered. "And I'm just supposed to take your word for it? It is common practice for witches and demons to hide their malice behind a facade of kindness and faith; but there are ways to test a witch that they cannot cheat."

'Noir, stop this!'

Shut Up! Noir snarled as veins of metal spiraled from his eyes and knuckles. He lifted the Malakh higher. "Let's prick you full of needles, see if you bleed. Or maybe we'll drop you in the river and see if you sink or swim, eh?"

"Noir!"

"What?" He snarled and spun on the speaker, killing the Malakh in his rage.

Adrian fell back with a yelp and scrambled away.

Noir's hands continued to spasm as he looked at her, but the metal corruption began to recede. Finally, he spoke, "I'm sorry, I have some ... bad memories of priests and the fanatics of God."

She inched forward. "Are you alright, now? You're not going to lose control?"

"Yeah, I'm alright." He released the corpse and considered Grim where he stood amidst the massacred Malakhim.

The Proctor swept his gore-stained scythe lazily up, and strolled toward the amassed soldiers. He paused beside Noir, absently folding his scythe into a seamless, arm-length rod. "I wonder what they hoped to achieve here. If they had been from the Second Sphere I could understand this absurd aggression, but Malakhim from the First Sphere? It's idiotic to believe they could even have scratched us."

Noir shrugged. "You can't find logic in anything Radiance's Angels do. Whatever he does to cultivate their appearances makes the nighttime madness bleed over into the day."

"So that's why they're so volatile." A spark flared in the Proctor's eyes and he grinned, speaking louder, "It makes me wonder what else you might know of the outside, Lieutenant."

Noir scowled. "If I wanted to talk with you, I'd say hi or kill one of your peons."

Adrian squeaked and darted behind him.

But Grim only smirked and left, hanging the rod from his belt.

Noir growled low in his throat and started toward the Doll District, Adrian following. "What was that about?"

"What do you mean?"

"Your reaction to Proctor Grim; one moment you're pleasant. Well, pleasant for you, and the next you're biting his head off. All he did was ask if you knew anything else."

"Look around, kid, what do you see?"

She glanced at their surroundings, trying to divine what he wanted. "I just see the Proctors' soldiers."

"And what do they look like?"

She blinked and missed half a step before reclaiming her stride. The soldiers were calm on the surface, perhaps a little rumpled from the recent battle. They looked no different from their usual selves: quiet, efficient people attending their various obligations. She almost relayed this to Noir, but one of the few idle soldiers caught her attention. He shifted in place and glanced over one shoulder toward his Proctor, who conversed with a lieutenant from the Gold District. Searching her environs a third time, Adrian finally noticed what Noir meant. A subtle tension brooded in the air, infecting everyone and restricting conversation to whispers as they all asked a variation of the same question: Who was doing this? It didn't seem to matter that the murders were dissimilar, the soldiers and probably most of Umbras subconsciously appeared to attribute them to the same perpetrator; a perpetrator they had no idea how to catch or, if they managed to catch him, how to defeat. "They're scared." Turning back to Noir, she found him several steps ahead and hurried to catch up. "They're scared."

"Of course they're scared. In this world, murder is like an annoying neighbor who stops by every day. Death on the other hand, at least the permanent kind, is almost a myth–"

'More of a boogeyman really.'

"—Except it's not a myth, not anymore. Permanent death has become a very real, very present danger. Right now these men are being swept away in a mighty flood; they're doing everything they can to find land or something, anything, that they might cling to; they're looking for something to trust."

"They can trust the Proctors. Can't they?"

Noir snorted. "Imagine that the soldiers are children. Now consider what death means to a child. They understand what the word means and cannot comprehend its absoluteness: an ignorance that both protects and frustrates them. The Proctors are adolescents. They understand what we're facing, but they're just as helpless. The Proctors can't protect them. Everyone knows we're trying to find someone who could kill a Tyrant, and they're terrified of what will happen when we do."

She glanced around again, watching the soldiers converse. "Some are probably hoping that we never find the murderer and that he just disappears."

"Yes, and probably trying to reconcile that desire with their obligations."

"But what does all this have to do with your reaction toward Proctor Grim?"

He scowled. "What do you think he meant by asking me what I knew about the outside world?"

She frowned and then realization flooded her. "He was accusing you of being a foreigner!"

"Yes, and in full view of those charged with the capture of a possible foreigner. The bastard just painted a target on my back."

"Well, that's why you should be nicer to people."

"What?"

'Hah, that's just what I was about to say!'

"Well, he probably did that because you insulted him the other day. If you'd been nicer, this wouldn't have happened." She flashed him a teasing grin.

"You sound like my brother."

"Oh." She looked away, her ears pulling flat against her head. A second passed before she spoke again, "How did he die?"

His jaw tightened. "The assholes locked him in a pit and set it on fire; too damned scared to attack us head on.

She hesitated before asking her next question, "Do you know who did it?"

He stopped walking and looked at her, veins of metal creeping along his irises. "Yes, and they'll find themselves in a very special hell when I'm done."

A tall man in a violet coat and a set of black lieutenant's tails stepped in front of them. "Oh my, those words certainly make you sound like the wild animal everybody thinks you are."

"What the hell makes you think I'll stand for your taunting idiocy?"

Grim's lieutenant smirked, his liquid, churning eyes glowing with mirth. "Now, now; there's no need for that. This is a neutral area, any violence you initiate here would be a declaration of war against Proctor Grim and a violation of Lock-And-Key's edicts."

Noir pushed Adrian behind him. "What do you want, boy."

"Boy? Ha, I was serving Proctor Grim a decade before his promotion. I hardly classify as a boy." The man flung his boast out with an ignorant grin, but his eyes twitched with something else: purpose.

"Having a brain doesn't mean you're not stupid and age doesn't make you wise, now stop poking dragons."

The lieutenant shook, his hands closing into fists and his lips spreading into a snarl, but the cold light in his eyes never wavered. "I have killed my share of monsters, both during the day and at night. I am not to be trifled with!"

Noir rolled his eyes and dismissed him. "Stand atop a mountain and shout it to the heavens; see if either the sky or the land cares."

'I remember when you did that, it was kinda funny to see both the land and the sky lose their shit.'

"And what if I say you're the murderer we've all been hunting."

He faced the lieutenant with slow deadly grace and found the man awash in thin, billowing shadows. "That's not something you want to say without evidence."

"I don't need evidence." The lieutenant's voice cracked as his shadows mutated into two forms. The soldiers and officials around them noted the brewing conflict and scattered.

Gritting his teeth, the lieutenant spoke as if he were reciting a poem, "Shadow Thrall: Soldier." The massed shadows on his right churned and solidified into the shape of an armored man. He spoke again, perspiration soaking his brow, "Shadow Thrall: Beast." The secondary mass of shadows warped and darkened, bending into the guise of a waist-high manticore. The lieutenant forced a smile even as he stumbled from the strain. "I don't need evidence. If you attack me on neutral ground, it would prove your guilt."

'It would also prove what a colossally stupid man our murderer is, and I had such high hopes for him too.'

"And since everyone already thinks you're a wild dog, they won't question me."

"So you're going to set your Constructs on me and tell everyone that I instigated the fight?"

'If you were just about anyone else, that would be incredibly smart. Except you are you, and he just won the award for grand nincompoop of the year.'

"Yes, unless you do as I say."

Noir caught a glimpse of Grim stalking through the crowd from a corner of his eye and grinned. Adrian, noticing the glint in his eyes, fell back a step and then several more.

Noir stepped forward, provoking the lieutenant's Constructs to drop into defensive postures. "Let me give you a little advice, boy; if you're going to threaten somebody on neutral ground, make sure they give a damn first."

The lieutenant's Constructs lunged forward, but Noir had already slipped past them, his right hand driving forward to impale their master. The lieutenant squirmed and gurgled, clutching at Noir's hand as he feebly sought the floor with his dangling feet.

Noir tossed the man aside, ignoring the disintegrating Constructs and rising screams, and spun to face Grim through the rapidly escalating brouhaha. Their eyes met and Noir shrugged, extending both hands as if offering a gift. 'Well, you have your war, Proctor; let's see what you do with it.'

Noir strode past Adrian. "Let's go, kid, I hear there's some wonderful cream and tarts at a stall just outside the Dollhouse."

"But you've just started a war!"

Noir shrugged. "Yes, and it won't start today; so we have plenty of time for cream and tarts."

'Yes! I love cream and tarts, especially when there's strawberries involved, ... but you don't seem that happy?'

Thornwood's Messenger of Wrath, Radiance's Malakhim, and Grim pulling the trigger on his war, all in a matter of days. I hate it.

'Why?'

Because it feels like circling vultures.

'Do you think they know something?'

I think they're involved.

Chapter Thirteen

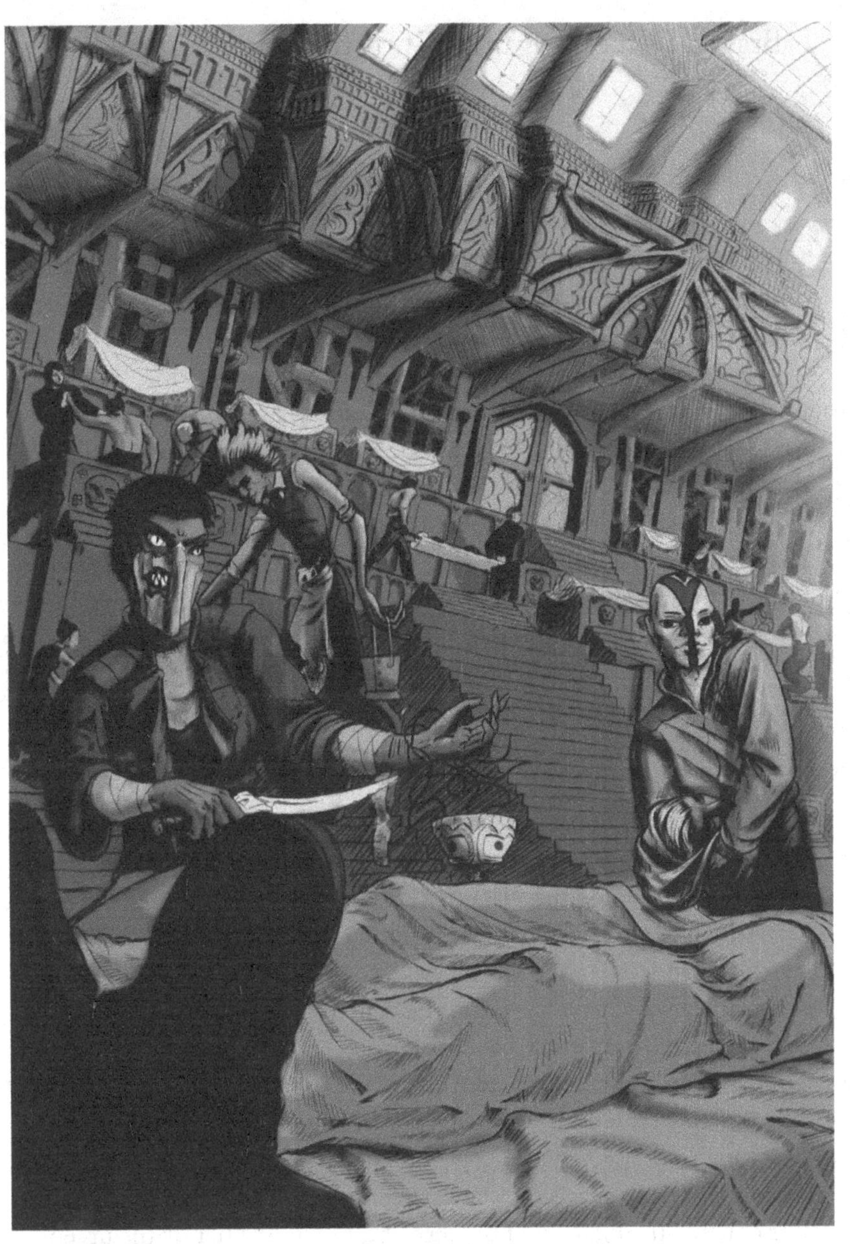

Brave a Den of Brigands, Cutthroats, and Smugglers?

At one of Doll District's bleeding stations.

Blood dribbled from the deceased hemomancer's wrists, pooling in depressions on either side of his prone body. The pathomancers flanked him, their veins engorged and sickly green where Adrian could see them. Gregorio supervised the bleeding from a seat at the table's head, his bleary eyes bloodshot from exhaustion and his hair, along with many of the small black feathers decorating his body, streaked white from excessive Necromancy.

A thin book resided in his hands, its rigid pages formed of Shadowsteel to preserve it from damage when the night fell. He flipped the page with a dull clank, but his eyes barely moved to glance at it before returning to their vigil over the proceedings.

The pathomancers gripped their subject's arms and inhaled, their cracked nails and rot-wreathed fingers digging into his pallid flesh. A bloom of noxious mist erupted from the hemomancer's pierced skin and twined up the pathomancers' hands, soaking into their bodies. The rot infecting their skin in vivid green cracks spiraled further up their arms, eliciting momentary grimaces as they continued siphoning the Plague's venom.

Adrian stood and began pacing along the entrance wall. Silas had yet to return from wherever he went yesterday. A full day gone and not a single word or rumor as to his whereabouts or health. No one else appeared perturbed by his absence, even Solomon who had expressly ordered him to remain in the Dollhouse. She couldn't fathom this reaction, especially with the scuffle between the Proctors and Radiance's angels earlier that morning and the subsequent declaration of war between Doll and Grim. A shiver of fear coursed through her at the thought, reminding her of the urgent need to kill Grim. The undertakers had to remove him from power before whatever machinations he intended came to fruition. Only, the undertakers couldn't find Lock-And-Key for approval, nor gain admittance to her palace. A deeper, more instinctual, shudder passed through her. Something felt deeply wrong in Umbras. She could feel it near her heart, like someone had buried a knot of thorns inside her; someone, or something, had intruded on the Pattern. She needed to speak with other undertakers on the subject, but had yet to find the opportunity.

"There's no need to worry about Silas, he'll work his way back around when he's ready."

She glanced over to see Gregorio watching her. "How do you know that?"

"Because he is very good at his job."

"What's his job? Consorting with underworlders?"

"He's our assassin. Oh, you wouldn't know it to look at him, what with his speech tendencies, but that man grew up on the streets in the night, killing to build himself an empire in the hours Proctors don't govern."

"But I thought Valerian…"

"Oh no, Valerian's our fighter, absolutely vicious in a straight fight, second only to Solomon Doll himself. But Silas, Silas is the scary one. He doesn't kill people fairly, he kills them in the dark when they're alone and can't protect themselves."

"Why would someone like him care enough to go out and avenge Hierophant? He hasn't shown attachment to anyone in the Dollhouse."

"That's the other thing about him; it may not look like it on the surface, but Silas would die before he let harm come to any of us."

"Why? What's his story?" She knew humans suffered a terrible existence, but that seemed to generally elicit an opposite effect; a habit of distancing oneself rather than the hyper-reliance Gregorio described.

Gregorio laid the book in his lap. "Silas comes from an abandoned precinct in the Doll District, several dozen skyscrapers that have never been used. Places like this are popular among underworlders and Night Princes as meeting places, operation zones, and resource storage. Because of that, they often become battlegrounds between the various factions. Silas lived in one of these along the lake, and had been there for who knows how long eating the Hydes that wandered into his territory just so he could survive. People knew he was there, they caught glimpses of him on the outskirts of the precinct every so often, but no one actually knew him. He lived like that for decades, killing anything that trespassed into his territory at night, and avoiding everyone else during the day. He left Umbrans alone though, and they ignored him in turn. Over time, people started calling him 'The Predator', and he became something of a ghost story." Gregorio rubbed his eyes and struggled to contain a yawn. "Either way, time passed and the underworlders started growing more brazen. New clans, organizations, and families cropped up across the district, sometimes as many as four a week. Their numbers multiplied over the course of a month, and the Night Princes followed suit. The old militia lost hundreds of soldiers to them, including officers, which only emboldened the different factions. Inevitably, they started preparing to overthrow the old Proctor. This created a market for powerful individuals, and one of the assorted kingpins decided to recruit Silas."

Adrian snorted a laugh. "I bet that went well."

"It went as well as you could expect with a half-mad, half-wild man; he slaughtered them and dropped the corpses off on the edge of his territory. When they woke after resurrection a couple hours later, the kingpin put a bounty on Silas. Literally hundreds of people went searching for him, drove Silas out of his territory through sheer weight of numbers. They hunted him for years, pursuing him from one district to the next, through the day and the night. He became a standing challenge over time: anyone who brought his corpse to a Proctor would receive an immediate officer position; and that was just one of his bounties. He had over a dozen before someone finally dragged him before a Proctor."

"Who caught him?"

"Rias Dorian."

"What? No."

"What's better, he brought him in alive. This was before Solomon Doll's ascension, so I can't say specifics, but the previous Proctor granted Rias the lieutenant's belt and demanded that he kill Silas. Rias refused both and instead spirited Silas away. That was the last anyone ever saw of Silas until Solomon overthrew the preceding Proctor. Silas butchered half of her officers in the span of hours without once stepping foot outside of her command center. He's been part of our group ever since."

"But that doesn't explain why he's so attached to all of you."

"Think about it, he lived alone for decades, if not centuries, and then spent years being hunted before Rias found him. After that, it was more years concealed wherever Rias had him. So, when we all accepted him into the Dollhouse, I believe we became something like a family. There's still something savage in Silas, and a deep-set fear of returning to solitude."

Adrian thought about Silas' story for a while, wondering what that kind of isolation must be like. She couldn't imagine it; undertakers lived in family units, there was always someone nearby who she had known since birth.

Adrian retreated from the unpleasant thought and refocused on Gregorio. "What's with your book?"

"This is our militia's rather questionable excuse for an obituary compendium."

"What?"

"Yes, we have an obituary reporter."

"It doesn't seem like he would have a lot of work…"

"He doesn't, which is why I think he takes a few liberties with the district's death tolls; he has one fellow—whom he describes as broody, burly, and darkly attractive—dying of flour inhalation and subsequent combustion."

Adrian smiled, strangely at ease despite the impending conflict. "I think he might be a little unsound in the head."

Gregorio hauled himself up with a low groan. "You may be right; I'll have to speak with Solomon about it." He walked to the dead hemomancer. "Is he ready?"

"Yes, sir."

"Let's get it over with then." Gregorio pressed his hands against the hemomancer's chest and exhaled. The hemomancer jerked back to life a second later and immediately dug his hands into the blood reservoirs on either side of the table. His blood rushed to meet his hands and slithered back up his wrists. Color gradually returned to his skin and he slumped back to the table.

Gregorio stepped back, his hair just a little whiter than before. "Rest there for a while, Kieran, you'll be ready to move again in about an hour."

The hemomancer, Kieran, gave a weak nod. His voice came out in a rasping whisper, "Th–… thank you."

"Don't mention it." Gregorio walked to the door. "Come on, boys, we have more to do before the Blood Moon rises."

Before he could touch the handle, however, the door flung open and Valerian swept in. "Ah, Adrian, perfect timing." The woman threw her arm over Adrian's shoulder. "Tell me, how do you feel about braving a den of brigands, cutthroats, and smugglers?"

"I feel like that wouldn't be wise…"

"No, but it's gonna be fun." Valerian grinned and propelled Adrian toward the temple's main entrance.

"I haven't agreed yet!" Despite her protests, Adrian liked the idea of spending the evening exploring low-life establishments with Valerian.

"As if you'd ignore this opportunity; plus, it's the Proctor's order. You'll be visiting the Madra District as a witness with Silas–"

"Wait! When did he return?"

"Just an hour ago. You and he are supposed to be–"

Adrian leaned in close to whisper, "What happened with Hierophant's attackers?"

"…They've been dealt with; don't worry, he didn't kill them permanently, but they won't be participating in the war."

"That's good to hear; they deserved whatever they got."

"Yeah… Anyway, you and Silas are going to visit several questionable locations in the Undercity, and I want you to promise to bring me back some souvenirs, like a tooth or something."

"Why aren't you coming? I know Silas is our Underworld contact, but this does seem more like your area."

"I tried! The Proctor just gave me more paperwork. Gah! Can you imagine it; I even offered to clean his office! Just think what that would have done to my nails. You'd think he'd forgotten flowers wilt when they don't get any sun." She despairingly fingered one of the flower blossoms, a lovely blue today, decorating her hair-vines.

They arrived at the Dollhouse where Silas waited at the top of the descending stairs. His features looked drawn and his eyes remained distant.

"Here you are, Silas, your wonderful new companion."

"Pickle my eyes, I can see that. Adrian, do you know what you're getting into?"

"Yes I do, sir. Though I don't think I have much choice about this situation."

"That makes two of us. Well, let's get going; the mercenaries won't salt and broil their own asses."

"What does that even mean, Silas?"

"They won't hire themselves, obviously." He strode off.

Adrian waved goodbye to Valerian and raced in pursuit. He led them toward the palace where, Adrian assumed, they would turn into the Madra District. Upon reaching the Doll District's main thoroughfare though, he took a right, leading away from the palace.

"Where are we going?"

"To catch a ride; I'm not steaming all of my hair off by walking to the Madra District."

"What about the trolley?"

"Left an hour ago." They crossed the thoroughfare into a large side road populated with curtained stalls and approached the first one. The door flap burst open with a discharge of steam as they neared, and Silas caught it. "Serfan, you here?"

A mouthless man materialized from the fog, wiping his hands on a fraying cloth. "What do you need, Corporal Silas?" He did not speak in a human voice, but in a barrage of intermingled chirps that somehow combined to fashion words.

"I need a ride to the Madra District; someone who can wait and isn't scared of rougher individuals."

"I heard about your war, and what happened to Hierophant; they connected?"

"No. Do you have a carriage?"

"Yes, just wait outside; I'll drive you myself."

Silas returned to the thoroughfare and seated himself next to Adrian on a pipe running parallel to the street. A minute later, Serfan emerged from the side road leading a towering man of copper and Shadowsteel. The machine, a steam golem with pipes jutting up its back and a bald head, dragged an open carriage by three fine chains. Moving to its left, Serfan yanked a lever on the golem's leg, and it dropped to one knee with a burst of steam. He grabbed a handhold and scaled up a series of rungs to seat himself in a nook between its shoulders "Well, get in."

"Did you have to grab the bigger model?"

"I thought it would be useful considering our destination." Serfan leaned forward, slipping his hands into a compartment of some sort on the golem's back. "Plus, this is new, moves like a small model except when turning, so it won't slow us down."

"What does it run on?" Adrian asked as she climbed into the carriage.

"Steam canisters bought from more social Aesians, and a little help from Shadowmancy. You see, copper alone is too heavy for the gears and steam to move effectively, so they use Shadowsteel where they can because it's lighter, and a shadowmancer can help propel it. That'd be yours truly." The golem stood with another burst of steam. "Ready?"

"Just go already."

Even by carriage, it took them several hours to reach their destination: an immense, circling stair that descended into the Undercity. A few animals and humans skulked along the outskirts, but for the most part it appeared desolate.

Silas swung from the carriage as it trundled beneath the red awning that shaded most of the courtyard, and stepped alongside Serfan. "You wait here in case this goes sour, all right?"

"That's why I brought Clementine."

Adrian broke into a startled laugh. "You gave it a name?"

"Sure did, it's better than calling them one, two, and three, etc."

"It's also crazy, let's go." Silas started down the wide stair.

"See you later, Serfan."

"You too."

She jogged after Silas and fell into step. He shot her a querying look as the partial sunlight gave way to buzzing, electric lamps. "Is there something I should know about?"

"What are you talking about?"

"You're acting differently, more cheery, less I'm going to freeze you all and stack you in a cellar as trophies."

"I never thought that!"

"Either way, what's up with that?"

"Nothing, I'm just trying something out, something my father said."

"Emarhine Gold?"

"You know him."

"Of course I do, he was part of Solomon Doll's coup. Do you know how he got that name?"

"No, never thought to ask; I just assumed he chose it."

"Some of us choose our names, some of us are given ours. I chose mine, Solomon and Emarhine earned theirs. Your father used the corruption in one of the old Proctor's lieutenants to mutate the man's blood to molten gold; cooked the bastard instantly even though he was a hemomancer."

"That doesn't sound like my father…"

"Six shoes to a foot, lots of people are about to do things that don't sound like them. We're there…"

They arrived at a doorway covered by a vast sheet of brown leather splashed with jagged lettering in a variety of greens and blues. "A word from the wise; be careful whenever you see color: it's a declaration of power. So stay behind me; you're just here as witness." He grabbed a corner of the leather sheet and lifted it for them to enter.

Adrian stepped into a pit of suspended walkways, water pipes, and wheels. The pipes protruded from the sheer walls all the way up to the ceiling, spitting a constant stream of boiling water into the seemingly bottomless cavity. The walkways—squeezed between the pipes wherever room permitted—ringed the walls, offering a claustrophobic collage of cloth rooms, make-shift tables, and people.

They followed the catwalk until they encountered a stairway and then descended it. Silas' coat earned them a few glances, some curious or frightened, and others ominous, but no one interfered.

Adrian inched closer, instinctively grasping her pistol. "I would have thought they'd be more cautious of you?"

"It's not our district; we can't do anything without Madra's permission. He, or whichever slumbag with peeled ears that rules down here, holds all the power. Speaking of which, can you walk through walls? I know some of you can do that."

"No."

"Pity, that would have made getting you out of here a lot easier. Over there." He pointed at a circle of tables hosting some dozen men and women.

"How do you know they're mercenaries?"

"I don't, but they're wearing that awful dagger sigil."

"The one that's on almost every wall here?"

"Yep, means they're part of whichever organization runs this turf." He exited the stair and approached them. "Is there anyone here of sufficient rank to do business?"

A woman with spines running the length of her back and arms stood. "Who are you here for? Yourself or your Proctor?"

"Proctor Doll."

"You looking for mercs?"

"Yes, an open contract, and I'll pay to have the word spread. Just come to the Dollhouse and we'll discuss terms."

"Word is Grim also has a contract out, started it early this morning; I doubt there's many left."

"We'll take what we can get, you just spread the message." He tossed a heavy purse onto the table. "Those are fresh from the Coin House, proctor-marked so they're good anywhere in the city."

She unwound the purse string and retrieved a stack of dense, square coins scoured with indents so they could be easily snapped into quarters. Each quarter carried Solomon Doll's rose embossed on its front and back.

She inspected it for a few seconds, then extracted a second, featureless, coin from her own purse and laid it on the table. Without hesitation, she flipped Solomon's coin on its side and smashed its edge into the plain coin, which snapped in half. "They're genuine, but pointless if you die in the next couple days."

"The coins themselves are still good; there just won't be any insurance on them."

"True. All right, we'll spread your contract through the Undercity. Most of our guys already signed on with Grim though."

"That's fine, we'll just kill them also. Let's go, Adrian." He departed the way they came, unperturbed by the evidence of Grim's moral delinquency.

Adrian caught up with him. "Grim fully intended the war to start today, didn't he?"

"Yes, but we have to give the citizens of our districts a grace period to leave the combat zone first."

"Will the other Proctors do anything?"

"Unlikely. Grim's actions violate no standing law." He slowed, glancing upward to the underside of the stairs as heavy boots thudded their way down, framed by the tails of familiar violet coats.

The front man of Grim's soldiers stopped and leaned over the railing with a grin. "Well, look at this, we found ourselves some Dollies. What are you two doing here so far from home?"

Silas' hand crept under his coat. "Do I need to remind you that the grace period is still in effect?"

"Oh no, we're perfectly aware of the fact, as is Proctor Grim. That's why we're here, and not up there." Still grinning, the man pulled his gun and rested it on the railing. The other six or seven men accompanying him followed suit.

Silas swung his own gun up, the firing bolt fully drawn. "Just think about where you are; one wrong step, or bullet as it stands, and you could go tumbling down into that pit with no hope of resurrection. You willing to make that gamble?"

The lead man, a sergeant by his coat tails, let his grin subside to a smirk. "Not really, but you can only fire if you're alive, and I'm pretty sure you're going to die before the chance arises." He waved and Adrian felt the muzzle of a gun press into her back. A glance at Silas revealed three other men, these from Grim's hired mercenaries, with guns poking his back and sides. "Now, I'm sure we can reach an arrangement if you surrender."

Fear prickled through Adrian's thoughts, but she pushed it aside and summoned the undertaker detachment. It swallowed her gently, silencing all the unimportant, badgering thoughts clouding her mind. She surveyed their aggressors, calculating odds and sight ranges. They couldn't win in this situation; Grim's soldiers held every positional advantage and outnumbered them drastically. They needed a distraction so they could run. But which option provided the best prospect of escape. She felt only one gun behind her, but there could be more behind the first, and there were three behind Silas. She glanced downward through the grating; the floor below them extended several feet further out. The drop appeared close to ten feet.

While she was assessing their environs, Silas spoke. "All right, we'll surrender if you guarantee our safety."

"Come on, now, you got to do better than that! Your surrendering doesn't do anything for us; we need something worthwhile."

"How about this, I have an information cache from Proctor Doll. It contains our plans, locations, and numbers; every officer has one."

"Let me see it."

Silas extracted a soft red sphere from his coat pocket and raised it for the sergeant to inspect. "It's opened with a drop of blood; any Doll-officer blood will do."

"Toss it up."

"Waste of time, it's encoded. You need me to translate." So saying, Silas lobbed the sphere to the sergeant, who caught it deftly.

He turned the sphere in his fingers for a while, his gun still trained on Silas and then dropped it back down. "Open it, I don't trust you."

Adrian slid her hand into her coat and grasped the butt of her pistol. "You're not going to harm me, I'm Umbran; so just let me go."

"I wouldn't be so sure of that; times are changing and you Umbrans won't be sacrosanct much longer. What's wrong with starting that process now?"

Adrian's hand tightened. *He knows about the outsider, or at least the coup. He has to, or he wouldn't be proclaiming the fall of Lock-And-Key so casually. We need to question him.*

"Enough stalling, open the cache."

Silas raised his hand and squeezed the pliant sphere. A single, needled-thin blade stabbed out from the sphere into his palm. Blood welled and then the sphere detonated into blanketing red mist. Silas exploded into motion, a thin, wicked knife appearing in one hand as his gun blasted Grim's soldiers with a salvo of bullets. His immediate captors fired blindly, but he was already in their midst, the knife flashing first black in the light and then red as it severed one man's throat and drove into a second's eye.

Without paying any thought to Silas, Adrian spun, knocking her reeling captor's gun aside and discharging her own into his stomach. He buckled and she dove around the nearest corner. The sergeant screamed something indistinct and gunfire erupted across the room. She couldn't see Silas, but she doubted he needed her help.

Across the way she saw the woman from earlier seated behind an overturned table smoking a pipe with a brace of three pistols draped over her legs. Adrian lunged forward, ducking from table to table until she slid beside the woman, who looked up from several neat stacks of coins. "Hello there–"

"Do you see the Grim sergeant over there?"

"Yes?"

"I have a job for you; bring that man to the Light Pillar Reliquary in the Doll District." Adrian snatched one of the woman's pistols and fired at the reeling Grim soldiers.

"Do you have money to pay."

"I'm good for it, whatever your fee, just bring us that sergeant." Adrian confiscated the woman's remaining pistols and dashed to the final table. There she stole a peek at the conflict and paused. A towering crimson creature rampaged through the Grim soldiers, its arms flailing about with imbedded swords as mist streamed from its shoulders and eyes. Bullets rent through its skin but seemed to cause the creature, a hemomantic Doll Adrian assumed Solomon had given Silas, no injury. Silas had probably carried it on his person, hidden to avoid spooking the underworlders, and activated it with his blood and a command phrase.

She scanned the obscuring red mist again and saw Silas crouched in a nook between two pipes along the wall. A trio of random thugs kept him pinned with a barrage of gunfire, several of their comrades lying dead or dying about their ankles. Several individuals, many of them bystanders, already lay injured or dead across the room, some bleeding from bullet injuries and others brutalized by the nameless creature. No one seemed to be paying Adrian any heed. *Not that there's much I can do,* she thought grimly. *I think I can give him a chance; Dark Father I hope he takes it because this isn't going to work twice.*

She aimed both pistols at the three men firing on Silas, took a breath, exhaled and squeezed. The pistols spoke, the diatribe of one finding its mark in a man's shoulder and the other ricocheting off the pipe in front of the soldiers. All three men vanished for an instant, one collapsing and the other two ducking at the unexpected fire. Silas did not hesitate, he dove for the edge and vaulted over the railing. Adrian shoved one pistol into her holster and followed suit.

She landed on the next floor down with a thud and buckled to the ground. Silas raced past her a second later, pausing just long enough to drag her to her feet.

"Where are we going?" she asked.

"Up, there's a side path just ahead; it'll take us to the surface." Bullets ricocheted all around them, rebounding off the walls, tables, and grating. Silas grabbed her arm and swung right, into a passage of the Undercity. She heard a thud as Grim's soldiers dropped after them, followed by a clang as more bullets bounced off the entrance to the passage.

"There!" Silas pointed at a ladder some forty feet ahead.

Adrian flung herself into a full sprint and reached the ladder just as the bullets started flying past their ears again. She snagged the highest rung she could reach and practically threw herself through the waiting hatch. Silas slipped through immediately after her, blood streaming from his right thigh, and she slammed the hatch shut, locking it.

He struggled to his feet and pointed the way they came. "That way."

"Do you need help?"

"I'm fine, you go ahead, find the exit."

She nodded and raced ahead, following the inclining path until she reached the great stairway they first descended. She sagged against the wall with a gasp and jammed a winder into her pistol. It started with a whirr, and she shifted her gaze to the leather curtain. Voices and sounds issued from behind it, but nothing that bespoke of Grim's soldiers. Her hyper-attention gradually faded and she slumped to the stairs, the pistol lying across her knees.

Silas staggered into view soon after, his leg bound with a makeshift bandage and his pistol likewise loaded. She went to help him ascend the stairs to where Serfan waited.

"What happened?"

"A couple of Grim's goons cornered us down below, it went sour. Just get us back to the Dollhouse as fast as you can."

"Wait, I'm going to need you to drop me off somewhere first."

Silas twisted to look at her. "Are you sure? This will have enraged Grim; while he can't attack Doll without a War Permit, that doesn't afford you any protection. Grim might try attacking you if he sees a way to do so without provoking the other Proctors."

"I'll be fine; take me to the Light Pillar Reliquary."

"Corporal?"

"Do it." He slumped back into his seat, one hand compressing his still bleeding wound.

"Let me help with that." Relinquishing her undertaker detachment as unnecessary now that the excitement had attenuated, Adrian knelt beside his injured leg and ripped a long strip from his pants to replace the first, shoddy bandage. "Can I ask you something?"

"Sure, I guess."

"Why did you disobey Solomon yesterday? He told you to stay, and you left anyway."

"Proctor Doll never told us to stay, he was telling us to go."

"How do you know that?"

"He withheld our titles."

"Then why not just tell you to go?"

"Plausible deniability; an unsanctioned act of violence by a Proctor's employee against another Proctor's subordinate is punishable by severe measures, but cannot result in the transgressing individual's execution; nor can the Proctor be held accountable. He forbade us to go before all those witnesses so Grim couldn't execute us or use our retaliation as an excuse for war."

"There's always something else with Solomon, isn't there? It's never what he says or does, it's always something else. How do you stand it?"

"Because I trust him to keep us safe, and to watch what I can't see or don't know."

"What about the murderer? It's been three days and we know almost nothing about him. How are we going to find him while warring with Grim?"

"We're a lot closer than any of us know, and when Solomon finds the bastard, we're going to bleed him dry. We're going to baste him in a pot of his own blood and send it to Grim as soup."

"That's awful."

"It's not enough. That 'thing' has executed people, Adrian, truly killed them. Their lives were just snuffed out. They will never speak or know anything again. They will never know a time when our lives are more than this." His head dropped to the seat and he looked up. "You can't understand it; as awful as this existence is, we are inherently safe. We die, but we're always resurrected again, and more importantly, we have a chance to live long enough to see a cure. This murderer shatters that. He cannot be allowed to live, and we cannot allow others to follow him."

She finished bandaging his leg and took a seat opposite him. She couldn't understand the depth of his emotions, but she understood that he felt them and that was enough. "We'll find him, and he will pay for his crimes."

"Damn right we will." He let the matter drop, but the fire remained in his eyes.

On their return to the Doll District, they dropped her off at the street to her home and exchanged farewells. She waved a final time and strode down the alleyway to wait at the entrance. An hour passed before a trio of ragged individuals rounded a corner and marched toward her, a struggling bundle in tow.

The lead man addressed her, "Here's your sergeant, where's the payment?"

"What do you want?"

"Do you have any Black Coins?"

"I will give you one, to do with as you please so long as it is not used to the detriment of Umbras."

"Done."

She dug into her pocket and flipped them a coin. They caught it and departed, leaving her with the bound sergeant. She left him where he lay and descended into the Reliquary, pausing only when she met another pair of undertakers. "Hello, Eamaan and Jiires, I have a favor to ask."

"What do you need?" Eamaan asked.

"There's a restrained human near the Reliquary's entrance. I need you to bring him down to the central room without releasing him; it's important."

"Of course."

"Also, can you tell me where my mother is?"

"I believe she's currently dining in the garden."

She thanked them and continued to the central room, where she took the doorway nearest to the Communion Chamber. The resulting passage ran about a dozen feet before ending in a screen of vines. Here Adrian paused to doff her shoes and place them neatly along the wall, adjacent to similar pairs, before parting the curtain and entering a room of tangled, feather soft roots.

Vines bedecked simultaneously with leaves both enormous and minute, and burdened with burgeoning sable fruit, draped from the ceiling in long, curtain-like walls. She advanced, stepping over the larger roots and fighting to maintain balance because the smaller existed in a state of constant, gentle flux.

"Mother, where are you?"

A faint response from somewhere to her left, "By the Seiccara." Adrian followed the voice, navigating the garden's maze of ever-shifting walls with ease until she encountered her mother on the rim of a fountain.

"Mother, there's something that needs your immediate attention."

"Oh? What has occurred?"

"Today I met a man, one of Grim's officers, who promised a change in Umbras. He said we would no longer be sacrosanct and then tried to kill me."

"And the only way he would know such things is if he was involved in Grim's coup, or with the man helping him."

"Yes. I had the man brought here so we could question him."

Her mother stood, dropping a half-eaten Seiccara onto the ground, where the roots promptly swallowed it. "I will bring him to the Matriarchs, and they will interrogate him." She moved toward the entrance only to pause before passing from Adrian's sight. "Thank you, Adrian." Then she vanished.

Adrian lowered herself to sit on the fountain. *It's done. We will find the evidence we need to condemn Grim; there will be no war with the Dollhouse, and we'll discover the outsider. All that's left is Noir and the murderer.*

Deep inside of her, however, that thorny knot dug a little deeper, sending a shiver of fear through her. She knew nothing physical afflicted her, but the mass remained, a gnawing dread she couldn't shake from her thoughts.

Chapter Fourteen

I Demand a Swanky Title

Later that night.

Noir strolled along a pipe through the Babylon District's skyscrapers, his nostrils flaring as he tracked a scent and his breath a white cloud in the icy air. An engorged rat scurried across the road below him, the scratch of its crooked nails coming to an abrupt halt as it noticed his presence. The creature hissed and dove into a hollow in the road, the ridges of its back scraping against the pipe.

An azure banner, one of thousands Babylon hung across his district, fluttered between two skyscrapers, its silver chalice visible on either side. Noir scowled. *I know Babylon's always been the Narcissist in Chief, but does he really have to proclaim his dominance on every street corner? I doubt his people are going to forget who runs the place.*

'Maybe he just likes the color blue.'

At this point, it's more of an infatuation.

'Well if someone must suffer from an infatuation, a particular color isn't the worst possibility. Personally, I'm romantically inclined toward green.'

I thought you liked blue?

'That was before it cheated on me with Babylon.'

Ahhh.

'In all reality, it's probably meant to confuse people and conceal the locations of his family's vaults. He's patient zero of that venerable disease known as paranoia.'

It's not paranoia if the danger's real. During my last visit, I heard of twelve separate cases where powerful individuals tried to ransack his vaults. His mouth curled into a grim smile. *The results were predictably bloody.* He grabbed a vertical pipe and scaled up its seamless length. *Considering that I wasn't actively researching the subject, it's likely another dozen attempts happened outside my knowledge.* He released his grip and dropped onto a horizontal, eastward-running pipe.

'Then why are you complaining about the number of banners?'

Just because I understand his motives, doesn't mean he doesn't exaggerate or that he isn't a narcissist.

'*If he's so bad, then why did you bring him here in the first place?*'

Noir glanced down an alley on his right, peering through the fog and tasting the air. *Because owning a collector is always wise; especially when it's a family occupation.* He continued forward, the scent slowly growing stronger. *You aside, it's a closely guarded secret and the reason why I make sure to drop by when somebody new dons the Azure Mask. Besides Madra, he's the only Proctor that knows my face.*

'*Why bother introducing yourself to him at all? You hardly qualify as social, and your friendliness factor verges on the negative.*'

To ensure they comprehend their situation. Both subsequent generations have strayed from their allegiance by interfering with the Umbrans or resisting Loc.

'*And what of their fathers, did you sing them a bedtime song and tuck them into a nice little coffin?*'

No. They sleep in the crypts beneath their vaults until such a time as they feel like waking again. Noir slowed as he caught sight of his destination: a collection of banners strung around a nest of pipe-work twenty-three stories off the ground to form a rudimentary abode. The whole construct reeked of ash—which simultaneously warded off flying Hydes and masked its inhabitant's scent—and wore a layer of ice, which blocked any potential heat signature within. Noir rolled his shoulders and leapt, vaulting between pipes until he landed outside the nest's entrance atop a make-shift balcony attached to the supporting pipes. He parted the curtain doorway and entered a lightless room, his boots thudding dully on a hard floor.

'*Oh, we're using the front door this time. Shouldn't you come bursting through the roof or something for effect?*'

Using the front door is more civilized.

'*Which would be fantastic if we were civilized people.*'

I can be civilized when the occasion calls for it.

'*In your case civilized is akin to an ugly hat, something you drop into the nearest sewer or foist on your arch-nemesis.*'

Harley straightened in a corner, a wave of surprise then fear coursing through the gray fur covering his body. "I really wish you wouldn't just barge in like that; it's rude and frightens the hell out of me." Despite his familiar tone, Harley's corded tail twined nervously.

"You're in no position to lecture me on propriety."

Harley flinched and nodded; his fear remained evident in every gesture, but the terror of their previous encounter had dissipated. Harley knew his worth, and he knew Noir's tolerance.

Noir glanced at the cluttered room, noting the bundles of packaged food, open wrappers, and discarded clothes. "One would almost think you're running from me, Harley."

Harley waved his arms with an emphatic shake of his head. "No. No, don't confuse hiding with running. I would have left Umbras long ago if I wanted to survive you."

"Not that it would help."

"Why do you think I'm still here?"

"What I think doesn't matter right now; I have a question for you, and you'd best have the answer." He leaned forward. "Where are they?"

"Yes, of course, um ... Lazarus is—"

"I don't mean Lazarus and Constantine; I want the person behind them, because they didn't do this alone and you're not running from the likes of Constantine."

Harley motioned Noir back with a clawed hand. "Okay, okay; I'll tell you." He scrambled to a trio of mounded bags and began rifling through them. "It's not just one person, it's a coalition of all the established Tyrants: Legion, Black Die, Radiance, Pandora, even Bubonic, and Seelie. They didn't start Lazarus on this path, but they certainly helped him along. I don't know how much each of them contributed, but I know it's larger than a couple of people stationed here." Harley shoved the leather rucksack aside, spilling ink jars, red paper, and quills. "I think the coalition actually predates Lazarus by some time, but it only gained real traction with his arrival; prior to that no one really had the balls to fuck with you and Alighieri. Ah, here it is." Harley produced a sheaf of paper and handed it to Noir. "Those are the names of people who serve the Coalition in Umbras. There's more, of course, and probably hundreds in the other cities."

"Why didn't you contact me earlier?"

"I wasn't ready; I didn't have all the pieces I needed for

everything to make sense. There's still things missing."

Noir tossed the sheaf aside. "I don't care what their names are, I just want to know where."

Harley frowned. "But can't you find them on your own?"

"No, I can't, and I've been searching for three days. Radiance must have concocted some form of repellent for the *Almas*, or they've been killing them, and I don't have the time to search manually."

"They're hiding out in the Doll District, an abandoned dye factory near the edge of Umbras. I don't know which one; people don't like brokering information about the Coalition, especially when they're so close. As for how their avoiding the *Almas*, they have to be killing them; Radiance doesn't have anything that would repel Shadowmancy without damaging it, my contacts would have informed me if he did."

Noir stood, *Almas* materializing around them and swarming toward the Doll District. "That's all I needed." He moved to depart, but paused at the entrance, one hand on the flap. "You're not forgiven, Harley."

"I know."

"Good." Noir exited.

'*So where to now: the Coalition or Constantine?*'

Constantine.

'*You know where he is?*'

In the Ambrosia District. Noir resumed climbing toward Umbras' utmost peaks.

'*What about after Constantine? The Coalition may be in the Doll District, but that's still a large area to search.*'

Don't worry about it; now that I know where to search and how they're deflecting my attempts, I just have to alter the Almas so they don't dissipate after death.

'*You're going to search for their bodies instead.*'

Yeah. He slowed as the piping attenuated at the sheer wall of another skyscraper, and raised his hand. The shadows wove down to wash over his hand, forming a bridge of shifting mist and pulling him onto it. He started climbing, feet finding purchase despite the steep gradient and the bridge dissipating behind him.

He pocketed his hands and cast his gaze out across the *Alma*-draped heaven. They numbered in the thousands, their fragile black wings glistening with inherent light as they flew toward the Doll District.

'*So what was that you said about playing it safe a couple days ago?*'

I don't want the Coalition interfering when I confront Lazarus.

'*So you're changing your beliefs based on the situation and how it best suits you? I'm not sure I want to associate with such a disreputable individual.*'

You don't have much of a choice; you are my little voice of madness after all.

'*I don't know what you're talking about; I'm perfectly real and not at all a figment of your rather tenebrous imagination.*'

Now you're the one who's changing details. Just the other day you admitted to being my madness.

'*I said no such thing! I'm really starting to worry about you, Noir. Maybe you should see a doctor.*'

Whatever you say, hypocrite.

'*You're always so mean to me; I don't know why I put up with you. In fact, one of these days I might start a coup and usurp your mind from you! What do you say to that?*'

Give it your best shot.

The voice subsided into murmured prognostications of the many horrible things that would befall Noir and faded from the forefront of his thoughts, leaving him alone in the night. He crossed the city via the suspended bridge, paying no thought for the embattled monstrosities below, and eventually reached an abandoned sector of the Ambrosia district.

He vacated the shadow bridge as it crumbled into Shadow-debris and landed on the roof of a skyscraper, phasing through the ceiling into a room gray with dust. He continued downward, traversing floor after floor that had never housed a living soul, his passage leaving a trail in the dust.

Finally he alighted upon the cavernous ground floor amidst a cluttered maze of tables, desks, and chairs overflowing with papers and all the other utensils one could imagine. He started toward the farthest corner, squeezing between stacked rugs as lights buzzed to life overhead and vermin scattered through the mounds of junk.

Almas trickled in through the walls and ceiling after him and dispersed across the cavernous room, searching.

Noir paused by one of the cleaner tables to sift through the notes strewn there. *Well, we know where the Shadow Poison came from.* He dropped the paper and continued as the *Almas* swooped in his wake, devouring the paper and destroying anything else Constantine might have used in his experiments.

An open door in the far corner lead into the Undercity, its handles, surface, and the floor beneath it clean of dust.

'If that's not an invitation, then I don't know what is; which probably means it's a trap.'

Noir shrugged and descended the unlit stairway, ignoring the door when it closed behind him. *Does he really expect that to hold us?*

'As we are? Probably not. There has to be more to this, maybe something with the Undercity?'

Noir stepped off the last stair onto the smooth, tiled floor of a featureless hallway. *This isn't the Undercity.*

'What do you mean.'

Well, we're in the Undercity, but were cut off from it. He's covered the

Shadowsteel here with something that reeks of Pathomancy. I can't touch anything outside this room. He crossed another invitingly open door into a dark room. "You might as well show yourself, Constantine. Even if I couldn't hear you breathe or smell your perspiration, I could feel the shadows draping your body and taste the rot you leave on the air."

A moment passed without a response, a silence broken only by the dull hum of electricity. Then the lights flickered on to reveal Constantine standing alone, a pair of copper-rimmed spectacles held loosely in the many-knuckled fingers of his left hand. "I take it your brother means nothing to you, then? ... Or have you come to agree? To set aside your shallow need for vengeance and serve the greater good?"

Noir slowly raised his hand, the shadows coiling into a lance. "Is this how you want to die? Preaching for the salvation of a world that cursed you?"

Constantine rubbed his eyes. "How can you be such a child?" The door slammed shut behind Noir. "After all the years and all that pain, how have you failed to mature, to realize others matter just as much?" More lights clicked on, the retorts of their ignition growing progressively deeper. Constantine dropped his hand. "It doesn't matter anymore, you will not see reason and I cannot die here, the world still needs me too much. But I need you to understand that I did not want to kill your brother, that I understand the inevitable cruelty of it. I wish it could have been different, truly."

"You seem to think you have a chance."

"I know why you might think otherwise; I've heard the stories, though I don't believe most of them." He laughed softly, revealing a mouth of clockwork machinery and copper teeth. "I cannot remember all the names they've called you: Tyrant, Demon, Ascendant, Transcendent, even God." His body spasmed, contorting with a dull click. "Even Brigadier, a Tyrant herself, cautioned me of your power. She called you a walking apocalypse, Ragnarok."

'Now that's just unfair, how come you get all the swanky titles?'

Because I'm the bad god. You're ... you.

'I reject your logic and demand a swanky title.'

You can be the Great Pestilence of this age.

'*Cool.*'

More lights flared on, burning at Noir's skin with their brightness and forcing him to squint. *Damn him, what is he up to?*

'*I don't know, but it's not aesthetics…*'

Grimacing, Noir pulled shadows over his eyes and refocused on Constantine. "I'll bite. What makes you think you have a chance?"

"That all your power lies within your Shadowmancy." Constantine ticked again, his eyes whirring in their sockets. "Without it, you are human and mortal. So if I strip it from you …"—the final lights flared on, routing the last shadows—"you will die."

Noir shook his head. "That's where you are wrong; there is always a shadow." The darkness within his coat swirled up into his eyes, thickening the protective veils.

Constantine ticked again. "That's … unfortunate, but Lazarus warned me you'd wriggle out." He extracted a mesh pouch from his coat and loosened it with a yank. The room, suffocatingly hot due to the lights, turned frigid.

Noir snarled, his breath misting, and stormed forward. "What did you take from him?"

"If you take another step, I'll destroy these bones."

Noir's snarl deepened, but he stopped, the lance dissipating.

"Did you know that this Plague is attracted to death? It thrives in old graveyards, particularly in the mass-graves resulting from diseases. Sometimes, the taint's so thick a *Rencensere* can't breathe without succumbing to the madness." He overturned the pouch, spilling twenty-eight human knuckles across the floor. "And what greater source of death is there than a necromancer? Every day, they resurrect the dead and send them out to die again in their thousands. Over and over again, they perpetuate the genocide of the human population, all in the name of prolonging our existence." Constantine pulled a dark vial from his other pocket and uncorked it. "That's why I needed your brother. I needed to understand how the Plague works, how to aggravate it, if I am ever to cure it." He upended the vial over the knucklebones, dousing them in a gray liquid that hissed and spat black mist upon contact.

Noir retreated with a low growl, shadows clamping over his mouth and nose to no effect. The mist blanketed him, and he felt the corruption in his veins explode, dragging him to the floor with a retch.

Fumes burst from his mouth and the tiles beneath him warped at their touch, first rusting then rotting. His shoulders snapped back, too far to be considered a natural motion, and his shadow-flesh split down the length of his arms and legs. Steel spikes sprouted across his knuckles and steel veins sprawled from the corner of his eyes. He clawed at the ground, drawing furrows in the tiling, and snarled.

'Noir, get a hold of yourself!'

Noir lurched forward and bit into his arm, flooding his mouth with the poisonous, acrid taste of his blood. It tore at his throat like razor blades, shocking him out of his transformation and into a semblance of control. Corrosive fumes still poured from his hand where the spikes of his transformation had punctured his flesh, however.

Eroded by his corruption, the room had fallen dark around them: the lights flickered in their distorted frames, the steel walls slouched beneath the ceiling as their steel rotted away, and huge swaths of the floor bubbled in a cold boil. Piping burst in the walls and the ceiling, its water hissing as it struck the corrupted fumes, and doused Noir and Constantine.

"They warned me that your most dangerous feature wasn't your Shadowmancy, your intelligence, or even your temper. But to think you would cause this much damage with just a fractional release..." Constantine combed his soaked hair back and flicked the water from his hands. "It makes me wonder how you and Alighieri can even be related. Lazarus told me how he died, and that man hardly deserved to be called a Tyrant."

Noir snarled and struck at him with shadow lances, but in that instant of distraction, his grip on the madness loosened and it roiled to life, swelling in him. He howled and pitched back, the shadow lances collapsing even as they assembled. Black, unformed metal spilled from his shoulders, shredding his coat and usurping his skin. He smashed into a wall and arched backward, fumes seething from his flesh and devouring the wall, rupturing another pipe.

Constantine leapt forward and kicked Noir's side, flinging him across the room into the far wall. "All the shadows in the world won't help you if you can't control them." He folded his glasses into a neat bundle and pocketed them. "Brigadier and Alucard were so obsessed with you they would speak of nothing else." He stalked forward, head ticking. "I tried to discuss the future with them, convey what your deaths would mean; but they didn't care, didn't realize this world is ending and that you were just the beginning of it. Without the Plague there will be no need for Tyrants, no need for the violence and power you embody. Then, finally, in their absence, the Copperwork Heart will be able to do what is right. Still, I regret the necessity of killing you and your brother."

Noir dragged himself from the wall's wreckage, slipping on the water and boiling floor. "Your god died years ago, Constantine, and there is nothing you can do to change it."

Constantine stilled, his eyes whirring with a frantic tick. "And that's where you are wrong. His body remains; we live in it every day, become part of it every night, and every one of us is born of him. His will endures, and someday we will rebuild him, even if I have to become him. You just have to die for it to happen." Constantine stepped forward, striking again.

Noir blocked and retaliated, hurling Constantine across the room with a kick to the chest. Even as the blow landed, his madness reared again, driving him into the wall as he clutched his head. A deep, pounding heartbeat ground through him, causing his skin to prickle and fumes to pour from his mouth.

Constantine surged upright and forward, driving a hooked blade of ticking clockwork through Noir's side. Fumes erupted around the blade but, manipulated by Constantine's Pathomancy, coiled unnaturally away from it, leaving it unharmed.

Half-blinded by the madness, Noir stabbed at him with one arm, but Constantine evaded it and slammed Noir's head into the ground. "Don't resist, just die. Join your brother." He wrenched the blade back and forth, tearing open Noir's side and releasing another cascade of noxious fumes. "He wouldn't want to suffer, to live in this hell without hope for salvation. He wouldn't want–"

Noir howled and lashed out, snapping Constantine's legs off at the knees with a metallic screech and toppling him. He lurched to press his assault, but a tide of fumes exploded from his shoulders and injuries, magnifying his rage and drowning his receding sanity. He screamed again and pounded the floor with his fist, nearly feral with rage as the fumes billowing from him multiplied.

'Noir! Get ahold of yourself!'

Noir howled again and stood, veins of steel crawling from the tips of his fingers up to the corners of his eyes. He exhaled a low, rasping breath of corrosive fumes and clenched his hands to fists, his nails digging into his Shadowsteel flesh. Slowly, painfully, the steel lines began to recede.

Constantine heaved himself up on his hands, gasping as blood pumped from his knees. A shudder coursed the length of his form, causing his skin to bulge in a wave. His mouth wrenched open and black fumes poured out, searing away his flesh to reveal a thousand copper gears.

Noir flinched as the fumes cascaded over him and covered his nose with a hand. Constantine groaned, his body swelling and building upon itself until it scraped the distant ceiling. Gear after gear forced its way to the surface, locking into sync and giving shape to a multitude of arms, renewed legs, and three immense heads.

The creature that had been Constantine settled onto the first of its arms and leaned forward and down toward Noir. Its clockwork eyes ticked in their sockets, spinning wildly in rows upon the half-moon crests that adorned each head. The creature blew a steaming breath and reached its arms toward Noir, filling his vision with its ticking fingers

Noir stumbled back, blood soaking his flank and the corruption aching in every muscle. He could smell the pathomancers who had molded Constantine's Hyde, amending and warping its nature over the course of decades until they achieved his desired form. Overlaying all of that, however, including his own leaching corruption, was Alighieri's scent: that of the ocean melded with rich soil, flowers, and spring.

Constantine struck in a sudden blur, some of its hands stabbing at Noir and others swiping. Noir dove forward through the storm of lashing arms and landed beside its colossal legs. He slashed and his claws, elongated by the corruption's increased manifestation, rent Constantine's armor but did little more than annoy it. In the instant it took him to strike, one of Constantine's arms struck him, hurling Noir crashing across the floor, snapping tiles with every collision and goring him on the shards.

Constantine lunged in pursuit, twisting awkwardly to shift its bulk in the room and reaching for him. As it leaned, however, one of its knees struck the rotting floor and the ground collapsed into the Undercity. Constantine's limbs thrust outward, latching onto the floor, ceiling, and walls to keep itself steady and from submerging further into the Undercity. Its fingers tore in the Shadowsteel, found purchase in the unaffected interior and heaved, dragging its bulk forward.

Noir hauled himself up against the wall, stepped forward and stabbed his hand through the rotting Shadowsteel floor, burying his arm up to his elbow in a nest of steel barbs. A savage grin twisted his countenance, and he released a concentrated thread of his corruption; not its full density, but enough to suit his purpose.

Steel veins lanced up his arm with an explosion of black fumes. The ground before him pitched and disintegrated, devoured by the corruption as it expanded outward from his arm. Noir yanked his arm out with a gasp and leapt back from the crumbling edge, clutching his mutilated limb.

Utterly berserk with his Hyde's madness, Constantine ripped some of its hands free and grabbed at Noir, spearing through the rushing black fumes only to shriek and recoil, its limbs disintegrating just as the floor had. But the fumes hounded it, enveloping the copper limbs and eroding them.

Constantine screeched again, its form now riddled with veins of the corrosive fumes, and shuddered with another violent tick. A gasp of steam escaped from its chest and something massive tore free of the collapsing behemoth.

Noir watched the vaguely scorpion-like creature scuttle down the lifeless husk of Constantine's body. *It seems he can evolve as the fight progresses.*

'*Be careful, he's a lot faster now.*'

Constantine, now roughly a third of its original size, charged, its arms and tails slashing with a whirr of blades.

Noir dove forward, twisting between its stabbing tails to land on his feet and drop beneath its sweeping arms. Constantine drew back for another strike and Noir shoved forward, rising just in time to smash Constantine's first leg. It recoiled with a seething, metallic roar, and he vaulted back, barely evading Constantine's whirring arm as it slammed down.

He landed and leapt, crushing Constantine's jaw with a kick. Constantine reeled back, lashing at Noir as he battered its skull with a flurry of punches and kicks until it tumbled backwards into the pit. Noir dove after it, caving its chest with another kick.

Constantine gave a final convulsion and subsided. Noir, kicking himself free, fell to the ground and stumbled back, copper shards from Constantine's machinery protruding from his leg like a hedgehog's spines. He slumped to a knee and began extracting the copper pieces, never once taking his eyes off Constantine.

Ominous fumes burst from the cracks in Constantine's body, followed by a crash as pieces of its form snapped off and tumbled to the floor. The corpse shuddered for an instant before crumbling into a pile of steaming rubble. Noir tore the last piece of copper from his leg and watched a humanoid creature liberate itself from the rubble. The twelve-foot creature shucked the final plate of armor from its chrysalis and emerged with a low growl.

Is there no end to this bastard?

'*His time's up, the mist is almost gone.*'

Yeah.

Constantine stepped forward, a knot of black, tuberous tentacles gently swaying between its shoulders. Noir flexed his hands and exhaled, releasing a final puff of fumes. The shadows converged on him, healing his injures and excising the remaining copper shards. He still hurt and the poison still roiled in his veins, but he could control it now.

Constantine reared, its maw opening wide in a gaseous howl. Noir struck, moving in a blur to decapitate the metal creature and then truncate all four of its limbs with lashing tendrils of shadow. Constantine crumbled to the floor with Noir crouched atop its quaking torso. He bore through the corrupted layers of iron and copper on its chest, stripping them away until he found the small, twisted creature within, its yellow eyes dark with the corruption's madness.

Noir leaned in close, his nostrils flaring at the greasy, infant sized thing. "Poor, misguided fool; you should have stayed in the Undercity." He reached one hand down and pressed an iron fingertip into Constantine's bulbous head. "Now return what belongs to me." Constantine gave a final, hateful shriek, and Noir dug into his skull, burrowing through the fleshy mass until he found a thin shard of bone. Extracting it, he stood and placed it in a vial of Shadowglass.

Shadows swelled around him, questing through the rubble until they found the twenty-eight knuckles. Collecting them all into a pouch, Noir leapt from the pit and retraced his steps to the surface as the shadows repaired his clothing.

Emerging outside, he slowed and exhaled, relinquishing the tension in his limbs and suppressing the last dregs of corruption. He dropped into a crouch with another breath, forcing his racing, fractured thoughts to calm. *That was harder than it should have been.*

'Yes, but it validates your decision to wait a day instead of confronting both him and the Messenger.'

Yeah, but I don't know how much of this was Constantine and how much was Lazarus. How much of Brigadier's trap was her?

'What about Alucard?'

That trap was all Lazarus.

'I wonder if he's testing us?'

Maybe, or maybe he's using me to kill them.

'Then why help them?'

So if they succeed they'd never learn his true intent, and possibly to weaken me as well.

The *Almas* descended around him, whispering of the Coalition and eliciting a grin. *We found them.* He straightened with a creak of warming muscles, and started toward the Doll District.

'*Who?*'

"Whoever it is that supplied Lazarus with the information and the power he needed," Noir responded aloud. "The ones who led him to Brigadier, Alucard, and Constantine."

'*Oh, joy. Let's invite them to a tea party!*'

"A tea party?"

'*Yes! What better place is there to murder a bunch of people than a tea party!*'

"You just want to eat more cakes, don't you?"

"Who are you talking to?"

Noir turned, shadows palpitating about his fingers, only to still and dissipate when he recognized the child from before. "No one you can hear." He resumed walking, his hands burrowing in their pockets.

The girl trailed after him, climbing onto the pipes as easily as he did. "Where are you going?"

"To send some old acquaintances a message about interfering where they do not belong."

The girl slipped between him and the wall and spun to face him, walking backwards along the pipe. "Where are you coming from?"

"From someone who had a piece of death that I wanted."

An *Alma* alighted upon the girl's head and others soon followed, perching upon every available surface until she resembled a dark-leaved bush. She made no attempt to displace them. "Why ever would you want a piece of death? Isn't there enough all around us?"

"Death? We are not surrounded by death; this is merely the life we have made for ourselves."

"Have you ever died?"

"No."

"Are you scared of dying?"

"No."

"Then what are you scared of?"

Noir hesitated. "Being alone."

The girl fell silent, but made no movement to change her course or to vanish as she had on their two previous encounters.

Thus, they crossed the city in silence, hesitating briefly only as they entered the outskirts of the Doll District.

Noir paused as he stepped beneath the white banners and raised his palm. A single *Alma* alighted upon his fingertips. "Show me," he said and the *Alma* took flight again, guiding him toward the edge of Umbras.

The girl trailed him, no more frightened by the occasional Hyde than he was. "What do you hope to find now that you could not before?"

Noir shrugged, the Shadowsteel grate clinking softly beneath his strides. "I am not looking for the same thing as before; I am looking for something that will betray its location."

The girl hurried to keep pace with him, her bare feet soundless. "You are not sending the *Almas* to find it; you are sending them to die."

"Yes, and the building where they die is where I'll find my foreigners."

"It is sad that so many of them need to die."

"Everything dies in one way or another."

He scaled a skyscraper, following a steadily growing current of *Almas* with the girl effortlessly shadowing him. They guided him across the Doll District toward the boundaries of Umbras until he could discern the shapes of Ferrymen reclining on the bank. There, a throng of softly chittering *Almas* fluttered around a single skyscraper.

Noir dropped to the ground level and crossed the street, a blanket of dead *Almas* crunching beneath his feet. The girl followed to the dead *Almas* and then paused. "Good bye, mister, I hope I get to see you again."

Noir glanced back as she vanished into the night, sparing her a final moment of attention before resuming his trek. He could sense the mingled Pathomancy and Shadowmancy that killed his *Almas*, a poisonous aura engineered specifically to kill them. Noir ascended a thin stairway, scowling to himself. The fools seemed to believe that *Almas* would leave no bodies when they died, as if they were nothing more than a casual Construct.

The door swung inward as he approached, its lock clicking open and slithering aside to admit him. He crossed its threshold into a dark room, grimacing as he felt Umbras grow distant; they had separated this skyscraper from the rest of the city. He flexed a hand and every shadow in the building shifted in accord. He felt the building's inhabitants surge to their feet, reacting futilely to the stirring shadows. He opened his other hand, causing the shadows around his own body to thicken and carry him up through the skyscraper. He felt his quarry frantically searching for any light they could find, desperate for something to quell the shadows in every corner and hallway. Many had already fallen, their bodies entangled in shadow.

Raising his eyes, Noir phased through the final floor and settled at the center of a brightly lit room. A crowd of Hydes intermingled with people surrounded him. The humans struggled in the grasp of diaphanous shadows while the beasts gnawed at their bindings or their own limbs in a desperate attempt to escape. Those who remained sane cried out and begged for help from the scattered few who had escaped entanglement. These individuals huddled in circles of light, barricading themselves with an array of candles, lanterns, and raw flames, anything that could banish a passive shadow.

They all became silent, ceasing their futile struggles, as Noir emerged from the floor. Those who cowered in the circles of light stood, facing him with raised hands or weapons. He smirked and the shadows collapsed inward, crushing them.

Noir spun slowly, assessing his captive audience. "...Black Die, Radiance, even Seelie; yes, I can see they all sent representatives." He snorted. "Did they even tell you who you would be facing, or did you all just piss them off at the wrong time?"

A rasping snarl pulled Noir's focus about to where a horse-sized canine thrashed in the Shadow webbing, its cavernous maw bleeding pathomantic energies. He faced the creature. "I must admit I am surprised you came in person Legion, but then again I guess you do have the bodies to spare. Don't worry; I'll deal with you shortly." He faced the segment of the room that held the most entangled people.

The serrated shadows convulsed, shredding most of the room's inhabitants into confetti. The massacre lasted seconds and ended with five survivors kneeling at the center of the gore-stained room. Of those that had been imprisoned, only Legion remained so.

Noir strode forward, and the released prisoners scrambled back, sliding through the blood and entrails with whimpering pleas. He waved his hand, calling the shadows to impede their flight. "I'm not going to kill you. No, I want you to take a message back to your respective Tyrants. Tell them to stay the hell out of Umbras, or I'll pay them a visit." He jerked his head. "Now get out of here."

They fled through the open door as Noir addressed the raging canine, "The same goes for you, Legion; send one of your bodies or peons here again, and I'll make sure all of you and your city ends up as a funeral pyre." The shadows constricted, grinding Legion into pulp.

Noir exited the skyscraper and returned to the Doll House.

Chapter Fifteen

Among all adept magics, Pathomancy is the rarest. Combine this with a universal reticence from the pathomancers themselves and it results in our general ignorance concerning their abilities.

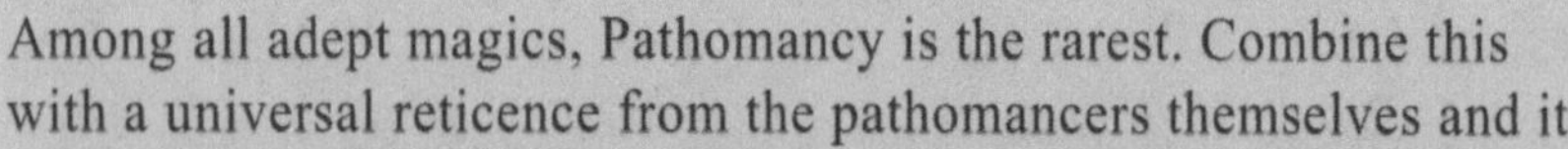

Plague saturation is quite important to pathomancers as it limits what features they can apply. More importantly, it also affects their ability to suppress and agitate the plague. The higher the saturation, the easier it becomes to agitate and the harder it becomes to suppress.

Pathomancers are frequently the most strange and strangely beautiful of individuals. They have the ability to manipulate how the plague affects organic material and so they tinker ceaselessly, striving for the perfect mix between aesthetic and utility. Consequently, they become quite dangerous as many will equip themselves with poisons or mesmerizing eyes.

He Must be Executed

The doors of the Communion Chamber swung open, spilling wisps of liquid shadows in a slow, airy descent and revealing her mother. Night had long since fallen on the surface, but undertakers still labored in the safety of their Reliquary. The Hyde's rarely ventured into the Undercity, loathing the eternal pipework, or more accurately the water it contained, and the cramped confines.

Her mother's gaze swept the assembled undertakers waiting outside the Communion Chamber and settled on her waiting near the back of the congregation. "Adrian, come forward, the Matriarchs wish to speak with you."

Adrian's breath caught and she looked up, doubting what she heard even as her mother stepped aside and prompted her inward with a wave. She had never conversed with the Matriarchs before, never seen them besides glimpses snuck through the Communion doors as they opened and closed in the mornings. This distance was not a result of prejudice, but from the simple fact that Adrian, being half human, could never achieve Communion with the city, and the Matriarchs never entirely surfaced from it.

Her mother laid a comforting hand on her shoulder as she passed. "Do not fear, they have loved you since before you drew breath." With that, they crossed into the shadows and the doors slid shut.

For an instant, all about her was darkness, but it was not the darkness of absent light. It was a physical weight, like water, that embraced her in a gentle, unrelenting pressure and seeped into her skin. Adrian advanced, noting a circle of illumination in the distance. The man she had captured cowered on the ground there, his hands clutching his head as he wept and pleaded. *He cannot see beyond that light,* Adrian realized. She glanced toward her mother. "How has he not changed?"

"The blood of the Matriarchs suppresses his Hyde."

"Can he hear us?"

"No."

Adrian paused when they came abreast of the light. "Why is he crying?"

"It's a result of these Matriarchal Shadows and the suppression of his Hyde, which unfortunately forces most humans into an unstable emotional state," her mother said, halting as well. "These shadows amplify his distress. There is something about their construction that fundamentally disagrees with humans; most of whom can't tolerate even to look at them. He's been trapped in their confines for hours, knowing that nothing else impedes his escape, no chains bind him. Yet, he cannot bear to traverse the shadows. Thus, faced with his cowardice and impotence, his spirit breaks. Come, the Matriarchs wait."

Adrian followed her mother until they came upon eleven female undertakers sitting on the ground in two ranks. The first rank, that of eight, looked up at Adrian's arrival and bowed their heads. The second rank, that of three, remained still as death, their eyes open and trickling shadows.

Adrian and her mother knelt; and a Matriarch, though Adrian could not identify which, spoke, "This man has conveyed many troubling tidings. He speaks of the coup and the intent to dispel the Pattern. These we knew before and, though validated, they pale against the confirmation of an outsider. He has taken root somewhere in the depths of Umbras, a cancer eroding at the foundations of our existence. We have all felt his presence in the Communion, but have recently started suffering its effects in the waking hours. First, we believed it no more than a manifestation of the coup, now we learn it is more."

"I think I feel what you do, but why would you speak to me of this?"

"We have a purpose for you, but first there is something you must ask for us. Harken to the man in the light, ask of him who gnaws at the roots of Umbras."

"Why do you not ask yourselves?"

"Because he fears us and is irrational because of our shadows;

you are human and may inspire him to divulge his final secret."

Uncertain of how to proceed, Adrian stole a glance at her mother before responding with a nod. Although doubtful, Adrian mustered her courage and shed her undertaker detachment.

The Matriarchal Shadows instantly closed in on her. Their pressure never changed, but their touch chilled her to the bone and their comforting embrace turned to drowning water. She staggered forward, unreasoning panic starting to erase her thoughts, and burst into the circle of illumination.

The man started with a muffled cry and looked at her with frenzied eyes. Recognition flashed in his gaze and his whimpers faded. "You...?"

She forced herself to breath normally. "Y–yes."

He stole a furtive glance at the shadows, frantic thoughts dashing through his features. "Help me..." His voice never rose above a fractured whisper.

"I don't know if I can."

"Please..." He wept openly, the tears spilling down his nose to splash against the floor.

"I ... I need something from you first."

His breath caught and a frail light gleamed in his eyes. "What?"

"Who's hiding below Umbras?"

The light died in his eyes, snuffed by a sudden unreasoning terror. "No ... no, please not that."

"It's just a nam–"

"No, I dare not! He would find me, kill me, consume me."

"Who?"

"The Godeater–no. No! I can't say."

"I can get you out of here."

"He'd kill me!"

"We'll take you somewhere safe, where he can't find you."

He shriveled in on himself and, after a long silence, dared a single name in a voice too low to hear.

Adrian leaned closer. "What did you say?"

He held his answer tight for a while, arms pressed against a shuddering chest. The shadows closed a little tighter and he finally spoke, barely louder than before. "Lazarus—"

His skin ruptured with a thousand cords of lashing blood. He screamed and flailed at them, but they plunged in and out of his skin like a storm of sewing needles. Adrian reeled back, screaming as he screamed, but his voice lasted mere seconds before he tumbled back, his injuries ragged and dry, utterly bereft of the blood that should have run through his veins. She watched him die in those few seconds, his body literally ripped apart from within, bones, muscle, teeth, and flesh. When it all ended, the blood converged into a single mass and slithered through the grating.

Her mother grabbed her by the shoulder and wrenched her out of the light. The shadows closed in, but she reached for her detachment and their burden diminished.

Her mother spun her about and gently touched her face. "Are you all right?"

"Yes, thank you for pulling me out." Relief flickered through her mother's face, and they both faced the light. "What was that?"

The answer came from a Matriarch, "Hemomancy; a cursed laid in his blood that would activate if he transgressed its boundaries. It is a powerful art, beyond the ability even of lieutenants. We have our answer, nonetheless: Lazarus. Hmm, that is not a name I know, and the First Born still refuse to waken."

Adrian looked at the three undertakers in the second rank. "What now?" she asked.

"We no longer need Lock-And-Key's permission to strike, so we will eradicate this Lazarus tonight. But first, we have another charge we would ask of you."

"What would you have me do?"

"Return to the Dollhouse and fight in Solomon Doll's war."

Her mother inhaled sharply, but Adrian's shock sent her voice into a shout, "Why?"

"However much he is a puppet, Proctor Grim is still a transgressor against the Pattern. He must be executed."

"What does that have to do with me? I'm no soldier, I can't fight a Proctor!"

"You will not fight him; you are merely temptation. If we are to destroy him with minimal sacrifice, we must empty his fortress; and what better enticement is there for a man seeking to break the Pattern than a helpless undertaker girl?"

Adrian's heart stopped for a beat. "You would tell him what I am?"

"Yes, and when he empties his bastion of reserves in pursuit of you, we will strike and eliminate him."

"…I can't…"

"We know we ask much of you. We know the risk you will take, but you would not act alone. We will guarantee your safety as much as can be. The choice, however, is yours."

"Adrian, I would advise you to deny them." Her mother spoke softly, but for the first time in her life, Adrian heard rage beneath the surface of her words.

Adrian pushed her fear away, immersing herself as deeply as she could in the undertaker detachment. "Do you disagree with their plan? Is it flawed?"

Her mother visibly flinched. "Their logic is cogent and the aim simple. It is likely to succeed, but please, Adrian, don't accept. It is too dangerous; Dark Father you would be in the middle of a war without your Scythe!"

Adrian looked to the impassive Matriarchs and thought, *I can't do this. I simply lack both the experience and the tools, and however much they promise it, they cannot guarantee my safety. But does that matter? My death or capture would be meaningless if they succeed; it would only last a matter of hours at the most, and by doing this I can save hundreds of lives. The war would conclude in hours, Solomon Doll would win and everyone would survive. All of this, if I'm just willing to risk pain.* She addressed the Matriarchs again, "How would you convey the secret of my identity to Grim without alerting all of Umbras?"

"We doubt he would share it with any but his most trusted advisors, all of whom will most likely perish through the course of his war. As for conveying the secret, that is a simple enough matter even at this time of night."

"…All right, I accept; what do I need to do?"

"Nothing, just return to the Dollhouse and linger there

throughout the course of the war. Your presence there will force his hand, compel him to assault the Dollhouse before he wins the District, else he would risk you escaping to the Reliquary as the conflict turns in his favor."

Her mother said nothing, but Adrian saw her hands tightening into fists and her Scythe twitching where it clung to her shoulder as an adornment. Adrian gently touched her hand in apology and reverted her attention to the Matriarchs. "Is there anything else?"

"Do you trust Lieutenant Noir?"

Adrian hesitated. "I do not know; superficially, he cares little for human life, but there is more to him that I cannot see." She thought about all she knew of him and nodded. "But we can trust him; he would never harm Umbras or the Pattern."

"Then with your permission we would appraise both him and Solomon Doll of our intent, and request that he protect you during the conflict."

A shred of relief flooded her; she doubted many of Grim's soldiers would dare confront Noir. "Do it."

One of the Matriarchs raised her hand. The shadows coiled into her palm and two miniature wrens sprang into the air. They circled once and soared through the closed door. "I have sent a messenger to request Lieutenant Noir's presence, we will await his arrival."

As one the Matriarchs lapsed into meditation, their eyes clouding with the shadows of the Communion.

Her mother addressed her quietly, "I wish you had not made this choice, but I cannot disagree with it." Her eyes closed and she turned her head toward the Matriarchs. "I wish we did not have to choose between the Pattern and family."

"I know." They said nothing else until the voice of quiet footsteps intruded on the dark.

Adrian shifted about, her eyes widening at Noir's approach through the shifting dark, the doors of the Communion Chamber tightly fastened behind him. She joined him midway.

"What do your Matriarchs want with me?"

She peeked around him, observing the closed doors again. "How did you get in here? The doors never opened."

"I phased through the ceiling—"

"How? I thought only Umbrans could do that? And what about these shadows, aren't they bothering you?"

"No. This"—he gestured at himself—"isn't me. This is a Construct I sent to meet with you instead. My real body's safe underground; as if I would risk venturing out at this hour." He snorted a laugh.

"But how are you speaking? How can you hear, see, or react to me?"

"We humans are just machines of flesh and blood; if I emulate their designs, I can achieve a comparative result. After that, it's just a matter of maintaining mental connection to the Construct, which allows me to perceive what it does."

"But how is that possible? You would need something organic, something alive to house your consciousness!"

"I imbue it with some of my blood, and store my consciousness in that. Now, let's get this over with."

He advanced under the Matriarchs' watchful gazes to stand before them without kneeling. "All right, what's this about?"

"We have a favor to ask of you, Lieutenant Noir. It is our intent to assist Solomon Doll in his war against Grim and have prepared a plan with that intent. The plan, however, requires us to put Adrian in some peril, more so than you might initially realize."

"Because she's female."

Adrian gasped. "What! You knew?"

He shot a glance at her. "Yes, female and male Umbrans feel different in the mind; any Adept shadowmancer could discern a difference if they just bothered to pay attention." His attention reverted to the Matriarchs. "What's your scheme?"

"We intend to betray this information to Grim, inciting him into a full assault on the Dollhouse, an assault that will leave his own fortress vulnerable. We are informing Solomon Doll of this currently."

"Why do you move against Grim? This is a concern of men, not undertakers."

"Grim and his allies have transgressed and continue to transgress on the Pattern. He imperils all of us and the city itself with his wanton avarice; we will not suffer his treason."

"What do you want from me?"

"To protect Adrian from all attempts to seize her. She must not fall into Grim's possession; such a result would reap devastation upon Umbras."

Noir fell silent, his eyes settling upon Adrian as his mind worked. Minutes passed before he finally resumed, "All right, I'll do as you ask; no harm shall befall Adrian from Grim's hand or that of any other."

"Do you need assistance? We cannot predict the course of a war, and Solomon Doll cannot keep one of his strongest weapons tethered to his citadel. Can you protect her even if you are called away?"

"Yes." He raised his hand and the shadows coiled into his palm, forming a single black butterfly. "This is my *Alma*, simply speak to one if you are in danger and I will answer." The *Alma* fluttered from his palm and vanished.

"You can invoke Shadowmancy from this distance?"

"Yes. Now if that's all, I'm tired and want to go to bed. See you tomorrow, kid." So saying, his body dissolved into Shadow-debris.

The Matriarchs settled their gazes on Adrian and her mother. "It is decided then. We suggest that you return home and find what sleep you can; tomorrow will tax you greatly. Also, Emarhine will lead our assault on Lazarus."

Adrian bowed her head and started to depart, but her mother delayed. "You go ahead; I wish to converse with the Matriarchs on another subject."

Adrian left, opening the doors a crack so she could slip out into the vacant central room. Not a sound disturbed the silence, or a flash of movement the stillness. Everything exuded an air of abandonment, even though dozens of undertakers had occupied these halls mere hours before. She shivered and continued toward her home. As she neared the appropriate passageway though, she heard footsteps. A light appeared ahead of her, revealing her father with an oil lamp in one hand.

He greeted her with a sad smile. "I heard what the Matriarchs asked of you."

"Are you mad?"

"No. Scared, yes, and very proud. So is your mother, though I doubt she will have said as much."

"Where are you going?"

"To join the others; they're mustering somewhere in the Undercity near the palace."

"They already told you?"

"Yeah, word travels fast when it's from the Matriarchs."

"Do you have any advice for me?" She spoke calmly, but fear plagued her despite the undertaker detachment. She knew, both on an intellectual level and an instinctive one, that she could likely die tomorrow regardless of the Matriarchs' and Noir's best efforts. That fear extended to everyone assaulting Lazarus; they had no knowledge of their foe, no concept of his abilities, or the strength he possessed. For all any of them knew, they could be invading the lair of a Tyrant.

He gently grabbed her shoulder. "The best thing you can do is keep your head down and trust Solomon Doll. You will be surrounded by men and women who have fought dozens, if not hundreds, of battles, and others who have survived wars."

She settled onto the wall beside him. "You've been in a war before, haven't you? You and Solomon both?"

"Yeah…" He stared into the passageway for a moment, his gaze heavy with memories, and then began, "It all started years before you were born, years before Solomon Doll ever ascended to the seat of Proctor. Back then, the White District belonged to a woman called Ivory. She was a shadowmancer, cruel, vain, and deeply jealous. Everything in the district belonged to her, and so long as you obeyed that concept, you survived with a relatively light onus.

"At that time, it was only Solomon, Gregorio, and me. We each worked our respective jobs during the day, and spent the nights harassing Night Princes for amusement. Solomon and I were powerful, even back then, but uninterested or just too lazy to join with a militia. Gregorio accompanied us mostly to ensure we didn't get ourselves killed. It was about this time that I met your mother; she killed me, thinking I was a surviving Hyde. I remember waking up after Gregorio's resurrection to her apology. I asked her out as a joke, but you know that story.

"This was when the trouble with the Night Princes started. Ivory lacked interest in controlling them so long as they paid homage to her, and in this lapse, they voraciously expanded their power. From mere empires at night, they evolved into gangs during the day, then organizations. She let this transpire without restraint, demanding only that they worshiped her and paid the tithes. Their organizations quickly began abusing the common people, terrorizing and exploiting them. The people begged Ivory to intervene, but she declined; the Night Princes were paying her a fortune. She wasn't blind, however. She secretly press-ganged the strongest Adepts in all districts, coercing them into submission with whatever she could find. Most came willingly, and only a few defied her. We three were among those few. Necromancers are taboo, of course, and the only thing I cared about was your mother, who she couldn't touch either. This left only Solomon, whose single most cherished secret was that he had a wife and daughter. No one knew about them but us. So we lived and denied her openly, desperately hoping all the while she never stumbled onto our secret. This drove her wild with anger, and she vowed to possess us one day. Her desire mutated into obsession, and we spent years fighting with her servants; well, Solomon and I did, Gregorio just filled double-shifts in the temples. All the while, her district continued deteriorating. The Night Princes expanded across the entire area and started claiming territory. Wars inevitably ensued.

"Throughout all of this, and despite the open aggression between us, Ivory consistently summoned us to her keep. She cajoled, threatened, and berated us for hours. Gregorio never bothered to respond with more than a nod. I would argue and trade rhetoric for hours before eventually abandoning it out of boredom or exhaustion. Solomon never relented. He assailed her word for word, heedless of who or what she threatened. As all of this transpired, however, Ivory changed. I don't know how, or what catalyzed this shift, but she grew infatuated with Solomon. It wasn't love, she was incapable of loving anyone or anything else, it was a need for Solomon to love her.

"We all noticed the change, Solomon most of all, and ceased responding to her summons, hoping that would dissuade her desire. It didn't work. Ivory became violent, bordering on the insane. She openly tormented the people of her district, often times butchering them for the slightest affront and then suspending their corpses from the flag poles for days as a warning. In was then, in the middle of this nightmare, that Ivory discovered Solomon's family.

"She imprisoned both of them in her keep and demanded that we submit. Solomon acceded without hesitation and bowed to her outside the doors of her keep. Only, Ivory wasn't content with that; she wanted Solomon to love her and knew that he would never do so while his wife lived. So she burned Irene, his wife, alive for all to see, and vowed to do the same with his daughter if he didn't swear to love her. Solomon didn't listen; he went berserk, slaughtered her soldiers indiscriminately and stole back his daughter before disappearing into the city. That marked the beginning of our war.

"We fought with her for years, both open combat in the streets and guerrilla strikes at night. We bought allies from among the mercenaries and accrued others from those who had learned to hate her. Every attempt to destroy Ivory or her militia failed, however. For all her failings, she was a Proctor and commanded the full support of the Night Princes in her district, all of whom needed her to maintain power until the opportunity for their ascension arrived.

"We killed, truly killed, almost seventy people throughout the war; she burned close to two hundred. Our one solace was that she rarely touched the innocent, and that her abuse of them all but vanished when Solomon started his rebellion. Nonetheless, we fought and people died until Solomon simply broke.

"He went to her mansion on one evening, sometime in winter, and vowed to love her if she would but forgive all transgressions. She agreed and, as proof of his devotion, he gave her a necklace of red roses and his daughter's bloodied doll, promising that she was dead. But this was a necklace and doll he had fashioned of his own blood, and when she accepted them, the doll and each rose came alive. Their thorns dug into her flesh, injecting her with parasitic blood, as the doll impaled her with a poisoned bone toothpick. She tried to destroy them, but they already served their purpose. She died in agony, unable even to muster her Shadowmancy through the pain.

"That concluded our war and ushered in Solomon's era. He hated the thought of accepting the Proctorship, but the thought of what would happen if he didn't, terrified him. He couldn't stand the possibility of anyone else suffering what he had, so he assumed rule over the White District and received the surname Doll. We eradicated the Night Prince factions over the course of a few years, and the district resumed a semblance of peace. His daughter's still alive, hidden away somewhere so no one can harm her."

Adrian released a shaky breath. "That's awful."

"Yeah, but I survived one war against a Proctor, so I'm sure there's no reason for you to worry." He gave her a reassuring smile and pushed off the wall. "Now, I have to go. You'd best go home and try to rest." He wrapped her in a hug and then left, joining a group of expectant undertakers at the entrance corridor.

Adrian watched them depart, unable to shake the cold dread settling over her.

Chapter Sixteen

Gregorio Taim
Hierophant
Rias Dorian
Valerian
Sylas June

Insanity or Necessity?

Standing in front of the bedroom's small mirror, Adrian fiddled with the buttons of her coat and adjusted her guns. The room housed a pair of beds, a mirror, and a small table. A washing bowl sat unused on the table while her bed sheets lay folded atop her mattress. A few of Noir's now ever-present *Almas* fluttered in the corner, silent but reassuring.

Still, a part of her wished he was beside her, his lips curling into a half-smile as he voiced some dry remark to usher her out. He wouldn't have given her the luxury of dithering over stupid buttons and hoping the war never came.

Taking a deep breath, Adrian slapped her cheeks. The stinging pain shocked her mind out of its stupor, giving her the energy she needed to emerge from her bedroom and start toward the main stairs.

After learning of their intent, Solomon Doll had advised that she and Noir sleep in the Dollhouse last night to both maintain appearance and tempt Grim. Noir had initially resisted, preferring that she stay with him, but ultimately capitulated when Solomon assured him they could ensure her safety. More than anything else, they needed her someplace Grim could reach; he couldn't attack her in the Reliquary, the other Proctors would annihilate him and his militia. Thus she would reside in the Dollhouse, and Solomon would inform the other Proctors she intended to resume her place among the undertakers in a few days. They hoped her departure would prompt Grim into a rash assault on the Dollhouse, thus providing the undertakers with their opportunity.

A call sounded from above her, contrasting the low rumble of many conversations below. "Adrian!"

She turned to see Corporal Valerian hastening toward her. "Yes, sir?"

The corporal paused, issuing a litany of commands to nearby

soldiers before readdressing her, "If you're looking for Noir, he's out with the Proctor. There's been another murder, this time in the Doll District." She adjusted one of the two packs she carried over her shoulder and grunted as her thorny hair caught in the Shadowcloth. She yanked her head free with a wince. "Though I don't suggest you go; they say it's pretty awful."

Rougher than four heads set on spikes? "Do we know who's dead?"

Valerian shook her head and resumed her descent. "No, and that's what makes it so bad." She looked back at Adrian, her lips assuming a thin smile. "If you do venture outside, be careful and don't go alone; we don't know how many thugs Grim has already snuck into our district." Valerian readjusted her bags again and hastened down the stairs, shouting orders as she went.

Adrian took another deep breath and touched a trembling finger to the butt of her pistol. She felt the anxiety of everyone in the Dollhouse and could smell how it antagonized the corruption in their blood. It wouldn't erupt of course, not while the sun remained in the sky to burn it away; but with so many contained in the Dollhouse, the scent became overpowering. Except, she realized uneasily, it could erupt; the Blood Moon would rise in a couple hours, and no one could predict the effects it would have on the hemomancers.

She shivered and continued her descent, slipping between the soldiers burdened with supplies, weapons, and assorted valuables, and repaying their greetings until she reached the fourth floor where Lieutenant Dorian gleefully exercised his inherited authority. Pausing in the doorway, she watched him and Corporal Silas June organize the war effort. Their voices failed to pierce the din, but they appeared confident, and the soldiers around them seemed determined. She continued, passing the teeming armory and vacant mess hall before squeezing through the packed entrance room.

Outside the Dollhouse, she found Sergeants Gregorio and Hierophant laboring on a series of barricades with a squad of soldiers. She began making her way in their direction but slowed as she saw who they conversed with—her brothers.

Black skinned like Noir, but with a mane of untrimmed white

hair coursing down their sleek suits, Eera and Jaysis towered over Gregorio and Hierophant. Their skeletal frames and bone masks did nothing to alleviate the discomfort Umbrans engendered.

Eera, the elder of her two brothers, hailed her from across the distance and waved.

Adrian resumed her former pace and reached them after a minute of weaving through the packed courtyard.

Eera spoke in his light, sibilant voice, "We have not come to fight your war, Sergeant. We are here to protect our brother." Eera's Scythe changed on the ground beside him, its humanoid shape first contracting and then shifting into a more feline guise, mimicking his unvoiced displeasure.

Gregorio scowled, eyes flicking to the Scythe before returning to its owner. "Then why not take him away from all of this?" Solomon had informed his officers of her true nature early this morning along with the undertakers' plan, but Gregorio had known her since birth and loathed the plan.

Jaysis shrugged. "Because that was not our command."

Gregorio's scowl deepened, but it was Hierophant who continued, "And you just do whatever you're told? No questions? Not even a twinge of doubt that war might not be the safest place for him?"

Jaysis interrupted with a gesture, the twin, curving blades of his Scythe swinging on their chains, "He's sworn himself to Proctor Doll, albeit temporarily; it is not our place to break or uphold his vows." He made a dismissive gesture, causing his Scythes to scratch the ground.

Gregorio raked a feathered hand through his hair. "Well, I can't argue with that, so I guess we should just be glad you're here." He held out his hand but neither brother accepted it. Gregorio switched his focus to her. "I'm not going to lie; the thought of those two watching over you does ease my mind."

Outwardly she shook her head and dismissed his concerns. "Don't worry, I can handle myself." Inwardly, she wished the Matriarchs had chosen someone other than her brothers, and that they were safe below. "Can you tell me where Noir is?"

Hierophant gave her directions—he always seemed to know where everybody was—and then she departed, slipping through the bustling soldiers with her brothers in tow.

They fell silently into step, and she abandoned her false baritone. "It's good to see you again."

"Likewise, little brother," Jaysis intoned with a sly wink, amusement at the whole deception almost bursting out his ears. Eera said nothing, but he had always favored their mother's demeanor.

They traversed the increasingly abandoned streets with caution, constantly appraising their surroundings until they found a small cluster of Solomon Doll's soldiers outside their destination. One of the guards, a woman with a third eye blinking at the center of her forehead, moved to forestall them as they approached. "I suggest you don't go in there, boy; it's not a pretty sight."

Adrian tried to peek around her, but the woman shifted her stance. "Is Noir in there?"

"Yes, he and Proctor Doll are here. But I still advise against entering, it's ugly enough in there that people are vomiting, and we aren't strangers to blood."

"We deal with your dead daily," Eera replied, "there is no brutality of man we have not witnessed."

The woman shifted uneasily, then consented with a forced shrug. "If you say so; the bodies are on the third floor."

They ascended through the building's dim interior to the third floor and slowed to a stop at the top of the stairs. A crowd of pale men and women clogged the slim corridor, but their clustered bodies couldn't mask the sheer amount of blood.

Adrian hesitated, then peeked in the room, instantly recognizing why no one could tell who had died; there was nothing recognizable left. She tiptoed over the littered gore to join Noir at the center. "What happened here?"

"What one would immediately suspect." He scraped some blood-soaked Shadow-debris aside with his boot, exposing the floor and uncovering deep lacerations. "I see you brought some goons."

She chuckled, his words forcing some amusement through her horror and disgust. "Those are my brothers; they're here to make sure I survive." Eera and Jaysis returned her wave with flat stares. "So, what happened?"

"Our murderer killed everybody."

"Yes, but what have we learned?"

"That our theory about this being a shadowmancer is probably correct. The only other kind of Adept with this much destructive power is a hemomancer. I guess a necromancer could, but not without time to prepare.

"Is there anything else?"

"Yeah, the crew we sent out to investigate Brigadier's death returned late yesterday. They found a huge swath of land bleached white and evidence of powerful Shadowmancy."

"What about these guys? Can they be resurrected?"

"What is there to resurrect?" He gestured at the devastation. "This is like twenty jigsaw puzzles shuffled together with broken pieces."

"And what about the people from yesterday?"

"Nothing we can do for them either. It's just like with Alucard and, I suspect, Brigadier. Whoever killed them destroyed their souls in the process." He scowled suddenly. "This wasn't the only murder, either. Somebody slaughtered another group of people over in the Ambrosia District. Though, most of them are being rez'ed as we speak."

"Shadowmancy again?"

"Yeah, though not anywhere near the amount or quality we've seen before."

"Oh, that reminds me, do you remember the shadowmancer from yesterday, Grim's lieutenant?" Adrian asked.

"What about him?" Noir knelt and sifted through a pile of crushed sundries.

"Well, he cast his spells without making a gesture; I didn't realize a shadowmancer could do that."

Noir leaned back from the mound, lifting a diminutive wooden cross to the light. "Almost any shadowmancer can do it."

She blinked, momentarily distracted by the cross in Noir's hand. "Then why don't they?"

Noir stood. "Because it makes everything ten times harder. Solomon!"

The Proctor deserted his own inspection. "Yes, Lieutenant?"

"At least one of these slaughterhouse fanatics belonged to Radiance"—he tossed him the cross—"and I saw what looked like a couple of ruined dice."

Solomon Doll frowned. "And I found remnants of Legion Flesh."

"What possible reason could three Tyrants have for holding a conference in Umbras? Much less for Legion to make a personal appearance?"

"I don't know, but I doubt they came here on Lock-And-Key's behest." The Proctor spasmed, the lines in his flesh flaring crimson. He snarled, one hand snapping out to brace against the wall.

Adrian drew back as her brothers stepped forward, a shiver coursing the length of their Scythes. Noir stepped forward as well, digging his nails into Solomon Doll's shoulder. The Proctor hissed, but the tension fled his body, leaving him slumped against the wall. Noir extracted his hand and flicked off the blood. "If the Blood Moon's started already, you're in for one hell of a night."

"At least Grim can't be having a much better time of it."

"I doubt he cares who dies in his fits of rage." Noir jerked his head toward the door. "Now come on, there's people that need killing."

Solomon relinquished his grip on the wall, his features still taut with the Blood Moon's effects. "Yes, there are." He adjusted his coat with a snap. "Lieutenant Noir, we will rendezvous back at the Dollhouse in an hour; most of Grim's sentries have disappeared from the border but it is too early for his War Permit to have been sanctioned. I find this concerning and wish to inquire as to the state of his Permit. You are in command until I return." He left, circumventing the gore as best he could and calling his guards.

Discarding the wooden cross, Noir addressed Adrian, "So, what brought you to this neck of the woods? There's not much out here that would interest you." A corner of his mouth twisted upward again. "Something tells me it's not my charming personality."

"Well, there is going to be a war, so I thought it best to join you before it really got started."

He grunted. "This isn't a war; this is a playground squabble."

"A conflict between Proctors is a child's squabble?"

"Anything that doesn't involve Tyrants, is a child's squabble, and be thankful that's all it is; Tyrants tend to rearrange the world." He started to leave, disregarding the blood soiling his boots.

Her brothers watched him exit with narrowed eyes, waiting to speak until they no longer heard him. "Be careful of that man, Adrian," Eera said, "he is full of a masked violence, and we couldn't stop him if he decided to harm you."

"Why do you say that? The Matriarchs never mentioned anything of the sort."

"For all their knowledge, the Matriarchs are not well suited to judging man," Jaysis replied, "they have too little involvement in the human world."

Adrian almost rebuked him but fell silent as she recognized the truth of his claim. "You think I should leave his company."

Eera shook his head. "We are not here to council you, Adrian. We are here to ensure that no human whim ends your life. Even if we were meant to advise you, we couldn't. We know less of that man's nature than you. All we have, is his vow to the Matriarchs."

"Well, you're a fat lot of help." She groaned theatrically. "You swoop in to spout dire warnings and then heave the entire mess into my lap without so much as a good luck."

Jaysis leaned over and patted her shoulder. "Good luck."

She shot him a withering stare, which he answered with a twinkling eye.

Adrian held eye contact for a second then relented. "I'll stay with Noir, but I don't want another peep from either of you." She hurried out the room, leaping from dry spot to dry spot, until she caught up with Noir.

They returned to the Dollhouse without delay and enjoyed a quick breakfast before Solomon returned and immediately called his officers to assemble. Noir, being the first to arrive, fabricated chairs for Adrian and himself. Gregorio and Hierophant arrived next, followed by Valerian, Silas and, finally, Dorian who slunk in as if expecting a death sentence.

"Relax, Dorian, I don't plan on killing you. Think of it as a welcome home present." Dorian hesitated then took a furtive step forward and with that everyone congregated around Noir's chair.

Solomon Doll spent a moment assessing his officers; Rias Dorian had reclaimed his usual hauteur, Silas regarded Solomon attentively, and Corporal Valerian almost vibrated with energy. Hierophant and Gregorio remained impassive, and Noir absently tossed a ball of formless Shadowmancy.

Ultimately, Solomon pulled the needle from his mouth and began, "I know that Grim used Noir's somewhat inadvisable actions to instigate this conflict. But that was merely an excuse and this was inevitable, so none of you will blame him for our situation."

Valerian laughed. "I don't think any of us would be stupid enough to challenge Noir. Don't know why the lieutenant even attempted it."

Noir snorted. "The man's fault derived less from his choice of actions, and more from his egregiously overestimated abilities. I doubt he expected to die at all."

"Whether or not the man expected to die is irrelevant." Solomon focused all of them with a look. "I contacted the palace about the War Permit, but they informed me that Lock-And-Key hasn't spoken to anyone or even appeared for a few months. Regardless, if the war begins, I do not intend to take their aggression passively. Three of you will raid the Grim District, where you will under no circumstance attack the civilians. This war is between us and Grim, understood?" They assented and he resumed, "Noir, Rias, and Valerian, you will all lead separate strike teams into the Grim District and attempt to raze his Citadel. Noir, I know you have concerns about Adrian's safety; but she will remain in the Dollhouse at all times, and I will do my best to ensure no harm befalls her."

Noir caught the ball of Shadowmancy as it fell. "Redeploy whatever troops you assigned to my company; they'll just slow me down."

"It would be smarter to mince my ass into seasoning, what if you get surrounded?"

"Have you ever heard the term 'mass grave'?"

"Alright. Noir goes alone, but there won't be help if you get in trouble." Noir shrugged and the Proctor continued, "The rest of you are assigned to protecting the Doll District. Your duty is to the people, even if the Dollhouse is burning, understood." They nodded. "Now, I will entrust each of you with a number of Terian Shards to augment your abilities, but by no means are you to challenge Grim if you encounter him. One Terian Shard may drastically increase your ability, but it is unlikely to equalize you to his natural abilities, and he will possess several Shards as well."

A low murmur swept through the officers, passing Noir by and concluding at Gregorio. "And how many will you be taking, sir?" He gestured at his fellow officers. "Our Shards will be pointless if you can't defeat Grim."

"I have three in my possession: two Hemomancy and one Bellua." He opened his hands, revealing two vibrant crimson shards implanted in his wrists and then bared the hollow of his throat and a third black shard.

Adrian leaned forward for a better look and heard Noir murmur something. She glanced back. "What was that?"

"Nothing, don't pay any attention to me."

She shrugged and resumed her inspection of the Terian Shards. Now that she knew what they were, Adrian understood why she smelled different Hydes in Solomon. Two of the new scents were identical, probably the Hemomancy shards, and the third reeked of violence: a Bellua Hyde for strength and endurance. Moreover, now that she knew it was there, Adrian could feel Solomon's increased power. The man could probably crush a rock with his bare hand. She leaned back, musing to herself. *No wonder people fought over them.*

"Bailey's waiting in the armory with your Shards; equip yourself immediately, this war begins the instant Grim get his permit, so we have to be ready. Elise and Temaria have your troop assignments."

The officers assented and migrated toward the armory. Adrian trailed them, striding ahead of Noir in her eagerness to see more of the Terian Shards.

She knew that the Terians, those who made the Shards, were themselves the artifice of some Tyrant, and that their Shards had defied every attempt at replication and understanding. Only the Terians knew their secret. The only information anybody had managed to uncover was that Terian Shards derived from Hydes.

They reached the armory and the officers filed in with the exception of Noir, who leaned against the entrance and crossed his arms with a twitching scowl. Adrian stopped as well, hammered by the scent of the Plague's corruption the moment she crossed the threshold.

"Stink, don't they?"

She retreated, one hand clamped to her nose and her enthusiasm wilting. "Dark Father, why is it so thick? Proctor Doll's stunk, but nothing like this."

"There's more here."

"You don't seem to like them very much."

"Those damn things have started more than one war, and I mean real wars involving Tyrants."

"So you don't like them?"

"No, I don't like them, just as I didn't like the bastard that created them."

"Past tense bastard? What happened to him?"

"The short version is that Terra Carrion started preying on the cities to make his Shards, and, well, the Tyrants back then didn't like him taking their subjects, so they split him into seven or eight pieces and burned him."

"Were you there? When they um ... diced him up."

"No, I was busy elsewhere. My brother stuck around though, even had a little something to do with the dicing." Noir gave her a savage smile.

"Why did Terra Carrion's poaching bother them? Couldn't they just resurrect whoever he killed?"

"That's the thing; they couldn't. Whomever the Terians butchered for Shards died permanently."

"So I guess it's something of a tender subject for humans?"

"Tender?" He gestured at the visibly interested officers. "Does that look tender? No, the Terian Shards are just another source of power and everybody always wants to acquire more. They're one of the few things that'll convince somebody to travel between cities."

"What happened to the Terians?"

"They're still alive out there in the wilds, probably waiting for their god to reawaken." He gestured at the officers. "Go on, they're about to get started."

She returned his nod, marshalled herself and ventured into the stench, breathing through her mouth. The officers had gathered around Bailey Utter and now waited as he flipped through a clipboard and referenced it against a series of pouches on his belt.

After an extensive period, Bailey extended his hand toward Dorian. "I'm to entrust Lieutenant Rias Dorian with three Terian Shards, one of Pathomancy and two Variatur." He deposited them in Dorian's waiting hand. "Be careful, the initial bonding is unpleasant."

Rias Dorian promptly squeezed a Shard into either palm and planted the third into his brow. Nothing changed initially, then he doubled over—retching—with one hand pressed into his gut and the other clawing at his brow.

Adrian felt the corruption in his veins stir, swelling up and thickening as the Terian Shards took root. She retreated, one hand pressed over her mouth and nose as the other grasped a nearby rack of armaments.

The initial surge of corruption dissipated as quickly as it appeared. It never truly abated, however, and when Rias Dorian straightened, everyone could see the jagged, black veins spreading across his eyes.

He looked down at his throbbing hands, a slow wolfish grin spreading his lips. "Yes, this is power! You have to feel it!" He grabbed a Shadowsteel winder from a nearby table and crushed it with a single hand. He giggled and threw the disfigured winder aside.

Bailey Utter worked his meticulous way through the impatient officers, bestowing upon each of them one or two Terian Shards. Ultimately, he arrived at Noir and stepped from the tight circle with three perfect black diamonds nestled in his palm. "For Lieutenant

Noir I have three Caelus Shards."

Adrian spun toward Bailey Utter, a reaction reflected by everyone in the room, except Noir. *A Caelus Hyde? Dark Father, who would be crazy enough to fight a Caelus Hyde?* She only knew the most basic laws governing Hydes, but even she recognized the danger a Caelus Hyde represented.

The Bellua Hyde favored massive, physically destructive bodies while a Variatur Hyde tended toward small, unusual creatures. The Conficta Hyde's were those that pathomancers had mutated. Caelus Hydes were the alpha predators of the wild, a race with such destructive potential that they were always killed permanently for the destruction they inflicted during the night.

Noir pushed off the doorframe and picked up one of the Shards. He examined it for a second and then tossed it back onto the pile.

Bailey Utter frowned. "Have you no desire for the Shards?"

"I have no need of borrowed power; save your crutches for the crippled." He strode from the room, heedless of the shocked stares hounding his steps.

Eventually, Rias Dorian managed to shift his attention back to Bailey Utter. "So who is to receive his Shards?"

"None of you." Bailey returned the Terian Shards to their pouch. "Proctor Doll specified that if Lieutenant Noir refused his Shards, they would be returned to the vault."

Corporal Valerian blinked out of her shock. "But why?"

"Because he feared their corruption would overwhelm you, even those who possess Evolved blood."

Rias Dorian opened his mouth to protest further, but Gregorio interjected. "No, Lieutenant, if this is the will of Proctor Doll, then we must follow it. There is no use in arguing, and we all have other obligations—namely, the war."

A soldier burst into the armory, almost crashing into one of the racks. He caught himself and, gasping, spoke, "Grim soldiers ... just seen ... across the boundary."

"What?" Valerian gawped. "The permit can't have been issued yet! They just requested it yesterday! That's like revolting against

Loc–"

"Forget about it," Rias barked, "we don't have time for this. Get your soldiers and get them moving. We can't let him harm the district." The officers spirited out, screaming commands and calling the soldiers to arms.

Adrian squeezed herself into a corner and then waited as a flood of soldiers streamed in and out of the armory, racing to equip themselves before dashing out into the city. It lasted several minutes and when it finally ended barely a man remained in the Dollhouse.

Moving hesitantly for fear of being crushed by another stampede, she ascended the main stair and knocked on Solomon's office. He gave a murmured admittance and she entered to see him hunched over a basin on his desk, a stream of blood flowing into it from his wrist. He smiled at her entrance, and greeted her brothers with a nod. "Hello, Adrian, have a seat. You too, Eera, Jaysis."

She took the seat in front of him and leaned onto his desk, inspecting the bowl. "What are you doing?"

"Divination." He twisted his hand as the skin crawled back over his slit wrist. "I requested some blood from my officers so I could observe them during the conflict."

"Even Noir?"

"Yes, but he refused with his usual candor. We'll have to rely on those butterflies he has stalking you." Solomon tapped the bowl with his wrist, knocking off the last drop. The blood rippled and an image formed. She saw Corporal Valerian rushing through the streets with a blade at her hip and a rack of pistols across her chest. The image changed, flicking through the various officers. After a few rotations, Solomon Doll nodded to himself and settled back. "There we are."

Adrian looked deeper into the blood and watched the war unfold...

At the Resuscitation outpost

Gregorio Taim crouched over a dead soldier with a pair of hemomancers hovering to either side and a mound of waiting corpses ahead of him. He barked something inaudible as bullets whizzed by and then hunched over the dead soldier. He ducked further behind the stacked corpses and flung the cadaver by its leg onto the nearest mound. More bullets whipped by overhead, ricocheting off the cobbles and smashing into bodies.

Green energy snaked down Gregorio's arms as he slammed his hands onto the cadaver, causing it to tremble. The hemomancers knelt beside him, pressing their hands alongside his with a pulse of red energy. The corpse quivered again and then jolted awake, his injuries healing and his body pulsing with death energy.

The soldier shook himself, nodded at the three Adepts in gratitude, grabbed a nearby rifle, and dashed to a nearby wall.

Gregorio barked another command, and the hemomancers dragged another corpse forward. Meanwhile, the man they had just resurrected jerked in a hail of bullets and crumpled. Behind them, another group of Doll soldiers crawled into view, dragging a cart laden with dead.

Somewhere in the Grim District

Corporal Valerian dove behind an overturned table, a pistol clutched in each hand and a wild grin splitting her features. Bullets ricocheted off the table as she smashed both pistols against her belt, locking in new winders. They came to life whistling, warning her this was their final charge. She just started ramming down bullets.

Two dozen soldiers in white surrounded her, crouched behind objects or around corners as they rushed through the loading and firing of pistols and rifles. One knelt beside her, shouting into her ear as he loaded his own rifle. She nodded and, still grinning, emerged from behind the table with both pistols leveled. Her arms lurched as the pistols discharged, and two men in violet crumpled across the street.

A bullet struck the man beside her, flinging him to the ground. She grinned wider and flung her pistols aside, her skin flushing unnaturally crimson as she activated her Hemomancy. The man arched beside her, blood gushing from his shoulder and streaming across the ground. It coiled up her legs and burrowed into her skin.

She straightened, her blade screeching free of its sheath, and vaulted over the makeshift barricade. A hail of bullets struck her, but she just righted herself and charged, her body ejecting the bullets as it healed.

At the Dollhouse Vaults

Hierophant breathed. In and out, and with every exhale he squeezed the trigger of his rifle, killing one of Grim's soldiers. Most of the violet soldiers cowered behind whatever cover they could find in Solomon Doll's meticulously clean streets. Hierophant's own soldiers crouched beside him at the entrance, a wall of overturned tables erected before them. He exhaled again and another violet soldier fell across the road.

One of Hierophant's soldiers slunk over to him, crawling over the tangled limbs of his dead fellows. He spoke inaudibly, gesturing at the flare gun hanging from Hierophant's side and motioning between the tightly massed Grim soldiers firing on them and the sky. Hierophant shook his head and leveled his rifle again, his words echoing clearly from the scrying bowl, "Our deaths do not matter, we can be revived." He fired again, killing another foe. The soldier beside him cursed and crawled back to his position.

A quiver pulsed through the Grim soldiers as they marshaled themselves and charged. They managed to cross half the distance separating them from Hierophant's troops before the ground erupted, flinging bodies, shrapnel, and acid in all directions.

Hierophant fired again on the routing soldiers, killing his fourth consecutive officer. He dropped behind the barricade, discarding the exhausted winder. He tapped something on the side of his arm and again his voice rang out clearly, "Proctor, you should know that not one of Grim's major officers have presented themselves. The highest ranked official I've seen is an ungifted corporal whose sole purpose seemed to be managing their troops."

Across the way, more troops in violet arrived...

Outside the Grim Vaults

Secreted in the shadowed entry of a skyscraper, Rias Dorian watched Grim's soldiers march past, their attention focused entirely upon one another. He snorted, his face contorting with contempt.

The quiet, buzzing mist around him hissed, evaporating in the sun. He flicked his hand open, expelling another burst of muddy green haze.

He slipped out from the entry way and crept along the building to its opposite side. There he dispelled his concealing miasma and entered one of the skyscraper's bottom rooms. His soldiers stood at the entrance, grabbing their weapons as they did so. One approached and asked him something.

Rias gave a dismissive wave. "Of course I did. I wouldn't have returned otherwise." He faced his assembled soldiers. "Listen close, the Grim Vaults are well-guarded but also vulnerable. The guards think themselves safe, surrounded by a small army and stationed far from the front lines." He swept a gaze over his troops. "I will use Pathomancy to conceal our approach, but this will also drain some of your strength. Once we are in position, we will engage with the Plague-grenades I prepared, so fasten your masks appropriately." He raised his own mask, and they responded in kind, almost causing the air to wilt beneath the scent of the herbs stuffed in their masks. He nodded. "Good, now Proctor Grim has assigned two Adept sergeants to guard his Vaults. You are not to engage them under any circumstance." They nodded. "Good, now let's see if you can do this without screwing up."

Somewhere near the Grim and Doll border

Silas June stalked along the piping over a street, twisting through labyrinthine struts and boiling steam. A platoon of Grim's soldiers slunk along below him, a dozen in number with a full pathomancer sergeant at their head.

Arriving at an intersection, the Grim soldiers paused to consult a map, and Silas June struck. He dropped into the midst of them, his skin shifting hues and texture to match whatever was behind it, rendering him nigh invisible. Grim's soldiers screamed and flailed, injuring one another in their panic. He ripped through them with poisoned knives, and in that confusion his platoon followed, betrayed only by the sound of blades puncturing flesh.

After finishing, they stripped Grim's soldiers of their coats and donned them. Then, guised in violet, he and his stalkers set out to find their next quarry…

The door to Solomon Doll's office burst open, unveiling a gasping soldier in white. "Proctor … Grim's here … outside the Dollhouse. You need to call the troops back … we don't have enough."

Chapter Seventeen

Adepts, however monstrous or beautiful, are entirely human. For Hemomancers that is less certain. Their very blood is different, it doesn't decay; it's more efficient, more unnatural. Hemomancers never fall ill, heal faster, and most need less blood to survive. Also, the more powerful the Hemomancer, the more exaggerated the effect.

One of a Hemomancers more useful attributes is that their blood is compatible with all others. However, if they do not consciously alter the nature of their blood, it will not assimilate with its new host. The Hemomancer will then be able to (at any time) reclaim it or turn it against the new host. One tyrant was said to have controlled her city by exchanging the blood of its inhabitants with her own.

Most Hemomancers have the ability to manipulate the warmth of their blood, cooling it or warming it to the point of melting skin. Others can freely mutate its chemical nature. Combined, they enable the creation of fire.

Unsanctioned War

"You need to leave," Solomon barked as he bounded down the main stairs, "take the Undercity route and get out of here."

"She can't, sir," the messenger gasped, almost tumbling as he missed a step. "Grim has soldiers down there. We tried to sneak a messenger out to call for help, and she was immediately gunned down."

"Damn! How did they get past our sentries? We should have seen them coming an hour off."

"I don't know, sir. And the energy signals didn't go off either."

"Blood in the well! Recall the troops anyway you can, this plan doesn't work unless they converge. Adrian, stay away from the fighting, I'm not going to tell your mother and father you died." He burst from the Dollhouse with a crash and sprinted up to the street. Adrian rushed after him.

A wall of crimson barricades lined the street outside, still gleaming with the luster of new Hemomancy. He hurried through them, climbing three distinct barriers before vaulting down to the open road. The few soldiers they had kept to guard the Dollhouse followed, most assembling on the final barricade while the substitute unranked officers dropped behind him.

Grim waited just past the fortifications, his soldiers arrayed in neat violet ranks, their faces impassive where his smirked. He advanced as Solomon emerged and flung two corpses at his feet, Gregorio and Hierophant. "I believe these are yours."

Solomon Doll spared them a glance before refocusing on Grim. "What is the purpose of this war, Grim? What prize do you seek? Even if you are victorious, Lock-And-Key will never grant you control of this district. You'll be lucky if she doesn't kill you for starting an unsanctioned war."

"And that's where you're wrong, Doll…," Grim purred Solomon's name, savoring it. "I've made a deal and it won't be long before I own more than just your district."

"With whom, Grim? What devil did you invite here?"

Grim laughed. "Now, now; you can't expect me to just spill my secrets, Doll, least of all to you." He kicked Hierophant's leg. "This is a courtesy call. I'm here to return some misplaced goods and give warning: I intend to burn your people when I'm done crushing you; it'll make the succession easier." A susurration of unease passed through Solomon's troops.

"You would deliberately end the lives of soldiers who only acted to uphold their oaths?"

"I am a man of my word."

"Damn it, Grim, this isn't how we fight wars!"

"Oh, come now, that wouldn't be much of a war, would it?" He began to retreat, then paused. "I should mention one last thing: anyone who leaves now or brings me the undertaker won't burn afterward." The murmuring soldiers stilled, caught between their oaths, his threat, and his promise.

Adrian watched all of this transpire from behind the outermost barricade. She could see the men in white shuffling and considering the open streets on either side. Her brothers waited beside her, Eera with his arms braced atop a barricade spike and Jaysis reclining against the barricade, carving a hunk of wood. He dusted aside a pile of wood shavings and motioned toward the soldiers in white. "If you don't act, sister, your Dollhouse will start losing troops, and our kin are busy besieging Grim's stronghold." He spoke calmly, disinterestedly, as if it had never occurred to him that she was powerless to affect the outcome.

Adrian forced her clenched hands to loosen. "I know."

"Then why do you not act? Is their loyalty beyond reproach? Do you balk from coercing them down a road they wish to avoid? Or do you hope someone else will do it?"

She shook her head. "Grim outnumbers us too much; we can't win an open engagement. We need a plan, something to overcome their advantage." She fiddled her pistol, her mind racing.

Eera, meanwhile, glanced toward Solomon. "So that's why your Proctor is parleying; he's buying you time to escape or devise a solution. Most probably he already has one; you just have to find it."

Yes, but how? I'm not Solomon, how do I know what he's thinking? Adrian pushed her emotions aside and scanned the Dollhouse for anything that might have caught Solomon's eye. It took her a moment, but she saw them: the *Almas*. They sat perched on every available surface in silent witness, numbering more than she had ever seen.

She dithered for a split-second longer, wondering if this was Solomon's intent, then moved to the nearest butterfly. "Please find Noir and tell him he's needed back at the Dollhouse." In the end, it didn't matter what Solomon wanted, this might save them, so she had to try.

Her message sent, she spun, drew her pistol and fired.

Her gunshot pierced the misted air, killing the rising murmurs, and split Grim's head.

The Proctor stumbled back, straightened, and looked up at her, his features distorting with rage. Adrian met his stare with undertaker detachment, refusing to cower.

He raised a hand, the flesh of his brow spitting the bullet into his waiting palm. "Kill them all." A cacophonous roar answered his command and chaos engulfed her.

Adrian ducked behind the barricade as a torrent of men and bullets surged by overhead. Soldiers in white landed all around her, their guns screaming and spitting steel. She grunted as one man climbed over the barricade and stumbled into her. He shoved off her with a curse, haphazardly firing his pistol at Grim's soldiers just before a bullet struck him.

He crumpled off the barricade, and she assumed his place, blood spraying into her face from either side as she aimed and fired. The pistol kicked in her hand and gave a sharp click, oddly distinct amidst the clamor. She threw it aside and grabbed another loaded one from a dead man's holster.

A litany of explosions shook the barricade, stemming both from Grim and Solomon's forces. She tasted blood in her mouth from where she had bit her tongue and spat it out. She scrambled to the side, crawling over a pair of writhing men, to reach her brothers.

"Well, aren't you going to help?"

Jaysis glanced at her coolly as a man in violet collapsed across from him. "And what exactly does it look like we're doing?"

She ducked as bullets peppered the barricade around her. "Sorry, I thought you were just standing there."

"A reasonable mistake," Eera replied, his Scythe diving at another of Grim's soldiers without him having to shift a muscle. Unaffected by the devastation raging around them, his gaze scaled the opposing skyscrapers. "How much we expend ourselves should not be your primary concern, though. There is something far more worthy of your attention above us."

Adrian followed his gaze and started. The city's Proctors observed the conflict from the overhead pipelines, attended by only their lieutenants: eighteen men and women dressed in coats of nine different colors.

Adrian slowly lowered her gun, a shiver coursing up her spine.

Eera continued softly, "They've come to bear witness and to judge the victor's power, and perhaps intervene if they deem their action warranted." Elis Madra wore orange, Syrian Fell crimson, Kore Byren black, and all the others their designated colors. She shivered again; alone they were powerful, together they rivaled a Tyrant. They could obliterate everything here if they so wished, erase the war and all its participants in the space of seconds.

Inevitably, Adrian followed their gazes down to the center of the battlefield where Solomon Doll and Grim faced off in a sea of writhing blood and wasted bullets. Even now, soldiers from both sides continued firing on them, as if they could achieve a different result through sheer persistence. Neither Proctor paid them any heed.

Grim advanced, slowly at first but gradually building momentum into a howling charge. Solomon wove aside, blood streaming to his hands from the ground and then plunging into the corpses around him.

The corpses spasmed and stood, their joints popping, their veins swelling crimson and their injuries clotting. Solomon flicked the strands, and his hemomantic puppets hurled themselves at Grim, who laughed gleefully and swept them aside.

Solomon spat a profanity and new tendrils of blood fountained from his fingertips, latching into the nearest hosts and dragging them back to their feet. Some of the bodies in violet coats weren't even fully dead yet. Most of Doll's appropriated soldiers charged Grim immediately, heedless of the hailing bullets; but two dawdled, their belts decorated with the regalia of officers.

Grim launched himself at Solomon, his form bloating as streams of blood coiled up his body and soaked into his skin. He swept at the puppet soldiers in his way, but they evaded his onslaught with unnatural agility and impossible contortions. He cursed and plowed forward. The puppets charged his back, hacking and slashing with Shadowsteel blades.

Grim roared and two Terian Shards woke upon his brow, blackening the veins on his face. He leapt skyward, scattering the puppets like cotton dolls, and dove at Solomon from three stories of height.

Solomon lunged aside, his own Shard waking upon his brow, but a burst of formless crimson energy from Grim's hand yanked them together. Grim's scythe carved upward to meet him, and Solomon reeled back, his body rent across from shoulder to hip. Before the cut even finished, blood swam up his legs and into the wound.

Righting himself, Solomon retaliated, smashing Grim's breast with an open palm. The two of them ricocheted apart: Solomon's arm shattered up to his shoulder, and blood spewing from the cavity in Grim's chest. Solomon slammed into the first barricade and shoved off with little additional damage. Grim hit the ground with a crunch and kept moving, his body twisting over itself and crashing against the ground until it finally came to rest in a distorted heap. Without pause, Grim's body gave a meaty throb and contorted back into shape. He stood, laughing, and advanced.

Solomon flicked his hand and one of the violet-coated officers he acquired earlier finally acted. The man raised his arms with mumbled words, commanding the shadows to coil around Grim and cinch tight, flinging him to the ground as they sprouted additional limbs which expanded into walls.

Grim snapped the bindings and surged to his feet, ramming against the walls of his prison and then battering them with his fists. A prison wall warped and then ruptured as his hand cleaved through it. The second Doll-controlled officer moved, lurching forward to impale Grim with a dozen Shadow spears that effortlessly traversed the box.

Grim roared, his body lurching as spear after spear struck him and then imploded. He strained against his prison, three Terian Shards now gleaming on his brow. Snarling, he pried the cage open. The walls simply reformed and shrunk, compressing him.

Solomon Doll spat more blood and closed both hands into a fist. The last two of his Terian Shards burst into life and began pumping corruption into his veins.

Another Shard woke in Grim's brow, and he pushed against the shrinking prison, ignoring the constant, vicious destruction and reconstruction of his body.

Solomon hissed as bullets ravaged through his flesh and stumbled forward, his body twisting and contorting as he fought with the corruption inside of him.

Slowly, painfully, the shadow prison shrunk again, inching toward Grim's obliteration. Then it exploded. Pieces of hardened shadows raked the courtyard, impaling soldiers on both sides. The two Doll-controlled officers collapsed, and a black, writhing, miasma billowed out from the wreckage, eating at the dead in its path.

Adrian gagged and recoiled, fighting the urge to vomit. She heard the screams as men were caught in the miasma and devoured by it, their skin melted by Grim's unleashed corruption.

She managed to swallow the bile in her throat and peeked over the barricade. There, crouched at the center of his dissipating miasma, loomed Proctor Grim: a towering, black-furred hare with clawed hands and a carnivorous maw. He stepped forward, brushing aside the lingering miasma with a sweep of his elongated scythe. His form pulsed with crimson energy and his eyes burned with it.

Solomon Doll retreated, all three of his Terian Shards seething in response to the five glowering on Grim's monstrous brow. A throb pulsed through the blood on the battlefield. Solomon raised his hands, his fingers splayed.

A thousand tendrils of blood pulled themselves off the ground and latched onto the first barricade. They snapped taut, held for a second, and then broke, removing massive chunks of the barricade as they went. The chunks swirled and crashed together, grinding into a vaguely humanoid form.

Solomon's lips curled away from bared teeth, and his Terian Shards burst into doubled brilliance, sending a tide of black corruption to every corner of his flesh. His ramshackle creation smashed to the ground and stood. The colossus shook itself, disentangling its limbs from Solomon's countless puppet strings, and shuffled toward Grim.

Grim howled and dove through the air with a reaping slash. The Shadowsteel of his scythe, glowing crimson with augmentative Hemomancy, sheared through Solomon Doll's puppet, dismembering an arm.

The goliath spun and struck at Grim, moving with surprising dexterity, but Grim's flashing scythe severed its striking arm. Without pause, Grim pivoted and lunged at Solomon, his form flooded with the borrowed power and corruption of the Terian Shards. The goliath collapsed behind him, eroded by the corruption his Hyde oozed.

Solomon Doll cursed and flicked his hands, releasing his own Hyde in a burst of noxious fumes.

His mortal flesh peeled away, crumbling to ash as crimson energy poured free of his discarded skin. He swelled before Grim, his form billowing out like gas before tightening into a form of roiling mist.

Solomon Doll levitated in motionless reassertion, the long ethereal fingers that adorned his many hands slowly solidifying into a bone-like substance. The Terian Shards remained in his brow, seething with volatile energy.

Tendrils shot from Doll's raised arms diving, not into the dead, but into Grim's living soldiers. The soldiers arched and screamed, their pupils utterly effaced by blood. A heartbeat of breathless horror passed, and then the possessed soldiers devolved into the thrall of their Hydes.

They swarmed Grim with all of the cursed strength coursing through their veins. He slaughtered them with impunity, crushing them underfoot, eviscerating with his scythe and impaling with his free hand. One, he threw at Solomon Doll, but the howling beast simply passed through Solomon's insubstantial form and crashed against the wall behind him.

But for every foe Grim obliterated, Solomon simply procured a new host in violet. Thus, by dint of sheer numbers alone, Grim's healing slowed. His injuries no longer healed instantly, they stayed open for split-seconds and heartbeats. That was all Solomon needed. One of his threads latched onto Grim, burrowing into a bullet hole even as it healed.

Grim instantly whirled toward Solomon and lunged, but a mob of his own soldiers converged on him. He shrieked and pummeled them, scattering their corpses with thoughtless desperation. Their assault never faltered. They clung and struck at him, slowing his advance as more of Solomon's tendrils wormed into his injuries. Soon, he stood wreathed in crimson veins.

A moment passed and the strings throbbed once in perfect unison. Grim reeled back with a howl and lunged forward again, scattering his possessed soldiers. The threads pulsed again, siphoning blood from Grim, harvesting his power and funneling it into Solomon.

Grim smashed through the final rabble clustered around him and charged forward. He flung his scythe at Solomon, the deadly weapon spinning end over end. It passed through Solomon without so much as a whisper and sheathed itself in the barricade behind him.

Solomon flicked his hands and the strings dug deeper into Grim. Grim slowed, his strides growing heavy with exhaustion.

He stumbled to Solomon and straightened with an effort, glaring down at Solomon Doll's ghostly form with bared teeth. Solomon levitated until their eyes met.

Grim struck, a sixth, damning Terian Shard flaring into life upon his brow. His claws lashed out, their tips flaring crimson with flecks of his own blood—blood that now coursed through Solomon's spectral veins.

Solomon lurched back with a cry, the blood he had siphoned erupting from where Grim struck him. Grim struck again, shearing through Solomon's threads and flinging him to the earth as diaphanous energy poured from his injuries. They grappled, but in their released Hydes, Grim possessed far greater physical strength and some influence over Solomon through his siphoned blood. He dealt injury after injury to Solomon Doll. Yet, these countless wounds were a superficial advantage; the true contest lay in their Hemomancy. Both had open injuries and both sought to bleed their opponent dry, robbing him of his strength and, far more importantly, his ability to regenerate. Despite that, and no matter Solomon Doll's skill as a hemomancer, he could not surmount the power of six Terian Shards.

Adrian cried out as she saw this, recognizing the end. She wanted to look away from Solomon Doll's last futile struggles but could not. She just stood there atop the barricade, watching in horror as Solomon's life guttered out, his form reverting to its old, corporeal self.

High above all of it, the other Proctors bowed once and left.

Grim pushed himself off the ground and faced the remaining soldiers in white. Towering three times the height of a normal man, he advanced and tore his scythe free of the barricade as he mounted it. What remained of Solomon's forces fled, but they could not escape Grim.

One of Adrian's brothers grabbed her collar and pulled her aside, dragging her from the approaching massacre. Soldiers in white and purple swarmed all around them, most locked in combat but many on both sides fleeing Grim's advance. Some of the soldiers attempted to impede their flight, but her brother's Scythes flashed in the deepening crimson of the rising Blood Moon.

Dusk was already falling, even though the day was merely hours old. She could feel the Blood Moon's corruption and madness mounting all around her. It affected everyone to some extent, though no one had suffered through a transformation yet. Hemomancers would suffer the most; this Moon augmented both their power and their madness, for they were the ones who made it. All four moons came from the Adepts: the Blood Moon from the hemomancers, the Bone Moon from the necromancers, the Curse Moon from the pathomancers, and the Dark Moon from the shadowmancers—although, no one had claimed to be its architect.

Adrian dashed into an alley, nausea twisting her gut into knots. She wanted to scream with rage, but her anger was only an ember when faced with her despair. The Dollhouse had lost. No one had the power or inclination to challenge that outcome, not on a Blood Moon with Grim in the full sway of his Hyde.

Adrian yanked herself from her brothers' grip with a cry of frustration and pounded the wall. They stopped a few feet ahead and watched her sag. She ground her fists into the Shadowsteel, hating her impotence but unable to refute the absolute truth of her powerlessness. Even if she had a Scythe, the three of them together couldn't defeat a Proctor, much less a Proctor who had released his Hyde.

She pushed off the wall, forcing herself to accept that she could do nothing but flee. It was then that she saw it: a single, silken butterfly circling overhead. She spun and there was Noir.

His chest rose and fell, exhaling a long, slow breath. "And to think I thought Grim was a fool to test Doll."

She stumbled forward, pointing behind her with a ragged plea, "Help them!"

"Why? They do not need a hero, they need a Tyrant, and Lock-And-Key is in no position to help them."

He turned away, but she dashed forward and around him to press one trembling hand against his chest. "Please, they'll die if you don't." Beneath her hand, the shadows that always clung to his person coiled around her fingers. Even as she said this, something clicked in the back of her mind, a suppressed doubt that she couldn't quite make sense of yet.

He paused at her touch, brows lowering into the hint of a scowl. "Everyone dies; you should get used to it. Twiddle your thumbs for a day, and they'll be back tomorrow morning."

She shook her head. "No! I mean they're going to die for real! Permanently—" But then she understood. She could not have said why it struck in that moment, only that it did. Her words died and she stepped slowly back, her hands falling to her sides. "You're the murderer." His evident power, his Shadowmancy, his knowledge of a dead language, his overarching hubris, and a hundred other small things that she couldn't really name. There was no way someone with his particular attributes could live in Umbras, or anywhere civilized, without being noticed. That meant he came from outside.

Her brothers dove at him, their Scythes moving in perfect silence. She heard the crunch as formless shadows caught and killed them.

"Very clever, Adrian, though I'm not surprised you figured it out first."

"Are you going to kill me?"

"Are you going to tell the Proctors who I am?" She gave no answer and he shrugged. "Then you don't leave me much choice."

She shuddered one last time and then forced herself to look at him. "You're a murderer."

He shook his head again, neither apologizing nor reprimanding. "I committed no crime; their lives were mine to do with as I pleased."

"No, they were free men. Whatever their crime, they had the right to be judged."

"They forswore such things as freedom when they stepped into Umbras, that is the law of Tyrants."

"This is Lock-And-Key's city, not yours!"

He snarled, "I made Lock-And-Key, and I made this city. They are mine to keep or to destroy as I wish."

She slowly collapsed to her knees, shaking her head in helpless denial. "It's impossible..."

"I will tell you why I killed those people; you deserve that much at least." He took a long breath and began, "I was born to a family of fanatic psychopaths who worshiped one of the old religions. They lived by its tenets, breathed its verses, and spat its lies without cease. Except it was an old-world religion and thus fragmented. But no matter, they filled in the blanks themselves. They were, after all, devoted followers and god would speak through them, ensuring they uttered his word perfectly."

As he spoke, Noir made lazy gestures with one hand, seeming almost amused by the beliefs of country bumpkins. "That was their world, and if something did not align with their precious beliefs, be it man or animal, that 'thing' must belong to the devil and therefore did not belong in the world. The only good thing that came out of that family was my brother." True, raw pain woke in his eyes, thickening his words ever so slightly. "He was younger by ten whole minutes, determined to follow wherever I went and the only person I ever loved. He did not belong in that house, neither of us did, but he even less so than I.

"It wasn't long before we learned to fear our parents and their bible; a discovery soon reinforced by the manifestation of our gifts. You can imagine how our parents would have reacted if they discovered our peculiarities, what would happen if they learned we were gifted." He snorted. "We managed to conceal our power for twelve years, but large secrets love the light. They found out and just like that we became witches, devil-worshipers, the spawn of Satan." His lips curled further, his eyes darkening but never quite losing the pain. "So I did what was required so my brother wouldn't have to.

"Advance four hundred years and a man approaches us, a sniveling little worm who wants to accompany us through the wilds. Being gods among men, we did not fear him; so we let him accompany us. But the man was a liar and led us into a trap. Fire rained down from the heavens, and the ground exploded beneath our feet. Fire and confusion became the entirety of my world. But, the true hell only came after, because I survived and my brother did not.

"They took his knucklebones, eyes, and skull; anything they could use to harvest the lingering shreds of his power. I have no doubt they reserved the more ... powerful pieces for themselves, but the little ones, the shards of bone or the odd tooth, these they sold to anyone with a desire for power. Tyrants, I've no doubt, paid especially well.

"There were four of them; Alucard, Brigadier, Constantine, and Lazarus, which you'll notice are the names of the murdered. All except one.

The last name stirred her memory, but she paid it no heed, she just looked at Noir, her eyes slowly brimming with tears. She stumbled forward, pleading in a choked voice, "Please, save them, I beg you. They are your people, your scions, please–" A sob interrupted her words and she broke down fully. "I don't want them to die! I don't want Umbras to change." Her head fell into her hands and she sobbed.

A moment passed and she felt his hand atop her head. "All right, I'll take care of them."

She looked up, making fists as she fought through her tears and a crumbling world. She managed to force words out of her tightening throat, hard mistrustful words, "You promise?"

He looked down at her, his steel eyes surprisingly soft as his free hand touched the skin above her heart. "Yeah, I promise." There was a flash of pain and then only darkness.

Chapter Eighteen

No Good Deed

~ There are some memories that never fade; moments, choices, and events that define or utterly rewrite the course of an existence. Noir had his share. The days he and Alighieri developed their gifts; the hour he murdered their parents before they could burn Alighieri for his gifts; the years he spent tortured and enslaved to Harridan Morr; and the moment Apollyon first addressed him beneath the boughs of Seelie's Forest... ~

A soft voice, almost mewling despite its burly depth, intruded on Noir's concentration, "Hello, are you the one they call Noir? Can I trouble you?"

He turned from the table of shifting, interwoven roots and glared at his addresser. "Who are you?"

The man quailed, shivers visibly touring the course of his body as he shrunk into an alcove of tree roots. "M– ... my name is Apollyon, sir. I beg of you, hear me out!"

"No. Leave me alone." He returned his attention to the table where an intricate, quarter-drawn map lay. He delicately grasped the waiting quill and leaned in close to blow. The quill's dry tip abruptly glistened with Shadow ink, and he touched it to the aged paper, adding roots to an incomplete mountain.

He felt the nuisance of a man stumble forward, his advance disturbing the fine shadowmantic particles Noir always kept orbiting about himself.

"Pl-please, sir." The man's voice grated on his concentration, but Noir ignored him. "Please, sir!" The man reached out, fully intent on grasping Noir's sleeve–

"I wouldn't do that if I were you." Alighieri's ebullient, musical voice sounded from above, drawing their attention to where he reclined in the boughs of a tree. "My brother has a very loose association with patience and mercy; they like to wave at each other from across the street."

The man, Apollyon, snatched his hand back and retreated hastily. His back foot caught on a root, upending him into a sprawling mess on the prevalent azure moss, startling up a storm of white and emerald Weir-Lights, their tinkling laughter barely more than a whisper. "What do you mean? Is he deranged? Is he safe? Shouldn't he be restrained?"

Alighieri laughed. "Due to unavoidable coincidences, I'm afraid we have to endure his little peculiarities." He dropped down and crouched beside Apollyon. "No need to worry though, he's mostly safe, just don't get handsy and try to avoid ruining whatever project he's working on; the maps in particular."

"Maps?" Apollyon asked it tentatively, but unmistakable excitement colored his tone.

"Yes, maps. Long ago he decided to document the places we've seen and the routes we traveled to get there. He's got pictures also and for some reason he insists on sketching everything by hand." Alighieri looked theatrically to the heavens as if in prayer.

"I draw them by hand because there's no artistry in using Shadowmancy." Noir's quill dissipated into Shadow-debris, and he lifted the map to blow on his latest addition.

"Still, you put too much time and effort in them."

"This from the man who spent two years convincing Legion he was the subject of a cult's worship in Labyrinth, and then another three creating said cult; all so you could laugh at him when he realized they were dedicated to his annihilation."

"That was different. It was for comedy; and trust me, I wasn't the only one laughing. You should try it sometime."

"Why? That's what I have you for." Noir glanced over his shoulder with a half-smile that died when he saw Apollyon. Nonetheless, he set the map aside. "All right, what did you want from me?"

Apollyon scrambled to his knees and clasped his hands in supplication. "Please, is it true that you've been outside? That you've traveled to other cities?"

"We just said as much; are you deaf or just dumb?"

"Neither, sir," Apollyon stammered. "I just wanted to ask if you would take me along with you? To wherever you're going? Please, I'll give anything you like!"

"And why would you want to leave Seelie's Court? Most would kill for admittance."

"Because I can't stand it anymore!" the man wailed. "I hate being eaten every week! You wouldn't know what it's like to have Seelie suck all your blood out and then eat eighty percent of your body every seven days!"

Noir sighed. "You can't even feel anything at that point; she has you so doped up on anesthetics you're barely lucid."

"It doesn't matter! You don't know what it's like to be nothing more than livestock, to only have value as dinner!"

Images of fire and blood flashed through Noir's mind, all set against a background of Harridan Morr's ghoulish ridicule.

Yet, it was Alighieri who spoke, "Trust me, there are worse fates than a day spent satisfying Seelie's lust, or an evening appeasing her appetite."

"I don't care, I want out."

"Then leave," Noir replied.

"I can't go into the Wilds alone!"

"Not our problem."

"I don't care where you take me; I'll go wherever you're going, just take me with you."

"All right, you've made your point," Alighieri said, shooing Apollyon away with his hands. "Now run along while we discuss this between ourselves."

Apollyon gave a final pleading glance before wandering despondently off into the forest. Alighieri waited for him to escape earshot, then seated himself onto a nearby root. "Well, I see no reason he can't tag along and do all the cooking."

"He wouldn't survive a day outside a Tyrant's sphere of influence."

"That's why he's asking you to help him."

"He's asking us."

"Yes, but I don't plan on doing any work, so in reality it's all on you."

"I don't want to babysit a whimpering infant across the Wilds, and I really don't want to petition Seelie for his release."

"Oh, I'll take care of that, she always liked me better anyway."

"That's because you keep pinning everything you do on me."

"True, but that's not the matter at hand."

Noir rolled up the map, asking in a resigned voice, "So you want us to drag his useless ass with us?"

"Yes," Alighieri responded without hesitation, his feet absently kicking. "We're two of the most powerful men in the world, known and unknown. We should be helping people more."

"Helping one straggler cross the Wilds is not going to save the world."

"No, but it's a start."

Noir slid the map into a protective casing and deposited it in a bag. "You should tell him the good news, I guess. Oh, and one other thing"—he raised his hand and a single white Alma descended through the forest to alight upon his fingertips—"this needs recharging."

Alighieri shook his head in mock despair. "You and your incessant paranoia." Nevertheless, he jumped off the root and proceeded to lift the Alma from Noir's hand.

"Just let it go when you're done, it'll find its way to somewhere safe." Noir swung the bag over his shoulder and started to leave, stepping carefully over the flowing roots and moss of Seelie's Forest. He managed only half-a-dozen steps before Apollyon appeared from behind a tree and snagged his sleeve.

"What have you decided? May I accompany you?"

"Enough already!" Noir yanked his arm free. "Yes, you can come with us. But bring your own food."

Apollyon dropped to his knees. "Oh, thank you, sir, you won't regret this! I'll take care of everything, just tell me what you need and I'll acquire it."

"You can start by leaving me alone; come back in a couple hours, or we'll leave without you."

"But won't that mean we're traveling at night?"

"Well, would you rather sleep at night?"

"Of course. I understand." The man dashed a couple of steps away then paused. "Uh ... where are we going."

"To Umbras."

"Won't I need a Black Coin to get in?"

"No, we'll take care of that."

"Oh, thank you, thank you!" The man vanished into the forest, leaving Noir to groan and massage his brow.

Alighieri came up behind him, grinning. "Perky fellow, isn't he?"

"I don't want to talk about it; just make sure to secure his release from Seelie. I don't want her banning us."

"Not like that would really deter you."

"No, but it's nice not having everybody hate me."

"Bah, that's what you have me for." Alighieri sauntered past, humming to himself and winking at Noir.

Roughly seven hours after leaving Seelie's Forest

The beast raged at Noir from where it hung suspended in his grip. Sickly black ichors leaked from cavities gouged down the length of its scabbed torso. Three pairs of splintered antlers crowned its brow and a lashing web of spiked tentacles its back. It bucked in his grip, clawing at him with its talons, gnashing at him with its oversized maw, and stabbing at him with its olive-colored tentacles. Noir absently observed it, theorizing that it—and its various eviscerated kin—had once been a herd of deer, judging from their antlers and general size. Unexpectedly, its tongue stabbed out from its mouth and smashed against his eye. Its bone tip snapped off at the base, but Noir still reflexively crushed its throat and discarded the cadaver.

He turned to where Alighieri lounged on a filth-encrusted stone paying no heed to the swath of dead avians expanding outward before him, all of them bleached white by his Necromancy. A hastily erected dome of black Shadowmancy sheltered Apollyon from the rabid, Plague-infected animals. Noir strode over. "Have you found him yet?"

"Oh, whoever are you talking about?" Alighieri unleashed his most innocent expression on Noir. Noir Just looked at him. Alighieri swung to sit up. "Do you mean to tell me that you believe this ravaging horde is under the influence of some bestial, untamed man? Some horrific, night-ruled savage of the Wilds?" Noir Just looked at him. "Oh, you must be right! There's no other reason for this herd to attack us so idiotically! I mean the wild animals tend to be smarter than that; it's only humans who would have such audacity or, conversely, such stupidity." Noir just looked at him. "Oh fine, he's over there about a hundred yards out."

"Thank you."

"Spoil sport."

A tide of Shadows swelled into the sky, blanketing the location Alighieri had alluded to, and smashed down, blanketing every tree, stone, or creature in the vicinity. A shudder passed through the surviving beasts, and then they fled with a terrified baying.

Alighieri inspected the covered ground for an instant. "Should I go resurrect him?"

"Do it in the morning, he'll just attack us again otherwise. Speaking of which"—Noir bent to grasp one of the deer monsters by its antlers and heft it for Alighieri to observe—"this is one of Seelie's beasts. What did you do?"

"I didn't do anything." Alighieri flashed his most innocent expression again.

"Alighieri…"

"What? I'm telling the truth! I didn't do anything!" The expression became mischievous. "Nothing at all. I never even spoke to her…" He grinned and bounced his eyebrows.

Noir dropped the corpse. "You never told her we were taking one of her subjects, did you?"

"Like I said, nothing."

"What if you had actually pissed her off?"

"That's what I have you for." Alighieri lay back and covered his eyes with a forearm. "Besides, it's not like she could actually challenge either of us." As he shifted around to find the position of best comfort, the rock under him bleached a little further, enough so that tendrils of white crawled into the dirt around his perch.

A knock sounded from the interior of the dome, followed by a muted, echoing voice, "Is it safe? Can I come out now?"

"Oh, yeah…"

The dome dissolved, revealing a rather disheveled Apollyon, who anxiously scratched his head and stole a glance at his surroundings. "Whew, that was close. Is it always like this?"

"For us: no, for you: yes. We don't have trouble unless something big wanders by," Alighieri said. "It's awful; I cannot tell you how many dreams of conquest, terror, and fame we've crushed while on our travels."

Apollyon groaned and clambered to his feet, wiping the dirt from his pants. "Well, should we go?"

"Not yet," Noir said while scraping a shattered tree stump clear of Plague-ridden moss. "We have someone to resurrect come morning."

"Who? Was somebody else assaulted by those creatures?"

"No, we had to kill the pack Alpha, a human of Seelie's Court." Noir sat on the cleared stump.

"Why are you resurrecting it if he's the one who attacked us! He would have killed us and left our bodies to rot! You don't actually intend to spare him?"

"He couldn't have killed us in a thousand years; besides, I'd like to maintain at least somewhat amicable terms with Seelie, and this was more a sign of displeasure than an earnest assault."

"How do you plan on me resurrecting him by the way? You kind of flattened him, and we have no accessible hemomancers."

"I didn't flatten him, merely suffocated him. Any damage he suffered from the blanket's descent will amount to nothing more than a superficial bruising."

Apollyon gaped. "You have that much control over your Shadowmancy?"

Noir shrugged. "What about you? Do you have any gifts?"

"Oh, no, no; I'm a pure third-class citizen, so nothing of note."

Alighieri leaned forward, intrigued. "Third-class?"

"It comes from Black Die and has migrated to most of the other cities. It's a caste system where your status is designated by the strength of your Hyde, your intelligence, and whether or not you're an Adept; basically, it's a means of quantifying your value to society. People with no discernible value are third-class, while those with a powerful Hyde, a gift, or superior intelligence are second-class. First-class are those with a combination of desired traits. Of course these are just designations for common civilians." He beamed. "I know this because I spent years researching the other cities in the hope that I'd be able to visit them one day; in fact, I probably know more about the Seven Cities and their respective Tyrants than you two do!"

"I doubt that." Noir reclined, shadows coiling behind his back to soften the stump's edges. "Your curiosity aside, is there a city you particularly fancy?"

"I want to visit Raikan's Tomb; you know Black Die's city."

"Yeah we know it." Noir glanced upward, judging the hour. "Well, you'd better get some rest; we'll leave while there's still light tomorrow to recuperate the time we lose tonight."

Apollyon shifted down to the moist earth. "What about you? Don't you need to rest?"

"No, and someone needs to keep watch."

"Well, if you insist…," Apollyon trailed off, rolled onto his side and soon fell asleep.

Alighieri waited until the man's soft snores filled the air before addressing Noir with a grin. "Admit it, you're starting to like him."

"Like is a strong word, let's leave it at not detest."

"No matter, I like him."

"Why? He talks incessantly, whines about almost everything, and fails to defend himself from anything."

"And despite all of that, he's out here traveling the Wilds; that takes courage."

"He has us."

"That doesn't matter, he's still out here; just give him a chance, he might surprise you."

"I don't like surprises."

"Yeah, yeah 'people only hide things they don't want found' and all that. Nonetheless, you should loosen up a little, maybe find yourself a lady, or a dog, or something. I'll even help you! Just make one of those transmitter things so you can always hear me, and I'll accompany you everywhere you go to share my wisdom and knowledge; you'll never want for a pick-up line!"

"Cause that's just what I need, your voice jabbering in my head at all hours." Noir stood. "I'm going to grab Seelie's man, you stay here and watch over Apollyon, make sure nothing eats him…"

Roughly twenty-three days since leaving Seelie's Forest

The behemoth rose, shucking earth, boulders, trees, and Hydes from its back. It tore the first of its many corrugated forearms free from the ground and slammed it back down, crushing a tree and hauling another foreleg free. It extended the first of its two heads, a bird-like skull attached to a sinuous neck, toward the overcast skies and screamed. Its second head, boasting numerous small mouths and a host of gargantuan eyes to adorn its vaguely apish shape, swung about to focus on Noir and Alighieri, the latter of whom waved at it. Apollyon, its unintentional disturber, clung desperately to the protrusive black scales that covered its six forelimbs and most of its underside.

Noir dropped his head into his hands. "Does he have to wake every Hyde we come across?"

"Oh buck up, it's only a middling Bellua."

"I know, I know." Noir advanced, shadows coiling beneath his feet as the night throbbed and yielded to his will.

The Bellua hauled its remaining bulk from the earth and straightened to its full height, carrying Apollyon thirty, forty, fifty feet into the air. It spun to confront Noir fully and screamed with both cavernous maws. Noir flung his hand skyward in response, hurling a barrage of lancing shadows. They pummeled its underside with staggering force, causing it to lurch and bellow, but not one pierced its dark scales.

The Bellua righted itself and lunged at Noir, snapping with its bird-head and swinging one of its arms in a wide arch across the ground. Noir leapt, vaulting onto a platform of shadows, which then catapulted him higher into the sky as a churning mass of shadows materialized to deflect the behemoth's stabbing head. Seemingly unfazed, it lashed at him with one of its four, stone-ridged tails. Noir contorted, his arms sweeping wide as shadows lashed the behemoth in a barrage of whips. One of the shadows diverged from the others to wrap about his hand and snatch him from the incoming tail's path, while the others encircled the Bellua from head to foot, ensnaring its arms, tails, and maws in a black web.

Propelled by the vine, Noir spun mid-flight and landed with his feet against the raging behemoth's side, his body parallel to the ground. The shadows clasped his boots, and he expanded his sensory net of shadows. Information inundated his consciousness, besieging him with temperature, noise, taste, visions, and touch. He discarded the unnecessary information, discovered his objective and launched himself from the behemoth's side in pursuit of the plummeting Apollyon. Behind him, the net tightened, strangling the behemoth.

He rocketed toward the screaming Apollyon, reached out and snagged the man's collar in passing. "Stop screaming already, I got you." He shifted his grip, placing Apollyon under his arm and arresting the man's personal momentum just seconds before they landed with a crash. Noir stumbled forward, his feet driving into and through the soft earth as his impetus expended itself. Ultimately, they ground to a halt some hundred feet from where Alighieri cheered loudly.

Noir dumped Apollyon on the ground and seated himself on an uprooted tree. Apollyon scrambled to his feet, still panting. "You saved me!"

"That kind of was the point behind traveling with us."

"But how did you survive the fall? That should have fractured every bone in your body! And you attacked the huge Hyde, how did you know that strangling would kill it?"

"I didn't, I just had to restrain it so Alighieri could kill it." As if on cue, a bitter chill swept across their surroundings, changing their breath to mist and the soft earth white.

Apollyon spun about to gaze upon the sagging behemoth and saw Alighieri standing beside it with his hand upon its bird head. A tide of white color expanded across its skin, granting it a phantasmal aspect.

"I try to avoid killing things when I can, as it tends to inflict irreversible damage to the body; Alighieri's method is much safer."

"Why even bother though? It's not like you're going to save whoever it is; you're not going to convey him to a city. Sparing his life is just … cruel."

"Maybe, but might also be a kindness; we cannot say whether or not this curse will dissipate, or if someone somewhere will discover a means of curing it. In that light, I cannot obliterate souls wantonly."

"But it's in self-defense!"

"Self-defense requires an element of bodily or mental peril; my situation seldom reflects either of those."

"So you just spare everyone that attacks you? Exact no retribution?"

"That about sums it up."

"I can't believe you; all that power and you just let anyone attack you. It shouldn't be like that, you shouldn't let it be like that; you have power, use it! Control what happens to you, force other people to follow you and not the reverse! Just think of all you and your brother could accomplish!"

"And that's just it," Noir said softly, "the lie that the small tell the large, 'ability confers responsibility'. They say power bestows freedom, but let me ask you a question: If a house is burning and there are two men, one who is resistant to fire and one who is not, who enters?"

"The one who could survive the flames of course."

"Then who truly had the power there? The one who could walk through fire, or the weak one who could not?"

"But the man didn't have to enter the house, the other man couldn't force him to do so; your logic is flawed."

"True, but what if there's a hundred men, and only one who's resilient? In that situation, the man has no choice." Apollyon fell silent and Noir smirked. "And that is why I do not strive to control this world: I do not want it; I want to be free of it. And the only way to be free of something is to exist beyond it."

"But you're not free of it! If you were, you would indiscriminately destroy everything that attacked you."

"Freedom from someone else's rules and freedom from your own are two very different things; I don't like killing people, its leaves a bad taste on my tongue, so I don't. This world won't enslave me to its rules."

Roughly thirty-eight days since departing Seelie's Forest

~Noir remembered every step of their journey through the Wilds, every look Apollyon cast, every word he voiced and every lie he attempted or succeeded in evincing. He had recognized some of the man's deceit even in the time of their utterance, but had not challenged him; every man harbored secrets, and he didn't fear Apollyon's. Now, the recollection of that hubris made him want to scream as much as weep. He hated himself for his failure with Apollyon, hated himself for the arrogance that led to Alighieri's death, hated himself to the point that his father's old avowals woke in his thoughts for the first time in centuries. "It is through pain that we achieve atonement." He had followed that adage even as his mind was breaking from despair and his heart turning cold, only to find no relief and only renewed hate for the man that sired him. He would rage and scream at the man's memory, cursing him for setting them on this road, enumerating all the horrors he had vicariously inflicted on them only to reach that final day when Alighieri died and for it to start all over again with him remembering every instant...~

The night draped everything in luxurious sloth, rendering the world uncommonly dark due to the strange absence of the Plague's luminescent corruption. The world seemed at peace; nothing stirred in the underbrush, no rabid creature burst from the trees, and no terrible monster uprooted itself from years of slumber.

A short distance ahead of Noir and Alighieri, Apollyon walked in a slow circle, openly basking in the quiescence. "By Seelie, this quiet is wonderful; I was starting to believe the Wilds never calmed down."

"They don't," Noir said and extended his sensory Shadow-particles, scouring every inch of the forest. "The only time the Wilds go silent is when something bigger than they are wanders past."

"Well, that would be you two."

"No," Alighieri interposed, "we try to maintain a low profile, restrict the signals we emit to a couple of feet around us, otherwise they tend to attract the bigger creatures."

Apollyon sobered. "So this is something else? Something that can repress an entire forest?"

"Yeah." Noir pushed past. "You'd best stay between us."

The shadows coiled as they advanced, forming *Almas* that flooded out into the night, accompanied by swarms of deceased rodents, small fowl, and insects, all searching for what stalked this region. Despite this, not a single chirp, click of bones, or rustle of wings interrupted the silence. It weighed on them, heavy as the nighttime darkness, an oppressive, suffocating pall of absence and ignorance.

Finally, Noir snarled. "I'm getting tired of this; let's just flatten the forest and flush this thing out of hiding."

"Now, now, isn't that a bit extreme…" A sudden sound intruded on Alighieri and the quiet, silencing him with a refrain of hushed music.

"What was that?" Noir asked, though his eyes remained fixed on where the music had originated from.

"I don't know," Alighieri replied, equally distracted, "but nothing of the Wild makes music like that: it's human."

"It's probably that Hyde you two were talking about, let's just leave it and go."

"Yeah…" Noir retreated a slow step from the noise. "Yeah, let's head west until the music fades and skirt around it."

"Wait, what if it's not the Hyde?" Alighieri asked. "What if it's someone else and they're just trying to break the silence; you know what it was like, you were ready to annihilate the entire forest after only a couple minutes."

"Yes, and?" Apollyon asked with a small gesture urging Alighieri westward.

"If it's not the Hyde," Noir said, "this music is certainly going to attract it, and whoever this is might not have the power to survive the encounter."

"We have to go help them just in case." Alighieri headed eastward.

"Come on." Noir said with a sigh and followed. Apollyon spent a second in disbelief then hastened in pursuit.

They passed through the forest in an anxious silence, the music gradually increasing in volume until its refrains echoed unchecked through the trees. As the music's full notes reached them for the first time, Noir ground to a halt. "Wait." His hand shot out, forestalling both Alighieri and Apollyon's advance. The music flowed around them, its smooth superficial notes obscuring a violent, discordant under-layer of unhinged sounds.

"What is it?" Alighieri brushed against his shoulders, surveying the bloated shadows for what Noir recognized.

"It's the music, I know it."

"Is it from a friend of yours?" Apollyon asked, peering around Alighieri.

"No." A coil of shadows slithered into their ears, sending a shudder under their skin with its unanticipated chill. "I'm covering your ears, but it might be imperfect, ignore the sound as best you can; this is not something you want to hear. Apollyon, prepare to run."

The music faded, leaving naught but the oppressive silence and a sudden eerie solitude. Noir strode forward, caution utterly discarded. They heard nothing and saw little, but the ground crunched beneath their steps, drawing both Alighieri and Apollyon's gaze to a field of desiccated rodents, vermin, and other small fauna. Apollyon paled.

Ahead of them Noir stopped, his silhouette outlined by the light of a clearing. His lips moved in the utterance of a word they could not hear, and his eyes flashed with a primal hate. Alighieri attained his side and again asked, "What is this?"

Apollyon crept forward last and stole a glance between Noir and the ghastly, contorted limbs of a tree. The only light derived from veins of Plague-light streaming through the ground, but it was a sickly illumination and barely touched their coat tails. It sufficed, however, to expose the field of progressively larger cadavers. Most were rotten, but the closest bodies to the center retained their corrupted, nocturnal states and bled profusely. This macabre vision displayed no rhythm, no sanity in composition beyond the progression in size and that they all faced the clearing's center. There, a horror lay in a mound of pink flesh, its coils thick and corded. The monstrosity boasted no head or secondary limbs, only the one main body and a legion of chittering, clacking, and snapping mouths. They protruded from its body on mounds or sunk into it with cavities; some harbored square, human-like teeth, others the fangs of serpents, the incisors of predators, the doubled maws of Hydes, or a knot of interconnected beaks, and even the baleen of whales.

"What is that?" Alighieri reiterated.

Noir's voice broke into their ears, transferred by whatever shadows filled them, "Nyagh'Garath."

Yet, it was not truly that creature, merely a fragment of it that had surfaced or grown here.

Noir did not respond further, he marched into the clearing, shadows descending from the sky to toss the cadavers aside. Alighieri rushed after him, but Apollyon retreated further from the clearing. Noir reached the horror and unflinchingly drove his hand into the mass. Noxious blood spurted fourth, coating and eating through his clothing and skin. He grimaced but plunged his hand deeper. Tendrils of shadows spurted from his burrowing hand, crawling through the creature's skin and shredding through its external layers.

Alighieri caught up with him and pressed his hand onto the mass as well. White cascaded across the skin, entangling itself with the black. The torn strips of flesh tumbled off, white, withered and lifeless, truly lifeless beyond any hope of resurrection or healing. In response, the tumid mass pitched; the countless small feelers of its body lashed at Noir and Alighieri while the larger, wormlike appendages struggled fruitlessly to shift its bloated core. Its maws stretched wide, emitting the awful music that had so entranced these animals and driven them insane when they approached. Noir pressed harder, tearing off pulsating thumbs of the creature and discarding them to the ground about his feet.

Suddenly, a crack rent the night air, drawing their gazes first toward the horizon where the first light of dawn was creeping into the heavens, and then down to where a finger-size fissure ran between them from one side of the clearing to the other. Noir lurched back from the creature, a coil of shadows snapping out to latch about Alighieri's waist, but the ground collapsed before he could do anything more and hurled both of them into a wild fall.

They landed with a splash as rocks and debris rained down around them. The awful creature tumbled into the thick, greasy liquid a second later, soaking the deep walls with waves of the red filth. Noir surfaced from the water with a roar and flailed through the shoulder-deep liquid for Alighieri, who surfaced a moment later. Noir rushed toward him. "Are you all right?"

"Yes fine, it'd take more than a cave-in to kill me."

Noir relaxed and raised a hand from the liquid to sniff. He frowned. "This reeks of Pathomancy."

"Then we'd best get out of it…," Alighieri trailed off, his gaze rising to the pit's mouth as a closing ceiling of Shadowmancy doused the faint light trickling from the surface. Noir followed his gaze and cursed as a wall of shadows slithered shut across the pit's opening. He tried to jump, marshalling shadows to pierce the barrier, but the liquid fastened itself to his body, anchoring him in place. A figure appeared above them, strolling calmly across the Shadowsteel wall: Apollyon. A match sparked in his hand.

Noir twisted with a desperate cry, wrenching his neck as he threw every shadow he could summon to cocoon Alighieri and create a secondary wall beneath the first, a shield between them and whatever followed. Apollyon just grinned and dropped the match. It tumbled through the air, an orb of Hemomancy burgeoning around it and shearing through all the impeding Shadowmancy. Noir had a final instant of horror to watch before it struck the liquid and everything exploded into fire.

All became fire and he screamed, stabbing at the surface with a spear of shadows while every other fleck he could summon converged on Alighieri. The fire ate through his barrier in seconds, and he threw more shadows at it, adding layer after fruitless layer. The fire consumed all of them even as it consumed his flesh and muscles. He couldn't see or hear Alighieri, and for an instant, he thought the worst had occurred, then he heard his brother scream as his barrier failed. His control shattered, the Plague billowed from his disintegrating body in a tide, but the fire just devoured it and burned all the brighter. He desperately reached out for his brother, but whatever trickle of shadows that survived in this tomb burned to cinder the second he called them. Nonetheless, he still reached, striving through the fire until his Shadowsteel body winked from existence.

His mind woke in another of his host bodies far away in a buried room, surrounded by more empty avatars. He threw his head back and wailed, all control obliterated as the corruption poured from every inch of his skin, annihilating his form and everything that surrounded him. The ground blackened and died, his Constructs and the room that housed them disintegrated, the trees clustered upon the surface melted and death roared into the open air. He did not transform, he could not in these bodies, so he just screamed until the day dawned and finally incinerated his untamed corruption, leaving him broken and voiceless in a wasteland of his own making as the reality that he had lost the one person in all the world he had loved drowned him.

Chapter Nineteen

The primary reason death has become such a transient force (aside from Necromancers themselves) is that complete destruction is necessary. So long as a fragment of bone remains, Necromancers can return a soul to its body. However, for a full return to happen, Hemomancers need an intact sample of genetic material from which to grow the blood and flesh.

Powerful Necromancers are rare in the cities for a variety of reasons, but primarily it is because they tend to develop a degree of megalomania. This leads most to venture into the wilds for an army with which to supplant one of the tyrants. We are fortunate however, in that these men and women frequently find themselves contending with each other, fighting massive unseen battles that delay their attack.

Shadow-law Apocalypse

~ *Noir lounged on a rock, bathing in the rare autumn sun as birds flew silently past, too frightened to utter their song. He ignored them as he ignored the corpses scattered all around him in tangled heaps, their injuries leeching black fumes.*

He exhaled a musing breath and turned his hand palm up to observe the ugly, puss-leaking scars. 'I wonder...' Shadows coiled up from beneath his tattered sleeve, encasing his arm. '...could I replace my skin with shadows, armor myself against this world.' He sat up, still considering his hand. 'But why stop there? Muscles, organs, nerves, bones, they can all be replaced; I could be invincible, never have to feel pain again.' He slowly closed his hand into a fist and then reopened it. 'But would I still be human then? Am I even human now?'

A thin string of shadows twitched in his other hand, warning him of someone's approach. He roused himself, sending his consciousness along the string to discover who approached, and grinned as Alighieri appeared across the field.

He leapt from the rock and jogged to his brother, who met him with a look of theatrical exasperation. "You do realize I have other things to do than clean up after you? Great, evil machinations and the like..."

"Of course you do."

"I do, and you calling me back every couple of weeks to resurrect those you've butchered does not help."

"Would you rather I leave them dead?"

"I'd rather you not kill them at all; it is considered rude in most societies."

Noir shrugged. "If I don't kill them, they just make a nuisance of themselves and attack me whenever I wander by. Plus, they never stay dead."

"Yes, but I'm exhausted from cleaning up after you."

"All right, I'll make a box and put them inside it so they don't bother me."

Alighieri flung his hands skyward with an exasperated, "Then they'll just kill each other!"

"I'll segregate them, keep them locked in with their packs."

Alighieri paused. "That might actually work." *He settled against a nearby tree.* "You could build a city, a place where people could live safely..."

Noir exhaled slowly. "I could, and I could make something to watch over them, a permanent Construct to protect them from Tyrants." He lowered himself to ground. "I won't do it now. I need to think on it, to perfect it."

Alighieri rolled his eyes. "To make it beautiful you mean…"

Noir shook his head. "No, this will be a prison, and a prison is an ugly thing. To make it beautiful would be to lie." ~

Noir watched Adrian crumple, her once vibrant eyes now colorless and empty. *That … hurt more than I expected.*

'Did you kill her permanently?'

No, she doesn't deserve that.

'And yet, you killed her anyway.'

Yes.

'Why?'

Because the city needs its Proctors, and I don't have the time to kill all of them. He raised his hand slowly, long, jagged strips of shadow streaming through his fingers to coalesce in his palm. Still moving slowly, he pressed his hands together and squeezed, ending the steam of shadows. A quiet deadness expanded from him, sweeping down through the floor and out across the skyscrapers as everything stilled: people, animals, banners, and even the Shadowmancy.

He opened his hands, revealing a sphere of roiling shadows, and spoke, "Shadow Law: Apocalypse."

The sphere exploded, roaring outward in a tide of all-consuming shadows, and neither the walls nor innate resistances offered any protection to those residing in the Doll and Grim Districts. They all died, their lives extinguished without mark or injury and only a dull black haze to explain why.

Noir dropped his hand and left, phasing down through the city grating.

'Why did you kill Adrian first? You could have waited three seconds and killed her with everyone else; several thousand birds with one stone and all that.'

If you are going to betray someone, have the courage to do it to their face.

'Still, the wise, the reserved, and just about everyone else would deem killing two whole districts a touch extreme.'

It was simpler, and painless. He rounded a corner, pulling aside a curtain of blooming Shadow vines. The garden he created upon first arriving in the Undercity four days ago had grown voraciously despite his inattention.

'It always surprised me how much actual life your creations had, not only the ability to grow or eat but also the ability to expand beyond the limitations you set upon them.'

Noir shrugged as he stepped over a massive lotus bloom. *Life is easy to simulate; all that something inanimate needs is a purpose, the potential of death and then the desire to be more.*

'So you're saying all of this is sentient?'

Yes, it's more fun and less predictable that way. A soft ticking sound called his attention to the left where a single gear spun in the wall, untouched by the rampant overgrowth. He continued on his way, watching gear after gear appear in the walls on either side of him, growing increasingly more numerous as he neared the palace. Eventually, gears and copper-work usurped the Shadowsteel walls, marking the point where the Copperwork Heart began.

The walls, floor, and ceiling churned behind a thin copper lattice. The countless interlocked gears clicked, while the piping and exhaust valves spat an endless stream of dark ash and smoke. A million tiny creatures, no larger than his fingernails, raced over the giant machine, their copper bodies gyrating and puffing little white clouds of steam.

Noir traversed the box-like passages of the Copperwork Heart without thought for its ticking walls or the robed Aesians he passed, most of whom knelt in prayer to the clicking machinery. As he advanced, however, corpses began to appear between the Aesians.

He crouched beside the first of them, an undertaker, and inspected the livid red injuries covering his body. *Lazarus seems to have been busy.*

'Can they be resurrected?'

I don't know and I have no inclination to figure it out.

The Aesians continued to grow more numerous as he progressed, but for every autonomous one he encountered two more remained ensconced in the walls, their gears and struts locked in sync with those of their dead god. Noir left them as they were, ticking away with closed eyes and the occasional shudder; they had imprisoned themselves of their own accord.

The deeper he ventured into the Copperwork Heart, the more complete the Aesian's mechanical transformations became. They were a relic of the Wild Years, the servants of a Tyrant who possessed no hemomancers to undo the damage inflicted upon them at night. Their Tyrant had repaired their injuries with his machinery, replacing severed limbs with arms and legs of copper and steam. He called himself Copperwork Heart, and they worshiped him as a god.

'You know what, it's still disgusting as hell whenever I remember that we're walking through somebody's entrails.'

Noir touched the wall on his right, causing the gears to tick with redoubled verve and exhale a burst of steam. The wall shivered and then separated to admit him. *If it makes you feel any better, he's not entirely dead yet.*

'No; it doesn't, that just makes it worse... But, if he's still got a head, we could sidle on up and pretend to be his conscience.'

The passage descended, expanding around him and the Aesians until it finally opened into a vast room. Here, Noir slowed, his eyes rising to the churning copper-heart suspended from the ceiling. The mass of grinding, interconnected gears churned without thought for the impossibility of it, revolving in and out of one another in a giant, tangled sphere.

Noir assessed it, watching the copper-heart for any sign that Lazarus had tampered with it. When the gears continued revolving without incident, he advanced into the room, weaving through the Aesians prostrated across every available inch. The gears clicked the quarter hour, and the Aesians rose to their knees in unison, raising their hands skyward with a murmured reverence. They held this posture for a moment and then prostrated themselves again as smoke burst from the ceiling and crashed against the floor, billowing out in a wave of soot.

Noir continued until he reached the hall's center and paused at the edge of a black pit. The Aesians knelt around it, their fingertips stopping just short of where the copper work gave way to shadowmantic pipes.

Noir crouched and extended a hand over the darkness, causing the shadows to convulse and froth up over the edge. A shudder passed through him and he exhaled. "Finally."

'Yes. And, by the way, I think it's only fair to warn you that you're going to get your ass kicked.'

Whatever you say.

'No really, you're gonna drop down, land in a storm of shadow tentacles and be all like—I'm the dark god of vengeance and retribution, and I'm here to avenge my poor brother!—Whereupon Lazarus will laugh with horridly overdone megalomania and launch himself into some long, boring rhetoric that'll remind us of school.'

We never went to school.

'Please, I've been schooling you for centuries now.'

Of course you have.

'Anyway, mid rhetoric you'll grow bored and decide to take a nap, whereupon you'll whip up a bed. Jump forward thirty minutes and you'll wake up just in time to intercept Lazarus' attack. What follows is a painfully drawn out brawl that finally culminates with Lazarus lying in a bloody heap at your feet.'

So far it doesn't look like I'm getting my ass kicked.

'Don't worry its coming. Just as you're about to deliver the killing blow, Lazarus reaches deep within himself, finds one last sliver of strength and manages to hurl a final attack, which of course fails. Flash forward another two minutes and you're walking away from his corpse; except as you do, the sound of singing angels fills the room. You turn around and there's Lazarus, shrouded with golden light and suffused with newfound power. This is where you get walloped into an eternal Monday, a far shorter battle culminating with your destruction and masses of rejoicing people rushing out to fill the streets.'

And why are you so certain this will occur?

'Because you're quite obviously the villain in this little Iliad; I mean who wants an underdog for a villain, and Lazarus is definitely the underdog here.'

So I'm going to lose because I'm more powerful?

'Yep, it's the only logical result. Now drop down and get what's coming to you.'

Don't rush me, I'm going.

Shadows swelled beside him, flowing through and around his body until they slowly resembled a humanoid shape. Noir jumped without waiting for them to finish.

He landed several stories below in a large oval room of seamless black piping that ran along the ceiling, down the walls and across the floor to form the base of a white Shadow-wood throne before vanishing below. A hundred, brilliant electric lights occupied the ceiling and walls, filling the air with a quiet hum. The hot piping trembled beneath him, displacing the sheen of condensation as the water pounded by inside.

A man sat in the throne. His cobalt flesh gleamed in the white light, and his fingers clicked with silver stone knives that grew from his bones. He slouched in the open backed throne, a dozen ugly red tubes protruding from his back and leading up to the ceiling where they vanished amid the piping. He dressed in loose purple silk, wore his crimson dreadlocks tied back, and dangled a yellowed skull by its eye sockets on the fingers of his left hand.

The man exhaled and steam poured from his mouth despite the room's already oppressive heat.

Lazarus looked up from Noir's throne with eyes of etched bone, neither orb seeming entirely at home within its socket. "So you've finally come for me." His triple jointed legs uncoiled, pushing him up beyond any normal man's height. "I suppose you wanted me to suffer, to languish in the knowledge of my impending destruction as you murdered my allies one by one and ruined all my schemes." He stepped down from the throne, causing the red tubes protruding from his body to slide along the ceiling between pipes. "Of course, what you don't realize is that this was the only scheme that mattered, the one that brought us together, with all of Umbras as the prize." The man shuddered, his breath hitching with excitement. "All it took was killing your brother and making sure you knew it was me. Then I just had to sit back and wait for you to follow."

His silk robes shifted aside, revealing his naked breast and a web of minuscule, white cracks. He spasmed as the cracks expanded and indicated his eyes. "As you can see, I have your brother's eyes and" —he lifted the skull—"Brigadier's power as well. Umbras will be well protected."

'Yawwwnnn, is it recess, yet? Man, this teacher is the worst.'

Noir snarled, his hands closing into fists and a thread of steel inching out from his pupil. "I did not come to hear you talk, Lazarus." His gaze flicked to the side at the sound of a step.

The small girl emerged from behind the white throne, seemingly oblivious to the coil of pulsing crimson energy about her neck. A single black vial swayed at the coil's ending: Shadow Poison.

The girl waved her hand. "Hello, I hoped you would come here."

Noir calmed himself with an effort. "You don't look too much worse for wear, Loc. Is there anything I should know?"

'She looks cute as a child; makes me want to plop fluffy socks on her feet, or perhaps dunk her head while she's taking a bath.'

The girl, Lock-And-Key, shrugged. "Probably, but I can't tell you anything"—she tapped her chest, indicating the crimson veins coursing through her body, no doubt containing some form of Shadow Poison to keep her in check—"and even if I could, I spent most of my time watching Grim." Her smile turned savage. "When you're done with this asshole, I intend to pay my errant Proctor a visit."

'Hmm, you'll have to talk to her about that language, we can't have a child running around spouting profanity.'

And what about her running off to eviscerate Grim?

'We shouldn't crush children's dreams; it's poor parenting and might stunt their growth.'

"Just sit tight, Loc, vacation's over."

Lazarus cocked his head, eyes clicking with a blink. "That's not for you to say, Noir, she doesn't belong to you anymore. She's mine." He took a flowing step closer, the Shadowsteel bleaching beneath his heel. "Moreover, while you were busy killing my associates, I have collected every drop of blood spilled in Umbras over the last week, so this city doesn't even belong to you anymore." The tubes protruding from his back throbbed grotesquely, pumping him full of blood. "I can be everywhere, know everything," he paused, "destroy everything if I have to..."

Noir answered with a long-suffering look, and the shadows

flashed, severing Lazarus' tubes in a fount of blood.

Lazarus just leaned back, soaking in the blood as crimson veins usurped the white cracks in his flesh. The severed tubes coiled toward the ceiling, growing as if they were living flesh to reunite with their other halves.

Lazarus' eyes flashed crimson and the blood at his feet expanded, coursing over the ground, then up the walls and across the ceiling, blanketing the entire room.

Noir kicked at the ground, splashing the ankle-deep blood, and noting the thin, fibrous tendrils connecting Lazarus to the floor. *It seems like he's converted this whole room into an extension of himself.*

'Yeah, kind of like what you did with Umbras, only in the pee-wee league.'

Lazarus ceased his advance, standing just shy of Noir. "So tell me, how do we begin?"

"By hurting you." The shadows exploded at Lazarus, stabbing at him in a hail of spears.

He twisted, his body contorting at an impossible angle around the spears and then flowing back as they slashed inward. "Brute power always was your preferred solution. It's simple, immediate, and effective. The number of individuals who could survive it number less than the fingers on your hand." The shadows receded, and Lazarus resettled into his normal shape.

Noir exploded forward, one hand dragging across the ground to leave a trail of shadows in the blood while the other launched a barrage of needles. Lazarus' form collapsed like water, black fumes erupting from his interior as he merged with the blood at his feet.

Noir wrenched to a halt and slammed his hand down, heaving the blood upward on a thrashing torrent of shadows that exposed the bare Shadowsteel beneath but revealed no sign of Lazarus. A stream of blood swirled up behind him and he spun, lashing harmlessly through it.

The blood swept around him: constricting his arms and legs, and yanking them outward. It burned with the distinct rot of the Plague but still failed to penetrate his skin. He slashed at the swirling blood with shadows, but they merely splashed through the liquid. Lazarus swelled up behind him, the blood solidifying into his upper torso, and stabbed down with a hand of elongated crimson talons.

Noir thrashed, the shadows surging up from beneath his coat and hammering out. Lazarus shot backward, blood gushing from his chest, as Noir buckled, coarse red lines streaking up his arms, eroding them where he had blocked Lazarus.

Damn it, he seems to have laced his blood with the Shadow Poison. Shadows coiled and struck, amputating his arms at the shoulder before the poison spread.

Lazarus, the blood streaming back into his chest, emerged fully from the pool and solidified with a puff of fumes, his clothing immaculate. "In the rare circumstance your first assault fails or you find yourself particularly enraged, you proceed into physical combat. Which is surprising, because I always thought artists hated to dirty their hands."

Noir straightened, flexing new arms as they formed.

Unperturbed, Lazarus strolled toward the throne, his robes trailing in the blood. "I spent years researching you before we ever met, all to achieve and prepare for this eventuality. I knew Alighieri would be easy to kill. But you, I knew you would survive the fire. I needed something more, something that could truly test you." He nodded at Noir's arms. "Regeneration that equals, or surpasses, that of a Tyrant-class hemomancer. A nearly insurmountable barrier, but susceptible to the same flaws. If you poison the blood, you poison the hemomancer."

Noir slammed his hands together, launching a massive, curved blade arching across the room. Lazarus just submerged again, further clouding the air with his corruption. The blade phased through Lock-And-Key and the throne without inflicting harm.

Unrelenting, Noir stomped, hurling a pool of rushing shadows out from his boot to carpet the floor. Lazarus reemerged a second later, first deforming then tearing the carpet. The rent shadows coiled and impaled his half-formed body, spearing him to the floor. Lazarus' form just rippled free, boiling with a cloud of fumes that rotted through Noir's shadows.

"If brute force fails, you test your enemy's pattern, extracting every flaw and strength before finally abusing their tendencies."

Lazarus finished materializing and snapped his hand forward, weaving the blood up Noir's legs.

Noir leapt, kicking at the blood and pulling the shadows into a platform beneath him, but Lazarus flooded the blood up Noir's chest and around his face. It pulled and stabbed at him, writhing at his flesh to no avail until it found and swamped his nostrils and ears. Shadows swarmed to his form and exploded, flinging the blood outward in a boiling tide. Even as it did so, however, a searing pain lanced through his heart.

He snarled, shadows surrounding him in a new shield as the blood surged back.

"The simplest strategy to beat you is to tear you apart from inside, pumping enough Shadow Poison into your body that you can't keep pace with the destruction." Lazarus' voice sounded inside Noir's head, inflaming the pain and sparking the Shadow Poison's advance.

Noir buckled, vomiting a globule of black and red blood. He snarled, pulling shadows in to restore whatever damage Lazarus inflicted.

"Again, when regenerating, your first response is simple brute force. You eradicate the damaged tissue and then inundate your body with shadows, repairing the damage and strengthening the rest. Fortunately, I had Constantine design the Shadow Poison to have a compounding effect; it destroys everything it touches, expanding outward and multiplying at an exponential rate. In other words, the faster you heal the faster it—"

'Oh hey, Laz, you're here too.'

"What? Who are you?"

'Sorry, but I've already rented this space, and I'm afraid you'll have to leave, go make somebody else crazy.' Blood erupted from Noir's skin, but the Shadow Poison remained, eating away at him.

"Who the hell was that, Noir?"

"Don't worry, it's just my personal madness." Noir pushed himself upright, his skin drinking in shadows as a net of crimson veins expanded across his shirt.

"Interesting that it sounded like your brother, not that it matters." Lazarus retreated, a hand delving into a pocket. "You say that a person can't kill a god, but I wonder if that holds true for another god?"

Noir leapt back, shadows repelling the blood; but Lazarus' hand was already emerging, a sparked match held between two fingers.

The blood ignited with a roar and engulfed Noir, hurling him against the wall in a mass of gory tongues. It swelled higher, eating through the Shadowsteel walls and causing pipes to burst as Noir screamed.

Lazarus staggered forward, one hand raised to shield his face and the other stoking the fire. "Fire failed to kill you the first time; but now your veins rust with Shadow Poison, preventing any chance of flight or regeneration."

The flames forced Noir to the ground, crushing him beneath an impossible weight. His skin turned cherry red, melting off his body as his clothing incinerated. His muscles, nerves, and organs followed, consumed by the flames until he crumpled in the hollowed-out wall, his body reduced to black bones etched with silver.

Lazarus relinquished the fire and grinned. "Oh, the things I will do with Umbras. You have no idea how long I've waited to own this place, the first city."

Water pooled from the ruptured pipes, hissing where it struck the lingering embers and flames. The steam billowing from it gradually filled the room, obscuring everything and dulling the embers' glow.

Lazarus faced Lock-And-Key where she reclined in the white throne, one of his hands extended as if to accept something, but stopped, eyes fixing on a wriggling thread of shadow. "There's always another trick..."

Noir stepped from the hollow, shadows still congregating on his person. "You are no god, Lazarus. You are just a parasite that has spent its life stealing and borrowing power. You don't even want Umbras because it's safe or developed, or because Alighieri butchered Terra Carrion. You want it because everyone knows of it and you want to use the Umbrans as a weapon." Noir gasped and caught himself on the wall as the Shadow Poison reasserted itself. *How? It burned in the fire!* Red cracks burst open along his hands and arms, eating away at his newly formed clothing.

"You must be wondering why the Shadow Poison persists despite the fire. It would have been quite an oversight on my part to not prepare for this eventuality. No, fire has more of an accelerating effect." Lazarus knelt, looking at Noir from the corner of his eye as he touched the blood. It ebbed out from him, stilling and becoming reflective. "In all my research, I discovered that only one individual ever survived your brute power and traps. In that instance, you simply obliterated every possible variable in a mile's radius and he happened to die in the process."

Noir pulled himself upright, teeth bared in a snarl. "Just die." The shadows rushed at Lazarus, scraping up all the blood in their path.

Lazarus liquefied again, a mirror sprouting in his place to catch the shadows, which struck, massed against and shattered upon it. Liberated, the amassed blood surged out from his position, rose into a second mirror and spat out a roiling storm of black and crimson energy. The seething mass hit Noir's chest and exploded, obliterating most of his torso and filling the rest with Shadow Poison.

"Bloody fucking hell." Shadows erupted around Noir, enclosing and healing him even as they shredded him in a barrage of knives, hands, and spears that excised every drop of Shadow Poison he could reach. It lasted seconds and ended with him on a knee, panting. *This is going be a problem.*

'Far more than you expect, anything you throw at him will just be reflected with more Shadow Poison. How can he do that, by the way?'

A crack split the left wall of his enclosure and he slammed a hand against it, repairing the damage. *He has a Terian, probably ripped it from some Hyde.*

A shudder rippled through the blood behind him and it swelled into Lazarus. "Rumor always said Shadowmancy was your greatest strength, but that's a lie isn't it? Shadowmancy isn't your strength, it's your shield: the only protection you have against your own Hyde. You can't release it without your brother to curtail the damage you'd wreak upon Umbras. How long did your little temper tantrum go the last time you lost control? I hear the sun can't even banish your taint. How long have its effects lingered, Noir? Days? Years? Decades?"

Noir twisted awkwardly and kicked Lazarus through the chest.

"Really? What do you hope to accomplish? You know physical blows cannot hurt me."

"No ... but my blood might."

Lazarus recoiled, yanking himself off Noir's boot as his back erupted in black fumes.

Noir drove his hand into the blood-soaked floor, dispelled the enclosure and released a thread of his corruption. The steel veins in his eyes snaked out and fumes oozed from his lips. The blood hissed and blackened. His arm collapsed into dust and the miasma of his Hyde seethed out, cleansing his body.

Lazarus collapsed, his skin eroding as the blood soaking the room evaporated.

The Shadowsteel floor and walls disintegrated, peeling away until they gave way to rock while the ceiling rotted into fountains of water. Only Lock-And-Key remained unaffected, for part of Noir's corruption thrived in her veins.

When it ended, and the miasma dissipated, Noir pushed himself to his feet. He ached, ravaged by the fragment of corruption he had released, but the Shadow Poison was gone.

Suddenly, a stream of blood shot up before him and rammed through his chest, forming into Lazarus' arm. "You know what? I'm starting to understand why you hate my kind." He twisted his arm, injecting Shadow Poison into Noir and pushing him to the ground. "You have lived too long. I don't care that you are a Tyrant. I don't care that you built Umbras. It is time for a new god to rule here."

Noir grabbed Lazarus and dragged him closer, baring his teeth inches from the man's throat. "*In meus left manus manus EGO incursio Partis of Oblivio quod in meus vox EGO habitum Sperma of Prosterno. EGO sum purveyor of obscurum, Archangel of nox noctis. Lucifer they accersitus mihi in hora of apocalypse, pro EGO extinguished totus lux lucis in meus obduco quod gave ortus ut a regnum of umbra.*"

"I don't speak that language."

It was Lock-And-Key who answered, "In my left hand, I clasp the shards of Oblivion and in my right, I hold the Seeds of Ruin. I am the purveyor of darkness, the Archangel of night. Lucifer, they called me in the hours of the apocalypse, for I extinguished all light and gave birth to a kingdom of shadows. Or something like that."

"More useless proclamatio–" Shadows flooded from the tunnel, inundating the whole room and crushing Lazarus as Noir shoved him off.

'You do realize that trying to crush Lazarus is pointless, right?'

Yeah, but it might suffocate him. Noir lurched, contorting as the Shadow Poison spread. He sagged to the floor, panting on the thin stream of air he funneled through the shadow mass. *We're running out of time.*

'What are you talking about? Just cleanse yourself with the Plague like you did last time.'

I can't. Noir crawled to the natural wall and sagged against it. He could feel the Plague within him pressing for release, and the Shadow Poison devouring his shadow mass. *It's everywhere now, and thicker. He's done something, augmented it with his blood or increased the dosage, maybe both. I can't control the amount of corruption needed to purge it all.*

A hiss sounded behind Noir, drawing his attention to a crimson light slithering through the shadow mass.

And you wonder why I hate hemomancers.

The shadow mass dissolved, eroded to dust by the poison as Lazarus formed at the room's center, his body half-finished flesh, muscle, and bone. He completed his formation with a snarl, and flung a ball of seething blood at Noir.

Noir heaved shadows up into a wall, but crimson veins devoured it from inside before it ever finished. Lazarus' ball struck him and exploded, throwing him to the floor and blanketing his body in the poison.

Lazarus stalked forward, ugly red vines sprouting from his footsteps and streaming to imprison Noir. They dug into him, drilling through his rusting skin to wrap around his bones and stretch him taut. He gasped and tried to break their hold, but his limbs barely moved: the Shadow Poison was already dissolving his muscles. Shadows coiled and struck, severing the vines only for them to immediately regenerate.

Noir retched, vomiting red blood. He heard Lazarus' steps and looked up through bleary eyes.

"No more deception or tricks, Noir. No more regeneration." He spoke calmly, not bored but content. "In your arrogance and rage, you came to a battle blind and now you suffer the consequences of that choice." He inhaled a long breath as if savoring the flavor. "I spent years hunting you, learning how to kill you, and then preparing for it. I never tried killing one of your kind before—a Homo Deos: a world-builder. You did not disappoint me. All those traps, poisons, and fetters I gave you, and even Brigadier couldn't so much as inflict one lasting injury. But I learned from all of them." Crimson light streamed to the tip of his forefinger. "This is something I fashioned with your brother's power, a Death-Spell keyed to you through my Hemomancy."

Noir snarled and pushed himself upright with shadows, more skin flaking away in the process. He tried to shift places with his shadow as he had done with Brigadier, but the Shadow Poison and Hemomancy vines retaliated.

Lazarus smirked. "Don't bother; even if you could escape, this spell would still find you." His smirk faded back into the look of apathy. "It's absolute, a perfect union of Hemomancy and Necromancy. You cannot block it. You cannot evade it. You cannot destroy it. It is instantaneous, so all the shadowmantic regeneration in the world can't help you. You simply die, and all I have to pay is a little exhaustion." His finger flashed crimson and Noir crumpled...

...Lazarus glanced at Lock-and-Key over his shoulder. "It looks like your savior's dead, and Umbras is now truly mine."

Lock-And-Key yawned, her feet draped over one armrest and her head reclined on the other. "I don't know whether it's sadder or funnier that you think you've actually won."

"What do you mean..."

Shadows flowed from the tunnel, curling about one another and tightening into limbs. They touched the floor and retracted, leaving Noir in their wake, newly formed and the steel of his hair, eyes, and nails gradually turning silver.

"How are you still alive? I killed you, your body's right there!"

"As if I would ever willingly fight blind. That was a facsimile, a harbor for my consciousness, nothing more." He rolled his shoulders and power rushed out from him. Shadows flowed from the tunnel, reconstructing the pipes and walls.

Lazarus snarled, flung his hand outward, summoning Shadow Poison in his palm. A Shadow swooped down and decapitated him.

"I'm not stupid, Lazarus."

'Well, the jury's still out on that assessment.'

Oh, shush.

Lazarus staggered to his feet, his still-forming body bloating with Shadow Poison. "But you wouldn't have been capable of infusing a facsimile with anything more than a fragment of your power!"

"True, but a fragment's generally more than enough."

Lazarus calmed himself with an exhale and raised his hand again. "No matter, I'll just kill all of yo—" Blood burst from his mouth, doubling him over in a retching fit. He looked up, blood streaming from his orifices. "What did you do to me? Where's my power?"

"I just told you. I'm not stupid, Lazarus. Did you think I was just sitting there, letting you beat on me for no reason? No, I injected some of my blood into those oh so useful blood reservoirs of yours. After that, it was just a matter of time. Whenever you accessed that blood, you poisoned yourself a little more. And, since my corruption is irreversibly mixed with your supply, there's no point in attempting to regenerate."

Lazarus moaned and stumbled back. "You're a fool, Noir! Killing me is pointless! It won't bring your brother back. This revenge earns you nothing! He is dead!"

"I didn't come for revenge, Lazarus, at least not entirely. You all took something from Alighieri, and I needed them back. And you should know very well that death is a covenant we broke long ago."

He tore the bone eyes from Lazarus' skull, leaving Lazarus to scream out the last moments of his existence. Noir pocketed the eyes and walked toward the unblemished throne. Lock-And-Key stood at his approach, discarding the Hemomancy necklace, and leapt onto his shoulders. He glared at her. "What are you doing?"

"I'm riding on your shoulders; what does it look like I'm doing?"

"Yeah, but why?"

"Because I know you hate it."

"Get down and change back to your adult self."

"Nah, this is more fun."

"I'm not staying in this body for long."

"Then I'll switch."

Noir sighed and launched himself up through the tunnel, the shadows accelerating him until he shot free several stories later. He hung suspended there as his momentum dispersed and then landed beside his prepared copy. It deconstructed into formless shadows and merged with his body, bearing with it the silver-etched bones he used to house his blood. The bones snapped into place and then he was bounding up through the Undercity.

Almas converged around them as they ascended, starting in a trickle but growing to a swarm by the time Noir exited the Copperwork Heart. He strode to the surface, almost sprinting through the Undercity's complicated roads.

He emerged just outside of the palace courtyard on the Doll District's main thoroughfare. A cold wind slithered through the empty streets, tugging at the forlorn banners and eddying over the dead. The palace guards scrambled behind the still present barricade and leveled their weapons. They recognized him as Solomon Doll's lieutenant, but they also knew someone had murdered everyone in the Grim and Doll Districts.

One of the guards presented his hand to forestall them, but his shadow and those of his companions decapitated him and his fellows. Meanwhile, the Shadowsteel barricade crumpled in on itself, grinding into a ball small enough to sit in Noir's hand.

Lock-And-Key tapped his head. "Try not to destroy my palace."

"I built the damned thing for you; I'll destroy it if I wish." A wall of shadows sprouted behind him, blocking every entrance onto the palace grounds. Shrieks and bellows soon followed, marking the sentries' deaths. Other screams rose as well, sweeping the palace with warnings that a foreign Tyrant had come to challenge Lock-And-Key.

The palace woke, its natural defenses stirring for the first time in decades. Noir kicked a nearby pillar. "Go back to sleep already, it's just me." It subsided, recognizing both Noir and Lock-And-Key. The men did not, however. Guards rallied to impede his advance, but the shadows struck all across the palace, suffocating any who abided within.

Reaching the massive front doors, he phased through and continued deeper in, traversing wall after wall until he reached a second courtyard. It was open to the sky, comprised of bleached Shadowsteel, and absolutely forbidden to all except Lock-And-Key. Countless *Almas* filled the sky, clouding out the Blood Moon and settling down upon every square inch the palace could provide. The hymn of their wings deafened all other sounds, but they never entered the courtyard. He started across it, every step bleaching his clothing and skin a little further even as they left a black footprint. Immense, sleeping Necromancy infused every inch of this courtyard, Alighieri's Necromancy.

A small marble island occupied the center of the courtyard amidst a ring of water, its surface glistening with moisture. Noir stopped at its edge and stared down for a long while before lifting Lock-And-Key from his shoulders. He set her down as a bridge formed over the water, and crossed to the island.

Up close, the island looked different from how distance portrayed it; cracks and dark smudges marred its surface, creating a checkered aspect. When Noir stepped atop it, he added to the island's various blemishes, each stride leaving a black footstep behind him and dark lines spearing across the marble to repair the cracks. He withdrew his hands from their pockets, spinning shadow tendrils around his fingers like yarn. A swarm of *Almas* landed before him, forming the rough shape of a man and then merging into a cohesive mass.

Shadowmantic saturation swept outward from him, eroding the courtyard's mostly pristine whiteness.

Noir flicked out his hands, sending his shadow tendrils to spiral around the *Almas*, tightening the cluster into a more refined shape. Another group of *Almas* materialized from the swarm on his right, bearing his pack between them. Another set carried the white Marrow Staff and laid it beside the bag.

He knelt, undid the straps to retrieve four vials and set them beside him. Next, he retrieved the staff and drove it into the ground beside the first group of *Almas*. This done, he refocused on the *Almas* and the human shape they had formed.

He stared at it for a long time, before reaching out with a tentative hand to stroke the figure's brow. At his touch, the figure changed. Minute details shifted, losing definition and texture or gaining them. Inconsistencies repairing themselves, fashioning the body until it echoed the memory of his brother.

Finished, Noir dug into a pocket and withdrew the bone eyes decorated by intricate runes. He pressed them into Alighieri's sockets and then immediately dug into his pack a second time for an equally decorated skull and a pile of finger bones. Both of these he carefully arranged inside the body, attaching them to the Shadowsteel bones within. Finally, he produced the vial of blood he had taken from Alucard and poured it down Alighieri's throat.

"First, we use the last fragments of his soul, the Terian Shards used to harvest his power." The vials dissolved in his hand, spilling white ether onto the body. "My memories of you, housed in a seed of madness, a sentient voice with your personality." He reached into his mouth, removed a black sphere and pressed it into the body's forehead.

The laughing voice that had crowded his thoughts since Alighieri's death, berating him incessantly, offering one idiotic notion after another, and bringing a shred of light into his wretched life, ceased.

"And finally"—Noir looked up into the teeming *Almas*, one hand raised to create a perch—"a last, small piece of you."

A speck of white light emerged from the boiling darkness overhead, trembling and flickering in and out of existence as it fought through the black tide of its brethren. It blinked out entirely for an instant and then the single white Alma alighted upon his fingers. It had survived Alighieri's death by a miracle, for Noir trusted no one and had sent it far in the heavens beyond the reach of any sane creature; any Hyde ruled by the madness would have cowered before so much as touching something so steeped in Alighieri's essence.

Noir trembled and slowly, carefully, caved forward to cup the pale Alma against his chest. If this failed, nothing would remain of Alighieri, not even the voice of madness.

Struggling against himself, Noir stretched out both hands and set the pale creature upon Alighieri's forehead. It perched there for a moment and then merged with the Construct, leaving a white stain upon the sable brow. Noir took a shuddering breath and touched his fingers to the Construct's lips. "Breathe."

An eternal heartbeat passed and then the Construct arched backward, its mouth opening into a painful gasp of air while its eyes snapped open, life and color filling their depths.

The entire courtyard, from the water to the island, turned white, even the *Almas*, as a massive influx of necromantic power washed the city. Noir's coat, stained black from his battle with Lazarus, flapped up into the air and then settled back down, pure white once again.

Despite this, Noir waited in breathless silence. He waited as the interminable gasp went on, waited as pain continued to wrack the Construct's body, and waited as it finally collapsed.

Noir endured one heart beat and then two, each second dragging a yawning pit of madness and despair closer. His hand barely moving a centimeter at a time, he reached and touched the now pale brow of his brother. "Are you–"

"Shhh, it's rude to disturb the dead."

"It's," he coughed, clearing his throat, and continued, "it's far worse to wake them and you used to do that on a daily basis, probably will again in the future."

"No, no, no; it's only rude for the living to wake the dead. Other dead people can wake the dead without fear. It's kinda like inviting your neighbors to a block party."

"So are you planning to open your eyes anytime soon?"

Alighieri cracked an eyelid, began to say something then sat up with a laugh. "Nah, I–wait; you actually went and got that useless thing!"

Noir blinked and looked at the staff. "What do you mean?"

Alighieri giggled. "I can't believe you trusted me enough to run off and fetch that stupid thing."

Noir's brow wrinkled and his voice turned dangerous. "Alighieri ... you told me to get it if anything ever happened to you."

"Yeah, I know, that's what makes this so funny." Alighieri rolled back, his laughter rising to a roar, before abruptly choking off as Noir wrapped both hands around his throat. "No wait, Noir, don't kill me, not yet–"

"I–Had–To–Step–Into–Mirage–For–That–Blasted–Staff.   And you know what a hell that place is!"

"Wait! I still have to resurrect those two districts you annihilated! Think about Adrian!"

"They can wait."

Meanwhile, Lock-And-Key leaned back against a column and smiled.

Epilogue

An Invitation to Adventure

Adrian woke gently, roused by the golden warmth of a natural skylight. Dust motes drifted past her eyes, filling an air that smelled of lemons and blood.

She pushed herself upright, examining the sparsely furnished recovery room of a necropolis with its one cupboard and piping-layered walls.

Noir sat at a table in the corner, scrawling on a sheet of bleached paper with his back to her. She tensed at the sight of him, then gradually calmed as the scratch of his pen and a vague sense of tranquility soothed her. He felt different, quieter, missing the pall of brooding violence that had always characterized his presence. Still, the sight of him caused her to shrink back, fighting the urge to scream.

"I can leave if you want me to."

Relief flooded her and she almost accepted his offer, but recognized that action as childish and resisted the urge; humans killed each other constantly and still managed to converse with one another. "Are you here to apologize?"

"No. I do not believe in apologizing for something I would not change." He laid his pen down and breathed on the ink. "I wish it had not been necessary though."

Her calm shattered. "Necessary? Necessary? You. Killed. Me!"

"Yes, I did."

"Why not just restrain me or something?"

"Because the proctors would have found you and then inevitably pursued me, which could only result in their deaths and immense damage to the city."

"Why are you here?"

"To tell you everything, if you want to know."

"You already told me why."

"I told you the gist, and you deserve more than that. So, here I am. Ask me anything, it doesn't have to relate to my actions here."

She kept silent for a while, just thinking and looking at her hands. There was so much she wanted to ask, her head buzzed with questions, and yet they all felt so irrelevant, inadequate after what had transpired between them. "I don't know what to ask. You're the Dark Father, you must know so much and all I can think to ask is why did you hide."

"I hid because while I know most of the Proctors, they do not all know me. If I returned and proclaimed myself Dark Farther without Lock-And-Key to verify my claim, they would have attacked."

"Why wouldn't she validate your claim?"

"She couldn't, Lazarus had infected her with Shadow Poison and the promise that if she ever resisted him, he would destroy her. It's a moot point, however, I would not have wanted to confront the usurpers together in the city; collateral damage on that scale is hard to control, even without ten Proctors in the mix."

"Wait! The Dollhouse? Are they–"

"They're fine, everyone is alive and accounted for. Grim was burned this morning."

"Why?"

"For treason mostly, but also for conducting a war without permission."

She slumped, breathing a sigh of relief. "Thank you for saving them."

He gave her the ghost of a smile. "Maybe save your thanks until after the full story."

"...What did you do?"

"I may have been a little lazy and just wiped out both districts."

"You what?"

"Killed every living inhabitant in the Doll and Grim Districts, concluding their conflict and ensuring no one died permanently. A tidy solution, and efficient."

"I can't believe you."

"Eh, I've done worse."

"...Do I want to know what you mean by that?"

"Probably not, but I'll tell you if you ask."

"No, thank you. I'm sure I can imagine."

"Unlikely, the world gets stranger the farther from civilization you get. Which brings me to this." He crossed over and offered her the sheet of paper.

She accepted the page, vainly trying to decipher the tangled mess of lines. "What is it?"

"A map of the outside world, everything my brother and I explored. Everything we've heard of, and everything we know about all of it; the Tyrants, their cities, and even the Wilds. It's all keyed to you. Just blow on it."

Adrian complied hesitantly and then gasped as the lines unfurled into mountains, forests, chasms, rivers, cities, and constructs she could not define: the shape of a world she had only imagined.

"It's not complete, there's more to the South and North we have to explore, but I will update it when I pass through."

"You've seen all of this?" she whispered in awe, running her hand just above the map's surface. "This must have taken years..."

"Yes."

"Why would you give me something like this?"

"Because I thought you might like it. Was I wrong?"

"No, it's beautiful."

"Thank you."

She touched the map gently, tracing the lines of Umbras and its surrounding lake. "What happens now? Will you leave?"

"No, we're going to monitor Umbras for a time, make sure the trouble's over. The city also needs some adjustments; I don't like the state it's in, and there's some people causing more trouble than they have any right to."

"We're?"

"Yes, we're. I didn't come here just for revenge, Adrian, I came for my brother. His murderers each stole a piece of him, and I needed those pieces back to resurrect him."

"Your brother's alive? But I thought they burned him?"

"We spent years devising ways to cheat permanent death, thankfully one succeeded."

"Where is he?"

"He's outside, waiting until you're ready."

"Why would he want to meet me? Isn't he like you? All powerful?"

"Yes, he's like me, just a lot nicer."

"But why does he want to meet me?"

"It's ... complicated. Better to just meet him, otherwise he'll start getting inventive."

"That doesn't sound so bad."

"And that's why you need to meet him."

"That serious? Then you should probably let him in."

"Only if you're ready; he'll understand."

"No, I'm sure. I want to know who I died for."

Noir opened the door without further preamble. "She's ready."

A near perfect copy of Noir entered the room, his skin, hair, and clothing all bleached necromantic white. "I may have caused a minor disaster outside and, on a completely unrelated note, Loc wants to see you." The man flashed a grin, at once unapologetic and reassuring as his bone eyes twinkled.

Noir exhaled a long-suffering sigh and stood. "All right, but don't overdo it while I'm gone, she's not used to you yet."

"You worry too much. The girl survived a week as your protégé; that's got to be a record."

"Oh, shut up. Adrian, there's one more thing you should know about the map; if you ever need help, write my name on the back and I'll answer."

The door closed behind him, leaving her alone with the strange man who stepped forward and extended his hand. "Hello, Adrian, I am Sir Alighieri of the Fuzzy Cat Ascendancy. Pleased to make your acquaintance."

"Umm, pleased to meet you as well?"

"As well you should be, I'm a very pleasing person." He flipped Adrian's hand over in his own. "You have lovely hands. Slim, ill-suited to manual labor but with excellent potential for delicate work. I can see why my brother likes you."

"He likes me because of my hands?"

"Among other things."

"I think you're mistaken, Noir doesn't–"

"Oh, he likes you. Otherwise you wouldn't have one of his maps."

"I hate to keep bringing it up, but he did kill me."

"And it hurt."

"How do you know that?"

"It's complicated, but we share memories from the last couple years. I'm missing a few but they're coming back slowly."

"Are they why you wanted to meet me?"

"Not entirely, I have all these memories of you, of our interactions; but I've never actually met you. I wanted to rectify that in case you decided to tag along."

"Tag along where?"

"To see the world. That's what the map signifies, it's an invitation to come with us. Not now, of course, but we'll probably meander back in a few years and he'll ask if you want to come with."

"For how long?"

"For as long as you like, to the places you've only imagined and areas we've never seen. Of course, we won't be leaving for a while; my brother is ever the perfectionist. But that just gives us time to become friends."

A Compendium of Terms

Hydes

Hyde: A general appellation for the transformation that befalls humans.

Bellua: A larger, more physically powerful breed of Hyde.

Variatur: A smaller breed of Hyde, but generally possessed of abilities and a more refined intellect.

Conficta: Hyde that's undergone pathomancer modifications.

Caelus: The strongest designation of Hyde, generally killed as a matter of rote. Manifests and exaggerates the qualities of Bellua and Variatur.

Evolved

Evolved: A rare group of individuals who have developed some control over their Hydes or transformations.

Sanitas: An individual who can maintain their sanity while in the midst of their transformation.

Rencensere: An individual who can resist the change to Hyde at night, and provoke it during the day for a brief span. They lose their sanity during the transformation.

Autorius: An individual that can both control and maintain their sanity during transformation. Extremely rare.

Adept

Adept: A human gifted with supernatural abilities divorced from the Plague.

Shadowmancy: The ability to manipulate shadows.

Hemomancy: The ability to manipulate and harness blood.

Necromancy: The ability to resurrect and enslave the dead.

Pathomancy: The ability to manipulate diseases, including the Plague to a degree.

Keegan and Tristen like to spend their time writing, drawing, reading, and gaming (both board-games and online) in Alabama.

Join our mailing list at kozinskibooks.com to receive buy-direct sales. If you would like to be an ARC reader, let us know. If you want our books to be in your local library, simply request your library to add it to their catalogue. If you want our books to be at your local indie books, request them to stock it.

If you feel so inclined, let us know what your favorite part of the book was.

www.ingramcontent.com/pod-product-compliance
Lightning Source LLC
Chambersburg PA
CBHW010546100726
47902CB00008B/2100